I0672770

"Do I look like an android...?"

...I looked her up and down, slowly, spending a lot of time on the graceful, incredibly long legs. I nodded.
"Yes..."

—from "A" As In Android.

ABOUT MILTON LESSER...

Born in Brooklyn in 1928, Milton Lesser was a prolific and versatile writer of Science Fiction and Mystery novels. He used many pen names but his favorite was Stephen Marlowe, which he adopted later in life as his legal name. He gained notoriety from his hard hitting detective novels but his Sci-fi works are here to testify to the enduring nature of his incredible imagination.

TABLE OF CONTENTS

MASTERS OF
SCIENCE FICTION

Volume 8

MILTON LESSER:
"A" AS IN ANDROID
and other stories

ARMCHAIR FICTION
PO Box 4369, Medford, Oregon 97504

For more information about Armchair Books and products, visit our website at…

www.armchairfiction.com

Or email us at…

armchairfiction@yahoo.com

"A" as in Android

The dancing girls fit the descriptions of androids, and that settled it, so far as Carmody was concerned. It also settled Carmody...

IT WAS ONE hell of a place for a nightclub. But then, Saturn's seventh moon, Hyperion, would be a hell of a place for just about anything.   Oh, Government had done wonders—and spent fortunes—giving tiny Hyperion a warm, breathable atmosphere and earth-norm gravity.   Outside of that, the jumble of rocky crags and powdered pumice might have been the space side of Pluto. I knew, because I've been there.

Now I heard the anxious stirring among the tough space-hands and miners as they waited for the first wonder of the Saturnian System—Hyperion's Dancing Girls. You couldn't blame them. Girls were girls, Andies or not, and the female of the species was about as common out here as an aardvark.

But frankly, I was more than a little sore at the over-patriotic deckhand who had reported the existence of the Dancing Girls to Tycho City on Luna. It meant I had to traipse almost a billion miles to collect the tax.   If the Dancing Girls were androids; if their maker had the money; if someone didn't put an end to the whole affair by deciding that a knife in my back might be distinctly better than paying a hundred bucks per head...

I saw those Dancing Girls. Let me tell you about them briefly. No, I won't go into detail. I remember they got my mind off all those morbid thoughts out in Hyperion City, and I don't want my mind to stray now, not while I'm trying to tell you this story.

They came out, about a dozen of them, and they danced. There wasn't a sound in the Hyperion Club. Not even music.

Not even breathing. I've never seen anything like it. And it took me a while before I realized just why those tall slim girls were so graceful. Well, graceful isn't quite the word, but then, no word exists in any language I know which can describe the something-more-than-grace which those girls had. They danced. All other dancing was mere walking, stumbling, clumsy tripping.

They had long legs. Not so you'd say they were nice long-stemmed chicks, but really long. Half again as long as they should be, or maybe more. But on them it looked good.

That clinched it. They were Andies, a dozen untaxed androids. I sighed and hoped the owner had his tax-money. I didn't want to impound these Andies for the government, not these dancers.

WHEN IT WAS OVER I didn't hear a sound. No clapping, no roaring, no stamping of feet. Not even shouts for an encore. Anything would have been superfluous.

I got up. I took my time walking across the now empty dance floor to a door which was marked, quite plainly, *Keep Out*.

I didn't. I walked right on through and a big guy with a seamy face stood in front of me, shaking his head slowly.

"Move, friend," he said, "can't you read signs?"

I told him that although I was not a college boy I could read, and would he please get out of my way because I had official business with the owner of the Hyperion Club. All he knew how to do was shake his head, but when I showed him the card in my billfold with the big letter *A* on it, the motion of his head changed. Now the seamy face bobbed up and down, but it looked worried. There's one thing about being in the Android Service—it sure can open doors for you.

Seamy Face ushered me through a corridor and down a flight of stairs. He only paused long enough outside a metal door to knock, and then I followed him inside.

The card on the desk said, *Mr. Tuttle: Manager*, and behind his thick-rimmed glasses Mr. Tuttle looked like he had insomnia. A little guy, and tired. He just wasn't cut out for the frontier. Maybe he should have had a curio shop in Marsport.

Seamy Face said, "This guy's from Android Service, Mr., T."

Tuttle looked up unhappily. He waved me over to a chair and I sat down, taking out my card again. "Carmody's the name," I said. "That's a nice act you have out there, Mr. Tuttle. Very nice. In fact, I've never seen anything like it. Androids?"

He didn't answer the question, not right away. Instead, he said in his tired voice, "A lot of people think so. Orders are beginning to pour in from all over the outworlds. There'll be thousands—"

I cleared my throat. "Andies will cost you exactly a hundred dollars a head, Mr., Tuttle. You know that, of course. What I want to know is this: why didn't you report the manufacture of your androids to the government? There's a reason for it, and for the tax, too. It isn't legal to upset the balance like this."

Tuttle sounded so tired I thought he'd fall right over into a deep sleep any moment. He said, "Who told you anything about androids? What makes you think they're androids?"

I smiled. "No stilts," I said. "Don't tell me they're wearing stilts. It's either that or androids, Mr. Tuttle."

Tuttle didn't answer that one either. Instead, he asked a question of his own. "How would you like to earn five thousand dollars, Mr. Carmody?"

I told him that was my year's salary, exactly, and I'd love it. Only I had a funny suspicion that whatever the offer was, I'd have to turn it down. Maybe we honest guys are fools; maybe ten years from now I'd still be earning exactly five-thousand, but at least I'd be able to live with myself. I'm no saint, but I've got a conscience.

"All you have to do," Tuttle said, "is this. Go back where you came from and say my dancers are not androids—for five thousand dollars, utterly no strings attached."

I asked him what I thought was purely a rhetorical question. "Are they androids, Mr. Tuttle?"

He was always answering a question with one of his own. "Define your term, Mr., Carmody. What is an android?"

I felt a little silly, and I said: "Why don't you ask your friend here?"

Seamy Face brightened. He said, "Well, an andie is kinda like a person, only it's made in a laboratory, not born. You know—chemistry, not biology." Seamy Face was very proud of his answer.

"Does that satisfy you?" Tuttle wanted to know.

I told him it did, and he said: "In that case, Mr. Carmody, I can assure you that Hyperion's Dancing Girls are not androids."

I JUST SAT THERE, hardly hearing Tuttle repeat his five thousand dollar offer. It didn't sound like he was lying, yet the whole situation smelled fishy. "Maybe you ought to let me see one of the—uh, girls," I told him.

"I wouldn't advise it, Mr. Carmody."

"Nah," Seamy Face agreed. "Better stay happy, friend."

"I'm stupid," I said. "I don't know when I'm well off. I want to see one of them."

Tuttle shrugged, pressed a button on his desk. "Tara, that you? Will you come in, please?"

I didn't have long to wait. In a few moments the door swung in, and the Dancing Girl closed it softly behind her.

She wore a pair of big gold earrings, with her long hair swept back and hanging halfway down to her waist. She had on one of those flimsy garments popular with the dancers these days, dark red and oddly metallic, with a bright gold sash. A lot of flesh showed, especially with those over-long legs. Android flesh. I was sure. She had an innocent face.

"What is it, Tuttle?" Nice voice, neither friendly nor hostile. Just plain nice. But no respect at all for Tuttle, the man who evidently had manufactured her.

Tuttle was sad, and afraid. "This man is from the Android Service," he told her. "I mentioned the Android Service to you, Tara. A matter of tax—"

"Why don't you pay the tax, Tuttle?" Even less respect this time. Still a nice voice, but haughty.

"I can't. You know I'm in debt, and I've been paying; I haven't got the money."

"Stupid of you," she told him, still in her nice, innocent voice. "You!" She turned in my direction, almost languidly.

"Me?" I said. Maybe Tuttle's fear was contagious, and I felt like seven different kinds of a damned fool. Only I was afraid, too.

"Yes, you. Do I look like an android?"

I looked her up and down, slowly, spending a lot of time on the graceful, incredibly long legs. I nodded. "Yes."

That set her back for a moment. "Come here, man. Come on. I won't bite."

Woodenly, I crossed the room to her. Don't ask me why, but I was plenty scared. Ever see a terrestrial dog on Mars, in the presence of some of the Martian fauna for the first time? Don't ask me why, but that's the way I felt. Worse.

The nice voice told me, "Touch. Go ahead, touch me."

I tried to act casual. I lit a cigarette, and I had to cup both my hands tightly around the match, so it wouldn't shake.

"Do you have to do that to touch me?" she demanded.

I stuck out my hand, foolishly. I grabbed her bare arm, high up, near the shoulder. I pulled my hand away, like it had been in fire.

She smiled. "Am I an android?"

I didn't say a word, not immediately. I just stood there, looking at my hand. What it had touched was cold—oh, not frigid, like a slab of ice, but cold, say, like the glass top on Tuttle's desk. Androids are just like humans; they're not hot, not feverish, but they feel pleasantly alive because they're warm-blooded. Tara's arm had a nice, rosy color, but it was cold.

STRANGE NOISES CLUCKED in my throat before I could say anything. My voice came from way down inside me, much too deep. "If you're an android, you're new. I didn't know androids could be—"

"Cold?" she smiled. "Not really cold. About seventy of your degrees on the Fahrenheit scale. That's not cold. Really, I find it pleasant." She shrugged. "But then, that happens to be the temperature of this room, I vary."

"She varies," I said.

Tuttle seemed a bit happier. "Well, now that you're satisfied she's not an android, I suppose you can go home and make your report. No tax, of course."

"Of course," Tara said.

If I ever get my conscience out in front of me where I could see it, I think I would kick it. Hard. "I'm not satisfied at all," I said. "She may not be an ordinary android, but she's not human. You're tax free for the present, but I'm going to order an investigation by some technicians."

Tuttle shook his head, sadly. Tara shrugged her cold rosy shoulders. "Borden, you will take him, please."

Seamy Face didn't like the idea, but he came at me ponderously, a great big slab of a man. It occurred to me at that moment that Tuttle's five thousand dollar offer had been about as sincere as a Venusian assertion of good will. We've been warring on and off with Venus for a hundred years. Because I realized, if Tuttle didn't have twelve hundred dollars to pay his tax then he didn't have five thousand to pay me. Any way you looked at it, it came out murder. Or, I hoped, *attempted* murder.

Seamy Face swung a big fist, which could have pulverized an adobe wall. I ducked and stepped inside of his flailing arms. They don't take weaklings for the Android Service, and I slugged away at his midsection, carefully. He grunted, and his guard came down, fast. Big men always do that. I stepped back, panting, and planted a right flush on his jaw, the way you see the Space Marines do it on video. Seamy Face shuddered and flopped about loosely for a moment, then he tumbled over on his face.

I felt cocky. "Who's next?" I demanded.

Tara's voice was still nice and innocent. "Why, you are," she said.

I should have known it would be the over-long leg. It started at the floor, long and graceful, and it moved so fast I hardly could see it. It caught me under the chin, and I think my feet left the floor. I had a quick, spinning view of Tuttle shaking his head, sadly, and then something crashed against my stomach. I remember sitting down, and I tried to get up. I could see the long legs standing over me, see the hands on feminine hips. I tried to reach out for those legs, only I never made it...

HYPERION IS ALMOST A million miles out, and I could see Saturn with her majestic rings in the port, the size of a silver dollar held at arm's length. That was all kind of hazy and far away, but it was enough to tell me I was in a spaceship before I blacked out again. Only I didn't quite black out, or, if I did, I had one crazy dream.

I remember Tara and half a dozen others stripping me, peeling off the jumper and the space boots as objectively as you might flay an extraterrestrial animal to study its insides, leaving me in my shirt and trousers, and then carrying me. One of them, Tara again, I think, took me over her shoulder like maybe I weighed thirty pounds, and then I remember a big bright room with a lot of machinery. I was on a table and loud noises buzzed in my ear and I felt oddly like a lot of sharp things were going inside of me. I don't mean inside my clothing—I mean inside me, all the way. My head, my chest, all over, with a gentle but outrageous insistency. Probing. Probing. Countless little knives, which were very sharp. So sharp that they didn't hurt at all. So utterly sharp that I knew they wouldn't leave any marks. Provided this wasn't some kind of an impossible, drugged dream.

The next part of the dream is even crazier. I sat up, still with too much fuzziness in my head to see clearly, and someone lay on the table next to me. That someone wore a jumper and heavy space boots. You could tell he was dead. You could tell—

I think I screamed, or at least I tried to scream. I saw everything through a fog, but the corpse looked just like me. Down to the last detail. Through all that fuzziness I could even see the little scar on the right temple. Me. A dead me, while the live me lay back and watched.

Someone was screaming and screaming, because the knives, which were so sharp that you hardly felt them, were going in again, doing their work. The someone was the live me.

"YOU FEELING ALL right now, Jones?" Tara asked me.

"My name is Carmody." My mouth tasted like someone had rammed it full of a lot of copper coins. "Carmody," I said again, stubbornly. I should have known I was wasting my breath.

"You want a mirror, Jones? It may help convince you." She gave me a big hand mirror, watched me with her innocent eyes.

I looked. I was twenty-five when Tara kicked me into her dream world on Hyperion. I looked fifty now. I didn't look anything like Mike Carmody. I had gray hair and dull gray eyes, a very red face with tight, thin lips. Trembling, I stood up. Mike Carmody is six feet tall in his socks. Tara is a big girl, maybe six feet herself. The top of my head didn't quite come up to her nose.

Something made me look at my right wrist, the inside of it, over the big blue vein. There was a bright letter *A*. Half an inch high. Capital *A* as in "Android." It was the law, I knew, for all androids to be so identified.

I grabbed Tara's arm and she didn't try to pull away. She had no letter *A*.

"You seem confused, Jones."

"I—" I couldn't say a thing. I just sat there.

"You were made fifty-three years ago, on Ganymede. You're a mechanic by trade, and a pretty good one."

I shook my head. I hardly felt like fighting about it, but I said, "I was born on Earth, in Chicago, twenty-five years ago. I'm an investigator for Android Service. Name's Mike Carmody."

She smiled. "While you were asleep, Jones, we landed back on Hyperion. Here's a newspaper." She handed the sheet to me, still smiling.

It was a newspaper, all right. The Hyperion City Gazette. I looked at the headline, and what followed:

ANDROID SERVICE INVESTIGATOR SLAIN HERE

At four p.m. yesterday, Earth Greenwich time, the body of Michael Carmody, Special Investigator for Android Service, was found in an alley connecting Dana and Bodini Streets in this city. Carmody had been slain some two or three hours before that time, in a bold daylight attack by unknown thugs who succeeded in taking Carmody's money, although his official papers were found on his person. Carmody, it is believed...

THERE WASN'T A THING to say. I was dead and my name was Jones now, and I'd better listen to Tara.

"So you see, Jones, you obviously couldn't be this Carmody. No, not you. He's a dead man, and you're a living android. Soon we'll put you to sleep again, and when you wake up, you'll understand. I can't blame you for being a little confused now, not really."

"You mean—you'll make my mind believe that story?"

"Yes, something like that. We erase the memory waves present and put in their place certain other—memories. Simple. Why?"

I thought fast. Hell, I didn't stand a chance getting off this ship alive, but at least I wanted to know what the hell was going on. You couldn't blame me. I said, "Well, if you're going to do that, maybe you can tell me the truth now." I meant it. I was a pretty resigned individual right then and there, and I wanted to know the truth as much as a man dying of thirst would want water. Even if the truth wouldn't stay with me very long.

Tara said, "All right, Jones. I suppose it won't hurt."

"Carmody."

"Carmody, then. What do you want to know?"

"Just about everything," I said.

Her voice was still nice and innocent. "Tuttle and Borden are dead. I had no choice. So now we need you, Jones—Carmody. Carmody is dead, too. You're Jones, an android. Soon you'll think that, too."

"Yes, but—who are you? The Dancing Girls—"

"I assure you, we are not 'girls,' Carmody. You wouldn't understand. You just wouldn't, not at all."

"Try me," I suggested. I turned idly to look about the room, and my eyes took in the port first. Outside, I could see Saturn's great bulk, low in the right side of the port, and much closer, so close that it couldn't have been more than a few miles away in space, was a ship. A ship! There were spacesuits here on this boat someplace, and if I could reach one, could kick myself clear of the lock and jet out to that ship...

"...Dimensions. Interlocking, say, like two soap bubbles, Carmody. You live in one; we live in the other. There aren't a lot of us—perhaps a billion—and if you saw our dimension, you'd know why we like yours better. Just a question of infiltration now—and what could arouse less suspicion than some innocent, wonderfully graceful dancing girls? We'll get popular, Carmody. It's starting already; so popular that there'll be a dozen dancing girls in every nightclub in the solar system. Then, in time—"

I was hardly listening. A door opened, and one of the other Dancing girls came into the room.

"Is he ready now?" she demanded.

Tara nodded. "I guess so. Carmody, are there any other questions before you're Jones, completely? No hard feelings, I hope. And even if you have them now, you won't—not when you're Jones. You'll have the memories of an android named Jones, who was made here, on this ship, a few days ago, but your memories will go back fifty years, and you'll be loyal to us. A publicity agent for us in your spare time, a mechanic otherwise. Any questions?"

I fiddled about for a question. I needed time. If they could take themselves from another dimension and assume their present, almost earthly shapes, if they could kill me and yet somehow not kill me, leaving my body dead in an alley in Hyperion City, but leaving me alive in the scrawny body of android Jones…

I HAD TO BELIEVE TARA. I couldn't doubt a word of it. So incredibly simple. Sure, no one would suspect a dancing girl of anything. What did you have to be afraid of?

"One more question," I said. I lifted a big bowl off the table and hurled it at her. "Just how strong are you?"

She stumbled back a few steps, trying to wipe some liquid from her eyes. She cursed roundly, and she may have been from another dimension, she may have assumed the shape of a girl here, but let me tell you she knew how to curse.

The other dancing girl leaped at me, and I sidestepped. I didn't want her to grab me, not when I remembered what Tara had done that day in Tuttle's office.

I ran out the door and I kept running. Behind me, I heard feet pounding down the corridor.

I don't know where they got the ship, but the single spacesuit I found hanging on a hook looked awful old. I hoped it would be airtight, and I didn't have much time to think about it one way or the other. I stepped into the suit and took down the plexi-helmet, and then someone spun me around and I saw it was Tara.

I swung my arm in a wide arc, starting from around someplace behind my back, and the helmet pounded against her face like a runaway meteor. It staggered her. The blow could have killed a man, but Tara just stumbled back a few steps, momentarily dazed.

The helmet fit in place snugly, the way it should, and I prayed again for air. Then I swung the lock door up, and I got a surprise.

There was no lock. Just cold empty space, with Saturn far off and the other ship hanging in space like a silver dart, much further than it had been before, but still close enough to reach with the suit jets.

I sensed the air wooshing out of Tara's ship, and I smiled. Maybe my worries were over. They had to be. You don't just go walking around in deep space, even if it's inside a ship.

Only Tara did. Her damned synthetic body—or whatever the make-believe dancing girl's flesh housed, could adjust to anything, instantly. She came for me, smiling innocently, still as if almost nothing was wrong. Maybe I'd been naughty, but that's all.

I kicked off from the hull and floated away from the ship a few yards. Tara stood in the simple doorway, and I felt a little giddy. I thumbed my nose at her.

It didn't last. She lifted a blaster and fired, and then I switched my jets on and began to soar away, darting, spinning, weaving—until I felt something like a gyroscope which lost its bearings.

The beam from her blaster zipped through space on all sides of me, but in a little while I was out of range, and by the time she could turn that ship around—even if she could withstand more gravities than a robot—I'd be in safe hands.

I smiled grimly as I swept closer to the other ship.

"LOOK," I SAID. "PLEASE, this is the fourth time I've told my story. It's been six months since the freighter picked me up."

The police officer shrugged. "What do you want me to do, Jones? We like to be nice to you andies—"

"I'm not an android!"

"We checked your fingerprints. There's the characteristic inverted V in the whorls. You have the android identification mark. You have your papers. Sylvester Jones, Android 1st class, Mechanic. So what do you want us to do? This Carmody guy is dead. He's buried now."

"Please. I'm Carmody—"

"Now, listen! We're going to have to put you away, Jones. We don't like to be hard on androids, but—"

"Carmody! Carmody! That's me, damn it—"

"Now, Jones, you'd better go away. We took you to Carmody's widow. She gave you the answer. Please, Jones, like a good andie." He frowned. "And that story you tell, better keep it to yourself. Dancing Girls invading the solar system. Ha, ha, ha..."

I stood outside in the streets of Earth. Chicago. Home town. It looked strange. I saw a billboard. "A hundred dancing girls in the Club Falcon. See them..."

The craze had swept the system. Every habitable world. Every club. They all had their long-stemmed dancing girls. Androids now, with little *A's* on their wrists, paying taxes properly, no questions asked. Infiltration...

Voices in the Void

*His papers were stamped "SF", and Space Fear meant that Craig
Reese could not look upon the stars and retain his sanity.*

*Once upon a time, it was believed that nothing existed between
worlds—there was nothing out yonder but empty "space." Now, we
know that it's nowhere near as "empty" as vacuums we can produce,
artificially, in our own labs.*

WITH THREE men and a woman, Craig Reese was
awakened and ushered out of the suspension room two hours
before the *Starcoach* roared down for planetfall on Gilhanna
II. A crewman lolled insolently in the corridor, snickering,
"Any of you people want to visit the lounge and take a last
look at space before we land?" he demanded.

He did not mean it. The suspension room was for SFs
only—for people afflicted with space-fear. Animation
suspended, they journeyed across space in their crypt, which
tradition placed adjacent to the eye-vault. Their more
fortunate fellows who did not hear the ghostly, impossible
voices of space, Reese thought bitterly, would always
remember the glorious dash across sixty-thousand light-years
of space from Sirius to the Gilhanna System, here at the hub
of the galaxy—would cherish their memory of hurtling suns
and mothers of suns that were nebulae, their memory of the
brief bright flare-up, which swept the *Starcoach* into hyper-
space, of the second flare-up that brought it out of the warp
and into view of the million-million gleaming stars, which
huddled together in chaotic confusion near the Hub.

But SFs heard voices and the voices could drive you mad;
so SFs slept in their crypt where the voices could not
penetrate their hypnotic slumber. The insolent crewman

knew this, of course. He also knew that not one of the SFs would ever venture near the star lounge, and some of them might choose mayhem as an alternative. But spacemen were a cocky lot, looking down their noses at planet lubbers in general and SFs in particular.

The crewman said again, "Sure none of you wants to come up to the lounge with me? Man, we're in a gorgeous sector of space. You should see the—"

"That's enough!" Craig roared, grasping the front of the man's tunic in big, powerful hands. "I saw a bright-eyed kid like you pull this same stupid trick on the Capella run two— three years ago. A lady got sick and she stayed sick, and if there's a cure no one told me about it. Any more of that, and I'll ram my fist down your throat."

Reese shoved the man back away from him and stalked into the baggage room to claim his gear. The *Starcoach* had cleared hyper, and by the time Reese assembled his luggage, shaved, showered and got a bite to eat in the 'low decks snack-bar, the ship knifed into Gilhanna II's atmosphere and made planetfall on time to the minute. A wonderful thing, space-flight—*if* you could appreciate it.

* * *

REESE gazed for a moment at the three suns in Gilhanna's sky, the white, the blue and the massive red. Here at the Hub, multiple star-systems were the rule rather than the exception, but Reese had lived most of his thirty years in the Sol- Deneb-Capella Sector far away on the other side of the Saggitarian swarm, which curtains the frontier worlds. It was all new to him, and breath-takingly beautiful, but he didn't have time for it.

He elbowed his way through the throngs of people on the landing apron, and the third sun, the big red one, brought a fine dew of perspiration to his skin before he reached the coolness of the administration building. There he told a pert receptionist that he had an appointment with Lee Sheraton and, after checking her schedule-book, she directed him to an elevator that whisked him to the fortieth level.

A second receptionist, and a third—both men—and then Reese waited while the door to Sheraton's office irised open and then blinked shut behind him like a giant eye over which the lid had been drawn.

Lee Sheraton turned out to be a woman. Tall, almost as tall as Reese himself, she wore a shimmering tunic, which fought a losing battle to hide the lithe proud curves of her body. Her eyes met his coolly, appraisingly; her blonde hair was close-cropped, frontier-fashion; she looked strong and hard, but she was also gorgeous, and if Reese ever had seen a more magnificent woman, then it was on Sol III, where the simple, decadent folk bred their women for beauty.

Lee extended her arm, shook hands firmly with Reese. She leafed rapidly through some papers on her desk, said: "So you're a warp-engineer, eh? Is the SF on your classification-visa a mistake?"

"No mistake. I have space-fear; so what?"

"So nothing." She shrugged. If he had seen a trace of contempt in her eyes, it faded away quickly, and he could have imagined it. "I was just thinking," she told him, "that it's a queer combination. A warp-engineer must spend a lot of time in space, naturally; doesn't it interfere with your work?"

"If it did, I wouldn't be a warp engineer, would I? A-1 rating, as the visa says. If you read some more, you'll find that I charted the original warp, which brings Sector One travel here on the new short route that skirts Ophiuchus—"

"Well a pat on the back for you! I can read, Reese."

His face reddened. He had not meant to talk boastfully; he merely wanted to justify his rating as a warp engineer, and it was hard enough to justify anything when the big letters SF were stamped in black on your visa. "I do your paper work," he explained. "I need a staff of space jumpers; otherwise, everything's nice and normal. You'll find recommendations—"

"I said I can read. But you look too big and too strong to spend all your time at paper work."

Reese gave her a wolfish grin. "I don't work slowly, so I have a lot of free time—and I don't use all of that for paper work." Instantly, he regretted it; she could stare that kind of grin down every day of the week, and twice on Sunday.

"I suspect we're straying from the point of this interview, Mr. Reese. What do you know about Gilhanna's warp?"

"Not a hell of a lot," he told her honestly. "Just what I read in the textbooks."

"Well, Gilhanna's warp is the only permanent hyper-space channel in the Galaxy. Starships shoot hyper all the time, sure: you couldn't have interstellar travel otherwise. But they use brief, temporary warps. Gilhanna's warp is more like a conduit, carrying water from this world to Gilhanna III, an arid desert of a planet on an orbit sixty million miles further out from that big red baby you can see through the window. It's complicated, Reese—you have to figure the syndoic and sidereal year of each planet, you have to account for the pull of three suns, you have to—"

"I know all that. What's the problem?"

"The problem is simple: it doesn't work. Something happens, we don't know what, and every week or so there's a breakdown. The fractured warp looses an awful lot of water into space, and that can't go on. Gilhanna II has a lot of water—only a fifth of the surface on this planet is land. But there's isn't enough to supply our needs, the needs of Gilhanna III, and a hole in space as well. Cigarette?"

Reese took the smoke and lit it. Some people claimed cigarettes went back almost as far as the game of chess, both of which rolled merrily along as man pushed back the frontiers of his universe.

"So I've got to see if I can find the flaw in the warp, is that it?"

The woman nodded. "More likely than not, you'd be chasing after shadows. Mr. Gilhanna thinks it's sabotage. We slapped down an abortive revolution two or three years ago, you know, but that was before the warp, and the five million mining families on Gilhanna III had to depend on shiploads of water for survival. The population out there has doubled since Gilhanna built his warp, but they're grumbling like mad now, because the warp started acting up. Any questions?"

"Yeah," Reese said. "I've got one; what happened to my brother?"

LEE SHERATON said, "Your brother? What are you talking about?"

"My brother, like I said. Name of Harold Reese. He'd be twenty-seven now; came out here five years ago to do tritium mining on Gilhanna III. Twenty-nine months ago, we stopped hearing from him. What happened?"

The woman snuffed out her cigarette, crossed to the window and looked for a long time at the monster red sun hovering on the horizon. "As I told you, there were five million mining families on Gilhanna III, roughly, twenty million people. That was two years ago. Now there are twice that number, and it would be pointless for us to keep records, Reese.

"You can go to Gilhanna III and look for him. It might work out very well for you at that, because a lot of your work will take you there anyway. But don't get too optimistic—when you reach Gilhanna III you'll find one of the really backwater worlds of the galaxy. Many places, they don't even have electricity, let alone atomics. In a constant state of anarchy, they don't keep records either, and—"

"Damn it," Reese swore, "you'd think that Gilhanna would keep his own records."

The woman smiled. "You don't know Garr Gilhanna. Probably, he's the galaxy's only quadrillionaire, Reese. This System's Gilhanna A—out here at the Hub there also are Gilhanna B, C, D and E; and Garr owns them all, down to the smallest chunk of meteor. He didn't get that way by watching out for every SF warp-engineer's wayward brother."

Alarmed, Lee turned away from the window when Reese's fingers dug into her shoulders. "Watch your step," Reese growled. "I didn't come sixty-thousand light years to hear you tell me my brother's not important. Understand?"

She took hold of his wrists with her own surprisingly strong hands, pushing them firmly down to his sides. "I understand, Reese, but you don't. You came here for a job—okay, we need a good warp-engineer, because before we turn in a verdict of sabotage and start knocking hell out of the miners on Gilhanna III we want to be sure. Meanwhile, you have a job. Anything you do on the side is your own business. You can turn III upside down and look for your brother; I don't care. But when you're on Company time you take your orders from me, and you don't talk back. You don't tell me what I can or can't think about your brother or anything else. Try it and you'll wake up one fine morning out in space, with a lot of emptiness all around you and all the little ghost-voices whispering in your SF ear. Is that clear?"

Reese shuffled his feet and looked down at the floor. He needed the job; he couldn't carry out an investigation for his brother without it. He said, "Where do you fit into the setup?"

"I'm the Executive Director of Gilhanna Enterprises for this System, Reese. You might stay here for a dozen years and never meet Mr. Gilhanna, but you'll see plenty of me, and you'll get plenty of my orders. Now, do you still want the job?"

"I'll take it," Reese said. He wasn't smiling.

CHAPTER TWO

AN UGLY little world, Gilhanna III, throwing bleak crags up at the somber red sky. The change struck Reese at once. Gone were the park-like islands of the planet, which housed Gilhanna's administration machinery. Gone, too, were the comforts of an interstellar culture. Reese had remained for a week on Gilhanna II, studying the theoretical aspects of the warp. He'd caroused a lot of that time outdoors, and the strong actinic rays of the red sun had bronzed his skin and bleached his hair.

A pleasant enough interlude, he thought now, as the dry winds of the third planet parched and irritated his skin like fine sandpaper. Almost, it had amounted to a lark, but Lee Sheraton had hovered nearby, observing, directing, commanding. The woman posed a problem for Reese, and he half-promised himself to solve it—along with a handful of others, which heaped one upon the other here in the Gilhanna System. Gilhanna's warp, which should have behaved itself and didn't; an abortive revolution and the role his missing brother had played; and a woman who seemed ornery out of all proportion to the situation...

The one thing he had no time to consider was his space-fear. After the interlude on Gilhanna II he'd taken up a warp-ship, one of those slow, ponderous vessels, which could hang precariously on the mysterious zone that separated hyper-space from normal space. Virtually every cubic foot of the warp had been investigated by his two jumpers, and he'd done a yeoman's share of paper work. It added up to nothing. Suddenly, without warning, the warp caved in upon itself, gushing a million tons of water into normal space every minute. He couldn't get near enough to investigate *that*, because the geyser spewed water, which became ice instantly, and the jagged particles of ice, which rocketed through space could be as effective—and destructive—as a meteor swarm.

So, rather than admitting failure, Lee had ordered him to Gilhanna III to study the receiving station.

The mining families lived in small communities, few of which exceeded a hundred thousand people. They lived primitively—only the tritium-extracting machinery smacked of interstellar culture. And at the outset Reese had no time to study the receiving station, a great artificial lake fed by one end of Gilhanna's warp. Instead, he found someone who remembered his brother.

* * *

THE MAN was a stocky, middle-aged miner who'd given up that occupation to become supervisor of the Lake. His office, buried deep among the generators, which pumped water from the Lake to all the communities of the planet, reeked of ozone, and by contrast with the dry cold of Gilhanna Ill's surface, the place was a Turkish bath.

He shook hands sullenly with Reese, then said: "Name's Jackson. Sheraton's office told us to expect you. But I'm a busy man, Reese; so whatever I can do for you, make it quick."

"I just want a few facts about the Lake here. But hell, if you're busy, I can get 'em myself. Lee suggested—"

"Bah! I wonder if that beautiful dame ever had a thought of her own. You know the story, don't you?"

"How should I know? I just got here."

"Well, Sheraton was a waif, orphaned when her folks died in a rough transit out of hyper. Don't ask me why, but Gilhanna took a fancy to her, raised her like his own kid. Now she thinks he's the Almighty, and the only life she knows is hard-boiled efficiency. That's what he taught her."

"I see." Reese stood up. "I don't want to impose, Mr. Jackson, so, if you're busy, I won't bother you. But I'd like to ask you one question."

"What'sat?"

"Did you know Harold Reese?"

Jackson rubbed the stubble on his chin thoughtfully. "Yeah. An eager kid, with some romantic notions about equality here in the Gilhanna System. I remember—"

Reese felt his heart doing a mad dance. Sixty thousand light years is a long way to look for your kid brother who went gallivanting off into deep space. "Where is he now?"

"Say, wait a minute! Your name is Reese. Umm-mm, wouldn't be a relation? What? His brother? Well, put 'er there, son." This time the handshake was vigorous, hearty. Jackson sat down, rapped his knuckles on the battered desk top. "Maybe you didn't come here to snoop around for Sheraton; maybe you came looking for your brother's grave, eh?"

"Oh," Reese grunted dully. "His grave—"

"Yeah. I'm sorry, Reese; he got it in the revolution two years ago, blasting a tin-can ship against Gilhanna's navy…"

"I came for both reasons," Reese admitted. "Lee Sheraton's paying me to kick around the warp and come up with something. But now that I found out about Hank—"

"That's rich," Jackson chortled. "Paying you to study the warp. Don't *you* know what's causing the trouble?"

Reese shook his head.

"Gilhanna himself, that's what. He figures if he can worry us enough with the threat of no water, he'll really have us groveling. Same thing last time, only then there wasn't any warp, so Gilhanna slowed the shipment by tanker. That led to the revolution—and to your brother's death."

REESE WAS confused, and he did not try to hide it from the supervisor. "That doesn't make sense, Jackson. Sheraton said you miners probably played around with the warp, sabotaging it."

"*What?*" Jackson's face turned purple. "We depend on the warp for life; would we sabotage that?"

"Well, Gilhanna depends on the warp for healthy miners to extract tritium and make him the richest man in the galaxy. You tell me which makes less sense."

"Are you serious?"

"Yeah. Yeah, I mean it. I think you're both barking up the wrong tree; I think something else is responsible."

"What?"

"That beats me. I thought I'd try to find out; now I don't know. I came to the Hub to see about my brother. You told me—"

"That's better." Jackson relaxed visibly. "I'd have hated to see Reese's brother working for them. You know, they say the only time Sheraton ever stood up against Gilhanna was during the revolution. She thought they could settle it without knocking off five thousand miners and bringing us to our knees, squirming in the sand for a cup of water. If it's true, she didn't do anything about it."

"I'll go now," Reese said, standing up again. "Probably, I'll draw my pay and get out of this system."

Jackson opened his mouth to say something, but a phone buzzed on his desk. He picked up the receiver, barked into it, "Jackson. Uh-huh, how're you, Mike? What say? What? Those damned butchers!" He hung up, and his hands were trembling when he faced Reese.

"Your pals, Gilhanna and Sheraton. Know what they did? They decided they were losing too much water into space. So they shut the warp down, and they won't start it again until they get to the bottom of the difficulty. We've got water here in the Lake for two weeks, for a month if we all go around with sore throats. After that, they say they'll be shipping by tanker, like in the old days—except that our population's increased so much that the tankers couldn't give us enough even for drinking purposes.

"Ain't that neat, Reese? I'd like to have that Gilhanna here. I'd like to see him living on a ration of a liter a day for all purposes. Damn his hide"

"Listen, Reese." The stocky man leaned forward impulsively, peering at Reese across hairy, muscular forearms. "Don't think we forgot about the revolution and what your brother died for. We don't want to bring Gilhanna to his knees; all we want is enough of a voice to make this slab of a planet livable. We got an organization, we got... Why don't you throw in with us, Reese, and finish what your brother started to do? There's Mike, who just called me. He wants a full-scale war, wants to come storming down on Gilhanna II in a bunch of obsolete spacers you could pry open with a pen-knife. And there's old Wilbur. He thinks we should arbitrate. Arbitrate—hah! That's a laugh. We've been arbitratin' for years, and what happens? Nothing. Me, I'm someplace in the middle. What do you say, Reese? Join us?"

"I'll think about it," Reese replied, moving toward the door; "Maybe I'll get in touch with you one of these days, Jackson. Good luck."

Jackson sat there, mouth agape, looking foolish. He seemed very disappointed. Well, there was a lot to what he said. Sure, Reese wouldn't mind at all finishing what his brother had died for. It wasn't his fight, he'd have to be a hypocrite to admit otherwise. Still, if his brother had died...

But of one thing he was sure as he emerged on the cold surface of Gilhanna III. He wouldn't cast his lot with a wild-eyed bunch of anarchists whose three leaders maintained three opposed points of view, not when it might place him one fine day in an old space boat with nothing between him and the voices of space but a one inch sheet of battered steel.

*　*　*

HE FOUND his two space-jumpers, a couple of scrawny old men who'd been licensed pilots before the Sector One schools started turning out polished young officers who knew hyperspace theory like the old timers knew asteroid hopping—found them drinking the fiery native liquor in a Lake City bar. He joined them for a drink or two, listening for a time to the angry conversation of the miners, keyed to fever-pitch by a woman agitator who favored the total-war solution. But Reese couldn't join the talk on anything like an equal level: his polished boots, smart britches and jumper with the big "G" emblazoned on its sleeve—these spoke too clearly of his employment by Gilhanna. And after he almost came to blows with a whiskered miner who mouthed a steady stream of invective at him, he took his two protesting companions by their arms and led them out to the space field.

Using its normal drive, the warp ship reached *Brenschluss* when Reese started hearing voices.

Sometimes it happened like that—sometimes even the six-inch hull of a new ship failed to offer adequate protection. Reese ran widely to the first aid locker, threw it open, reached in for the hypo that would put him to sleep.

The voices tore at the fibers of his brain, twisting through the convoluted paths, probing insistently, clamoring...

He depressed the plunger, held the hypo up to the light. It was empty!

Babbling now, Reese tumbled back into the control room. Sure, space-fear was a comparative rarity and drugs here in the Gilhanna System were at a premium. He'd neglected to tell the clearance officer on Gilhanna II of his affliction, and somehow the man had missed the SF on his visa.

Now he could do nothing but take it for four or five hours, until the ship reached Gilhanna II's shielding atmosphere. Take it—take the voices. Half a millennium before, when mankind first blasted out into the void between the worlds, they'd discovered space-fear. They knew no cure; in Sector One they spent a billion dollars yearly to find one, but the money dissolved into space as surely as water from Gilhanna's leaking warp.

The familiar giddiness swept over Reese, the all-consuming desire to hurl himself from the lock and merge with the ghost-voices. Not voices, not really, although people called them that. Just the suggestion of a sound, and the suggestion of tired bitter thoughts, which somehow belonged to the sound and somehow did not. Reese could not understand the thoughts, not entirely. No one could, and the savants considered them purely subjective, on the fringe of lunacy, delicate, razor-sharp pips of madness welling up from the unconscious mind.

Grimacing horribly, Reese tugged at the airlock mechanism. Some sanity remained, some slight sanity, which the discord of humming and half formed alien thoughts could not reach, and it told him to stop. He cried out, "Damn it, hit me! Hit me..."

The ship was on automatic, and now the two space-jumpers came running from their quarters. They'd been around long enough to understand. They took one look at Reese and leaped toward him. Their scrawny frames hid deceptive strength, and they battled him away from the lock, threw him to the floor where he continued his babbling and struggling.

One of them held him down... *The insane fool! The voices beckoned, beckoned. He merely wanted to go out and join them. What was wrong with that? Why couldn't these two idiots leave him alone? Stop! Get your filthy hands off me! Look out now, look out— ummm...*

One of the jumpers held him there on the floor, one pounded at his jaw, over and over again, smashing his fists against it until the knuckles were raw, then smashed again. Reese was tough and Reese could take it, but eventually he subsided...

CHAPTER THREE

"HOW DO you feel?"

"Lousy, thanks. What happened?"

"They brought you down okay, Reese. You've been here in the hospital for a couple of days; your jaw was dislocated."

"Ow! You're telling me." His whole face felt stiff, like it had been packed in ice for a year. Lee Sheraton sat on the edge of his bed, looking as beautiful as the first day he'd seen her. But all unruffled. Things happened fast in the Gilhanna System, and he figured a lot had happened with explosive force since his accident, yet the woman appeared as coldly efficient as ever. He wondered, suddenly, if she had looked that way when she ordered his brother's death.

"I found out about my brother," he said.

"Yes? Tell me."

"Nothing to tell. You know that revolution you told me you slapped down? You slapped him down with it; he's dead."

"Oh."

"Yeah, 'oh.' Are you ready to do the same thing all over again?"

"Don't jump to conclusions. The revolution wasn't my idea. Once it started, Mr. Gilhanna had to put it down, of course. I still didn't like it. I kept out of the picture."

"You kept out of the picture. I think that's swell. But you didn't lift a finger to stop it, huh? You just watched. Nuts!"

She changed the subject. "Mr. Gilhanna wants to see you."

"Is that so? What for? I thought he doesn't see anybody."

"There's trouble on Gilhanna II, Reese. Your space-jumpers told me you saw it yourself, but now it's worse. Mr. Gilhanna's hands are tied; he can't give them water—"

"Doesn't want to, you mean. Hell, the guy's a quadrillionaire, you said so yourself. So he can waste some water, so it costs him a lot of cash—so what? He can afford it."

"Doesn't want to, then," she said acidly. "Have it your way, Reese, but you've not been in the System long enough to be a policymaker. Will you shut up and let me talk? Good. He's decided to abandon the warp until you locate the difficulty. He wants to see you about that now. Think you'll be up to it this afternoon?"

"Damned right I'll be up to it."

She leaned forward, lit a cigarette, gave him a drag through the bandages on his face. "Don't worry about those swaddling clothes on your mouth, Reese. They come off today. What I want you to keep in mind is this: Mr. Gilhanna favors doing some slapping down again, that's the way he is. I'm not, and I don't. I'd like to see you find the answer. If you do, it can prevent a lot of bloodshed—"

"Sure, so I go spinning merrily off into space again!"

"I know doctors recommend a year of planet lubbing after an—attack, unless you go out on one of the big liners and get your animation suspended. Still, I thought you might like to prevent some mass murder, like your brother…"

"Shut up. When I decide to prevent anything, I'll let you know. What time at Gilhanna's office? Three o' clock this afternoon? I'll be there."

Deliberately, he turned over on his side, did not look up again until the door irised shut behind her. Then he picked up the phone and ordered some food.

* * *

GILHANNA'S offices pierced the clouds on the tower atop the administration building. Three levels, which did business in nothing but precaution supported it. In the first, Reese was stripped. He went one way and was questioned by a psychologist; his jumper and britches went another way, carefully studied for any signs of a lethal weapon by a staff of experts. He met them and donned them on the next level, while a trio of female receptionists stood by indifferently; asking questions, which in many cases coincided with those of the psychologist, then checking them by phone. Another searching on the third level, this time less thorough, and a complete briefing on how to act in the presence of the Great Man.

Then Gilhanna himself.

Like everyone who had ever met the man, Reese did not know what to expect. A craven coward in the isolation of his tower, protected by his three levels of scientific bodyguards? A big mountain of a man, bathing in luxury, scenting his soft body with the alien perfumes of a dozen worlds in bondage, sipping from a selection of exotic liquors and wines, which made champagne taste like dishwater?

Gilhanna was neither. Reese met a thick-thewed giant with a handclasp like two iron jaws clamping together, with close-cropped gray hair and a superbly-muscled body, which proclaimed constant vigorous exercise. With two burning eyes that pierced into you and seemed to strip your mind of its most secret, cherished thoughts. Mostly, Reese was aware of the eyes, and he did not like them. Eyes of unwavering purpose, but twin orbs of evil, flint-hard, coldly calculating— eyes, which perhaps had studied Lee Sheraton as she grew from an infant to a girl to a woman, guiding her, clamping her in an inflexible mold, which turned out a polished, efficient Executive Director for Gilhanna...

The woman was there too. "Craig Reese," she said, "this is Garr Gilhanna. You will call him Mr. Gilhanna."

"Okay, *Mr.* Gilhanna."

"Reese, the girl's crazy. She thinks if you can repair the warp, we can prevent revolution on Gilhanna III." He spoke of the planet, which bore his name with a studied lack of pride. And that, after all, was the really prideful way. Gilhanna System—why, naturally! "Now, Reese, I'll make this perfectly clear. First place, I don't like the idea; I don't think you can fix a thing. "

"I didn't say I could."

"Lee said you could."

"Well, I still say it. It's certainly worth a try."

Gilhanna waved a hand for silence. There was silence. He said, "Further, I actually favor the revolution. Sure, let 'em get smart, let 'em try something—we'll knock 'em down thoroughly this time, and when the pieces are picked up and put back together again, I'll hold 'em in the palm of my hand. I'll balance 'em on the edge of my little finger. I'll—"

"You told me," the woman reminded him softly, "that you'd give Reese here a chance."

"I did, and I will. I—"

"Nobody said I wanted the chance," Reese stated, smiling when Gilhanna's eyebrows shot up in disbelief.

"Good!" the Great Man said after a time. "Splendid! Then we can call the whole thing a closed issue and I'll just wait until the miners take their dinky crates up and try something. Like the last time—"

"What about the last time?" Reese wanted to know.

"Simple. Ridiculously simple. They blasted off in four converted freighters. We waited till they reached *Brenschluss*, then popped 'em out of space—*ping, ping, ping, ping*—just like that. Two ships wanted to call it quits, but we had to teach 'em a lesson, had to slap 'em down good. Eh, Lee?"

"No," she said. "It wasn't my idea; it wasn't necessary." Her eyes implored, yet she looked not at Gilhanna, but at Reese... It was as if her eyes said: *Please; work again on the warp. He'll kill again if you don't, like he killed your brother...* Then Gilhanna's tutelage had given his ward everything she needed to be a first rate Executive Director, except the ruthlessness of the master himself.

Reese said, "I think I'll take a crack at it. When can I start?"

"At once," Gilhanna muttered. "The sooner you admit defeat, the sooner I can take my own measures. A promise is a promise, Lee—but you'll see that we're wasting time."

"We'll see," she told him, as Reese got up to leave without waiting for Gilhanna to dismiss him.

* * *

In the weeks that followed, he tried. He studied the warp when it did not conduct water; he had them pump water through it in a continual torrent; had them shoot the liquid through in short blasts. He tried everything, and the warp behaved perfectly, a channel of hyperspace tucked into normal space on a path, which followed Gilhanna II and III on their journeys around the red sun with mathematical perfection.

And then it broke down, suddenly. No cause. No reason. It simply broke down.

The miners on Gilhanna III grumbled, went on half-rations, grumbled some more. Rumor had it that their fleet consisted of a dozen over-aged ships this time, culled in by sympathetic businessmen outside the System who wanted a hand in Gilhanna's quadrillion-dollar enterprise.

Lee Sheraton warmed to Reese. In his spare time he saw the brittle shell of her efficiency wavering. Two or three times she spoke in open rebellion against Gilhanna's plans. She'd not stand by and let him slaughter thousands of miners again, despite everything. Her zeal almost communicated itself to Reese, and many times he found himself thinking that he'd be on hand when the final reckoning came. Except when he thought of the voices in space, and the terrible things they could do to his mind. Even his two space-jumpers must have sensed that, because now they treated him like a delicate piece of china, soothing him in space, keeping him occupied with tall tales of their exploits before the bright young Sector One pilots came along and took their jobs away, reminding him whenever he got morose that they had a loaded hypo on hand this time.

Back on Gilhanna II, Reese saw Gilhanna's preparations for small-scale war. A hundred shining warships were fitted for action, and they waited, long, graceful teardrops, in orderly rows on the space field. All he had to do was press a button... No, probably he'd blast off with them to witness the carnage firsthand. After that, he'd spend many a comfortable hour with his memories of the way he'd slapped down the second abortive revolution.

Once, Reese got a call from Gilhanna III, Supervisor Jackson. The man wanted to know if Reese had considered his proposition, if he were ready to act as inside man. Reese told him his hands were tied. He was not in a position to work from the inside, even if he had wanted to. He advised Jackson to have patience, to wait and see what might develop, but the words sounded empty, without promise, even to his own ears. Jackson cut the connection contemptuously.

* * *

The next day, Lee Sheraton stormed into Reese's hotel room without warning. "Craig," she cried. "Craig, I don't know what to do! I—"

"*You?*" he demanded. "You don't know what to do?" Immediately, he was sorry. She'd come to him because she thought he could help; she certainly did not come for ridicule—

"Stop fencing with me all the time, Craig. Please. Do you know what's happening? The miners sent their dozen ships up today, and they're rendezvousing a million miles this side of *Brenchsluss*. They don't have warp drive, just the old normal stuff. Gilhanna's going to shoot his hundred ships through hyper and surprise them while they're coasting. They won't have a chance."

"All right, okay. You don't want to see it happen. At first, that surprised me; it doesn't any more. I don't want to see it happen either. But what the hell can we do?"

"You'll see, Craig. It took me a long time to see through Gilhanna. I almost did the first time, but he sugar-coated everything for me after that, and I forgot. Now—well…"

"I said, what can we do?"

"You'll be getting a call from Gilhanna any minute now, I—uh, arranged a fight with the only other warp-engineer in the System. I got him in an alley and hit him with a big piece of metal, Craig. He fell and he was bleeding and I hope I didn't hit him too hard and—"

"My gosh," Reese said letting her babble against his chest, "you're human after all. I'll bet you'd make a nice gal-friend now that Gilhanna's veneer is washing off. I'll bet—"

"Not now, Craig. Gilhanna will need a warp-engineer to chart his course through hyper. You're it. Maybe you can trick him, or—well, you know more about that than I do."

Reese didn't have time to think about it. The phone buzzed, and Gilhanna himself was at the other end of the connection. Could Reese meet him at the space field in thirty minutes? Excellent…

CHAPTER FOUR

"SHE COMES with us," Reese insisted, and Lee nodded her head vigorously. "I'm not kidding, Gilhanna. If she wants to come, she comes; otherwise I don't!" There might be danger, there probably would—but if Lee still felt like being on hand, there'd be nothing better than that to wipe the last traces of Gilhanna's training from her.

Gilhanna shrugged his massive shoulders. "All right, both of you then. Let's go."

The hundred ships gleamed like rubies in the bright red sunlight, and when Gilhanna's pilot took the first one up, the others followed, roaring their thunder as they cleared atmosphere in less than three minutes.

Space—cold and bleak and silent. And voices? Sometimes you heard them, sometimes you didn't. Now Reese couldn't be sure. Faint mutterings nibbling at the corners of consciousness, but certainly nothing more. For the present, at least, he was safe. He shuddered when he thought of the last time…

"Now," Gilhanna told him, "you'll chart us into hyper. I want to reappear with this fleet a thousand miles this side of the rebels, Reese. These are their present coordinates—" He flicked a switch, and a tri-dimensional graph swam into view.

"Sure," Reese mumbled, studying them. "I'll have us into hyper in a minute." He thought: *Ah-hah, about half a billion miles off course. That'll give the rebels their chance to land on Gilhanna II, and they can take over the planet without force before Gilhanna can get back.*

"…Oh yes. I wanted to tell you something else," Gilhanna was saying. "There are two vials of hypo aboard this ship." He held a slim tube containing an amber colored liquid. "This is one. The other I have hidden away." He brought his arm down with a swift motion, and the tube shattered on the floor, its contents spreading in a shining stain. "If you somehow confuse the warp, I'll do the same thing to the other vial. How would you like that?"

Reese said that he wouldn't.

"Further, if that isn't enough, I'll make you a promise, Reese. I keep my promises. If you foul up this venture, I'm going to leave you in space with enough air in your plastisuit to last you a good long time. You'll die, of course—but that would be a horrible way for an SF to die, wouldn't it? All alone in space, with the voices closing in around you, with nothing under your feet but a lot of vacuum—and voices… Think about it, Reese.

"For now, I have business up front with the blasting crew. I trust you. So whenever you're ready, you can take us into hyper. Incidentally, did you know that they say space-fear is particularly strong here at the Hub? Well, I'll see you in a few minutes."

* * *

A MILLION million stars. The center of a galaxy. Still, space wag empty—one feeble candle in a forest glen at midnight would cast more light. And then the stars twisted and spun, leaped about chaotically, danced crazy dances and faded into a murky whiteness. Reese sighed, spun around in his chair and faced the woman.

"Well?" she said.

"Well what?"

"We're in hyper—but heading where?"

"Where Gilhanna wants. A thousand miles this side of the rebel fleet. What could I do, Lee? The voices are faint now, so faint that unless I think of them overtly, I hardly hear them. But they can increase. They can— Lee, you couldn't know what it's like!"

"No?" Wordless, she reached into a pocket of her tunic, came out with a billfold. "You'll find my visa in there."

Dumbly, he opened it. The big black letters "SF" stared at him boldly, mocking—

That could explain so much.

She said, "You can't change it now, can you?"

"N-no," he admitted. "We're warping through straight on course, I couldn't alter that if I wanted to. Lee—" He reached out for her, wanted to take her in his arms, to kiss her, to show her in that way that he was sorry, maybe to hold onto her for strength, he didn't know. But she evaded him, flicked a lever and waited for the door to iris open. "I'm going forward to the blasting room," she said.

He followed at her heels, half running to keep up with her. In his mind—and in hers too, he now knew—the voices grew louder.

A warships lethal weapons are located in the blasting room. They're mounted in such a way that they can swivel a hundred and eighty degrees, and for that reason the blasting room is not closed off like the rest of the ship. Yawning circular ports are spaced at regular intervals, and the blasters are so calibrated that they will not fire until their snouts coincide with one or another of these holes, which peer out into space.

In the airlock adjacent to the blasting room, Reese donned his incredibly light plastisuit, the spaceman's answer to the bulky vacsuit of the previous century,

TECHNICIANS checked their guns.

Gilhanna strutted back and forth, staring every moment out into the murk of hyperspace.

"Ah!" he called. "Reese. Will we be out soon?"

Reese grunted something into the radio strapped to his chest, and then, all at once, the whiteness disappeared. In its place—the speckled vault of space, and a dozen tiny mibs straight ahead, reflecting the blood red sun...

Gilhanna's fleet closed in. The mibs grew to tiny teardrops, to ships, old gutted ruins for the most part, patched up for a final glorious—and hopeless—dash for freedom.

The voices plucked at Reese's brain—then plucked more insistently. He hardly saw Gilhanna shouting orders to his technicians, hardly was aware of the first rebel ship splitting in twain nearby, the debris cascading out from its sundered ruin. He sobbed and he looked at Lee. Her mouth hung open as if she were screaming, but he heard nothing. She'd turned down her radio, accidentally or otherwise, and her mouth hung open. Her eyes bulged. Silently she screamed and screamed...

The well-known impulse came again, and Reese fought it. *Jump out, come on, now—it'll be a cinch. Just step through one of those yawning ports—* Voices plucking, tugging, pulling, vague shadows of thoughts, which might become clear if he could join them there in the vault of space!

For Lee the summons must have been more insistent. One moment she stood there, swaying, staggering. The next, she stepped up onto the sill and dropped out into space.

Reese ran to the port, peered out. Lee floated almost within reach, held by the slim bonds of the ship's gravity. Below her, a second rebel ship caught a fatal blast from one of Gilhanna's warcraft, and it split in two like a rotten stick. The voices clamored, but for the moment at least, Reese fought them off, leaned half out of the port and stretched his arms toward the woman. He missed by inches, stretched out farther still—but then a near miss by one of the remaining rebel ships knocked their own gravity haywire, and when Reese picked himself off the floor. Lee floated in space, tumbling end over end slowly, a hundred yards away.

Reese moaned, ran to the wall, pulled down a jet-belt, fastening it about his waist with trembling hands. He stood poised at the port for a moment. Gilhanna was shouting something, he couldn't tell what. And then he leaped.

When he reached Lee and took her in his arms half a mile from the ship, the voices began to make sense. Nothing slow, nothing gradual about it. Suddenly, they formed words which spoke inside his head.

We've been a long time contacting one of you creatures of flesh.

He looked at Lee, asked: "Do you—hear it?"

She returned his stare mutely, her radio still not working; but she'd stopped her screaming.

You live on the surfaces of planets, we live in space. You know, for a long time we doubted your existence. It's caused quite a stir...

"What are you?" Reese's mouth was very dry as he spoke.

We are life. We are sentience. So are you. Is it so strange? More strange, indeed, that life can exist in a tiny, grubby thing like you. Take my body now—that's what you would call it, a "body". It fills a cubic light year of space, but it weighs only—ah, one ton.

"That did it," Reese said aloud. "I couldn't stand the attack this time. It drove me insane!"

That's ridiculous. And what attack are you talking about?

"Space-fear. Voices, half-formed thoughts, which pluck and pull and twist—"

By space! Then our thoughts exist on a frequency which some of you can grasp. If they damage, we'll change them, of course. We did not know. How wonderful it is that there are creatures of sentience as wide apart as we are. A great gulf between us, and yet, and yet...

REESE WAS beyond disbelief. The voice was there, talking to him patiently, as to a baby, and he could do nothing but accept. "But how can you exist in a vacuum?" he said. "Tell me that and maybe I'll believe—"

How? Who said anything about a vacuum? There is more matter drifting about freely in interstellar space than there is matter in all the stars of your galaxy. What do you need for the creation of life, my friend? A spark, a brief spark—which can be obtained at the core of certain nebulae; just as it can be obtained in your oxygen atmospheres. No, the stranger thing is that you can exist, planetbound except for your puny metal carriers...

Yes, Reese had read that somewhere—more matter in the void between the worlds than on the worlds and their suns.

It was true. And wouldn't it be foolish to reject the further revelation, of life? Where there was carbon and hydrogen and oxygen and nitrogen—and where cosmic forces could touch off a spark...

A bargain. We are prepared to make a bargain.

"Huh? What say?"

A bargain. Service for service. Our thoughts bother you?

"Damn right they do. About one out of fifty of us, actually, but it's enough."

Very well. We can retreat with them to a different frequency.

Reese felt giddy. Somehow, the space-fear had left him, and the voice spoke lucidly, simply, softly. But what price could a totally alien being demand for the removal of a blight that made life uncomfortable for millions of people?

It is a small thing, I assure you. You have something which you call a warp of space—something which bridges the gap into a new dimension and then out again? It disturbs. It creates images of horrible solids, of confining spaces, of cubes and globes and prisms.

The voice carried with it an aura of loathing. *Stop it. Oh, not the brief transient flashes when one of your metal carriers darts momentarily through hyper-space. I refer to the more permanent form, to the space-warp here at the Hub. Destroy that can you?* Alarm crept into the voice. *Can you do that?*

"You bet I can!"

A sigh, a sigh of pure ethereal contentment. *Then farewell. You'll not hear our disturbing voices again. You know, we consider them quite beautiful. Well, good luck, creature of flesh...* The faintest suggestion of a chuckle, and then the voice faded, was gone. Reese knew he never would hear it, or anything like it, again. Nor would Lee. Nor would anyone, ever.

Lee in his arms, he jetted back to the spaceship.

HE PUSHED her ahead of him through the port, tumbled in himself right behind her.

"Five ships blasted," Gilhanna sneered. "It's slaughter, as I expected. Won't those fools ever learn?"

"That's enough," Reese told him.

"What do you mean, enough?"

"I mean the war's over. Now!" He moved forward quickly, backing the bigger man into a corner. But then Gilhanna laughed.

"You puppy—you stupid little puppy! I'll break you in half."

They came together, their plastisuits pushed back against their clothing by the contact. Reese got the second biggest surprise of his life when he felt himself lifted high overhead, felt Gilhanna's massive hands digging into his flesh. Then he was hurled across the room, and he crashed with bone jarring impact against the far wall. Gilhanna roared, "Do you think I got where I am today by pussy-footing around?"

Reese stood up groggily, and they plunged together again, grappling. He caught a brief glimpse of Lee holding the two technicians at bay with a hand blaster.

Gilhanna found the going more difficult this time, but he got Reese down on the floor and he sat astride the warp-engineer, his fingers groping through the thin plastic for the neck. Reese squirmed and twisted, struck short hammering blows at the face leering into his own. With an oath, Gilhanna released him, and they tumbled over and over again.

Reese came out of it on top, pounding his fists at Gilhanna's head. The man could take it, could—no, now he was relaxing!

A trick! Gilhanna reached around to the back pocket of his plastisuit, came up with a knife. Reese blanched. The vacuum of space filled the blasting room. Gilhanna wouldn't have to deal him a mortal blow at all. He'd merely have to rip the suit...

Sweat ran down Reese's forehead into his eyes. With both hands he forced Gilhanna's wrist back, back. The knife gleamed dully. Just a scratch...

Gilhanna lunged upwards, and Reese caught the blow on his heavy gloves, deflected it. Gilhanna's hand fell back toward his own chest, and horror contorted his features as he tried to check its momentum. It sliced home—just a six inch tear.

Gilhanna's hands darted jerkily toward the rip, tried to force the edges back together. He died that way, a quick layer of frost covering him under the plastisuit with a translucent sheet as the cold of space licked in and condensed his body moisture...

* * *

"CONTACT their leader," Reese told Lee later. "He'll call it quits when you do. Then we'll have a meeting on Gilhanna II and decide what's to be done. This System's rich enough to ship sufficient water to III by tanker, and the answer's probably something like that."

"First thing," Lee reminded him, "is to destroy the warp. Sure, I heard everything out there too. Probably, although they couldn't destoy the warp, they could damage it at times. Amazing, isn't it? I mean, creatures like that—"

"Hell, that isn't the amazing part of it. Like they said, matter exists out there too, so why shouldn't life? Here's what's amazing: they gave us space-fear without knowing it, and we gave them their equivalent—I guess you'd call it solid-fear—the same way. Sort of poetic justice, huh?"

"Sure, but—"

"Will you stop talking and let me see if I was right about what kind of a gal-friend you could make now that you're not ornery anymore?"

"Me, ornery? You, you mean—and listen, someone's been pushing me around all my life, and now that that's over I don't want—"

"Shut up and let me kiss you."

As it turned out, they both liked that idea. Immensely.

The Double Occupation

No man was ever more inhumanly trapped in a body not his own. Could the star-bright heritage of Earth strike away his bonds?

IT WAS Corporal Ralph Cook's first tour of occupation duty and as he stood waiting on line at the T. M. checkpoint, stiffly ill at ease in his unfamiliar body, he felt slightly sick to his stomach. But that was to be expected so soon after transmigration. At any rate, he told himself with some small sense of relief, his stomach occupied approximately the same anatomical position in the complex entity that enveloped him.

What's your line of work? he asked the host mind, which shared the exoskeletonal Jaycee body with him.

The responding thought was truculent, arrogant. *I am not required to answer that question at this time.* Evidently the Jaycee host knew his Interstellar Law—which might be good or bad, depending on the creature's attitude. Right now, it looked bad, and might quickly become terrifying.

I was just trying to get acquainted, thought Ralph, holding his anger in check. He expected a reply, but was not too surprised when the Jaycee failed to answer him.

The long line of Jaycee soldiers, looking a great deal more like giant praying mantises than the lobsters they were supposed to resemble, advanced slowly toward the head of the checkpoint, their thin, delicate antennae quivering in the breeze, which was whistling through the tall reeds at the edge of Lake Comoy.

A human major and a master sergeant stood at the head of the line, and as the officer asked questions, the enlisted man made notations on a pad.

Overhead, Jayc's twin suns scorched a yellow-green sky. The larger, saffron orb, hung suspended almost at the zenith, while the smaller green one—actually blue, the Troop Information lecturer had pointed out—epicycled erratically behind it.

Ahead of the line and beyond the checkpoint, the mounds and towers of Comoy City, bomb-scarred but still bustling with Jaycee activity smoldered in the noon-day heat.

As Ralph and his host neared the head of the checkpoint, he wondered anxiously if the Jaycee would cooperate in the routine interrogation. It was hardly his problem, for they could easily substitute another host and confine the ornery Jaycee. But he knew he would be very ill if he had to undergo the transmigration ordeal again.

"Name?" asked the major, a bantam-rooster of a man, trim and neat in starched khaki, his bull-neck thrust sharply forward beneath his close-cropped head.

He was not exactly a physical paragon, this major. But Ralph envied him the familiar bipedal body, and facial features, the hands with their opposed thumbs, the five-digited feet—everything a man takes for granted until he gets occupation orders.

"Corporal Ralph Cook, sir," said Ralph, the voice box smoothly encapsulated between his head and thorax translating the clicks and clacks into their human equivalents.

The master sergeant scribbled and the major stared, frowning a little: "And your host's name?"

Ralph waited tensely, releasing his hold on the speech centers of his brain, waiting for the Jaycee to answer. Suddenly he was clicking again, and the voice box blared: "Desmar Kaloy, *sir*." There was too much emphasis on the "sir."

"Your occupation?" demanded the major, strutting around Ralph's new body in a circle, hands behind his back, examining the mantis-lobster minutely, although he had seen a hundred others like it that very morning.

"I am a school teacher, elementary level," Ralph heard himself replying, both in the clicks and clacks, which he now could understand, and in artificially vocalized English as well.

The major looked at the master sergeant and chuckled. "They have the same classification and assignment troubles we have," he said. "A school teacher in the Infantry." Then he told Ralph's host:

"Kaloy, the alternative to successful cooperation with your guest is confinement for the duration of the occupation. Is that understood?"

"Yes, sir. I was told that at the Prisoner of War camp, north of Lake Comoy."

"Very well, Kaloy. I trust you will not allow yourself to forget it."

Ralph could sense his host withdrawing from the centers of speech, and even from consciousness. But the Jaycee mind was there, lurking, listening—

"All right, Cook," the major was saying, "you're a school teacher. According to your form twenty, you've an impressive scholastic background. Do you think you can teach school here on Jayc?"

"I can try, Major," Ralph said, not caring to remind him that teaching a Union history of the Civil War in the deep South on Terra would have been a less hazardous undertaking.

"Don't sound so glum," the major said cheerfully, while the master sergeant continued with his scribbling. Apparently the voice box could translate Ralph's emotions along with his clicking speech. "Your tour of duty will only last six months. Then you'll have six more of rest and rehabilitation on Arcturus IV before you return to Earth for discharge. You're not a career man, are you?"

"No, sir," Ralph said, too hastily to please the master sergeant, who looked up quickly and glared at him.

"Well, good luck," the major said. "No matter how bad it gets, remember there are compensations awaiting you on Arcturus IV. Move along."

Arcturus IV was the Garmisch-Partenkirchen of the Army, complete with mountains loftier than the Alps towering over azure, tropical seas, and carnivals the year around. It was famous for its I.S.O. hostesses—and an up-to-date hospital, which treated, primarily, psycho-neuroses and associated nervous disorders.

The master sergeant removed Ralph's voice box from its capsule sheath at the top of his thorax and placed it in a neat row on the warehouse steps. Ralph checked a foolish impulse to stoop and retrieve it. Somehow, it represented his last connection with his own people. For the next six months he would be a Jaycee, living the Jaycee way of life. Desmar Kaloy, school teacher. Provided Kaloy played ball—and Ralph could bring charges and have the Jaycee confined if he proved stubborn—none of the other Jaycees would be aware of the masquerade.

Masquerade? Parasitic relationship would cut closer to the truth, Ralph told himself bitterly. Two million Earth soldiers, rotated at six month intervals, whose task it was to occupy and peacefully indoctrinate a planet which had, for some obscure reason, lost its respect for the interstellar moral code, and gone to war with a neighboring world. Why did Earth have to draw occupation duty whenever a few billion "bugs" needed re-indoctrination? It was infuriating to realize that Desmar Kaloy might very well be secretly laughing at him.

CHAPTER TWO

Purchasing a ticket on the monorail in Comoy City at his host's direction, Ralph was soon carried aloft in the gleaming, air-borne train. For interminable minutes the pale green waters of Lake Comoy tilted up crazily behind them as if they would spill into the busy city, and then, all at once, the silent monorail had climbed the range of hills beyond the city, and was swooping down with incredible speed into the green-brown lowlands, whizzing along so fast the landscape blurred, and the bushy blue trees became inverted pyramids. As Ralph stared, the occasional mound houses and the small settlements along the monorail merged even more miraculously into a blur of pastel color.

Ralph shared his compartment with two male Jaycees and a female. The males wore their traditional yellow sack-like garments, but the female was naked, her exoskeleton buffed and polished to a uniformly dazzling sheen, and stamped here and there with an intricate abstract design—her clan symbol.

Each of the Jaycees, Ralph included, had an irregular, branchlike stanchion in place of a seat. It was a grotesque way of traveling, but Ralph had to admit that the supports were not uncomfortable. Theoretically it should have been impossible to relax when perched upon an artificial tree-limb, but theory simply did not square with the facts.

"Going far?" the female clicked at Ralph.

He squirmed warily on his perch. This was his first contact with a Jaycee other than his host, and though he knew it to be purely a routine question, a manner of passing the time of day it put him on his guard, and made him uneasy.

"All the way to Central Terminal," Kaloy supplied the answer for him. "My home is in Plainview Heights."

"You're lucky, then. That far from Comoy City, the Army of Occupation should be spread thin."

"Why?" Ralph asked. "Do they bother you?"

"Where on Jayc have *you* been?"

"Studying in the University at Porgriny," Ralph answered, quickly. Had he admitted serving in the Jaycee Army, her suspicions would have been instantly aroused. After all, one out of every five Jaycee soldiers were now serving as hosts for Earth's occupation forces.

"Overtly, I suppose the Terrans are all right," the female admitted. "But don't you see, it isn't *their* war? They don't even know what caused it—what it was about. They were merely assigned here to occupy us and—well, to indoctrinate us. There's just no other word for it."

"Should there be? I mean, isn't interstellar cooperation important—not just for Jayc, but for an worlds?"

The female clicked wordlessly for a moment, then said: "I won't argue with you. Let's keep this a pleasant trip, shall we? I suppose you're a confirmed interstellarist?"

"I have an open mind," Ralph told her. Instantly Kaloy's sentience stirred within his own, saying, *What's the matter with you? Do you want to get me confined through no fault of my own? She'll see right through us in another minute. Just keep quiet and let her do most of the talking.*

On sped the monorail, the suns of Jayc sinking toward the horizon behind it, and casting quick dark shadows ahead across the flat country. By the time a mauve-streaked emerald dusk descended, Ralph had learned that the female, whose name was Ayd Setay, was a psychological social worker in Central Terminal. Her job, ironically was to rehabilitate Jaycee soldiers *after* they had spent six months as hosts!

The two males were members of a plumbing syndic in Mountainvale, a small city a few miles from Central Terminal. One of them had a nephew who attended school in Plainview Heights. Had Ralph, by any chance, ever heard of him? Not that he recalled.

Dinner for the Jaycees, who, like men, were omnivorous, might well have been quite palatable by human standards—although it was almost impossible to tell. At its conclusion, the monorail began to climb at an ever-increasing angle and a busily, whirring heat-device quickly dispelled the ensuing chill from their compartment.

"We'll reach Mountainvale before morning," one of the males said. "Elevation is almost fifteen thousand feet, so you can rest assured it's cold. Have you been to this part of the country before, Mr. Kaloy?"

"Only passing through," said Ralph, noncommittally.

"Well, I think you'll like it. Mind, I'm no chauvinist, but the mountains around here are unspoiled. We're still a hundred and fifty miles from Mountainvale, and more than twice that distance from Lake Comoy. It isn't good farming country, but some day the government is going to discover its value as a resort area. Meanwhile, if you're thrilled by an unspoiled wilderness, take a look outside. You could walk for days without seeing anyone, especially when it snows."

Ralph peered through the oval window and saw large, slow-drifting snowflakes falling in the glare of the monorail's lights. Horizon-piled clouds had swept up swiftly with the coming of night, or—more probably—had been waiting for them in the higher mountains. The snow made him feel uneasy, even though their monorail compartment seemed warm and secure.

He couldn't understand the feeling until he remembered that the Jaycee breathing apparatus was located on the outside of the body, on the exoskeleton itself. The fear was Kaloy's and probably subconscious—akin to a man's fear of falling, but unquestionably worse. The snow, freezing on an unprotected exoskeleton, could strangle a Jaycee in short order.

"Well," Ayd Setay clicked comfortably, "I'm going to turn in. Perhaps I should look at the brighter side of things; Kaloy. After all, the Earth occupation has now gone through three rotations. I rather imagine they'll consider their job finished before too long."

It was a factor Ralph hadn't considered. His six months on Jayc might well be the last any human would have to spend on that bleak world. Better still, they might recall the entire occupation force before the six months elapsed.

"I'd certainly like that," he said.

So would I, Kaloy told him grimly.

The two males from the plumbing syndic had lowered their heads in repose until their sharp chins rested on their tiny, crossed forearms. Ayd Setay began clicking a little tune, as if singing herself to sleep. Soon she was silent, slumped and relaxed like the others. Even Kaloy's consciousness retreated almost beyond Ralph's ken.

If he shut his eyes—damn it, the Jaycees were not endowed with eyelids—he could almost picture himself back on Earth somewhere, speeding along in a train, with the ceaseless click-clacking lulling him to sleep, and dispelling irrational fears of fine powdery snow dogging his breathing pores, of strangling ice coating his exoskeleton, and of ever more feeble forearms and mid arms clutching, clawing, sliding in its relentless embrace—

A strident whining sound awakened him as the monorail suddenly attempted deceleration too rapidly. He was thrust from his branch-perch and tumbled headlong to the floor of the compartment. Twisting over on his back he saw an expressionless Jaycee face appear in the doorway, and heard in frenzied, anxious clicks: "Fasten yourselves! The rail's out up ahead. The ice snapped it like a twig!"

The face was gone. The others stirred in wild alarm—the two men from the Mountainvale plumbing syndic lodged against the front wall of the compartment, and Ayd Setay still clinging precariously to her perch with one set of hands while she fastened a belt around her body with the other.

"Secure yourselves!" she clicked excitedly. "You heard what he said!"

Ralph tried desperately to follow the example set by the two plumbers as they scurried back to their perches. But he was soon forced to surrender control to Kaloy, and was able to observe his own ascent on the artificial branch with surprising objectivity while the monorail went on whining and decelerating.

Straps were quickly fastened about the juncture of his thorax and abdomen. Overhead lights and the monorail's outside beams winked out. Ralph looked through inky darkness toward where he thought the oval window was, but could see nothing.

"It's still snowing, I think," one of the males clicked.

The snow bothered them more than anything else. The whining had faded away, to be replaced by a hissing, sliding sound. The break-neck deceleration of the monorail had surrendered to an irregular, almost gentle swaying.

"We're safe," said Ayd Setay, clicking with relief.

She spoke too soon. They swayed far to the left, hung for the barest instant suspended, and then plummeted down, hurtling end over end, dislodging the branch-perches from their floor-moorings, ripping the safety straps from Ralph's lobster-mantis body.

All the lights in the falling monorail went out, plunging the passengers into darkness.

The last thing Ralph remembered was an agonizing burst of pain in his head—and the fact that the fear of falling had replaced fear of snow, even for Kaloy.

CHAPTER THREE

Ralph had a vague nightmare memory of snow, of Jaycees calling back and forth across a dazzling white expanse. It grew sharper, and became a memory of snow spilling down all him, of hands—not his own—brushing the snow away, of mournful clicks, of blankets and slick mountains of tarpaulins, of pain in four of his six host limbs and a terrible inability to move. Sharper still, and he grew aware of waves of suffocation, which ebbed and flowed, of hands massaging him. Hands? Claws. He clicked and clicked and wanted to scream.

Someone prodded him.

"Here, drink this."

A container was tilted to his mandibles. It was scorching stuff, but he drank. Another liquid was sloshed about his exoskeleton, then vigorously rubbed into his tracheae. For a tormenting instant his whole body seemed afire and he clicked outrageously. But afterwards he could breathe more easily, although his senses were drifting off vaguely as if they'd rubbed him down with some narcotic.

There were voices—or rather, clicks. The semantic difficulty, he thought, would always remain.

"Can we move this one?"

"He ought to remain still."

"He can't stay here. Anyway, the hospital in Mountainvale is already full."

"There's an extra bed and some medical supplies at the weather station on Halbady Peak. But I don't like the idea of moving him."

"We have no choice. Here, you! Bring that sledge. Easy now."

The pain was so violent when they lifted him that he passed out. He next was aware of a not unpleasant trundling motion and an expressionless face—he thought it was Ayd Setay, and Kaloy confirmed this—hovering over him. She clicked sympathetically and he fell asleep, dreaming of his own endoskeletal body, bipedal and all at once the most beautiful thing in the world—until Kaloy, unfortunately not asleep, banished the dream with a distasteful click.

There was a mountaintop eyrie, glass-domed and utterly isolated, looking down on a world of snow and jagged peaks and valleys only dimly visible through an encircling golden haze. There was a solitary Jaycee who lived there, casting off weather balloons, checking wind velocity, listening to book-tapes and munching a stimulating dried leaf, which after many days he gladly and graciously shared with Ralph.

There was even a perch, reclined at a comfortable forty-five degree angle, and all the good food Ralph Kaloy could consume. There was not much talk but there was no real need for talk in the first few weeks. There was need only for rest.

With rest came a growing realization of the extent of injuries sustained, of the shattered, twisted exoskeleton—comparable to a multi-fractured spinal column—and the damaged tracheae which would heal with time. And there were occasional visits by the doctor from Mountainvale, whenever the weather permitted his passage through the mountains.

"You're a lucky fellow, Desmar Kaloy. There'll be some scars. A limp, perhaps, I don't like the looks of that left rear leg at all. But you'll be all right in time. As long as you don't go jumping over these mountains like a hopper during the next year or so, you should be fine."

There was the slow, quiet friendship of the meteorologist, a taciturn old Jaycee with a surprising fount of stories, which kept Kaloy fascinated and Ralph interested. And there was the setting in of deep winter, as the Jaycee mountaineers called it. It came one night in a wild storm, which threw together clashing thunder and lightning with a steady fall of snow, and damaged the meteorologist's radio equipment so thoroughly that communication with the outside world was made impossible until the coming of spring.

There was Ralph's impatience as the weeks rolled slowly by and his strength returned, and his impetuous insistence that the meteorologist try to repair the equipment.

"Very well, young fellow. It's your job."

And every day Ralph would spend most of his time on the damaged radio instrument. Transistors had not yet replaced vacuum tubes on Jayc, but the radio was basically familiar. Kaloy's lack of experience with any form of electronics, however, was to hamper the work, and it was not until the first spring thaw had reached the valleys far below, puffing billowing clouds of vapor toward the eyrie, that Ralph succeeded in his task.

Why was he so fiercely impatient? He didn't know. His tour of occupation duty had been a lark, with four of his six months already gone. Surely the attitude was an unreasonable one, for Kaloy's still crippled body was only his temporarily. He'd be whole—and a human again—before he knew it. Still, had he fingernails, he would almost certainly have resorted to biting them.

Kaloy's increasing truculence may have had a great deal to do with it. The Jaycee host, when he wasn't listening to the stories, which could be drawn after much coaxing, from the meteorologist, would spitefully sulk in a corner of their mind.

When Ralph requested some not readily available information, Kaloy would balk, and finally cooperate—but only with reluctance. Ralph gathered that the Jaycee blamed his uninvited guest for the accident—which, at least, may have been partly true, for if Ralph had not occupied him, Kaloy would not have returned so soon to Plainview Heights.

It became worse every day, and by the morning Ralph had repaired the radio, Kaloy would hardly bother to answer his unspoken questions, unless, in so doing, he could go into malicious tirades about the men from Earth.

"Well," the meteorologist told Ralph, after speaking to Mountainvale for the first time on their repaired instrument, "I have to congratulate you. It's as good as new, Kaloy. They missed our weather reports, sure enough. But there wasn't anything we could do about that. Weather's fine in Mountainvale. A little cold, but not *this* cold."

"I guess I'll be heading down that way pretty soon now," Ralph told him.

"Well, now, I wouldn't rush things. Why don't you wait for the supply sledge, and travel back down with the team, safe and sound. Not much happens around these parts anyway, so you won't miss much by being cautious. About the only thing of importance that happened all winter, as far as I could learn from Crispay at the station, is something which ought to make a lot of Jaycees happy. Not me, though. I never minded much." It was a long speech for the meteorologist—when he wasn't telling stories.

"What's that? What happened?" Ralph demanded.

"No more occupation. The Earthmen left Jayc, every last one of them."

Ridiculously for a moment Ralph was aware of laughter echoing silently inside his head, mocking him. Kaloy's sentience, all at once, seemed sharper than it had been for a long time. It was as if the meteorologist's statement had stirred the Jaycee host from the fringes of a kind of cataleptic trance which he'd only left, of late, to ridicule and annoy.

Ralph's own emotions surfaced seconds later, wildly incredulous. It was a mistake—an insane rumor. It *had* to be a mistake.

"What are you talking about?" he cried. "Withdrawal of the occupation forces is impossible, and you know it."

The meteorologist clicked indifferently. "I don't care, either way. That's what they told me. Why, does it disturb you?"

Not me, thought Kaloy. *You've ruined my life, Earthman. This is an unexpected turnabout, is it not?*

Laugh now, Ralph told him bitterly. *Go ahead and laugh. We'll be sharing this body the rest of your life. Laugh if you think that's funny.*

You're going to be a monster. Kaloy went on mocking him. *The rest of your life. You always considered me a monster secretly, didn't you? You're a crippled monster yourself now.*

Shut up, said Ralph. Then, aloud: "Sure, it disturbs me. Here, let me at that radio."

Kaloy, who apparently believed the meteorologist, did not try to stop Ralph as he frantically beamed the call letters of the Earth occupation headquarters, repeating the signal over and over but getting no response.

"Can't this radio reach Comoy City?" he finally asked, an almost human tremor in his Jaycee voice.

The meteorologist clicked in thought, then said, "Only rarely. The waves are short and are usually trapped here in the mountains. Is it important?"

"Do they have a news station in Mountainvale? Call it for me, please." And, moments later, Ralph was saying anxiously, "This is Desmar Kaloy at the weather station on Halbady Peak. No, I'm not the meteorologist. I was a victim of the monorail crash."

Would the Jaycee never stop asking questions? "I'd like some information," he went on urgently. "Yes, you'd call it routine news. He wanted to shout, *it's not routine to me.* The Jaycee was switching him to someone else. Would he wait? Damned red tape, as bad as the Army's.

"Ah. Yes, this is Kaloy. I know. I was referred to you by the operator. Thank you. What information do you have on the departure of the Earth occupation forces?"

Kaloy had retreated again, burrowing deep into the stratum between conscious and subconscious. Ralph had learned the trick, too. It was like sleep, but far more restful to the mind, and it affected the body, the shared body, not at all. There, in that strange half-state, you could conjure up dreams at will. At first Ralph had thought it an attribute of the Jaycee brain, but in more pleasant days, soon after the crash, Kaloy had assured him it was the result of two minds sharing one body.

"Here we are," said the Jaycee in Mountainvale after a brief pause. "Sixteen days ago, after being so ordered by the Interstellar Confederacy, the Earth Army of Occupation was withdrawn from Jayc. The removal from their host bodies of almost two million alien Earthmen was carried out without serious incident. A preliminary psychological examination of the hosts indicates that one-third of them will need psychological readjustment and the Jaycee Government has therefore put into continuous operation its forty-six rehabilitation camps all over the world. Dr. Ruy Orty, director of the camps, declared that—"

"No, no!" Ralph clicked. If Jaycees had possessed sweat glands, he'd have been bathed in his own perspiration. "Don't you have anything else on the Earthmen?"

"Well, let me see. Yes, here's something. Lieutenant-General Willis B. Eichler, Commander-in-Chief of the Earth Army of Occupation, extended his heartfelt thanks to the authorities and people of Jayc, saying, 'Your sincere cooperation assured the success of this mission. It is hoped by the people of Earth and the other worlds of the Interstellar Confederacy that Jayc is now ready to take its place in the community of worlds as a morally responsible member planet. We wish you all good luck for the future.'"

"Anything else?" Ralph clicked desperately. "Were there any snags, any delays in the withdrawal?"

"I seem to remember something. Are you preparing a thesis? Splendid subject...ah, here we are. A final survey by the occupation forces revealed that eight hundred and seventy-six occupation soldiers were unaccounted for. This number was reduced drastically when rural area reports filtered into the Earth caretaker forces—"

"Caretaker!" Ralph gasped. "Is someone left?"

"I'm coming to that. Rural reports revealed that some seven hundred and forty-three hosts had died natural and violent deaths during the occupation, their Earth 'guests,' of course, perishing with them. Unaccounted for: one hundred and thirty-three occupation soldiers. Considering the scope of the operation, the Occupation Information Office said that the casualties were..."

Ground static drowned out the Jaycee's clicking while Ralph twirled the dials in a frenzy of frustration. When the clicking Jaycee's speech could be heard again, it was faint and hard to follow, "Such negligible losses...cooperation of the Jaycee people. It has been speculated...fifty percent of the so-called casualties...adjusted to Jaycee life and refused to return."

"I can't hear you," Ralph pleaded. "I can't hear you. What about that caretaker force? Are they still waiting?"

"...detachment of Earth specialists at the T.M. Station, Comoy City. Stragglers...are asked to communicate with...them at once. Any Jaycee with information leading...of the stragglers...will be rewarded."

"How would you like some of that reward money?" Ralph cried. "You see, I'm an Earthman. I've been trapped here on Halbady Peak since the monorail accident and—"

"Hello, Halbady Peak. Hello, Halbady! Can't hear you. Mountainvale to Halbady Peak. Hello, Halbady Peak. Halbady—"

"You've got to hear me. How long is the caretaker force going to stay on Jayc? *How long?*"

Squawk. And a rushing sound, as of wind...

CHAPTER FOUR

"I couldn't help overhearing you," the meteorologist said. "If there is something I can do to help—"

"You can do plenty," said Ralph.

A pleasant if monotonous lethargy had possessed him since the accident, but now he felt suddenly vital and alive. If Kaloy had been aware of the conversation with Mountainvale, the Jaycee gave no indication. Perhaps, Ralph abruptly found himself thinking, Kaloy had been responsible for the lethargy.

"You can tell me the best way to get to Mountainvale. You can try to repair this radio, and contact the authorities. You can..."

"I'll do everything within my power," the meteorologist interrupted. "But it's very common for the cold to snap our aerial, and outdoor boosters at this time of the year. You'd better do what you have to do and forget about the radio, although I'll be trying to fix it after you're gone."

The meteorologist hopped to a cabinet and returned with a map of the area. "Take this with you. Of the three passes between here and Mountainvale, the one on the east is usually the best in late winter. The distance is almost two hundred miles though, and in your condition I wouldn't advise the trip."

"What do you want me to do, be stranded here?"

"He mentioned a caretaker detachment—"

"And didn't say how long it would stay. They're liable to take my own body back to Earth, over three hundred light years away. Or destroy it, I don't know which."

"What do they do with your body while you're a Jaycee, anyway?" the meteorologist asked.

"It's kept in a suspension vat," Ralph replied while he studied the map . "Womb-like. Its breathing is stopped, its heart slowed, and it is fed and given oxygen through an artificial umbilical cord. All the perception areas of the brain are blanked out so that only that part controlling heartbeat and other automatic functions remains active. There's no perception at all. They can keep it up indefinitely, and the body hardly ages at all. But it's expensive and .after they give all the stragglers enough time to reveal themselves, or after they conduct a search, all the remaining bodies will probably be destroyed."

"Pardon me for saying so, but that sounds cruel."

"Yes and no," said Ralph. "For the individual, yes. For his family, his wife if he has a wife, it is merciful. You see, his family does not know if he's dead or alive. Not knowing, they can't live normally, so he's declared missing in the line of duty, then declared dead after a certain amount of time has elapsed."

Once more, Ralph had that odd feeling of unexpected objectivity, as if he were talking about someone other than himself. It was, he surmised, the location of sentience, which counted. Right now he was far more interested in the well-being of Desmar Kaloy's exoskeletonal body.

A while ago it had been quite the other way around. But that had been strictly an I-don't-want-to-admit-I'm-not-human response. If Kaloy died, he would die. He wanted to return to his own body and would use Kaloy to any extreme short of death to do so. But...

Shouldn't I have something to say about that, Ralph Cook?

Did you hear our conversation?

Most of it, I'm not sure I liked what I heard.

Surely you'd be glad to see me go?

I'm not sure. You'd better look to your own welfare.

Ralph found himself walking with the odd hopping gait of the Jaycees to a mirror on the far wall of the room. He stood there and turned slowly, examining himself.

I see you're unimpressed. Just as you would be if an animal of your world had a shortened leg or a limp, or a twisted body. It may be injured, but you don't regard it as an ugly cripple or freak. You only regard your own species in such a light. To you I'm a damaged vehicle. In my own eyes—in the eyes of my people—I'm ugly, deformed, someone to be stared at and pitied.

Ralph thought, *I don't see what that has to do with my staying or leaving.*

I was going to take a vacation, to forget the war, down at Seaside Moors. I never would have taken the monorail for Central Terminal. It was your fault. If I have to live with this deformity, why shouldn't you?

"I can give you heavy mountain garments and a supply of food concentrates," the meteorologist was saying. "There is a sledge and two *ixors*, hibernating, in the basement. You can start out any time you wish."

"At once," said Ralph. *Ixors*, he knew with knowledge borrowed from Kaloy, were almost man-sized insects of burden, which ordinarily burrowed underground and slept through the winter. "How do we wake up the *ixors?*"

"With stimulants. It's dangerous, and they usually don't survive very long. But it's done in emergencies."

Tense moments later, Ralph was wolfing down a hot meal, his last until the *ixors* pulled his sledge through the pass to Mountainvale. The meteorologist was busy stirring the giant insects from their season long slumber and Kaloy had retreated again to the edge of the subconscious.

The injured Jaycee, Ralph suspected, might pose a problem more vexing than the snow and ice. If Kaloy really wanted him to stay—it seemed incredible, but the Jaycee evidently needed psychological help—the difficulty might develop into a contest of will between them. And the Jaycee, being more familiar with their body, might be expected to gain the upper hand.

Bundled in a bulky, shapeless garment, which was fastened by draw strings at each of his six extremities beneath an overlapping water-proof slicker, Ralph waited impatiently for the meteorologist in the numbing wind outside the eyrie. Securely attached to the back of his thorax was a pack of food concentrates, emergency medical supplies and a reserve slicker. The toboggan-like sledge, its long graceful sweep of surface flush with the snow for increased distribution of weight, was barely wide enough to accommodate the broadest part of Ralph's Jaycee abdomen.

Presently the meteorologist emerged from the lower level entrance of the eyrie, which reared its gleaming dome massively over their heads. He was coaxing along the still-sluggish *ixors*, which resembled huge, stubby grasshoppers, with thick, brittle hind legs folded almost double down the length of their abdomens.

"Do they jump?" Ralph demanded anxiously.

The meteorologist clicked humorously. "You bet they jump. You'll be strapped in. A soft Earth body couldn't stand the ride. A Jaycee can. I don't know about an injured one."

"I'm healed."

"Perhaps. Don't expect the fractured junctures to be as strong as the rest of you, though. I only hope you don't rebreak part of your skeleton." The meteorologist commenced harnessing his *ixors* to the sledge with thick, leathery thongs.

"They're usually quite docile," he pointed out. "But under the influence of the stimulant, they're somewhat unpredictable. Here you are." And he handed Ralph a small packet containing a dozen tubes of amber liquid and a long-needled syringe. "If they display torpor, inject this at the base of the thorax armor. Don't try any other place or you'll snap your needle."

Ralph nodded, fastening the packet to his slicker by means of a barbed hook . Then he settled himself on the toboggan, secured himself with the double strap fastened to its edges and firmly grasped the thongs trailing from the *ixors'* harness with his forearms.

"Well," he said. "I guess I'm ready."

The meteorologist checked his straps, draped a blanket across his abdomen and clicked with concern. "Good luck to you, Earthman," he said. "And, for the mutual good of our people, take care of your host."

"Thank you," Ralph said. "I'll try."

You'll never make it to Mountainvale in time to contact your friends, Kaloy told him spitefully.

Ralph released the harness, jiggling it experimentally up and down. The eyrie leaped away from him, the ground streaking down and back on either side. To his utter consternation the sledge alighted fifty yards away with a tremendous jolt, shaking his exoskeleton. Fearfully he shook himself, and found all areas intact. But before he could regain his composure the *ixors*, far from torpid, were underway again.

CHAPTER FIVE

Jayc's twin suns had come out brightly here in the high mountains for the first time all winter, kindling the snowy peaks with fires of green and saffron yellow. The pass to

Mountainvale was a steep-walled gorge, possibly the bed of some ancient frozen river, which had carved its way down to the foothills, melted and rushed on across the plains to Lake Comoy or to the sea far beyond.

But now the gorge was bare-walled, its rock strata reflecting the green and yellow suns in dazzling brilliance. The icy bed itself was a blinding saffron mirror, except where some of the taller sunward peaks cast their cold dark shadows across its gleaming immensity.

The Jaycee exoskeleton, Ralph soon learned, could cushion most of the shock of the *ixors'* great, fifty-yard leaps. The insects seemed tireless, pausing only long enough to gather their strong hind legs under them before taking off. Incredible seemed the ease with which they alighted on their runner-like thighs, and glided silently across the ice for several hundred yards, the sledge trailing easily behind them on its taut harness straps.

Down behind the western mountains dipped the suns of Jayce, summoning first emerald twilight and then dusk and darkness. Ralph halted the *ixors*, munched on some food concentrates with stiff, frozen mandibles, activated the sledge's small heating unit, wrapped himself snugly in blanket and slicker, and fell almost instantly into the dreamless asleep of utter exhaustion.

When he awoke, the *ixors* were lying motionless on the ice. All of his prodding and shaking could not stir them. But almost miracuously the syringe of stimulants had them hunched, and ready in a matter of minutes. While eating, he probed his mind for Kaloy's consciousness, but he could not find it. The Jaycee still slumbered, although dawn had long since fingered the higher peaks with green, and the brittle cold air was knife-edged and invigorating.

On the second night, Ralph dreamed that the *ixors* still labored forward in seven-league leaps. When he awoke, feeling hardly rested at all, he saw that a light, powdery snow had fallen. He dreamed the same dream on the third night; and the fourth. He felt exhausted, as if he hadn't slept in days. He attempted to evoke Kaloy's consciousness, but was not successful.

He had estimated the *ixors'* progress at some fifty miles daily at the very least, which meant that they should have already reached Mountainvale. Since there was no way out of the pass, it seemed incredible that they could be lost.

Kaloy, he pleaded. *Kaloy, can something be wrong?*

No answer.

Kaloy, listen to me. We'll have no food left if we don't reach Mountainvale soon.

Still no answer.

There was nothing to do but inject the *ixors* with stimulants again, and keep moving. He poised the syringe over the first insect's thorax—and deliberately held it there, not actively resisting the downward motion, or the plunging of the needle into the flesh at the base of the creature's exoskeletonal armor. The needle slipped in almost instantly, the syringe was depressed. Kaloy was in no trance, cataleptic or otherwise.

You did that. I didn't, Ralph thought. Stop playing games.

Why don't you let me sleep? came in spiteful protest.

We slept all night.

There was the thought of laughter. Then: *You slept all night.*

What about you, Kaloy?

I have been sleeping days.

The enormity of what Kaloy had done did not at first occur to Ralph. *Then I did not dream that the ixors moved by night! You drove them at night. Thank you.*

More laughter.

But in that case, we certainly should have reached Mountainvale long ago.

Our food is almost gone, Ralph Cook. By one third of the distance we are closer to Halbady Peak than to Mountainvale. We best return there before we starve.

Do you hear, Ralph Cook?

When Ralph understood, he slammed his forearm down in blind rage and frustration on the surface of the sledge. He longed for his own bipedal body. He wanted to stand there, at home in it, and throttle Kaloy. But you couldn't strangle a tracheae-breathing Jaycee by choking him. Nor could you expect a Jaycee's motivation to be clear to you, even if you shared his alien body.

You've doubled back on our trail every night, Ralph accused his host. *After the first day, we went practically nowhere. Why did you do it?*

There was an explanation, but to Ralph it seemed monstrous. Ralph had said that the caretaker force couldn't be expected to remain at Comoy City forever. Kaloy had been injured—crippled—and he held Ralph responsible. Kaloy wanted Ralph to suffer too. Kaloy thought that, in time; Ralph would come to accept the alien Jaycee body as his own. Then Ralph would suffer with his host.

There would be time enough to think about Ralph's own Earth body later, if at all. If it wasn't too late already. Did Kaloy think it was too late? Kaloy didn't know. Ralph knew more about such matters than Kaloy did. Kaloy was quite willing to let circumstances unfold themselves in their natural and inevitable fashion.

It's your body, Ralph pointed out. *Mine only temporarily. When you volunteered for occupation, you promised to cooperate.*

The occupation is history. I am a free agent. How was I to know I'd only be interned four months more if I hadn't volunteered?

Was it self-pity which motivated the Jaycee?

Well, Ralph thought again, *it's your body. Your body, my vehicle, call it what you choose. We're going to Mountainvale. I'm not going to sleep at all and the food won't last. But we'll get there. You brought this on yourself.*

But I'm convalescing. I can't take the strain, the lack of food—

You should have thought of that sooner.

The *ixors* bounded forward. The harness straps tightened. The sledge leaped away.

He was, after all, as much Desmar Kaloy physically as Kaloy was himself. He ached atrociously from the exoskeletonal armor of his thorax to the stout claws of his hind legs. Every time the sledge alighted he wanted to scream but, lacking vocal cords, had to settle for clicking instead. And hunger twisted his entrails and tightened nerves, which already overloaded with the intolerable animosities of two conflicting personalities, threatened to snap altogether.

The newly-healed body conveyed messages of sleep. The tired brain wanted to accept them, but Ralph rebelled. Soon he came to distinguish between two different kinds of sleep, and so could manage an occasional uneasy nap. When the demands of the body became too great, when his muscles were possessed by a leaden lethargy, and his head lolled against his thorax, it was safe. For then Kaloy must sleep too, and Ralph only had to worry about awakening ahead of him.

But when it was the brain which thought of sleep, conjuring images of Ralph's own slumbering body which somehow—like a poorly executed painting—were not quite correct, not fully in proportion, not altogether human—then he had to remain awake at all costs, often rubbing his sensitive antennae stalks with snow until Kaloy's attack passed.

Once Kaloy had awakened from the body slumber first, and when Ralph became aware of his surroundings was calmly and expertly smashing the syringe against the edge of the toboggan, maliciously spilling its amber contents on the snow. A disaster more dreadful could hardly have been imagined. The *ixors* were in stupor and would remain in stupor—either perishing that way or going into deep hibernation again. There was nothing to do but leave the sledge and set out on foot with barely enough energy remaining to take each painful hopping stride.

Fatigue crossed the threshold of perceptive awareness . The ice, the snow, the jagged peaks, the coming of dusk and the desperate, brief moments of slumber, the first green suggestion of dawn, and the ordeal of plunging on—all became a hazy, obscurely experienced nightmare. Kaloy had, for the time being, given up any attempt to interfere. Kaloy, who could thus sleep through it all, was lucky.

In a dream-like torpor, Ralph followed the pass as it angled sharply down and to the left. Perhaps, he thought vaguely, in their native state before they had conquered the environment and themselves, the Jaycee were accustomed to hibernate. Perhap...

The cliffs on either side of him dropped away. The pass—a road now—became clear of ice and snow. Ahead were small hills. No—the mounds of a settlement! There was the rich verdant green of seasonless mountain plants, the evergreen smell as of some magically transplanted valley of Earth. And there were figures coming toward him, Jaycees, reaching out and catching him before he could stumble and fall.

There was something he wanted to tell them. Something more important even than rest and sleep and a warm soup to drink. There was something... If only he could remember! He slept.

He was feverishly dreaming again. In his torment he sensed that much time had passed, and had half-formed memories of a Jaycee hospital and of a long, drug-induced slumber. No, he was not dreaming in a total sense. He could now feel the difference between a dream and an action of his Jaycee body while he slept. Kaloy at least was awake. He had come a long way through streets embanked with snow, through dimly-lit passages, which he suspected, were taking him ever deeper underground.

He wanted to wake up completely, but could not. But Kaloy was awake and thinking, I'll *stop him once and for all. If he tells his story, the authorities will be contacted, and we'll be on our way back to Comoy City.*

At last he stood in a warm, damp chamber, thick with a moist greenish haze, which hid the high-vaulted ceiling and shadowed the far walls. Suspended from the unseen roof and hanging within reach of his forelimbs was an intricate network of crisscrossed girders, with a thick, leathery pod as big as his body attached to each angled juncture. There were scores of the brown-gray things, hundreds of them.

He probed Kaloy's thoughts desperately. Cocoon? Chrysalis? An earlier stage of Jaycee life, developing underground, undergoing metamorphosis, waiting to emerge with the blossoming summer as full-grown Jaycees? He had never seen Jaycee children. Were these, then, the children, the earlier stage? He wished he had paid more attention to his Troop Information lecturer. He sincerely wished he had.

His right forelimb was clasping a long knife. He was reaching swiftly upward now, grasping one of the giant pods, pulling the swaying leathery thing down toward him. Desperately he tried to awaken, to stop the quick, thrusting motion of his limb. But Kaloy fought him back.

Ralph plunged the blade home, ripping a slash in the pod. The instant he stepped clear a pulpy yellow liquid began to drip from the opening. Faster it spilled and faster, gathering into a spreading hideous pool at his feet. He clicked loudly and insistently, and soon other Jaycees were hopping frantically toward him, taking the knife from him, wrestling him to the damp floor as he struggled.

If only he could make them understand, if only he could tell them it was Kaloy, not Ralph Cook of Earth who had done this horrible thing. If only he could let them know there were two of them, fighting for control of the shared, tormented brain. But he fought on, and they carried him, writhing and kicking, from the vault. As if in compassion someone administered a hypodermic, and he relaxed at once. He could think for himself now, lucidly. But the Jaycee body would not obey his commands. Frustrated, he could do nothing but wait.

He was deposited on a reclining perch, then drugged again. Didn't they know that time was working against him? Why wouldn't they let him talk? He lost consciousness.

CHAPTER SIX

Ralph Cook awoke to see Jaycee faces peering at him. Mandibles clicked excitedly, forelimbs waved in his face. He listened, numb with horror, utterly sick at heart.

"The pupa he attacked is dead."

"He's ill. He couldn't have known what he was doing."

"Well, we've sent for the regional psychologist from Central Terminal."

"You still think he should be tried and executed?"

"I do. The circumstances indicate cold, cruel premeditation. You don't just stumble into the incubator vault."

"No, you don't. But if he's ill and—can be cured—"

"I suggest we let the psychologist decide."

"If he can be exorcised—"

"Don't tell me you believe that story we got from Halbady Peak? I'm not blaming the meteorologist, understand. But if he's an Earthman, why didn't he say so before? He was there four months."

"He's waking! He hears us!"

"I *am* an Earthman," Ralph said. "I didn't say so because I was under command of absolute secrecy."

"There, I told you! We ought to send him to Comoy City to be exorcised."

"We'll let the psychologist decide. I think the Earthmen are already gone, anyway."

"Call them," Ralph pleaded. "Please call them. Maybe there's still time."

"All right, let's assume you tire an Earthman. Did you kill the pupa? Surly your host wouldn't have done it."

"I did not," Ralph told them. "Desmar Kaloy was trying to delay me. I guess he thought if he committed so serious a crime I'd never get away."

Try and persuade them to believe it, thought Kaloy.

"What you say doesn't make sense on two counts. In the first place, why should a Jaycee kill one of our pupa? In the second place, even assuming your statement to be true—which I don't grant for one minute—why on Jayc would he want you to stay? He'd want you to be exorcised, and good riddance."

See? came triumphantly from Kaloy.

"Are you from the police?" Ralph asked.

"No but my companion is. I'm a doctor."

"I demand that the caretaker detachment of Earth occupation forces in Comoy City be notified."

"You're not in a position to demand *anything*. We've sent for a psychologist who, with the necessary apparatus, should be able to determine your identity."

"And meanwhile I just wait?"

"You just wait."

"But in even a few hours it may to be too late."

They ignored him, turning their backs and clicking in low tones between themselves. The room was white and bare, unfurnished except for his perch. He asked Kaloy if the psychologist really would be able to tell. When the answer was a glum and reluctant affirmative, he began to feel somewhat better. It was a minor victory, anyway.

Half an hour later, the psychologist arrived, unclothed. Obviously the Jaycee was a female. Even when he borrowed Kaloy's familiarity with his own people, Ralph still found it almost impossible to tell one Jaycee from another.

"Desmar Kaloy!" the female psychologist cried in surprise. "Is it really you?"

Ralph suddenly remembered that the female he had met on the monorail had been a psychological social worker. Psychologist? In Mountainvale the terms would be synonymous. What was her name? Ayd—Ayd Setay.

"Hello, Ayd Setay," he said. "I'm glad to see the accident hasn't left its mark on you."

"I was just shaken up a bit. They let me care for you as far as the eyrie. Then I went on to Central Terminal alone. We've been busy rehabilitating former hosts, and won't be finished for a long time. What seems to be the trouble with you?"

"Look at me," he clicked despondently. It was not Ralph now, but Kaloy speaking. "Look at me. Scarred, hideously crippled—a monster. They—should have let me die."

Ayd Setay clicked her sympathy. "A little exoskeletonal surgery can do wonders, after you're fully healed."

"That wasn't me," Ralph clicked in alarmed protest. "I never carry on like that."

But Kaloy added, "It's just that I must be a pitiful sight in your eyes."

Ayd Setay clicked something—barely audible—about a split personality, then went into conference with the doctor and the police officer. Presently another Jaycee entered the already crowded room, carrying a small drum set, with graph paper and stylus, on a metal stand.

"I'd rather you didn't do this," Ralph heard himself saying.

"It's harmless," Ayd Setay assured him. "Won't take a minute. There, now."

A metal brace went swiftly over his head and was clamped tightly at the sides with a sticky salve. From somewhere, he heard the hum of electricity. The drum began to rotate slowly, the stylus to trace a line on the graph paper.

A few moments later, Ayd Setay was telling the doctor: "An electroencephalogram doesn't lie. Earthman and Jaycee share Desmar Kaloy's body."

Unperturbed, the doctor said, "Then it becomes a question for the courts to decide. Unless, through careful psychological testing, you can determine who actually was guilty of the crime."

"Perhaps I could. But it might well take months—unless they both cooperated. As a psychological social worker, my first allegiance is to the Jaycee, Desmar Kaloy. But as a citizen of Jayc my first allegiance must be toward our world."

"I don't follow you."

"We'll have to do what is right in the eyes of the Interstellar Confederacy," clicked Ayd Setay. "Desmar Kaloy can be rehabilitated—or punished—later. But first the shared body must be sent to Comoy City to be exorcised."

"You'd let the Earthman go free after destroying one of our pupa?"

"This wasn't Earth's war, but her people have suffered several hundred casualties."

"You're talking like an Interstellarist…"

"I don't think so. I'm trying to do what's best for Jayc. I'm taking the Earthman—and Desmar Kaloy—to Comoy City."

"Is the caretaker detachment still there?" Ralph asked anxiously as the apparatus was removed from his head.

"I've heard they're getting ready to leave," Ayd Setay clicked. "But we'll call and tell them you're coming."

"And they'll wait?" It was Kaloy asking the question.

"There's no reason why they shouldn't. Of course—"

But Ralph answered himself emphatically. "Of course they'll wait."

Ayd Setay clicked her interest. "My scientific curiosity says I ought to keep him here. What a study he would make! You'll notice the way the two personalities, Jaycee and alien, argue in the one shared brain."

"I'll tell you all about it," Ralph promised. "Just call Comoy City, and get me there."

"It is clearly the court's right to decide," protested the doctor.

"Hardly," clicked Ayd Setay. "I'll sign a writ of *dokay maj*, if that will satisfy you. Desmar Kaloy is not responsible for his actions and is in need of mental treatment."

Ayd Setay was gone for perhaps half an hour, while doctor and policeman clicked together, obviously debating. Kaloy was sulking again, especially when the policeman was heard to say that the writ was perfectly legal under the circumstances. Kaloy was losing ground.

The deeper Kaloy burrowed into funk, the more optimistic Ralph began to feel. It seemed completely a matter of routine now. In days—and perhaps less—he would be safely back in his own body, rocketing toward the rehabilitation center on Arcturus IV, the whole nightmare of Jayc forever behind him.

Once there, solaced and healed by the sunlit tropic sea, mellowed by heady Antarean wine, he might even feel sorry for Desmar Kaloy, who had never been able to adjust to the occupation.

When Ayd Setay returned, she signed the writ giving her control over Kaloy until such time as his psychological rehabilitation could be completed.

"Incidentally," she clicked, "I've contacted the caretaker detachment in Comoy City. Incredible as it may seem, they want to give me a reward."

"I want to be punished," Ralph heard himself clicking. "I murdered a pupa and demand to be punished. You can't make me go to Comey City."

"There," said the doctor. "You see?"

"That was Kaloy," Ralph protested. "Not me—Kaloy."

Ayd Setay clicked, "I've already reserved our perches on the Comoy City monorail, and the sooner the Earthman is back where he belongs, the sooner we can start with Desmar Kaloy's rehabilitation."

"And eventually punish the wrong individual," protested the doctor.

"That's quite enough," Ayd Setay clicked impatiently. "I'm going to pack a few things. I'll call for the patient later this afternoon. Meanwhile, give him this sedative, and please don't disturb him any more than is necessary."

The sedative was injected into Ralph's quivering thorax. He slept.

CHAPTER SEVEN

He dreamed of Arcturus IV, where he was telling an attractive hostess from Earth all about his adventures on Jayc, embellishing them considerably, and enjoying every moment of his triumph to the full. Presently, however, the Earth girl's long-lashed eyes were replaced by lidless Jaycee orbs, the full red lips by clicking mandibles. It was the Mountainvale doctor, leading him along the streets of the small city.

This was no dream, Ralph suddenly knew. The doctor was saying, "I called the caretaker detachment and apologized, telling them it was a false alarm. There is a doctor I know in Central Terminal who can exorcise you properly. He is the man to call upon under the circumstances."

"Why are you doing this?" Kaloy demanded.

"Because it seems incredible to me that you could have committed that crime. Because in exorcising you our way we will also execute the Earthman."

"Perhaps I don't want that."

"Now you're joking."

"I'm not. Just look at me—an ugly cripple, for life. I want the Earthman to suffer with me. In time he'll accept this body as his own, and realize how terribly deformed he has made it."

Ralph's struggle was hardly physical, but it left him exhausted. He struggled desperately to awaken, to protest, to point out that now he was legally Ayd Setay's charge, and that anything they did with him would be illegal. He remained aware only—sentient but powerless. For the first time he found himself siding with Kaloy. His host's way would at least give him time. The doctor's way was a short monorail trip to Central Terminal—and death.

"I'm not questioning the legality of what you propose," the doctor clicked. "Morally, however, I believe I am doing the right thing. It will be my way or not at all."

Ralph groaned inwardly.

"But don't you understand? I have no desire to live unless the occupation soldier can live with me and learn to suffer as I must."

"You're being melodramatic," said the doctor. "Once exorcised, you'll feel better. Come along."

"Please. Just hide me somewhere, until the caretakers leave Jayc. I'll work out my own future."

"Your mind is possessed," declared the doctor superstitiously. "Come along with me and be exorcised."

"He's stirring," Kaloy clicked. "I can feel him trying to waken."

"Then hurry."

"If he goes free I have no wish to live."

"He won't go free," the doctor promised. "He'll perish."

"I want him to suffer."

The debate had cost Kaloy his control over Ralph, who could feel it slipping slowly, who could feel his way along the nerve fibers again, and through the motor regions of the brain. Control came not all at once but slowly, and he wondered if Kaloy could feel the extent of his returning powers.

I'm winning, he thought.

Abruptly he turned and fled down the street, the doctor's frantic clicking fading swiftly as he darted around a corner and kept going. Kaloy fought him furiously every step of the way, frustrating the muscles, issuing contradictory orders.

He stumbled on, wondering a little wildly if the Jaycees ever became intoxicated and deciding that if they did he must have presented the aspect of a thoroughly drunk individual.

His whole body burned painfully as, like laboring lungs, the tracheae gulped increasing quantities of oxygen to keep him going. He realized fully then why the Jaycees were a comparatively sedentary people, and hoped the doctor would not pursue him too vigorously. Of course, the doctor could call ahead to the monorail station, but the law was on Ayd Setay's side, even if public opinion might not be.

The city of mound-like dwellings bounced and tilted crazily about him as he hopped along from street to street, the motion rendered more erratic by Kaloy's attempt to thwart his flight. He paused just long enough to ask a pedestrian the location of the monorail station, then plunged on.

Officials met him at the station and held him while he clicked and swore, and informed them they were breaking every law on Jayc and in the Interstellar Confederacy as well if they didn't let him contact Ayd Setay or the Earth caretaker detachment in Comoy City. The doctor had called, they said. The doctor had told them to hold him if he appeared at the station. They would listen to the good doctor.

The doctor, as it turned out, was Ayd Setay! Eschewing her billowing wraps as soon as she was warmed by the station heaters. Ayd Setay said, "When you weren't at that doctor's place I didn't know if they had taken you somewhere else or if you'd come here to meet me, or even if that split-personality of yours had acted up. I rushed right over."

"A little of each," Ralph said, explaining what had happened.

The caretakers—by now somewhat bewildered—were called again. Everything, including Ralph's body, was in readiness. Now they said they were from Missouri, Ayd Setay informed Ralph, whatever that meant. First he was, then he wasn't, then he was again. Would he please hurry?

He certainly would. With Ayd Setay he boarded the monorail and was soon whisked across the Jayc landscape, suspended almost a hundred feet off the ground on the monorail cable, watching the great mountains and then the fertile plains of Jayc unfold below him.

The war, Ayd Setay admitted, had been a Jaycee mistake, an impetuous attempt at imperialism in an age of interstellar cooperation. The resulting occupation, if anything, had brought Jayc closer to the main stream of interstellar civilization. For that her people were grateful, and hoped to make the most of it. Would he carry that message back to

Earth and the rest of the Interstellar Confederacy? He would be delighted.

He settled back comfortably and watched the scenery below him—and fought against Desmar Kaloy's hatred.

I'll never let you get away, Kaloy had thought, and kept on thinking. It sounded fantastically like the vow of a lover.

Kaloy would take no food. Ralph wasn't hungry.

If you can't suffer, I don't want to live. I should have let the doctor kill you.

Ayd Setay sympathized with Ralph but admitted her first concern was for Kaloy's welfare. The Earth caretaker detachment would administer to Ralph's needs soon enough. Kaloy, however, refused to talk with her, even after she had Ralph recline on his perch in their compartment to try free-association.

Ralph grew hungrier but couldn't hold down his food. It was not for many hours longer, he told himself. See the bright side of things. Be cheerful. You'll be leaving Jayc for good soon.

I'll kill you first.

"Perhaps the death-wish is for himself as well," Ayd Setay suggested. "Minds are sometimes damaged during occupation. He refuses to adjust to his deformity and blames it on you. Would you care for a sedative?"

"Thanks, but no." Ralph had had quite enough of Jaycee sedatives. He would remain awake all the way to Comoy City if he could help it. Time enough for him to worry about the mental fatigue later.

The afternoon wore on and faded into emerald dusk. Ayd Setay took her evening meal in the passageway adjoining their compartment since the sight and smell of food now made Ralph ill. He had needed sleep ever since his wild night through the streets of Mountainvale to the monorail station. But now he would forego it until they reached Comoy City.

He'd sleep in his own human body, all the way to the Arcturus System if necessary. No, he'd gorge himself on good food first, on succulent roast fowl and pork shoulder stuffed with good old Earth chestnuts and—he gagged and thought of something else.

Kaloy laughed inside their head, then was silent. Entirely too silent.

CHAPTER EIGHT

Ayd Setay was asleep on her own perch, an ungraceful lobster-mantis in repose. It was hardly possible to think of her as a sentient creature—which foolishness, Ralph thought wryly, was probably responsible for the Jaycee war in the first place, with the Jaycees casting the same anthropomorphic limitations on their nearest interstellar neighbors.

He found himself half dozing and wished he had thought to take along some reading tapes. He slid back the ground observation panel, but could see only vague shadows flitting by below in the faintly greenish moonlight. He tried the skyport and had better luck.

The rush of air on his face, the crisp cool night air of Jayc, the faraway roaring of wind, parted by the first car of the monorail. He tried to shake himself awake—and failed. He was acting, moving about on Kaloy's volition; not his own. Trying to remain awake so long had been a mistake. He should have trusted Ayd Setay, who was becoming an Interstellarist without realizing it. Now it was too late.

Now Kaloy had left their compartment and was in the passageway paralleling it in the monorail car. In the dim light, Ralph could see doors leading to other compartments, all closed. The only open door led outside, to the moonlight, to the rushing wind, cold and green and to the ground far below.

He wanted to shout. No, to click. Damn semantics, anyway. The fascination was his as much as Kaloy's as he approached the doorway and poked his head out into the knifing wind.

A shudder passed over him.

It was exactly like fighting dream-impulses, he thought with the frightening objectivity, which at times was part of his strange parasitism. In a dream you stood at the edge of a cliff and you knew you were going to fall. A part of your mind, dim and labyrinth-lost, but half aware of the fact you were dreaming, tried to stop you. You groped forward with one foot, letting it dangle. You waited.

This was no dream. This was Desmar Kaloy's death-wish, and death for the final member of the Army of Occupation. His own personal occupation swirled by in seconds, the long line at the checkpoint, the first monorail journey, the crash, the mountain eyrie and the months of healing on Halbady Peak. Then the long trek to Mountainvale, which had almost ended in death, Kaloy's crime, the ethnocentric doctor, Ayd Setay's test, his flight, Kaloy's death-wish and his inability to eat or even think of food, and now this—

He was leaning out over green darkness, buffeted by the wind. It would make a wonderful story to tell over a few tall ones on Arcturus IV and later back on Earth, but he would never tell it. He would die here on the plains of Jayc and for a short time be grist for the mill of interstellar politics until he was forgotten. He would never see his own body again, let alone dwell in, it. He would never explore the worlds with its five senses, never eat the foods he had dreamed about until Kaloy's death-wish had precluded all thought of food.

He paused on the brink of nothingness and retreated a fraction of an inch. Kaloy's hold was weakening, for some inexplicable reason. Kaloy was rested, he was not. Kaloy should have exercised his influence without too much trouble, yet for one moment Ralph had felt control in his own hands.

The food.

He dreamed of eating, of being served dish after dish by armies of uniformed waiters on Arcturus IV. He breathed the aroma of food and fingered it with his hands and wallowed in it and rolled over and over in cooked mush, steaming and pungent.

He retreated another step and gagged. He gagged on steak, on gamey Arcturan antelope, on sauces and wines and rarebits. He gagged again and retreated and thought of maple syrup, straight from some New England tree, sweet and viscous, of milk, frothy and animal-warm, of a milking stool and a bucket there in the barn, with the smell of fodder thick in his nostrils.

He gagged and was sick there in the passageway. He made it back to his compartment and had Ayd Setay fetter him to his perch and didn't let her untie him all the way to Comoy City, although Kaloy pleaded and cajoled.

They met him there by the lake, the bipeds, the men of Earth, familiar and beautiful. Soon they took his body from a vat and there was a complex apparatus, which could separate the electromagnetic vibrations of his own sentience from Kaloy's and restore them.

And soon he was standing and stamping his feet and pinching himself in delight and demanding a mirror so that he could see himself and more mirrors than they had, and all the mirrors in the universe.

Ayd Setay led Kaloy away and he felt a brief pang of regret before he realized Kaloy was Ayd Setay's problem, not his. He let the men of Earth lead him to the spaceship where they plied him with endless questions.

Instead of answering, he followed his nose to the galley.

No-Risk Planet

*Sam had sold life insurance to every race in the galaxy. But on Halcyon
he found a people who not only didn't want it—but didn't need it!*

Interstellar Hotel
Halcyon City
Halcyon

Mr. Herman Spottsworth
Interstellar Division
Terran Insurance Co.
Baltimore, Md., Earth

Dear Boss:

The natives got a big kick out of it when I told them what
the name of their planet means in English. It means peaceful.
From what I could gather, the first Terran to land here fifty
years ago was so impressed with the balmy climate and
pleasant rolling terrain and almost tideless oceans that he
named the planet Halcyon. The only catch is, the natives
have all the food they want and all the natural resources and
just about everything. So, they have nothing to keep them
occupied except fighting wars. They haven't been able to
string three peaceful years together since the beginning of
recorded history here, two thousand years ago. It's kind of
like a game with them.

That being the case, I ought to establish a new record for
the Interstellar Division. I've got to sign off now because the
air-raid bell just rang. Regards to Joanie.

Cordially,
Sammy Trumple

Interstellar Division
Terran Insurance Co.
Baltimore, Md., Earth

Mr. Sammy Trumple
Halcyon City
Halcyon

Dear Sammy:

Glad to see you've arrived O.K., and are so impressed with the sales potential there. Remember the motto of the Interstellar Division: IF YOU CAN PLANETFALL, YOU CAN SELL...

Yours in sales,
Herman Spottsworth

P.S. Regards from Joanie.

Interstellar Hotel
Halcyon City
Halcyon

Mr. Herman Spottsworth Etc.

Dear Boss:

That air-raid was murder! You'd better double my own life insurance policy. Take the premiums out of my salary, please. Incidentally, your letter almost got lost because you forgot to include "Interstellar Hotel" in the address. It's a fifty-room fleabag, boss, but they got pride. Please take good care of Joanie.

Cordially,
Sammy Trumple

Interstellar Division
Terrain Insurance Co.
Baltimore, Md., Earth

Dear Sammy:

You've been on Halcyon three weeks now. How come you wrote up no policies yet? You aren't taking the sights in like a tourist, are you—on a Terran expense account?

Yours in sales,
Herman Spottsworth

143¼ East Scjulak Street
Halcyon City
Halcyon

Dear Boss:

Please note the new address. The Interstellar Hotel was blown to bits in the last air-raid. I'm scared, boss. There are air-raids around the clock, with Halcyonians dropping off like flies.

And that answers your question, incidentally. There are no tourists on Halcyon. It's too dangerous. Better quadruple my own life insurance policy. And tell Joan I love her.

Frantically,
Sammy Trumple

Interstellar Division
Terran Insurance Co.
Baltimore, Md., Earth

Dear Sammy:

I've quadrupled your policy. I'm taking care of Joanie. I'm awaiting your first sale.

Spottsworth

143¼ East Scjulak Street
Halcyon City
Halcyon

Dear Boss:

I'm trying. I'm trying my head off. With those big premiums to pay, don't you think I could use the commission?

There's something fishy going on here on Halcyon, but I can't figure it out yet. The way they get killed off in these wars, the Halcyonians ought to snap up insurance policies. In fact, I don't even know how much profit the Company could expect to make from them, but that's your department. It's funny, though. The Halcyonians don't want life insurance. They don't even know what life insurance is!

To give you an idea of what I mean, I'll quote verbatim a conversation I had with a couple of Halcyonians right after this morning's air-raid, which leveled every building on their block except their own.

ME: Good morning, folks. You're mighty lucky people, yessiree.

FIRST HALCYONIAN: Why are we lucky?

ME: You're the only survivors on your whole block.

SECOND HALCYONIAN (shrugging): So what?

ME: So what? So you could have been killed in that air-raid, that's what.

SECOND HALCYONIAN (shrugging again): So what?

ME: (tuning my language translator to its most cheerful pitch): I'm from the planet Earth. Did you ever hear of the planet Earth?

FIRST AND SECOND HALCYONIAN: No.

ME (hopefully): It's also called Terra. Near Sirius?

FIRST AND SECOND HALCYONIAN: No.

ME: Well, anyhow, I represent the Terran Insurance Company, Interstellar Division. I'm here on Halcyon to offer your loved ones financial protection from the ravages of war, via life insurance.

FIRST HALCYONIAN: Which insurance?

ME: Life insurance. The special, triple indemnity war and disaster policy of the Terran Insurance Company.

FIRST HALCYONIAN: I never heard of life insurance. What does it do?

ME: I have here in my hand (this required some explanation, boss, because the Halcyonians do not have hands) a blank policy for you to look at. Life insurance, you see, pays a stipulated sum to a party of your designation in the event of your death. All you do is pay small yearly premiums, and...

SECOND HALCYONIAN: Oh, like the fellow from Fomalhaut.

ME (gasping): What? There's another insurance salesman in my territory? Someone's poaching?

SECOND HALCYONIAN: He's been here some time now, but we couldn't possibly be interested.

ME: The Fomalhautian's policy offers you more?

FIRST HALCYONIAN: Really, we couldn't be less interested. But the answer to your question is no.

ME: Is he still here in Halcyon City?

SECOND HALCYONIAN: Who?

ME: The insurance salesman from Fomalhaut.

SECOND HALCYONIAN: I think so. His name, I believe, is Lar Luk. You could look him up in the city register.

ME: I sure will. And thank you, folks.

FIRST HALCYONIAN: You're wasting your time, Mr. Terra.

ME: No, that's my planet. My name is Trumple.

FIRST HALCYONIAN: Well, Terra or whatever your name is, you won't sell any of those dohinkuses here.

Well, that's the conversation, boss. Half an hour later, the two Halcyonians got their breathing vents ruptured in the air-raid and died of strangulation. I'll bet you're glad I didn't sell those two policies!

Yours still hopefully,
Sammy Trumple

P. S. I intend to look up this guy from Fomalhaut.

Interstellar Division
Terran Insurance Company
Baltimore, Md., Earth

Dear Sammy:

Six weeks now without a sale. What's the matter with you? Getting soft? Homesick? Joanie is all right, I assure you. Hell's bells, man, IF YOU CAN PLANETFALL, YOU CAN SELL. And by the way, you go right ahead and sell 'em. Let the boys in the actuary department worry about having to payoff immediately. We're sales, Sammy. Sales.

Why don't you go out into the grass roots somewhere, where this bird from Fomalhaut hasn't tried his hand? Maybe he's soured all the Halcyonians on life insurance with the wrong approach. Overaggressive or something.

Buck up, Sammy. I've still got a little faith in you. Explore. Consider. Sweat. Sell.

Yours in sales,
Herman Spottsworth

Rmpldecroidesanspertxkle
Halcyon

Dear Boss:

I'm out here in Rmpldecroidesanspertxkle trying your suggestion about the grass roots. It's a small town, population under two thousand, without an important war industry. You'd think it would be safe from air-raids, but it's not. As I told you when I first reached Halcyon, they have no real reason for war. War is like a game with them. Their best bombers are sent out after hospital ships, I understand. Tennyrate, tomorrow I'm going to try my luck here in Rmpldecroidesanspertxkle.

Meanwhile, I have something of interest to report. Remember that guy I mentioned, Lar Luk, the insurance salesman from Fomalhaut? I met him in Halcyon City before I took the monorail to Rmpldecroidesanspertxkle, and we had a long talk.

"I said, "I hope you don't think I'm poaching on your territory Mr. Luk." I then turned down the translator to soft obsequious. "I assure you that's not the way Terran Insurance operates. We didn't know you were here."

"That's quite all right," Lar Luk told me. "YOU can have the whole planet for all I care."

"Are you going back to Fomalhaut?" I asked hopefully.

"Goodness, no. I had my savings shipped here to Halcyon and started a munitions plant. I'm making a fortune."

I next asked Lar Luk (translator on shocked voice) about his Company Loyalty. He said, "That's a lot of (CENSORED BY MY TRANSLATOR)! When in Rome, heh-heh…" It seems every civilized planet has an author who said something like "when in Rome, etc."

"You didn't happen to try the grass roots, did you?" I asked with my translator in indifferent because I didn't want Lar Luk to get the idea I was eager and maybe try it himself.

"Friend," admitted Lar Luk, "I tried everything. Without any success. Say, why don't you come into munitions with me? There's a whole colony of extra-halcyonian insurance salesmen going into munitions here. I could use a partner."

That ended our conversation. I'm going to cold-canvas Rmpldecroidesanspertxkle in the morning. I'll keep in touch.

Pessimistically,
Sammy Trumple

XXX—SUBSPACEGRAM—XXX FROM HERMAN SPOTTSWORTH INTERSTELLAR DIVISION TERRAN INSURANCE COMPANY BALTIMEARTH XXX TO SAMMY TRUMPLE RMPLDECROIDESANSPERTXKLE HALCYON XXX DON'T GO GETTING ANY IDEAS FROM THIS LAR LUK FELLOW XXX REMEMBER YOUR COMPANY LOYALTY XXX REMEMBER OUR MOTTO XXX REMEMBER ALL THOSE PREMIUMS YOU HAVE TO PAY XXX THE CHIEF OF SALES WANTS RESULTS SOON XXX I WANT RESULTS SOON XXX OTHERWISE HE'LL HAVE MY HEAD XXX I'LL HAVE YOUR HEAD SPOTTSWORTH XXX TRANSMITTED VIA ALPHA CENTAURI SUBSPACE STATION XXX SEND FLOWERS BY SUBSPACE TO ANY PART OF MILKYWAY GALAXY AT NO EXTRA COST XXX QUARTERLY SPECIAL: ARCHENAR III DRAGON BLOSSOMS XXX ALPHACENT XXX

Rmpldecroidesanspertxkle
Halcyon

Dear Boss:

You don't have to worry about *my* company loyalty. But still, no sales. Unfortunately, half of Rmpldecroidesanspertxkle was wiped out yesterday in an air-raid. I'm lucky I came through it with a whole skin. I went through the hospitals and first aid stations to canvas what was left of the population. They're just not buying. They can't—or refuse to—grasp the meaning of life insurance. The following conversation is typical:

ME: But in a devastating war like this you need protection. Most other insurance companies wouldn't issue policies under the circumstances. You can consider it an interstellar public service by Terran Insurance.

IT: What do I need life insurance for?

ME: Don't you have a family? Loved ones? People you'd like to see cared for after your—uh—that is, if you're suddenly not around to take care of the bills and things, if you...

IT: You mean if I drop dead?

ME: Yes, sir.

IT: What the hell for?

ME: One never knows when he is going to, uh, drop dead.

IT: No. I mean what the hell do I want an insurance policy for?

ME: Statistics demonstrate that everyone wants the security of a life insurance policy.

IT: I don't.

So, that's the way it goes. I've had another idea, though. How does this strike you, boss? The local Army commander has his headquarters not far from Rmpldecroidesanspertxkle. Since the whole planet is under military rule because of the constant warfare, I figure if I can sell a policy to General Multacni. I could then sell every dogfoot in his command. How does the idea strike you?

With a glimmer of hope,
Sammy Trumple

Interstellar Division
Terran Insurance Co.
Baltimore, Md., Earth

Dear Sammy:

Now you're firing away on all jets, boy! Now you're good Terran Insurance material. You're darned tooting, sell the general. We'll have it made after that.

Enthusiastically,
Hermie

P. S. I take back everything I may have said about you in haste, dear boy. You're A-1 Terran Insurance all the way. P. P. S. Joanie is languishing, she misses you so much. Make a couple of dozen sales to cover your expense account and we'll think about getting you home on the next ship.

MILITARY TWX FROM SUPREME COMMANDER HALCYON SUBDIVISION THREE CMM OFFICE OF MILITARY JUSTICE CMM TO CLN MR H SPOTTSWORTH CMM INTERSELLAR DIVISION CMM TERRAN INSURANCE CMM BALTIMEARTH DASH PENDING TRIAL OR APPEAL OF YOUR STATE DEPARTMENT CMM WHICHEVER COMES FIRST CMM WE ARE HOLDING TERRAN CITIZEN S TRUMPLE UNDER PROVISIONS OF ARTICLE SEVEN CMM HALCYON CODE OF MILITARY JUSTICE PD PARA ARTICLE SEVEN READS CLN QUOTE ANY INDIVIDUAL ATTEMPTING SUBVERSION OF

MORAL WELFARE OF OFFICERS OR ENLISTED MEN CMM THIS COMMAND CMM IS SUBJECT TO IMPRISONMENT FOR NOT MORE THAN TWENTY FIVE HALCYONIAN YEARS PD ENDQUOTE PARA PLEASE ADVISE PD PARA FOR THE COMMANDING GENERAL CMM LIEUT DASH MAJ ROG GO FURL CMM HALCYON SUBDIVISION THREE CMM OFFICE OF MILITARY JUSTICE PD END TWX

Subdivision Three Stockade
Halcyon

Dear Boss:
Lar Luk of Formalhaut is forwarding this letter for me. Help!

Sammy Trumple

Interstellar Division
Terran Insurance Co.
Baltimore, Md., Earth

Commanding General
Subdivision Three
Halcyon

Dear Sir:
With Terran State Department approval, I am writing you in regard to the case of our employee, Mr. S. Trumple of Earth. With full State Department backing we insist that you permit Mr. Trumple to tell us, uncensored and in his own words, what has happened, in order that we may take steps to defend him as a citizen of Earth.

Very truly yours,
Herman Spottsworth

Subdivision Three Stockade
Halcyon

Dear Boss:

Lieutenant Major Roggo Furl informs me that I'm permitted to write you an uncensored letter. Boss, I'm in the dregs of despair. Please take good care of Joanie. It's cold here in the stockade. The food stinks. The other prisoners are all Halcyonian military deserters. Get me out of here!

But I better calm down and try to tell you what happened from the beginning. As I already told you, I decided to try and sell General Multacni a life insurance policy. It took me two hours working my way through the chain of command before I could even get to see the General. When I finally did, I found myself facing a huge figure in military uniform— huge even by Halcyonian standards. General Multacni is probably nine feet tall.

At first he was courteous. He listened politely, taking time out every now and then to direct a bombing raid by radio, while I explained to him exactly what life insurance was and what he could expect from the Terran policy.

Like everyone else on Halcyon, he said he didn't need life insurance.

"See here, sir," I said, translator polite but not obsequious. "War is dangerous business. You never know when your number is going to be up."

The General's office rumbled with laughter as he said, "Mr. Terran—" they all call me that "—I'm indestructible." As you probably know, that's a typical military career man's attitude. They all think they are indestructible. The other fellow will die in the trenches or the raids, not them. Even on Earth we have trouble selling our policies to the military.

I tried a different tack, the one approved for military customers on Earth. "Well, General," I said, "someday this war is going to be over. Someday you're going to retire to a farm somewhere in the good rich land around Rmpldecroidesanspertxkle. You'll raise chickens—" which the translator translated to the Halcyonian equivalent, of course "—and bounce your little grandchildren on your knee. And then, way off in the dim future, General, years and years from now after you've lived a rich, full life, you're going to succumb to natural causes. And, if not sooner—and we certainly hope it won't be sooner—that's when your family will need this insurance policy I have for you."

"The war isn't going to end," General Multacni told me.

"But someday, when your side is victorious, and—"

"Victorious?" His translator buzzed, repeating the word syllable for syllable. "What is that?"

"When you win the war."

"Win it? But we're not going to win it, Mr. Terran."

"Things can't be that bad," I consoled the General giving him my best you're-down-in-the-dumps-now-but wait-till-later smile. "Maybe the enemy has you on the run just now, but you'll emerge victorious—you'll win—in the end." Of course, I would have told the same thing to General Multacni's opposite number in the opposing camp. I'm no authority on Halcyonian military matters, but under the circumstances it seemed the correct thing to say.

General Multacni stood up. "I must consider this interview at an end, Mr. Terran," he said frostily. "And I advise you to keep such subversive thoughts to yourself in the future. I'm a broad-minded Halcyonian, but—" And the General let his voice trail off ominously.

I figured he had battle fatigue, boss. Nobody could talk like that in his right mind, not even a general on a planet which is engaging in warfare almost constantly. Anyhow, I had to find out. Wandering through the military reservation on my way back to Rmpl, I chanced upon a noncommissioned officer's club. Here was the place to find out once and for all! I would speak to the NCO's who probably had families and probably were in danger of shipping out to the warfronts at any time.

I went inside and I spoke. Maybe I made too much like a soap box orator, I don't know. I don't know. I told them they would need insurance during the war, and after the war. I told them our policies would give them solace in these trying times, mitigating some of their worries during the necessary horrors of their struggle for existence. When finished, there wasn't a sound in the whole vast room. Boss, I thought we had them. I brought out a pad of policies and was ready to start scribbling names.

Then the military police came in and arrested me.

You know the rest. How I was taken to the subdivision stockades, given a medical exam (for some reason, a small slice of flesh was taken from my rump I won't miss it, but I couldn't sit down for two days), told that I was being held under the provisions of article seven of some kind of code of military justice. Me, subversive. When all I want to do is sell insurance policies. Boss, please get me the heck off this nutty planet.

Tragically,
Sammy Trumple

Terran Consulate
Halcyon City
Halcyon

Department of State
Halcyon Subdivision Three

Sirs:

Please explain the charges under which Terran citizen Samuel Trumple is being held in military prison.

Walter M. Foggarty
Asst. Consul

Department of State
Halcyon Subdivision Three

Mr. Walter M. Foggarty
Terran Consulate
Halcyon City

Dear Mr. Foggarty:

We hasten to respond to your note of yesterday and wish to thank you for the diplomacy, tact and patience you have displayed in this matter. We of Halcyon are firm believers in reincarnation of the individual after death, as you may know if you've read Stoy's ANTHROPOLOGICALLY SPEAKING: A Study of Sixty-Seven Galactic Societies, or attended any of our religious services.

Now, since we believe in reincarnation (off the record, I'm a free-thinker, myself) and since every individual certainly can't be born with the proverbial silver feeder in his mandibles, death is an adventure eagerly anticipated by most Halcyonians, who have hopes that their station in life will be improved in their next incarnation, although they believe, of course, that they will maintain their individuality, their *elan vital*, if you wish, in the subsequent incarnation.

Terran Citizen Trumble was guilty of the worst sort of subversion when he spoke of an end to warfare. Naturally, there are some atheistic pacifists on Halcyon who would like to see war abolished and more people live out their current incarnations, but this dangerous minority is constantly hunted down. However, we recognize extenuating circumstances in the case of Terran citizen Trumple. He is, of course, unfamiliar with our way of life. That being the case, I have recommended to the military authorities that he be pardoned without trial. I will keep you informed.

Most sincerely,
Aleg Trogonommo
Sec'y for resident extra-Halcyonians

Terran Consulate
Halcyon City
Halcyon

Mr. Herman Spottsworth
Interstellar Division
Terran Insurance Company
Baltimore, Md., Earth

Dear Mr. Spottsworth:
The enclosed communication from Trogonommo is self-evident. Feel better?

Foggarty

Interstellar Division
Terran Insurance Co.
Baltimore, Md., Earth

Dear Sammy:

Keep your chin up, boy. It's only a matter of time now. Jeanie's fine.

Hermie

MEMO:
TO: The Commanding General
FROM: Lieut-Major Roggo Furl, Office of Military Justice
SUBJECT: The Terran Sammy Trumple

1. Trogonommo of State wants us to go easy on the prisoner, Trumple.

2. It is my feeling, though, that in the best interests of Halcyon, an example should be made of the Terran Trumple. The General realizes, I'm sure, that the colony of extra-halcyonians on Halcyon is growing. They must learn to. Consider Halcyonian culture as inviolate.

3. Accordingly, I recommend we go ahead with trial of Terran Trumple.

Signed
Roggo Furl
Lieut-Major

MEMO
TO: Lieut-Major Roggo Furl, Office of Military Justice
FROM: The Commanding General
SUBJECT: The Terran Sammy Trumple

1. Sorry, Furl. Trogonommo has more political friends than a Veterans' Legion Commander.

2. However, I quite agree with you. An example must be made of Trumple.

3. But not through a military court of justice. That's political dynamite.

4. I'd like to suggest that Trumple be allowed to make an attempted escape. He can be killed while fleeing. That should teach everyone a lesson. Trumple included.

5. The details of this attempted escape are in your hands. I suggest you use Lar Luk of Formalhaut as a go-between, however. And make sure Trumple is killed!

6. After you read it, burn this letter.

Unsigned

143¼ East Scjulak Street
Halcyon City
Halcyon

Dear Boss:

Have I got news for you!

A few days ago, Lar' Luk—the ex-insurance salesman from Fomalhaut—visited me at the stockade. You could tell something was going on because Luk, usually a loud extrovert, spoke in conspiratorial whispers.

"They are going ahead with your trial," he said.

"How do you know?"

"I am in a position to know. I think you're being treated unjustly, Sammy. I came here to do something about it."

Boss, I was desperate. Despite your encouraging note, I didn't know which way to turn. I said, "Like what?"

And Luk leaned forward to whisper, "Like helping you escape."

He clamped a flipper over my mouth before I could blurt out something which would give us away. I calmed down and said, "Can we do it?"

"We can try. We have to try."

"When?" I asked.

"Tonight, after I leave, after it's dark. I had to get special dispensation to visit you. They won't let me visit you again."

"But what...how..." I'm no intriguer, boss. I felt like a pawn in this game—but a pawn who was about to be checkmated unless he did something about it.

"Here," said Lar Luk, thrusting something into my hand. "This is a Formalhautian freezer, Sammy. You'll stop anybody dead in his tracks with it. When they come to your cell tonight and bring your meal..." Lar Luk didn't finish the sentence.

"You'll be waiting for me outside?"

"Yes. With a jetcopter, my friend. It won't be long now."

And Lar Luk was gone. I examined the weapon he had given me. It looked deadly, all right, with a dull metal finish and a wicked, funnel-like snout. I was ready, but I didn't see how I would get through the afternoon.

I tried to sleep. I couldn't. I tried to think of you and Joanie and what it would be like back on Earth. I couldn't concentrate. It grew dark slowly, the way it does on Halcyon. I thought they never would come with my supper. I thought they were starving me before the trial so I would confess readily. Then I began to think that maybe someone had seen Lar Luk give me the weapon. Perhaps the cell was wired and every word we said was heard in the stockade commander's office.

Then I heard footsteps in the corridor. It always sounds like more than one person, the Halcyonians having more legs than we do. I stood there at the door of my cell, waiting. I could feel my heart fluttering around inside me, like a bird.

The cell door opened.

At first I was going to use Lar Luk's weapon, but I didn't know what kind of noise it would make. He hadn't told me.

Instead, I used the butt of the gun, banging it down across the guard's head. He slumped at my feet. I hoped I hadn't hurt him too badly. I even hoped Lar Luk's weapon was effective but not lethal. I had nothing against the Halcyonians, I just wanted to escape.

Out into the corridor I ran, passing three cross-corridors before I reached the stockade quadrangle. In the halls, I met no one. So far, I was lucky. But then...

"Halt! Who goes there?"

A guard in the quadrangle challenging me!

I was trembling so much I had to hold Lar Luk's weapon in both hands to fire it. It made a noise like a siren.

The guard didn't fall. He kept corning.

I fired again.

It was a siren.

Lar Luk had tricked me.

You can imagine the pickle I was in, boss. The siren summoned more guards, who came at me from all directions. I tried to get away, pounding across the pavement of the quadrangle. From somewhere, a searchlight cut a bright yellow swath across the quadrangle. It found me and held me.

One of the guards fired a blaster, hitting me in the base of the skull and killing me instantly.

Cordially,
Sammy Trumple

Interstellar Division
Terran Insurance Co.
Baltimore, Md., Earth

Dear Sammy:

I'm glad you managed to get away, but quit pulling my leg, will you? So the guard killed you—and then you sat down and wrote me a letter. Please tell me what really happened.

By the way, I have great news for you. Joanie had a litter of four pups, all spotted brown and white and cute as the dickens. I'm sending two of them to you by Subspace Express.

And let me know what happened, will you?

Yours in sales,
Hermie

Rmpldecroidesanspertxkle
Halcyon

Dear Hermie:

This letter is being smuggled out to you by a friend because it never would pass the Halcyonian censor. They have a good thing and they want to keep it to themselves as much as possible and I can't blame them.

Thanks for sending along the pups. I'll be waiting for them. Give Joanie a pat on the head for me.

Incidentally, cancel all my insurance policies. And I quit the company, effective immediately. I'm staying here on Halcyon.

I wasn't pulling your leg, Hermie. You remember I told you a slice of flesh was taken from my rump at the stockade. That's how the Halcyonians have developed their reincarnation process. They've learned a way to duplicate an individual artificially using a sample of his hereditary genes from the slice of flesh. Every Halcyonian has his slice on file of course. The new embryo is then grown rapidly, in a matter of a few days.

Lar Luk and I figured it's about time heavy industry came to Rmpldecroidesanspertxkle. We're opening a new munitions factory here, which suits the Halcyonians fine. Most of them are in favor of war because they'd like to better their position in life and might do it next time around on the new incarnation.

This reincarnation sure as hell beats life insurance, doesn't it?

With fond regards,
Sammy

The Music of the Spheres

Mayhew knew it was impossible for him to return to Earth—
unless he wanted to spend his life in prison...

MOMENTS BEFORE making planetfall on the
unknown world, Mayhew saw the other spaceship.

It was coming in twenty-seven degrees galactic north of
Mayhew's own position. It was coming incredibly fast, but
Mayhew still could have shot it out of the sky. He didn't only
because the design of the ship was entirely alien to him: he
knew the ships of Sol system and those of Sagittarius and
those of Deneb—but this square, tubeless, ungainly cube of a
ship was of a type the Earthman had never seen before.

Entirely alien?

Naturally, it was possible. Someday, the scientists of Earth
and Deneb and Sagittarius said, we will meet up in the infinity
of space with an alien culture. In the first five-hundred years
of spatial exploration, though, the human explorers had
encountered nothing but a parade of ruined worlds. Planets
where civilizations alien to us *had* flourished, but did not
flourish now. Planets, which had been ravished by war,
which were pock-marked and glazed by H-bomb craters, as if
the hallmark of intelligent life in all the ruined cities on all the
ruined worlds was a dirge of death and destruction.

This meant much to the scientists and theologians, but it
meant nothing to Mayhew. For Mayhew was an escaped
convict who had broken out of Luna prison a thousand light
years behind with a life sentence hanging over his head. The
supply ship he had taken was not the fastest and sometimes
he considered it almost a miracle that he had not been
captured. But he had kept off the startrails, heading for the
fringe of the arm of the Milky Way galaxy in which Sol

System is located. He knew a return to human civilization was barred to him forever: but he also knew he preferred freedom to captivity and the fact that he would probably never see another human face did not greatly disturb him.

Now Mayhew watched the strange cube of a spaceship hurtling toward him. He failed to realize they were heading on a collision course until it was too late. When he did realize it, when the strange ship filled all space to starboard, Mayhew cursed and heard the screaming whine of the radar warnings and punched frantically at the control board. But he was too late, for the cube-shaped ship—it was fully ten times the size of his own, Mayhew realized—came on inexorably. Mayhew had a split second to curse himself as a fool. He should have landed on the unknown planet that revolved about its lonely sun here in the backwaters of the galaxy, and to hell with any alien ship. But he knew from experience that if the planet below them harbored life, if it had ever harbored intelligent life, that life had probably already destroyed itself in suicidal war. It was the pattern the scientists spoke of: and Mayhew had seen it in his travels.

The cube came on, filling all space to starboard and fore and aft. Grimly fascinated at the prospect of his own imminent death, Mayhew stared at the viewport. The cube flashed there, dazzling, bright. Mayhew steeled himself for the crash and the moment of pain before death.

There was no crash.

The alien ship seemed to engulf Mayhew's small cruiser, as if—lifelike—it had opened a maw to its digestive track and swallowed the smaller ship, Mayhew and all. Incredulously Mayhew watched the dials of his control board. Absolute spatial speed was reduced from thirty miles a second—a little more than landing speed but still deadly in a crash—to zero in a split second. External pressure built from the zero of deep space to seventeen pounds per square inch in the same instant. And Mayhew felt only a gentle cushioning effect, as if his spaceship was a toy and had been dropped from a height of a few feet on a feather bed.

He got up and, amazement stamped on his hard features, made his way to the airlock. He had already strapped on his blaster. He was going to see the alien after all. It seemed that the alien had an unexpected trick or two up his sleeve, but that didn't bother Mayhew much. He considered it a challenge. It was why he had not fired on the alien ship: to an alien Mayhew would be no criminal. In the alien's civilization—wherever it was—Mayhew might have a chance to start life anew.

Mayhew worked the airlock tumblers. Suddenly he lurched forward, hitting his head against the inner door. He began to black out, and called himself a fool even as he did so. The alien ship was corning in to land, wasn't it? Mayhew's ship, with Mayhew, was inside the alien ship. Mayhew should have strapped himself into the blast hammock...

He lurched again, struck his head again. Space became brilliantly white. In this eye-paining whiteness a tiny black dot appeared. The black irised open and swallowed the white brightness, swallowing Mayhew with it.

MAYHEW OPENED his eyes. Sunset, he thought. There was a red glow in the air, a sunset glow. He had forgotten how beautiful the colors on Earth could be.

Sunset? No. Mayhew looked around. He sat on the edge of a high bluff overlooking a ruined city. The sun was high in the sky, but a somber red color. It was a red sun. Mayhew sniffed at the air experimentally, then told himself that wasn't necessary. He'd been breathing it, hadn't he? The air had a sweet smell, a smell of growing things. There were green plants on the bluff around Mayhew, and little star-shaped flowers wonderfully fragrant after the canned air of the spaceship, the air, which was reprocessed over and over again and was breathable but hardly more than that.

Mayhew stood up and the long vista he saw to the horizon after the confinement of the spaceship made him giddy. The ruined city dominated the view, of course. It was spread out below the bluff, on which Mayhew stood and beyond it was a river. Across the river were the stumps and skeletons of three bridges. The city itself was battered and smashed as if a legion of giants had trod across it. The tall once-graceful spires were bent and broken, the elevated streets were buckled and twisted. The city was a dead place, like a dozen dead places Mayhew had seen on a dozen once-civilized worlds.

"A pity, isn't it?"

Mayhew whirled at the sound of the voice. In his concentration he'd almost forgotten the alien. Behind him was the great cube of a spaceship. Now that Mayhew saw it stationary he realized how truly big it was. It was the largest spaceship Mayhew had ever seen, possibly half a mile across each way and half a mile high. "What have you got in there," Mayhew said, "an Army, equipment and all?"

"Your first thought is of violence, I see. That is a pity, too."

The alien was naked. His body was a slender, incredibly graceful trunk of pale blue flesh, like a tongue of flame. There were no limbs, yet the tongue-of-flame body seemed so fluid, so mobile, that Mayhew knew at once no limbs were necessary. Atop the blue flame of a body was a perfectly round sphere, featureless as the body was limbless. The sphere was not entirely opaque, however. There was the vague suggestion of translucency, as if the alien needed no eyes, no ears, no nose or mouth because his brain—or whatever he used for a brain—could focus these senses, and perhaps others that man did not possess, through the translucent shell of the head.

"Where's my spaceship?" Mayhew asked hostility.

"Inside. In good shape, don't worry."

"How the hell do you talk my language?"

"I talk any language I wish."

"Where are you from?"

"Shouldn't we rather both be interested in this world we decided to land upon?"

"It's a dead world. I'm interested in living things."

"Perhaps; if our interests differ, we had best each go his separate way."

"Sure," Mayhew said sarcastically, "that's why you captured my ship." Abruptly he clawed the blaster from his belt and leveled it with a steady hand at the alien. "Look," he said. "Maybe you have a few tricks up your sleeve I've never seen, but you don't scare me. If you're protoplasm, this blaster can hurt you. So, let's you and me put our cards on the table where they can be seen. You especially. Why did you capture my ship? What do you want?"

The alien did not waver. The flame-tongue of a body seemed steady as a rock, and though no wind was blowing, it looked gracefully insubstantial, as though the slightest breeze would waft it about.

"I'll answer your questions," the alien said. Mayhew could see no mouth on the featureless face, no opening anyplace at all. He wondered where the voice was coming from. He had the vague idea that it was originating, at the alien's direction, inside his own head. "But first, Mr. Mayhew—" here Mayhew started, for the alien knew his name—"I would like to prove something to you. Fire that thing; go ahead, fire it."

"At you?" Mayhew wondered what this bluff was all about.

"Certainly at me. Go ahead, I'm waiting."

"But—p"

"Shoot me!"

Mayhew frowned—and pulled the trigger. The blaster leaped in his hand, butt slapping against his palm. The surge of raw energy flashed out at the alien—and through him. Mayhew actually saw the beam strike rock on the other side.

"Now do you see?" the alien asked. "For all intents and purposes, I am quite invulnerable. Do we do things my way?"

For a moment Mayhew did not answer. Then he heard himself say one word: "Yeah."

"Splendid. To begin with, there is no Army in my ship. I am the sole inhabitant. The ship is so big because it is filled with sufficient automatic control machinery and supplies to ensure a perfectly safe journey for the balance of my life. Since my life span is measurable in scores of thousands of your years, that means a big ship. Other questions?"

"What happened. I mean, did we crash?" The arrogance had gone from Mayhew's voice, to be replaced by an emotion to which he was thoroughly unaccustomed. That emotion was awe.

"No, we didn't crash. My ship landed. You were not prepared for the instant deceleration. You died."

"WHAT?" gasped Mayhew.

"You died. When I got to you your skull was split, you had a broken back, a broken pelvis, two broken limbs. You had lost almost all your blood. Fortunately for you—"

"Died..."

"Fortunately for you, I could repair or synthesize all of those things. You're all right now."

Mayhew felt himself gingerly. He felt whole. There were no aches or pains. He walked. He did not feel stiff. He looked at the alien and did not speak. What the alien said made no sense. Yet he believed.

"Look at this world," the alien said. "Beautiful, isn't it?"

Mayhew said it was beautiful.

"And the city?"

"Dead," said Mayhew.

"Dead," repeated the alien. "By its own hand. A civilization whose science outstripped its moral values by several generations: result, racial suicide. This is not the only—"

"Yeah, I know," said Mayhew. "Practically all of them."

"In my own survey, Mr. Mayhew, ninety-seven worlds out of every hundred are destroyed by their own hand. Self-destroyers. The reason is always the same. It never varies. Is your world going to perish by its own hand too, Mr. Mayhew?"

"What do you know about my world?" Mayhew felt a sudden intense longing to see Earth again, and wondered if the alien had implanted it.

"Planetary suicide," said the alien. "Reason: a failure on the moral level. Reason: an inability on the part of morality and social science and the general culture level to keep up with the physical sciences and a consequent ability for self-destruction without the moral fiber to curb it, to prevent war. Reason: constant battle between science and theology, productive only of death."

"Listen," Mayhew said. "I—" Obscurely, he was going to attempt a defense of distant Earth, but the alien silenced him with a dancing undulation of the flame-tongue of a body and went on:

"That is the case on ninety-seven of a hundred worlds. I haven't visited your world yet, Mr. Mayhew, although now we're hardly more than a thousand light years from it, is that correct?"

"Yeah," said Mayhew.

"I don't usually visit a world. I send an emissary, one of its own citizens. Are you listening, Mayhew? Do you understand?"

"You mean, you want me to go back to Earth for you—with some kind of a message?"

"Precisely."

"I can't," said Mayhew.

"You must!"

"Can the message—well, you know, will it cure them?"

"If it's given them in time."

It was cool there on the bluff above the dead city, but Mayhew began to sweat. He believed everything the alien said. There was no possibility of untruth. Somehow, with utmost finality, Mayhew could sense that. Yet what could he do? To return to Earth would mean returning to lifelong imprisonment.

"I'm an escaped convict," Mayhew said flatly, tonelessly. "They'll put me in prison for life if I go back there."

"Foolish man, not with the gift I give you!"

"What do you mean?"

"Do you believe everything I say?"

"Yeah," Mayhew said promptly. He meant it.

"In precisely the same way, they will believe you. If you return in time with the gift I will give you, you can save your human race from suicide. You understand that, don't you?"

"If—if I don't go back there with your message they're going to kill themselves off, like this world and all the others?"

"Yes. Overwhelming pride in their glorious attainment, Mr. Mayhew. Your ancient Greeks called it *hubris*, I believe. Pride in their science. Refusal to slow down, to let their morality catch up, to heed the word of their own theology."

"What can I do?"

"Mr. Mayhew, did you ever hear of the music of the

spheres?"

"I—yeah, I think so. Some kind of crazy legend about celestial music made by all the stars and planets in their motion through the firmament. The most beautiful music in the universe. Heavenly music. Divine. It sure sounds corny."

"Corny, Mayhew? The legend of the Music of the Spheres can be found in almost all your sub-cultures, can't it? Like your universal legend of a flood?"

"If you say so."

"I tell you, Mr. Mayhew, the Music of the Spheres is the message of salvation, if only you can understand in time, if only your people can."

"I don't get it."

THE ALIEN laughed for the first time. It was a simple laugh, melodious, at once friendly and serene. "Remember, I said an unresolved conflict between theology and science means destruction. This is what has happened on ninety-seven of every hundred habitable worlds throughout the galaxy. Needless to say, it: is the rule, not the exception."

"But what can I do?"

"The Music of the Spheres exists, Mr. Mayhew. It is known to your people as it is known to all scientific races. The Music of the Spheres is its theological name, but it has a scientific name as well. Under that name you are familiar with it. Every spaceman must be. The scientific name for the Music of the Spheres, Mr. Mayhew, is radio astronomy."

"Radio astronomy!" gasped Mayhew.

"Certainly. Radio astronomy."

Mayhew thought: hell, yeah, I'm familiar with it. Radio astronomy. With it you picked up radio beams from stars you couldn't see. Invisible stars, hidden behind dust clouds, in nebulae, in glowing swarms too far and too close-packed for a telescope to separate. Or dead stars, which emitted no light but gave off radio waves. Radio astronomy, Mayhew knew had been known on Earth for hundreds of years. Since the middle third of the twentieth century, as a matter of fact. Yet what had radio astronomy to do with this alien's message—a message which could save Earth from the self-destruction that seemed the rule of the galaxy?

"What has radio astronomy got to do with the Music of the Spheres?" Mayhew asked.

The alien said: "They are one and the same thing. On ninety-seven out of every hundred worlds, Mr. Mayhew, the electromagnetic signals of the radio-telescopes are regarded simply as radio waves. But on three worlds out of every hundred—on the worlds which will survive and put an end to internal strife—the message of the radio waves can be read. I will give you the ability to read this message, and you will bring that ability back to your people. You will bring them—the Music of the Spheres."

"It's actually some kind of message?"

"Precisely, Mr. Mayhew. As I have said—theology and science. No longer making war on one another, but wedding eternally in the Music of the Spheres. Or, to put it another way the Music of the Spheres—a product of radio astronomy, one of your most advanced sciences—for once and all time will establish as true the tenets of your most profound theology. You understand?"

Mayhew said: "I guess I'm kind of out of my depth."

"You won't be, once you see for yourself. Are you ready?"

"Yeah," said Mayhew. B ut he looked doubtful.

"Then come."

The alien turned, went to the enormous spaceship. As he approached it a port appeared magically in the side. A ramp materialized. With Mayhew the alien went up it and inside the ship. The ramp disappeared. The port closed. There seemed to be no seam in the hull of the cube-shaped ship.

THE MACHINERY was elaborate, labyrinthine. It meant almost nothing to Mayhew. He saw his own small spaceship, nestled in a cocoon-like cradle. He made no comment. They passed it in silence and entered a small chamber. Mayhew recognized the radio astronomy equipment. It was something he could understand.

"Put on the earphones," said the alien.

Mayhew did so. At first he heard nothing, then the alien pressed a switch. The familiar beeps filled his ears.

"You hear it?"

"Sure. Radio astronomy. Sixty cycles, isn't it? The commonest of wavelengths. The radio astronomy sound of hydrogen, the commonest element in the universe. So what?"

"That is as you have always heard it. That is as ninety-seven out of every hundred worlds hear it—and perish. But the remaining three... Listen." Another switch was pressed.

And Mayhew heard.

All at once his face went rapt. His eyes widened. Tears stood in them, rolled down his cheeks. A radiant smile lit up his hard, cynical face and he fell on his knees before the alien. The tongue-of-flame-body wavered in embarrassment and Mayhew climbed to his feet.

"Please," the alien said. "I am not who you think. I only hear the message, as you do. You understand?"

"Yes!" cried Mayhew tremulously. "Yes, yes, yes!"

"And you will take it back to your people? They can study this single receiver and duplicate it cheaply enough."

Mayhew said that he would do it. He was trembling with emotion, for he had heard—and understood—the music. The Music of the Spheres. An enormous wave of kindness and altruism engulfed him. He wanted to do things for people, to spend his life helping them, to serve mankind…

In a dreamlike trance, Mayhew watched as his small spaceship was disgorged by the larger one. He went outside with the alien. They stood together for a moment, staring down at the dead city.

"In the proud, cynical perfection of their upstart science," said the alien, "if a world can see lucidly and for all times with the very tools of their science that their pride as creators and artificers is one and the same as the humility and self-effacement of their theology…"

"Yes," said Mayhew. He understood. His face was still raptly serene. He took his earphones and entered his ship. A moment later he blasted off.

The alien stood until the red sun went down, gazing across the ruins of the city. Here, he thought wearily, he had been too late. Too late with the word. And—for Mayhew's Earth? He did not know. He had his hope only: that he was in time.

But it was up to the Earthman Mayhew. He knew that. He sighed, returning to his big cube-shaped spaceship with a gentle burning motion. A thousand light years—that was the journey Mayhew had to make. And with so many worlds to visit, the alien allowed himself only one try at each. It was Mayhew for Earth—or Earth was lost.

A thousand light years. With a ship such as Mayhew's, the chances of surviving the journey were exactly one in two. On the way out, Mayhew had been lucky. The alien wondered if he would be equally lucky on the way back. He did not know. He was not omniscient. If Mayhew made it, Earth would survive. If the odds of one chance in two worked against Mayhew somewhere in the depths of interstellar space—in fiery collision with an unseen dark star or heat-destruction in a suddenly engulfing nebula or failure of the subspace drive—then Earth would perish.

The alien went to the radio cabin and tuned in the instrument. He had not heard his radio astronomy all day, and he longed for it. The music swelled. Even by itself it was the most profoundly beautiful sound in all creation that ever was and ever would be. It was at once glorious and humble. It was God and creature and the starry universe. And the words—the words which were the same for all stellar languages, the simple words chanted to the music of the radio astronomy, the Music of the Spheres, the words so simply and so obvious and believed at once and for all time, the words that could save a world...

Would Mayhew bring them back to Earth—or perish trying?

The ethereally beautiful words were: *LOVE THY NEIGHBOR.*

Code of the Bluster World

*Establishing friendly relations with a new planet was usually routine
work. But on Qadak it was impossible—unless you were prepared to
die!*

FROM the moment the government cruiser *Milky Way*
shuddered into the invisibility of subspace, I began to expect
trouble.

"Ned, you're a regular worrywart," Ambassador Hurley
said.

Ned, that's me. Ned Talbert's the name and don't get me
wrong. I'm no diplomat, no foreign service career man. I'm
an explorer and it's got so I'm not happy unless there are
more parsecs between me and civilization than there are
square light years in a globular cluster. It was just my luck to
know more about Qadak III than any other terran.

"I'm sorry, sir," I told Ambassador Hurley as two taciturn
members of what passed for the Qadakian diplomatic corps
drove us in what was nothing more than an ornate wagon
toward the new Terran Embassy. "I just don't think the
Qadakians are ready for diplomatic relations. They don't
understand what it implies."

"Really, Ned," Robin Hurley said. Robin was the
Ambassador's daughter, and on the long subspace trip out
from Ophiuchus, where the closest Terran colony lies, Robin
and I had become good friends. When I thought about it,
Robin almost made shackling an explorer to a diplomatic
mission—to the first diplomatic mission ever accepted by the
Qadakians—worthwhile. "Just because the Qadakians are a
stage or two below us in culture—"

"A stage or two," I said as our wagon climbed a series of
terraced hills pulled by two surefooted bipedal beasts of

burden, which looked enough like enormous submen to make the Qadakian believe *we* were a stage or two below *them* in biological development. "A stage or two is nothing. They're barely civilized at all. I don't think the government ship should have stranded us here until we were sure the Qadakians understood exactly what a diplomatic mission was."

"Some optimist you are," Robin said.

Qadak III was not a place for optimism, but I didn't tell her that. It was a small rugged planet of a binary star system. The sky was as pale blue, as watery-translucent, as a Martian sky. Neither the small red sun nor the slightly larger white sun gave as much heat as Sol gave Mars. Together, they put Qadak in an energy range midway between Earth and Mars— which meant that as the wagon took us toward our Embassy, Ambassador Hurley, Robin and I were bundled to the ears in warm clothing. The Ambassador and I wore shapeless parkas and hoods but Robin wouldn't hear of such a thing. She wore a ski outfit which might have been fine on one of the Himalayan package tours, but here on Qadak her teeth were already chattering and the tip of her pert nose looked blue.

"You should have dressed more warmly," Ambassador Hurley told her. "Can't have the official hostess of the Terran Embassy down with a case of frostbite."

AMBASSADOR Hurley's banter hid serious concern. The Ambassador doted on his daughter and Robin knew it and the knowledge usually made her behave like a petty tyrant toward her father but what could you expect of a pretty and spoiled twenty year old?

The struggling bipeds bore our wagon higher into the craggy hills of Qadak, where the clear air was numbingly cold. Snow clung to the rocky floor of the deepest ravines but Qadak was a dry world and the mountains were lifeless and bare. Far below us, the sparse timberline was only faintly—reluctantly on Qadak, I thought, if you can call a timberline reluctant—green.

There were three Qadakians in the wagon with us, and just looking at them could give you the willies. But I was an explorer and Robin was an idealist, so if anybody got the willies it was the Ambassador himself, but Robert Hurley could mask his feelings pretty well. The Qadakians look like rubber-skinned dinosaurs, man-sized with huge heads and fantastically large jaws and teeth that could bite your arm off and a tail one swipe from which could knock over a three-ton jet mobile, let alone the flimsy wagon, which was our official vehicle of state. The Qadakians had newly adapted our custom of wearing clothing although their rubber-like skins were perfect insulators against the cold of their world and they only wore the clothing as a gesture of friendship, but it was hard to see what view of what part of a dinosaur's anatomy would shock even the primmest of Terran girls. And Robin Hurley, make no mistakes, was far from prim.

The wagon finally hit a stretch of level ground. The Ambassador beat his parka-clad arms across his chest. The cold had made his nose run and there were particles of ice in his moustache. His face looked a scrubbed schoolboy pink in the clear freezing air.

"I—I th-think we a-arrived," Robin chattered, her jaw numb with cold.

I grinned at the Ambassador, but he gave his daughter a stern fatherly look. She winked at him and skipped from the wagon as it rolled to a stop at the entrance to a large cave. Her ski-suit was the color of flame and it would have looked fine in a cheerful skiing lodge in the Himalayas especially since color-crazy Bhutan has been going after the tourist trade, but on stark, bare, colorless Qadak it stuck out like the proverbial sore thumb.

The Qadakian wagoneers clucked something in their native tongue and led all of us into the cave.

"Hey, I remember this place," I said. "It's what passes for a palace around here. They haven't taken us to the Embassy, sir. They've taken us to the palace probably to impress us with a show of strength."

"Shall I act impressed or indifferent? You know the Qadakians, Ned. That's why you're here."

"Act indifferent. Act indifferent as hell. They're megalomaniacs, pompously and fantastically convinced of their own importance. It you don't try to deflate them from the very start you'll be the yes-maningest Ambassador in the history of galactic relations."

The Ambassador nodded. Robin had already ducked inside the cave. I began to trot because I didn't want to lose sight of her for long. Trotting on Qadak is something to see. The planet is midway in size between Mars and Mercury and a fairly athletic man will get the hang of the gravity differential almost at once with the result that he can jump around better than any kangaroo that ever came out of Australia.

IT was unexpectedly warm inside the cave. On my third jump I alighted next to Robin, who had already stripped off her ski-suit. Under it she wore a dark blue flannel shirt and tight levis. The shirt was open at the throat and against the dark blue of the shirt, framed by her gleaming black hair, Robin's face and throat were very white and very lovely.

"It almost looks like something out of a medieval romance," she told me.

She had a point there. Torches thrust into niches in the cave wall lit the huge cavern with an eerie, pulsing crimson light. Hundreds of Qadakians were assembled near us in two long torch-bearing rows, awaiting their *numin* or king. When he finally appeared a chant rolled across the vast floor of the cavern, building in volume as it came until it seemed to shake the walls with vocal thunder by the time it reached us.

A voice in Qadaki and another repeated in accented English for our benefit: "The Great King arrives!"

The hundreds of Qadakians bowed, scraping the muzzles of their great jaws against the bare rock of the cavern floor. The Ambassador looked at me but I shook my head—which meant that we should do no bowing.

The Qadakians carried rawhide shields—hide of the gigantic manlike beasts of burden, I realized—in their small forelimbs. As the Great King came down the living aisle they had made for him they shook their shields and it made a noise like the cavern roof collapsing. Finally the Great King reached a high stone platform at one end of the cavern. Thick-muscled tail dragging, he mounted it and lifted his forelimbs for silence. The shields rattled once more, then were stilled. The Great King began to speak in a deep booming voice. The translator intoned:

"That you of Earth should take the trouble to send an Ambassadorial staff halfway across the galaxy is a tribute to the awe you must feel for the great civilization of Qadak, the most wonderful our galaxy has yet produced. We acknowledge this tribute as one we justly deserve, although in truth we had expected gifts and riches to accompany your Ambassadorial staff."

"Already they want to get on the interstellar gravy-train," Robin whispered.

But I shook my head. "It has nothing to do with that. The Qadakians are really megalomaniacs; that just wasn't a way of talking. But usually they lead up to it slowly." I added in a worried voice, "If they start off like this, I wonder what they'll finish up with."

The Great King had been talking all this while. I picked up the translators words with: "...must obey the Qadakian laws of diplomacy while here, not the Terran laws, since the Qadakian laws, developed here, are obviously superior."

"That's impossible," Ambassador Hurley said in a furious whisper. "The Terran Embassy always follows the interstellar covenants to the letter, not the system of some backward, out-of-the-way planet."

"The *Milky Way* is en route back to Ophiuchus," I pointed out. "It looks like you'll do whatever the Qadakians say. If you think I'm' kidding, listen to what their Great King is saying now."

The translator intoned: "I therefore expectorate upon your culture. I cast the dung of our beasts of burden upon it. My people are mighty. I am mighty. The Qadakian civilization is older than the stars and brighter, and older even than the nebulae, which spawned the stars before your paltry Earth, your insignificant Earth, was born.

"There are certain concessions we shall want in the nature of interstellar trade from your planet. It is a custom of Qadakian diplomatic procedure to hold for ransom a valuable asset of the delegation in question until such time as the concessions are granted. As Great King I therefore impound, since you have brought no treasure with you, the female member of your staff."

IT hit us like a thunderbolt. Ambassador Hurley's face turned purple with rage. He was so angry he couldn't speak. Robin gave me a weak smile as two Qadakians came clomping across the rocky floor toward her on their pillar-like hind legs.

I got my hand on Robin's shoulder and pulled her toward me, then behind me. I had spent a month on Qadak on my trail-blazing expedition. I knew something of the Qadakian customs and now I hoped it would be enough. I knew you had to push the Qadakians a long way, but there might be a point beyond which was fatal. For Robin I had to find that point.

"Hold!" I shouted, consciously trying to ape the Qadakian Great King's flowery way of speaking. "You of Qadak are not worthy of the dung of your beasts of burden," I said, as the translator put my words into Qadaki for his ruler. "You are not worthy of the dung of the fleas that inhabit the hair of your beasts of burden. You mock a civilization, which has spanned a thousand thousand parsecs of space and challenges the doors of infinity itself, yet you have never lifted a clumsy foot off the face of your pebble of a planet."

I expected a shocked silence on the part of the Great King. But he didn't even bat a figurative eyelash as he countered, "Interstellar travel holds utterly no fascination for the great Qadak people because on Qadak is the sum of all that is worthwhile in our galaxy and all that can ever be worthwhile. Take the woman, please."

"Hold!" I cried again as the two Qadakians lumbered in our direction once more. But the Great King merely waved a forelimb for silence. Firelight wavered and danced all about us. I had removed my parka and stood there in jumper and slacks, a high-powered atomic pistol strapped at my waist. I pulled it clear of the holster and challenged: "Now you'll stop."

The Great King spoke. The translator said: "Kill the young Earthman." His voice sounded utterly indifferent, but you never could tell about a Qadaki voice.

A spear blurred through the air at me, whistled by my face, inches from the jawbone. Another tugged at the synthetic fabric of my jumper sleeve. Robin screamed. The Ambassador, weaponless, shook his fist and ranted.

I dropped quickly to one knee, took dead aim and blew the heads off each of the two advancing Qadakians. The dead decapitated bodies fell at our feet with two clearly audible thuds in the complete silence that had followed the two explosive roars of the atomic pistol.

The Great King spoke and the translator translated. "You believe for a moment this impresses me? Two lives? Merely two? Behold."

The King roared some orders and the translator remained silent. A troop of archers trotted up from an alcove to the King's left, stationing themselves below his high rock platform and strung their bows. I thought we were finished. I thought I had gone too far—although I hadn't been able to help it: I had merely killed my own executioners. The archers had come to finish the job of execution, not merely on me but on all three of us.

The Qadakians let their arrows fly.

And sent them winging toward the thickest part of the Qadakian crowd!

A score of Qadakians fell, dead or dying. There were great hissing screams in the audience and the translator screamed: "See! Our Great King is mighty. For two that you have slain, he has killed fifty."

FIFTY was an exaggeration. Twenty was more like it, but the point was well made. I killed two Qadakians. In terran terms it was murder, if defensible murder since the Qadakians had been my executioners. But in Qadakian terms it wasn't murder at all. In Qadakian terms, it was merely a challenge cast before the Great King. *I have killed two of your subjects, the challenge said. Can you top this?*

The King had topped it all right. And we were in the same hole I had been trying to yank us out of, for the Great

King said: "Take the woman so that I may present our demands."

Two more Qadakians advanced. I got down on one knee again with my atomic pistol, but Robin placed her slim fingers on my wrist and said, "Please, Ned. What good would it do? If they want to take me, they're going to take me."

"Over my dead body!" Ambassador Hurley roared.

"You too, Dad. You couldn't stop them. There are only two of you."

"Is that so?" The Ambassador said. "Ned's done a fine job of stopping them so far. Hasn't he?"

"At the cost of twenty lives," Robin said. "We don't want that. We didn't come here to fight a war with the Qadakians. We came here to start diplomatic relations with them, to welcome them into the expanding interstellar culture, to—"

"I'm beginning to think Ned was right," her father told Robin. "These creatures aren't ready for diplomatic relations with us or anyone. But right now—"

"Right now," Robin insisted, "you're not going to lift a finger when they take me. They only want me for a hostage; they're not going to hurt me."

The Qadakians were very close now, but they were watching my atomic pistol and advancing warily. I looked at the Ambassador and shrugged. I wasn't in charge of this expedition.

He shrugged too. "Do as she says," he told me finally.

Robin ran to him and kissed him on the cheek, then came to me and nestled for a moment in my arms after I had buckled away the atomic pistol. She kissed me on the lips and darted away, confronting the Qadakians boldly, unafraid. They took her by the arms and led her off toward the alcove from which the archers had emerged. The archers formed a double file and followed them inside.

"She goes willingly," I told the Great King, and it was translated for him. "She goes willingly so as not to humble you at the outset of our relationship. We demand, however, that she not be harmed in any way."

I was told, "You are not in any position to demand." For the first time the Great King's boast was pretty close to the truth when he added, "With your weapon you were able to kill two of my subjects, but with the primitive weapons at my disposal I slew twenty—ten times two—in the same period of time. For I am mighty, mightier far than you."

"We demand," I repeated, "that she not be harmed."

"That depends on you," we were told. "When we present our demands—"

"Present them now," I said.

"Tomorrow, at our first meeting of state."

I leaped swiftly toward the alcove through which Robin and her captors and the two files of archers had vanished. I said, "Then I go with her until tomorrow."

As if by magic, three archers appeared in front of me, bowstrings taut, bows arched, arrows pointing at my chest.

"She goes alone," the Great King said.

I walked slowly back to where the Ambassador was waiting. My twenty-foot leaps in the direction of the alcove hadn't impressed the Great King at all. Or—if they had impressed him—he hid the fact very well.

"If they hurt her in any way," Ambassador Hurley told me, "I'll never forgive myself!"

"If they hurt her," I said, trying to bolster the Ambassador's confidence, "they'll have to kill me first."

He looked at me gravely. He didn't say anything, but the look said: if they want to, they will.

THE next day, the Qadakian Great King presented his incredible demands. They were presented in the same palace cavern after a sleepless night in which the Ambassador and I had paced back and forth in the small, dark, damp cave allotted to us, but this time thousands of the Qadakians had squeezed in to hear how the Earth representatives would be humbled.

The Great King said:

"We of Qadak demand to have a representative with full voting power on every Terran voting body in existence, from the Senate of United Earth on down."

I got out the word "'but'"—and was interrupted.

"Actually," the Great King said, "this is more of a favor than a demand. Since we of Qadak are so superior intellectually to you of Earth, it will do your Senate and your other voting bodies a great deal of good to have the stabilizing influence of a Qadakian in their midst."

Patiently I tried to explain that by common interstellar tradition each world remained sovereign despite intercourse with other worlds but that the well-being of the denizens of each world was enhanced by free trade, competitive interstellar trade on a private enterprise basis, between worlds. It made a lot of sense to most worlds but it left the Great King of Qadak as cold as the deepest snow-filled ravine slashing the highest mountaintop on his planet.

All he said was, "We of Qadak do things differently. Naturally, ours is the correct way. Our second demand is that you permit our surplus population of some three hundred million Qadakian families to settle on some of your out-worlds. This too can hardly be regarded as a demand from your point of view. It is a favor since your people will clearly benefit from rich personal contact with ours."

"What are we going to do?" Ambassador Hurley whispered to me. "The demands are impossible. We can't even relay them on, can we?"

"I guess not," I said. "You're the diplomat."

"You wouldn't know it—here."

"Will they let us use a subspace radio?"

"Probably. They don't quite understand what a radio does. Why?"

"Call the *Milky Way* back from Ophiuchus. We may have to evacuate."

"But what about my daughter? I'm not going to think of leaving without her."

"Did you think I would?"

"I'm sorry, Ned. I'm very upset, I guess."

I addressed the translator: "Before we can consider your insignificant demands, the customs of our own diplomatic procedure make it mandatory that the Earth girl be returned to us."

"That is impossible," said the Great King, "until all our demands are met."

"Tell them anything," the Ambassador said. "We don't have to go through with it. Obviously, Qadak isn't ready for diplomatic relations with civilized worlds."

"I'm not the Terran Secretary of State," I said, "and neither are you. But if the Terran Secretary of State tells us something—"

"He's never been here. He hasn't seen what it's like."

"Look, Ambassador. I agree with you. I was against this mission from the beginning. But since we're on it, I think we ought to do what we can. We ought to work under the assumption that the Secretary of State wants diplomatic relations maintained unless we hear otherwise."

"But my daughter—"

"I'll get your daughter," I said. "I have an idea, Ambassador. You know those motion pictures we studied on the *Milky Way*, the ones explaining Qadakian ceremonies and customs—"

"Yes, of course. But this is no time to talk about motion pictures."

"Ask for a recess. Go to our quarters and bring the pictures here. And bring a projector. I think I have a way out of this." I didn't want to tell the Ambassador what my plan was. It seemed farfetched even to me, and I had dreamed it up. But I was beginning to think it was our only chance.

AMBASSADOR Hurley asked for and was granted the recess. I waited until he was gone, then headed for the alcove through which the Qadakians had taken Robin. A bowman seven feet tall, his great dinosaur mouth leering barred my way.

He said something and the translator boomed: "You are not to pass!"

"Tell him to get out of my way or I will kill him," I said. The translator spoke in his native tongue. The bowman strung an arrow. He stood not fifteen feet in front of me and pointed his arrow at my chest.

From somewhere behind him, Robin cried: "I can see you, Ned! Don't do anything foolhardy, please. I think they've been given orders not to hurt me—so far."

"Then scream," I said.

"Scream?"

"Scream," I repeated, and waited as she did so. It was a man-sized bellow for a slim girl like Robin, and it brought the Qadakian guard's dinosaur head pivoting around on its immense neck. I sprang forward and slashed the butt of my pistol across the base of the large skull. At first there was utterly no reaction and I was afraid the Qadak had been immune to the blow. But then he wheeled to face me slowly, dropping the bow as he came around. When we stood again face to face the Qadakian collapsed at my feet.

I leaped over his great body and sprinted down a dim passageway. It twisted to the left and widened into a small bare room with a single cot against one wall. Standing at the entranceway was Robin. I hugged her quickly, then she withdrew and I took her hand and said, "Your Dad should be outside now with his projector."

"You mean movie projector?"

I said that was exactly what I meant.

"But I don't see—"

I tugged her toward the main gallery of the cavern. I wasn't sure I saw it either.

As we reappeared near the body of the still-supine guard, the Great King roared something and the translator said, "Since you have disobeyed me, you must die."

"Oh, Ned," Robin cried. "Why did you have to—"

But I called out in a loud voice: "I issue a challenge, O King. Can you have me killed before the challenge is accepted?"

"No a challenge will always be honored."

I was banking on that. Qadakian pride had saved my life—for the moment. But would it save the day for us?

The Ambassador appeared lugging a trim modern motion picture projector and a reel of film. I set the machine up on a small outcropping of rock and began to check the connections when the translator said:

"We of Qadak couldn't possibly be interested in your childish gadgets. Kill this man."

Archers advanced, but I held my hands up and spoke swiftly, knowing I had no more than seconds. "Hear me, O King. Yesterday I slew two of your people in self-defense. You immediately killed ten for one, showing how great your power was compared to mine."

"That was but a sample," came the translator's words after the Great King had halted the archers in their tracks with a wave of his hand. "I can kill a hundred to one. I can kill a hundred of my subjects for each you slay. I am mighty."

Robin looked at me with sudden anger in her eyes. "You'd kill them in cold blood, just to—"

"It's his life or theirs," Ambassador Hurley said, but I shook my head and told them:

"I hope it's neither!" I shouted. "And if you cannot, O Great King? If you fail?"

"That is an impossibility."

"Nevertheless, if you fail?"

"Very well, if I fail we will conduct our relationships with Earth and the other planets of the galaxy according to your foolish traditions."

"Can you trust him?" Ambassador Hurley asked me.

"I think so. If he fails, his pride will be hurt. He'll be craven. There's no middle road, not right away, for a megalomaniac."

"But if I succeed," the Great King said, "your life will be immediately forfeit. Is it a bargain?"

"Yes," I said. My hands shook as I threaded the motion picture film. It was archaic twenty-first century style film because I had taken the pictures myself on my first exploratory trip to Qadak and an explorer has to watch his budget and will often make do with outdated, second-hand equipment. Soon a square of yellow light appeared on one wall of the cavern.

"As near as I can figure," I told the Ambassador, "there's one shot here that shows a hundred thousand Qadakians marching toward this palace through a deep valley, which leads here from their capital city. When the film reaches that frame, stop it. Project that frame on the wall and hold it there. You understand?"

"Yes, but—"

"O.K.," I said, and started the machine.

The Qadakians oo'd and ah'd as lifesize images of themselves appeared on the wall. Even the inscrutable king seemed impressed, although he tried to hide it.

"Watch," I said, "as with Terran magic I make your people spring to life from the naked rock wall of this cavern. You believe in this magic?"

"It is a magic I have not seen before," the Great King admitted. Coming from him, it was a mighty concession, but he immediately added, "I await your challenge, Earthman. I will kill a hundred of my subjects for each one you slay. If I fail, we bow to your diplomacy. If I win, you die."

The old projector purred on. Half a dozen archers advanced and took their positions ten yards ahead of us, arrows strung and ready. If the King succeeded, I wouldn't survive his success more than a few seconds.

I wasn't even watching the film. I knew it by heart. There would be a series of shots on Qadaki—local customs, then the climactic filming of the great march of a hundred thousand Qadakians on the royal palace-cave. And then, success or failure. Life or death.

"Here it is," Ambassador Hurley said finally. "Here it is, Ned." He touched a switch and the projector ground to a stop. I looked up at the wall and saw the square of light projected by the machine showing a huge gorge a mile or so down the mountain trail. The gorge was packed with Qadakians. My first estimate of a hundred thousand had been conservative. There was no telling how many Qadakians were assembled there, but I figured the number was probably closer to a hundred, and fifty thousand.

"Out of nothingness, O Great King," I cried, "I produce this vast throng of your people. You see?"

"I see," the Great King said. You could tell he was awed.

I turned a switch for the sound track. The roar of the crowd and the thunderous stamping of their great feet came to us.

"Now watch, O Great King," I said. I didn't have to say it. He was watching, all right. His small eyes had grown very round. They were practically popping from his dinosaur head. Even the archer-executioners looked interested.

As calm as I could—but my hands were trembling—I lit a match and touched it to the motion picture film. The film curled, I looked up at the wall. Great brown blisters appeared as if by magic, consuming the vast throng projected there. In a moment it was over. The wall was now a blank.

The Qadaks rattled their shields. The archers waited, motionless, for their orders.

As far as the Great King knew, I had killed some hundred and fifty thousand of his subjects. To win our wager, he would have to slay some fifteen million of his people. He said nothing at first. He stared at the wall for a long time, trying to conjure an image of the square of light as it had been, filled with his subjects. Then, slowly, he stepped down from the high stone platform and came stomping across the cavern toward us. The archers parted before him and he advanced as if they weren't there. When he reached us he stopped and stared at me harder than he had stared at the wall.

Finally he spoke and the translator said: "This great feat I cannot match, let alone increase a hundredfold."

"So?" I said arrogantly.

"So I am yours to command."

And he prostrated himself on the floor of the cavern before us.

THE next day, the *Milky Way* returned in answer to Ambassador Hurley's urgent radio summons, but he told the captain:

"I guess it was a false alarm. It's all right now. Everything is all right, thanks to Ned Talbert."

The captain nodded. "Confidentially, that's why State sent Talbert."

"But how do you know?" the Ambassador demanded.

"Because I work for the State Department. You see, Ambassador, they knew the Qadakians were megalomaniacs. At the beginning, an ordinary embassy staff couldn't hope to cope with them. To match their megalomania we needed someone who was supremely independent and self-confident—who, in short, but an explorer who always has to rely on his own initiative? Who but Ned Talbert?"

"Listen," I said. "That doesn't mean I'm going to stick around indefinitely. There's a lot of uncharted space to be explored and I want to do my share."

"Not alone, you won't," Robin said, holding my hand.

"Not alone," I told her.

The *Milky Way* Captain said: "We'll need you for a few more months, Talbert. You're our guarantee. The Great King was humbled by you. There's no middle road for him right now, you see? He's either master or slave. He'll be slave until Qadak begins to understand the ways of interstellar democracy, then you'll be free to go where you will. All right?"

I said it was all right if that was what the State Department wanted. I told him he could explain the rest of it to Ambassador Hurley and walked off with Robin.

There was another kind of exploration that could be done right now, and I wasn't any better at it than any other man. It was high time I began to explore the beginning of my life together with Robin...

All Flesh is Brass

When you put lead into these warriors it might stop them and it might not. And you always wondered what would fly out of their heads—nuts of brains...

SOMEWHERE on the Northern Front, January 1. I think the Ivans are beginning to learn they have nothing on us with their famous Russian winter. Until recently they had never tried the good old United States variety, served North Dakota style. Now that they have, they'll learn.

I'm a fine one to talk.

I'm with the Regulars and I was born and bred a city boy. Place called The Bronx, although now The Bronx is the northeastern lip of Manhattan Hell Hole, spilling radioactive rubble, down into the H-Crater.

At least, that's what some of the Replaces tell me; I wouldn't know myself: I haven't been there in fourteen months.

But let's get back to this North Dakota Winter. It's cold. It's so cold that every other thought of coldness you ever had just doesn't mean anything. It's the kind of nerve-chilling, bone-numbing cold that separates the men from the boys in a hurry. It comes in great, frigid gusts from the northland and it's too cold to stamp your feet or beat your chest. And whatever you do, the winter manual says, don't let the metal parts of your rifle come in contact with your bare skin. A guy I know tried it accidentally. He's been cleared to the hospital in Fargo, but they ought to keep the rifle as a warning. You don't have to come very close to see the strip of skin three inches by one inch stuck to it.

So, it's cold. But I'd better knock off this kind of thinking before I get morbid.

January 1, later. Last night was New Year's · Eve. God knows where they got it from, but at about twenty-two hundred the medics came crawling and stumbling through the snow, leaving a pint of whisky in each fox hole.

A couple of minutes after I opened my pint and started drinking, I had a visitor.

A girl.

She wore the uniform of an Irregular—that is, she had on a helmet and a white armband which said U.S.A. The shoe-packs were strictly homemade, the denim trousers frozen stiff, the mackinaw, which came almost to her knees, covered with snow. She came tumbling into the foxhole so fast that had she been an Ivan, I'd have been dead.

"Mind?" she said, plunging her rifle-stock into the snow and hunkering down beside it.

I shook my head. "Two bodies will make this hole warmer than one." I gulped another mouthful of the whisky, discovered with no particular interest it was rye.

Her mittened hand closed over mine. A small hand. "Please," she said.

I looked at her. She had a nice face, which however, would have failed entirely to inspire an artist. "Where you coming from?" I asked, taking another drink.

Her hand stayed put. "Please." She snuffled and wiped her running nose on her sleeve. "Up front a ways, Patrol action."

"They taking many girls?"

"As many as will join. I can shoot this gun; I guess that's all they're interested in since the Ivans started pouring over the Canadian border. Please."

I cursed softly and handed her the bottle. She hardly paused to breathe, downing the half-pint which remained in four gulping swallows. She blinked, she wiped her lips, coughed, tossed the empty pint carelessly up over her shoulder and into the frozen night.

"Thanks."

"Damn it! Why'd you have to show up?"

"It makes you warm. Doesn't it?"

"Yeah. Yeah, I guess. How long you been fighting?"

"Three days."

"No training?"

"No training. My husband—"

"You married?" She looked so young.

"I was. My husband got back from the English Evacuation with one arm shot off. Three days ago the Ivans found us and killed him. I fled south and joined up. Smoke?"

When I nodded eagerly, she got two cigarettes out of the breast pocket of her mackinaw, lighted them, passed one to me.

We smoked and talked till my watch said twelve o'clock.

"Happy New Year," she said.

"Happy New Year."

Then we got some sleep. A year ago I never would have believed it. There we were, bundled up like couple of Eskimos but still trying to keep warm. We lay huddled together, breast to breast, and I could feel her heart thumping. We spent that night as close as a couple of logs in an ice jam—and just as dispassionately.

She was up with the first gray streaks of dawn. She clambered up the side of the foxhole three times and slipped back down the slippery snow each time.

"Here," I said. She started up again and I got both my hands under her fanny and heaved. She went up and over and plowed head-first into the snow. She turned around, looked down at me, grinned. She waved and was on her way.

Probably I'll never see her again. It was an hour till I remembered I'd forgotten to ask her name.

JANUARY 5. Colder still, but no fresh snow. The Ivans laid down a brief artillery barrage, but it was enough to splash purple and orange flame all over the tundra. Rations giving out. I'll have to get some company soon or starve to death.

JANUARY 7. Great news! I'm being shipped to the rear for two days of rest and warmth. Chaplain came around and said so, and I felt like blessing *him!* He tells me I'll have a bed back there, in a house with four walls, although probably the ceiling's been blown off. I'll settle for the bed alone as long as it has a blanket. Well, I'll find out pretty soon.

JANUARY 8. This is the life. Hot soup this morning, with savory hunks of meat in it. Served in bed, if you please, by a gal with looks. And Chaplain was pessimistic: there's a ceiling here!

But the guy in the bed next to me dampened it all with a sordid story. I can't make up my mind if it's true or not.

"Are you a Replace?" he said. He was a short, gnarled man, balding, with deep-set eyes, red-rimmed and unhealthy-looking. Replace? That's short for Replacement.

I told him no, I wasn't.

"Good. Good. But watch them Replaces. Oh yes, keep your eye on them, you mark my words."

"What for? You mean because they're green?"

"No. Not on acounta that. Because some of them ain't human."

I told him I thought he was joking.

"I'm not joshing, young feller. Name's Ben. You think old Ben would josh about a thing like that? I read the Book and I'm a God-fearing man and don't you forget it. But some of the Replaces, they ain't human."

I smiled. "Now, if you said the Ivans weren't human, I'd agree with you. They're like machines." I still thought he was joking. But that stuff about the Ivans isn't so funny. The way I understand it, top brass suspects most of them are cokey. "But shoot," I went on, "they probably eat hashish instead of C-rations and heroin instead of K."

"I doubt it," the small, gnarled man named Ben said very seriously. "They probably came up with the Invention sooner than we did, that's all." He said it like that. Invention. Like it should have a capital letter.

"The Invention?" I asked Ben. "What invention?"

"A new kind of Replace. Awful." Ben grunted and sat back complacently, as if because he'd told me that much now it wasn't his worry any longer.

I leaned over and prodded his shoulder while the nurse brought me another cup of soup. "What kind of Replace?"

Ben shrugged. "Not sure. Mechanical, though, instead of human."

"You mean robots?"

"Didn't say that."

"Damn it, say what you mean then!"

"Not sure I know. But there's a rumor—troube is, son, you've been at the front too long. You get to miss what's going on. Like the Good Book says—"

"Never mind what the Good Book says. *You* said something about robots."

"Did not. Mechanical Replaces, not robots. There's a world of difference, son. All the medical outfits are staffed with a lot of cybernetics men, too. You know, thinking-machine stuff. Man comes in from the front. Dying. If they get him quick they have ways to duplicate his body and reproduce the complicated electrical impulses which make up his mind. He thinks he's a man. He don't know no better. But he's a machine. A better fighting man, sure. But a machine. If the Ivans have them too, it gives you a kind of creepy feeling. Fighting machines which think they're men." Ben shuddered, lapsed into troubled silence.

JANUARY 10. Well, I'm on my way back to the front. Funny guy, Ben. He didn't say another word till right before I left. I tried to get a conversation going a couple of times, but he merely grunted and averted his head. Before I left he said goodbye, and that was all. January 11. I'd better run some of these entries together like this because I'm running low on paper. After two days of warmth, the front is colder than ever. I wonder, do pleasure and pain always buck each other that way? January 12. Snowed all day and all night. A couple of Ivan's jets flew over, but apparently just on reconnaissance. They came in real low because the snow brought visibility down below the level of the treetops. I think one of the jets got into trouble with the AA boys a couple of miles from here, but it's hard to tell.

JANUARY 14. Still snowing.

JANUARY 16. Talk about your miracles. Miss New Year's Eve came back today, quite by accident. Her name is Beth and she's been delivering messages until they shoved her back into the infantry. Mine was the first fox-hole she happened to find. This time *she* had the whisky and *I* did the grubbing, but Beth didn't mind at all. If I knew Beth could keep me supplied with whisky like that, I'd ask her to marry me.

JANUARY 17. Beth tells me she's scared. At first I thought it was what the aid-man said when he brought up some chow. Rumor of a big Ivan push coming, despite the snow and the cold. Kicking off tomorrow at dawn unless G2 got some cockeyed information. But Beth says that isn't what's worrying her.

Dames, I thought. But then she made like what's-his-name—like Ben.

"It's the Replaces," said Beth. "More and more of them with that stony-eyed look, almost like they weren't alive, Charlie." That's me, Charlie.

"I know," I said, and laughed. "They're machines. Carbon copies of men who got theirs on the front and died. Good copies, but machines. Terrible stuff."

"Why, yes! That's just what I had in mind, Charlie."

"You're nuts," I told her. "I heard the same thing from a nut in a rear area."

Beth insisted, "You'll hear it every place you go. A thing like that gets around."

"I haven't heard anything."

"You have too. From me and—and the rear area nut."

"It's smoke from the embers of a dung fire," I said, borrowing an expression from the Ivans which had got popular with our boys. "I don't believe a word of it." I snickered. "Next thing you'll be telling me, you're one of the robots."

Beth shook her head. "Of course I'm not. But not robots, Charlie. One of the worst part of it is, the Replaces don't even know. They think they're men. Only they're not afraid like men, and they don't get so cold, either. The sober rumors say they last about a year or two and then break down.

"But I thought of what you said. Right after I began to put two and two together about the Replaces. I had to make sure. I—I experimented on myself. I went without food and I got hungry. I cut my hand with a knife and I bled."

"That's funny," I said. "You really believed it."

Beth shrugged in the cold, leaned toward me, took my hand. By the time I realized something funny was going on, it was too late. Beth had my mitten between her teeth, and she bit. I yelped and pulled away, but the experiment had already been conducted to her satisfaction. Blood welled up sluggishly, stained my mitten a dull red and froze an almost chocolate-brown color a few moments later.

"You're human," said Beth.

I didn't answer. I felt good and sore, sore enough to cut my nose to spite my face. I didn't bundle with Beth that night. She stayed put on her side of the foxhole; I curled up, shivering with the cold, on mine. I slept poorly, but so did Beth. Damn her, though—my hand throbbed all night.

JANUARY 18. It's late afternoon now, and G2 hit it right on the head. The sky all around us is pulsing with that purple-orange glow which spells out, clear as anything, rocket barrage. And I got the chance to shoot at some Ivans this morning—that is, before I had to high-tail it back a mile with Beth. The line is stabilized there, more or less, but the Ivans are still mounting their power for a thrust at our center— about three miles west of here. The artillery is pounding and thudding off in that direction, and kicking up great splashes of snow. I got me two Ivans, I think, and Beth claims one. But Regulars and Irregulars dotted the snow all around us as we ran, and Beth cried a little. More later.

JANUARY 18, later. God! I still can't believe it. If a girl were brought up in a cloister and then introduced to the facts of life by a brutal sex-fiend, she might feel something like this. Trouble was, I didn't believe. I didn't *want* to believe what everyone told me. I believe now. I have to. I saw for, myself.

It happened like this. Beth and I were hacking away at the frozen ground under the snow with our bayonets, for even a shallow hole would be some protection against the wind and the cold. About half an hour after we got started, someone began crawling over to us. Beth saw him first, dragging himself across the snow and yelling. We both ran to him, but I got there before Beth did.

There was a hole where his chest should have been. A gaping hole with plenty of snow in it. He should have been dead, but he dragged himself along, yelling. The hole went all the way through to his back and the snow came out there. A nice clean hole with white snow going in the bottom and coming out the top, still white.

Beth saw him and screamed. He clutched at his chest and screamed back. The hole was smooth and even, but that could happen if a high-velocity rocket passed through you cleanly. Of course, you wouldn't live to tell about it.

This man did.

Something gleamed against the snow as he tried to raise himself on his haunches. Metallic. A coil of thick wire, but twisted and bent. Protruding from the hole in his chest. He looked at me and said, "I swear I didn't know—"

I carry a pistol which I got from a dead Ivan officer. I took it out and felt it slap back savagely against my palm as I shot the wounded man's head off. Literally. In pieces. Metal pieces. I was sick after that, and so was Beth.

I think I'll make love to Beth tonight. It will help some. Probably, though, it won't help enough.

JANUARY 19. *Boom! Crash! Blat!* I can hardly hear myself think. Trust those Ivans to out-guess the guessers and come up with something foxy. They raked the center of our line with zero'd-in artillery so that we concentrated our reserve behind it. Then they cut away quickly and drove their salient three miles away—*here!* They tore through our line like it was paper and they cut around and halfway behind our reserve before it could deploy itself properly.

I've got to put down this pencil for my rifle, says Beth. More later.

APRIL 14. That's right, April 14. Beth is dead. It was January 19 when it happened. During the big Ivan push. She got it quick and clean. I don't think she even knew what hit her. I'll miss her.

I got mine the same day, with an old-fashioned recoil rifle, of all things. Somehow, a couple of aid-men found me, carried me to the field hospital. The way I understand it they did some emergency work there, then shipped me to Base Hospital in Fargo. Today's my first day back at the front. They really rush things, those medicos.

Incredible as it seems, we somehow managed to stop Ivan in his tracks. Skillful leadership? Plucky foot soldiers? There are all sorts of answers, but I've got one of my own. Ben knew what was going on, and Beth. The Replaces. More and more of them every day. Metal men. Duplicates of men who died in battle, every tiny aspect of their brains and physical features copied to the last detail. Metal men who can go on and on because they don't get tired like mere humans. Evidently we can make more of them than the Ivans can. So now we're winning.

It's not a secret any more. Too many of the metal men have been blasted by artillery at the front. Too many have been strewn over an acre or so of ground, their tiny, intricate metal parts gleaming more brightly than the snow. The Replaces will never be forgotten. They're going to win this war for us, and then they'll die. All of them. In a year or two, for they're not constructed to last longer than that. A couple million metal men—looking like humans but with different drives and different joys—would be quite a strain on peace-time social structure.

APRIL 15. The snow has begun to thaw in the northern hills. The winds are still icy, but they haven't bothered me. Been thinking of Beth again.

APRIL 26. We've cleared Ivan out of continental U.S.A.! That calls for a celebration, especially since the men in New Pentagon declare they'll be out of the Western Hemisphere inside of six months. Wouldn't be too surprised if the counter-invasion of Fortress Europe got under way before Christmas.

MAY 14. Peculiar change in the Replaces we're getting here in central Canada. The metal ones are proud of it. They let you know right off, saying they're better than flesh any day. Fights more and more frequent, with the Replaces coming off best, naturally. I don't like it.

MAY 15. I don't like it at all. I saw my first metal versus human battle today, with a couple of hundred soldiers on each side. At first I thought it was strictly behind U.S. lines— but about an hour after the fracas started a few-score metal men breezed in from the *other* side of the front. Metal Ivans fighting with metal G.I. Joe's against flesh-and-blood G.I.'s. Artillery finally got the Replaces, but not before they'd killed about seventy-five men.

MAY 28. At an Eastern P.O.E. Looks like I was wrong. The Invasion of Fortress Europe—words on everyone's lips—will come a lot sooner than expected. I'm shipping out tomorrow or the next day. Destination? Probably Iceland. The British Isles will be part of the free world again by September. Unless the Replaces become a serious menace. Right now I don't know what to think.

MAY 31. At Sea in the North Atlantic. The Replaces are everywhere. Two-thirds of the troops aboard ship openly admit their identity.

JUNE 1. We're turning back in mid-voyage. I don't understand. The Replaces are jubilant, though.

JUNE 4. In the Catskill Mountains. The War is over! Nothing to applaud about, however. For there's a new war and one, which from all indications, will be worse. Metal-man versus flesh—to the death. The Replaces bombed New Pentagon and the hush-hush laboratory nearby, and now they don't have to worry about death in a year or two. At least, that's what they say. It has something to do with a storehouse of electrical records in the lab. The bombing destroyed it completely—and with it, flesh-man's ability to kill metal-man at will.

New York was in Replace hands, but it was comparatively easy to escape to these hills a hundred miles northwest of the city. Everything's so disorganized. One thing is clear: the Replaces are fashioning recruits. *Something* has to account for the fact that one man out of three seems to be metal. According to one newspaper I saw in the city—the last paper to be printed before the Replaces took over—almost every army man who was severely wounded some time during the past sixteen months was turned into a Replace, most of them with no knowledge of the transformation at all.

And now the Replaces roam the countryside at night, capturing recruits. You can't create artificial men at will. You've got to copy a flesh-man first. And it's said the Replaces are choosy, too. They'd like to kill off a good percentage of the population, save the remainder for slave labor, and live the metal life of Riley. They might do just that. Pretty grim…

JUNE 6. How dumb can I get? It was staring me in the face all along. I won't say till I'm sure, though. Objective note on the doings of the day: the Replaces are winning everywhere. Mankind, the original mankind, is doomed.

JUNE 10. To hell with waiting any longer. I'm going down from the hills into the large town of Liberty this afternoon. I should have realized it long before this. I've been fighting on the wrong side! A new and glorious future awaits *homo superior*, the man of metal. *I am a Replace.*

JUNE 11. Liberty, New York, is a nice town. The Replaces accepted me, their brother, with open arms. More about this later.

JUNE 11. Later. The last few humans are being dragged from the hills around Liberty for execution. If the New Order is to get off to a flying start, there must be some bloodshed. But an amusing thing happened a few minutes ago. Interrogated by an Intelligence Officer, I was really given the third degree:

Q. Do you know for a fact that you are a Replace?

A. Of course I'm a Replace. (Details about my front-line injury and what followed.)

Q. That strikes you as proof enough?

A. Naturally.

Q. There are simple tests. Will you submit to them?

A. I don't have much choice—but I don't have anything to worry about, either.

So that's the status. They've arranged for me to be tested tomorrow.

JUNE 12. *Homo sapiens* has surrendered unconditionally! Our poor half-brother had no choice, really. We sprang up on all sides of him. We abducted a wife, killed her, copied her. An hour later she returned, armed, to slay her unsuspecting husband. Our Replace husbands brought their wives in bodily for destruction and copying, provided they merited it. The new Era dawns... It says precisely that on a proclamation issued this morning. But more about it later. Right now, I must take my test.

LATER. Last entry. The test was simple.

Someone held me. Someone else hit me. Repeatedly. In the nose. I learned my lesson: never jump to conclusions.

I bled...

It's Raining Frogs!

George didn't like the idea of little red frogs raining down on him from a clear sky. But a pretty girl falling into his arms was quite another matter!

We shall pick up an existence by its frogs... Wise men have tried other ways. They have tried to understand our state of being, by grasping at its stars, or its arts, or its economics. But, if there is an underlying oneness of all things, it does not matter where we begin, whether with stars, or laws of supply and demand, or frogs, or Napoleon Bonaparte. One measures a circle, beginning anywhere." – Charles Fort, LO!

IT was raining. There wasn't a cloud in the sky, but it was raining. George wished it were raining cats and dogs, but it wasn't. Anything would be better than this. It was raining frogs. Little red frogs.

It was strictly a local rain. The frogs seemed to germinate from a spot somewhere above George's head, and then they spread out and came tumbling down in a cone shaped area some fifteen feet across. The worst part of it was that George was in the center of the cone.

The frogs fell on him. They seemed to be concentrated most heavily in the center of the cone, and a good percentage of them landed on him—mostly on his head—and then bounced off to fall on the sand. George didn't like it.

He moved. He got up off the sand and ran half a dozen paces closer to the surf, but he still felt the little red frogs striking him. The spot was still directly over his head; George was not sure how high up. He was still the center of the cone.

"Myra! Hey, Myra," George called his wife. He could see her head bobbing up and down in the waves and the powerful strokes of her arms through the water showed George that she had heard him call. But she would be angry. As soon as he shouted, the frogs stopped falling. First the downpour became a drizzle, and then there were no frogs at all. Myra would be very angry. She was all wrapped up in this new idea of hers, and she would be angry. If he hadn't yelled, more frogs would have fallen—and there's no telling what else, George thought.

The Bikini suit was not in style this year, but Myra wore it because she knew she looked good in it. George watched her run toward him and watched her shake her dark hair loose after she removed the bathing cap. Then he looked at her figure and he knew it was good, so good that he unconsciously felt the spare tire beginning to blossom out around his waist, and he blushed. That was another trouble, he always blushed. Not only that, but he was very fair-skinned. They could spend the entire summer at their seaside bungalow in this secluded area, and Myra would be bronzed like an Indian maiden. But George would turn red and then he would peel. Then he would turn red all over again and then he would peel again. And he had freckles all over.

But he stopped thinking of that now. It was a general consideration. The specific consideration bothered him more: there was one circular area of little red frogs, fifteen feet across. Then there was a trail of little red frogs on the sand, five running steps long. And then there was another fifteen foot circle of them. Most of the frogs were still, but some of them hopped about, and soon the circles had become irregular areas.

Myra came up to him breathlessly. "Oh, George!" she cooed. "You're magnificent, really magnificent. Frogs this time. Little red frogs. You're so—so *Fortean.*"

George sighed. He had a lot of friends, and many of them complained because their wives would call this or that thing

Freudian. But they had sympathy: a lot of men had wives riding the Freudian merry-go-round. This was worse. To Myra things were *Fortean*. George had seen pictures of this man Fort—a nice enough looking guy with a cherubic face and a ruddy complexion, a turned up nose and big bushy eyebrows. A mild, harmless man. He had passed away; for some twenty years now he had been dead. But he could impress people. His work had impressed Myra.

He thought we're *property*, or things are teleported from one place to another, or we're being fished for, or you can tell a world by its frogs, or science is whacky and word-nutty and sophistic hooey... George had heard it all dozens of times. Myra had told him. Myra had told him so much that he thought he knew Fort's philosophy by heart. A lot of ridiculous hogwash—until the rain. How could he call it ridiculous now?

"SEE?" Myra said triumphantly. "See, George? This time it's frogs. Yesterday it was beetles, and the day before, those little birds—and everything was red."

"Maybe they're communists," George suggested feebly.

"Oh—"

"Well, that's as good an explanation as any."

"No, it's not. Red is the predominant color of whatever world they come from, so they're red. Or else it could just be coincidence, but I doubt that. And I told you you were a good catalyst."

"So I'm a good catalyst. So I can make rain. They could have used me back East a few months ago—if they wanted a rain of frogs."

"Or beetles or birds," Myra reminded him.

"Yeah, Beetles and birds, too." George said this matter-of-factly, but then he felt his knees start to tremble. It was the inevitable aftereffect. This was *strange*. It couldn't be happening to him. It never rained that kind of rain, even if Fort had said that it did, and even if Myra believed that Fort was right. How could it rain like that? George knew what caused rain, and by no stretch of his imagination could organic matter be the result. Any sort of organic matter. And least of all little red frogs. He always associated frogs with mud—and the idea of little red frogs coming from the sky was too incredible to consider.

But there were the frogs on the beach.

George stroked the sand gingerly with the toes of one foot, clearing frogs away until he had room to sit down. He sat.

One of the little red frogs jumped into his lap, and he stood up again—so fast that he almost upended Myra.

"My gosh, George. You may be a good catalyst, but after that you're hopeless. That's where I come in."

George was sorry he had decided to play along with his wife. She had given him a test, and that part he enjoyed, for all he did was shoot dice for several hours. Something about psychokinesis, Myra said. And George scored high. So high that Myra had cried: "You're positively Fortean!"

And then had come the birds, the beetles, and the frogs. All red.

"Listen," George said. "This is the last time. This is positively the last time."

"The last time? Last time for what?"

"The last time that I let you use me as a—a catalyst. I can't go around making it rain like that. We're in a deserted spot out here, so it isn't too bad. But what if this happened when people were around? What then?"

"Silly, why do you think we came to this bungalow for the summer? And besides, even if people were around, why would they think you caused the rain? If you insist on calling it rain."

George did not like the way she said *you*. It was as if he didn't amount to much—but she always spoke to him like that. He knew he was no world-beater. He had an adequate job and he made an adequate salary, but he just didn't stack up like some of the men he knew. Or some of the men Myra knew. It always got him angry when she said *you* that way.

"What do you mean, why should they think I caused the rain? Who else can cause it, that's what I want to know? Who else can cause it?"

She smiled, and if it was a smile of triumph, George pretended not to notice it. "That's what I mean," she said, putting her arms around his neck. "You're so wonderful. Only you can cause it. Let's go into the house, George."

He grunted and he disentangled her arms. Then he took her hand and walked back across the sand to the house. And he held his head very high so he wouldn't have to look at all the little frogs on the beach.

THEY sat in the living room and the sun was setting, throwing long shadows across the room through the big picture window. George sipped his bourbon and then he put his glass down. Two drinks on an empty stomach always put that dreamy feeling in his head. He wanted to get up and pour himself another, but it was so pleasant just sitting here and thinking of nothing that he decided against it.

"You're ready now," Myra told him . "Oh, you're really perfect now. Remember, George, just think of nothing. Don't think of a thing. Lean back, relax, and keep your mind a blank . It shouldn't be too hard."

There was that undertone of scorn again, but now George didn't feel like doing a thing about it. She was right: it wouldn't be too hard. He had had his two drinks of bourbon, and now he would just sit back and relax, like Myra told him. Besides, he had nothing to worry about. It couldn't very well rain anything inside the house.

"It's just like the poltergeists," Myra was saying, but George hardly heard her. "There are so many cases of poltergeist phenomena on record, of the little mischievous ghosts who throw dishes or stones or who cause pointless little accidents. And in each case, there's a catalyst. Usually it's a little child, and more often than not, a girl, but that isn't always the case. The important thing is, there has to be a catalyst."

"That's me," George said proudly.

"Yes, that's you. My George, the best damn catalyst that ever lived." Myra had had her bourbon, too. "You know, science always explains away the poltergeists, but they do a pretty awful job of it. A lot of people aren't satisfied. Like Fort. Like me."

Was that a compliment? Was any of it a compliment? George thought so, but he couldn't be sure. His mind was fading into a pleasant haze of deep red, like the sunset. His eyes were opened and he was looking into the sunset, and that's why he saw the deep red. But then he noted a fact which would have startled him, only it didn't now. He was tired and he closed his eyes and still the deep red persisted, stronger than ever. It didn't startle him because he was too perfectly relaxed, and because the deep red was so soothing...

"Were you calling me?" the voice said.

GEORGE jumped up. He thought he had heard the voice, but he couldn't be sure. Now the sun had set completely and a heavy dusk settled over the room.

"What did you say, George? George, did you ask me anything?"

George said no, he didn't, and he got some slight satisfaction from the fact that Myra's voice sounded frightened. But then a slow chill crept up his spine and spread all over his body. Myra had heard the voice too.

"Well, were you calling me? Come, come, I haven't got all day, and if you weren't calling me, then I'll go home."

George gulped, and he heard Myra choke off a little whimper in her throat. Then George smiled. Hell, one of their friends from down the beach had come, and he decided to act mysterious here in the darkness. It was Andy. Andy would play practical jokes like that. Andy, the life of the party.

George strode jauntily to the light switch. "Hah, hah, had us fooled for a minute, Andy old boy. And nope, the answer is that we didn't call you. But you're always welcome here, you know that. Come on and join us in some bourbon."

His hand was on the light switch now, and he flicked it up. The room was bathed in the pale white of the fluorescent lamps, and George turned around to say hello to Andy.

He stood in the center of the room. He stood there regarding George with a half-smile on his lips, a playful smile. You couldn't tell his age and there was nothing special about his features. But the half smile remained on his lips like something permanent. He was definitely not Andy.

"As you can see, I'm not this Andy person."

"No. You're not," said George.

"Now, then. Wh. called me? Which one of you called me?"

Myra's voice was husky. The way it sometimes was at night, after a few drinks. The way George liked it. Only now she was scared. "I guess we both—called you."

"I wouldn't have come myself, of course, except that the message was so urgent. The call has never come out that strong before. I'm not just speaking about that from memory, of course, I'm king now but I haven't been around that long. There are records—and your call is twice as strong as any of the others. I could have sent an assistant, naturally, but I figured if the call was this strong I'd come myself."

HUMOR him, George thought. He's just a nut who came in off the beach. Only the reasoning was lousy. It stank. The door was locked and the big picture window was locked from the inside, so he could not have come in off the beach. George sighed.

"This is silly," the man was saying. "You put through such an urgent call that I come here myself. Then, when I arrive, no one will tell me what for."

"I know!" Myra cried. "You're from the world of the red frogs."

"What say?"

"I said you're from the world of the red frogs. You rained."

"Yes, I reign. I've been reigning for eleven years now, ever since my father died. Actually, though, it's open to question. While I'm the titular head, there's my wife to consider. She does a lot of reigning herself. In fact, she'll be pretty angry when she learns I answered the call myself. Below my dignity or some such thing. She always wants me to be dignified, but that's stupid, because she's anything but dignified herself. You know, I often think it isn't any fun to be king."

"That's nice," George said.

"I mean," Myra said, "you *rained*. Rained—r-a-i-n-e-d, like the frogs."

"Oh, the frogs. Yes, they would come through first, of course. Something about making sure the co-ordination is right. A messenger could go straight through at once, but that would be dangerous, and if the co-ordination were off, he'd be a sorry mess. Frogs or bugs or sometimes birds, we send anything through to make sure. Anyway, what do you want?"

"Now that you mention it, I don't know. I guess we don't want anything. We were just experimenting," Myra explained.

"Experimenting? Will you stop kidding? With a call as strong as that, experimenting? I wasn't born yesterday, sister. Look, don't be afraid of my wife. She doesn't know where I've gone and it will be some time before she can find me, so tell me the truth."

"That's the truth. I knew we'd get something, but I didn't know what. We got you. My husband is very psychokinetic."

The man shrugged. "He hardly looks it."

"Oh, don't let George fool you. He's potent that way."

"That's me," George said. "I'm a terrific catalyst. Ask Myra."

"He is," Myra said.

"Well, then I see it was all a mistake. Do you think he could get me back?"

"Of course he could get you back. You said yourself this was the strongest call on record. Get him back, George."

George smiled. He was beginning to like this. It all depended on him. The man with the enigmatic smile knew exactly what was going on, Myra knew to some extent what was going on, George knew almost nothing of it, but everything depended on him. "Why should I?" he demanded. "He only just came, and I'm not in any hurry to send him back."

"Please," the man said, and for the first time the smile began to fade from the corners of his mouth. "It was all a mistake, and now I'd better get back home before my wife finds out."

George felt cocky. "Well, it was your mistake, not mine, and I don't feel like sending you back yet. So guess you'll stay right here."

"You're not serious?"

"Serious? You bet I'm serious, I don't even know where I'm supposed to send you, but I'm not going to. At least not for a while yet."

"Now, look. You've got to send me back. I'm the king."

"Send him back, George. You don't know what you're playing around with. Send him back."

"No."

"I'm the king."

"Send him back, George."

George got up and took a long drink of the bourbon. His stomach was still empty, except for the previous bourbon, and the drink sent a warm glow through him. "No," he said.

THEY sat there in the living room, the three of them. George on the sofa, Myra on a straight-backed chair, and Arl cross-legged in the middle of the floor. The king's name was Arl, he had told them that. And then afterwards, he was silent. He was sullen, and George smiled. He was in trouble and he did not know what to do and it all depended on George.

"Listen, George," Arl was trying another angle. "Maybe if I tell you what this is all about, then will you send me back?"

"I doubt it, but maybe I will. Just a slight, improbable maybe. But I guess you're grasping at straws now. Say on."

"Better send him back, George," Myra said. "I got you into this and you don't know what it's all about, but you better do what he says."

"Do *you* know what it's all about?"

"No, I don't. But I know more than you, and I know that you better not horse around."

"Well, I'll listen to what he has to say. But I better tell you now that I doubt if I'll send him back. I didn't really call him, you did. Now *you* send him back."

"If I could I would, I don't want to play around like this. It can cause trouble. If he loses his temper, George—well, just don't say I didn't warn you."

"Unfortunately," Arl admitted, "it takes me a long time to lose my temper. It never used t. be that way. But Narka—that's the queen—has tamed me. A king should not be so impetuous, she told me, only she's as impetuous as hell. That's the trouble. She's all the time telling me to do things, which will make me more polite, more refined, more cultured—none of which she does herself. The result is that I've become more of a figurehead, and she's the real power. It's regrettable."

"That's not an uncommon situation," George assured him. "But just what are you titular king of?"

"Then you do want to hear my story!"

"Yeah, yeah, I said I wanted to hear it. I didn't say I'd do something about sending you back, but go ahead and tell me if it will make you happy."

"Okay, I'll begin with a question. Do you know anything about the fourth dimension?"

GEORGE was silent, but Myra said: "I know all about the fourth dimension."

"You just think you do. Actually, you don't know a thing about it. A lot of fuzzy thinking here in the world of three dimensions, but you really don't know a thing about it."

"Oh," said Myra.

"You tell her, Arl, old boy," George said. "You tell her. That guy Fort didn't know what he was talking about."

"Fort? Fort? Oh—yes he did. He knew *what* he was talking about. But he didn't know how or why. This is a world of three dimensions, right?"

"Uh-huh."

"Well, let's assume you had a world of two dimensions. Of length and breadth, but no thickness. How would you get a world of three dimensions?"

George said, "Search me," but Myra went into a long explanation which George didn't understand at all.

When she finished, Arl shook his head. "Just what I thought. A lot of fuzzy thinking. Unfortunately, you're way off the beam. It's really simple. You have a world of two dimension—length and breadth, and all you have to do to get a world of three dimensions is extend that world in a new direction—perpendicular to the first two. That direction is up or down, as the case may be. Either way, it's a direction at right angles to the first two, and the result is a world of three dimensions, this world."

George said he understood. "But that doesn't mean I'm going to send you back," he added.

Arl was all wrapped up in his explanation, and he ignored the remark. "Now, then. The same situation applies. The same relation exists between a world of three dimensions and one of four. You merely extend the three dimensions out in a direction at right angles to them—a direction which is perpendicular to length, breadth and thickness, and the result is a world of four dimensions. That's my world."

George was feeling chipper. "Well, a pat on the backside for you," he said. "Now I suppose you want me to send you back?"

ARL waved his hand. "No. I'm not finished. Let's go a step further. If a world of two dimensions existed—a whole world spread out perfectly flat on this table, with no dimension other than length or breadth, a flat world—if that world existed, do you realize all the power you, as a three dimensional being, would have over it?"

George said that he didn't.

"Well, suppose something was enclosed in a square on that table. Just four lines, a square. That would be the equivalent of a cube in this world—say, of a safe. Say there was something in that square that the people of the flat world wanted to get out. But the square was locked. It was just four lines, forming an enclosed space, but because there was no such thing as up or down in that world, they couldn't get over those lines and get out what they were looking for. It was utterly inaccessible.

"Now, then. You're a three dimensional creature. All you'd have to do is reach down, pick the item up, transport it through the third dimension, and put it down again outside the square. You would have done the impossible. You would have taken something out of an utterly inaccessible place and put it elsewhere. Mysteriously.

"So, just change the situation a bit. A four dimensional being would have the same power over this three dimensional world. He could make things appear and disappear easily, simply by transporting them through the fourth dimension. And that, my friend, explains everything strange and unreal and impossible, which this man Fort reported. It was simply the intervention of a four dimensional being. One of my subjects. When the call comes through, your people are not even aware that they give it. But when it does come through, we answer. And here the call was the strongest on record. I'm the king and I came through myself. But we can't come through and we can't go back without the call. That's you, George, and it was all a mistake. Now will you send me back?"

George smiled. He enjoyed this situation. He thoroughly enjoyed it, and he watched Myra's face turn white as he said one word:

"No."

"BE reasonable, George. If you don't send me back, there'll be trouble. I won't tell you what kind of trouble, but don't say you were not warned in advance."

"Well, maybe you ought to tell me. What kind of trouble?"

"Narka trouble," Arl said, and George could see that the man's hands were trembling. "When my wife finds out, she'll be mad. When Narka's mad, she's very mad. And not just at me—she'll be on the warpath with you, too. She'll come here and—"

"How can she come here, without your call?"

"Oh, she'll find a way. Getting back is the difficult part. Please, George."

"No. No. I don't think so. Myra started all this, not me. I told her to stop but she didn't want to. Now I think I'll let the two of you stew in your own juice for a while. You can't blame me. In a sense, I'm just an innocent bystander who happens to be a top-flight catalyst. But this could be amusing. I'll just let things stand."

Arl turned to Myra. "Myra, do you want me to go back?"

"Yes. Yes, I suppose so. You know more about this than we do, but my husband can be so obstinate—"

"I'm not being obstinate. This was all your idea, and now I want to see what happens."

Arl said, "There'll be quite a mess. Not only will Narka be angry with us, but the call will be coming through from all over, and none of our subjects can go over without my permission. You know what that means?"

George asked him what.

"That means that there'll be a lot of situations where poltergeists should have appeared, sort of like the old *deux ex machina* of your early literature, only they won't. That, my friend, will cause a mess."

George laughed. "I don't know. I've known a lot of people to get along well enough without your poltergeists. Everyone I've ever known, in fact. All my life."

Myra shrugged helplessly. "Honest, Arl, I'm sorry. It's just that George is so ordinary."

George scowled. He had been on the verge of relenting. He definitely had been on the verge of relenting. But that did it. He wouldn't relent now.

"Can't you make him?" Myra demanded.

"No. That's the difficulty. I can't. The caller must either be unaware or willing, and your husband is neither. There isn't a thing I can do about it until he changes. Ordinarily, I could do many things so that he'd see it our way—but that would necessitate popping in and out of the fourth dimension, and without George's help, I can't do that. It all rests with George."

"Well, maybe we can make him cooperate."

"How do you mean, make him?"

"I mean physically. There are two of us and one of him and maybe we can make him."

MYRA advanced, and Arl was a little slower, but presently he got the idea, and he too came toward George. "Stay back," George warned. "Keep away from me or I'll never change my mind, and then you'll be stuck here forever."

"He's right," Arl said.

"No, he's not. We can make him. We can force him to change his mind."

Myra was so close now that George could reach out and touch her. He backed up a step. Myra was young and strong and she was athletic. Every curve of her lithe body was deceptively strong and beautiful at the same time, and George was developing that spare tire around his middle. It was small but it was there and George knew he was anything but athletic. He did not want to fight with Myra, especially when Arl, who was a head taller than George, would be helping her. It definitely was unwise.

Myra's first attack was merely speculative. She pushed George to see if he would fight back. He backed up two or three steps, and then he was sitting on the sofa.

Arl was much less speculative. He reached down and yanked George to his feet. Then he began to shake George.

"Hey, stop it!" George's voice sounded like a rattle.

"We won't stop until you change your mind," Myra told him, and to show that she was serious, she poked her fist in George's stomach, hard. He felt the air *woosh* out of his lungs, and then he was sitting on the sofa again. At another time he might have thought this was getting monotonous, but he didn't think so now. When Arl picked him up again, he tried to cringe away, but Arl held him tight.

He butted his head at Arl, and the king stumbled back and away from him, losing his grip on George's shoulders. George didn't back up; he stalked after the king, and when he reached him he balled his right fist and struck out with it.

THE contact was a bit painful, but George was happy with the result. Arl stumbled and fell. He was all stretched out on the floor, and he didn't try to get up.

"I did that," George said.

"You stinker. My own husband, and what a stinker you turned out to be."

"Now, my dear—" George began, sure of himself. But the words caught in his throat. Myra threw herself at him, bodily, and George sat down. He was sitting on the floor and then he was down flat and Myra was sitting on his chest, and those two hammers hitting his face were her fists. They hurt.

Myra and George had had fights before, George was not a violent man, he knew that. He always wanted to settle things with words, and whenever Myra lost her temper he would make it a point not to be around because he thought she could beat him, and if she did that once, there'd be no living with her. But now he couldn't make it a point not to be around because Myra was sitting on his chest and he couldn't get up.

George heaved up and over, and he felt Myra roll off him. Then he sat up and he pulled Myra across his knees. She struggled, but he held her down with one hand and with the other he did the only thing that a husband should do in a case like this. He spanked her. At first she was volubly indignant, but then she began to whimper, and George didn't stop until she was howling. He pushed her away and stood up, smoothing the crease in his trousers. Arl's head was propped up on one elbow now, and Arl had a dark discoloration around one of his eyes, but the look he gave George was one of pure admiration.

"I wish I had the nerve to do that to Narka," he sighed. "That's what she needs. I can see it now. That's what she needs."

George strode around the room jauntily. "You can if you want to, Arl. Just because you're a king doesn't mean that you can't." Then he turned to Myra. She was just getting up, blowing her nose in a dainty little handkerchief.

At first George couldn't quite fathom the look she gave him. She was angry, of course. But she was something more than angry. "George," she said, and his name came out in a long sigh, and he knew that for the first time he had made a conquest of his wife.

"I'll be in our city apartment," he told her. "If you want me, that's where I'll be. And I guess you both realize my mind is made up. Arl will remain here until I'm good and ready to send him back. Good night."

George went outside, got into the car, drove it down the dirt road to the highway, and headed for the city.

He was whistling.

GEORGE sat on his stool at the bar and ordered a straight bourbon. He had changed his mind about going to his apartment immediately. Instead, he had gone to this bar. He had something to celebrate. Something told him that this business was far from finished yet, but he didn't care. It was incredibly fantastic, but he relished the prospect of more dealings with King Arl, and with Myra, too.

He lifted the tumbler of bourbon to his lips and sipped it. But then he set the glass down on the bar, hard, and it toppled over. Something had plunked on his head.

"Hey," the bartender roared. "That's good bourbon. You just spilled it all over. Now you'll say it's my fault and you'll want another."

"No," George said absently. "Forget it."

Something plunked on his head again. He put his hand up and plucked at his hair. The thing was wet and slimy. It was a little red frog. George held it out in front of him and then he placed it down on the bar.

"Now, look," the bartender was getting angry. "You think you're a wise guy or something? Who ast you to bring them little animals in here? This is a respectable joint, and I got my customers to think of."

George said he was sorry. Plunk! Another frog came down on his head. He felt it hop off, and then he saw it alight on the bartender's shoulder.

"Yoiks! Cut it out, bud! I'm warning you, cut it out." He was a little fat man with a bald head and his face was all red, almost like the frogs. "You stop that, bud . I don't wanna play games with you."

George said he was sorry again and he watched the bartender brush at the frog with one hand. It landed on the bar then it jumped twice and landed on the hand of a customer two stools down from George.

It was a lady but she let out a very unladylike howl and stalked out of the bar.

"She went out without paying her bill!" the bartender told George. "So you owe me for it. Three-fifty."

George wondered about this. Arl said he was helpless without George's call, so this couldn't be Arl's work. Someone wanted to come through from the four dimensional world, and that someone had been receiving the call from George. He had been sipping his bourbon, minding his own business, yet he had given the call. He had been unaware of it but he had been giving it, and that could be embarrassing. As it was now.

"Three-fifty," the bartender said. "Three-fifty or I'm gonna force myself to call a cop."

George handed over the money and left hurriedly.

HE sat near the front of the trolley car, hoping that no more frogs would fall. He could have walked home, but that would have taken much longer, and there might be more frogs. This way, he was taking a chance that they wouldn't fall in the trolley car, and, if they did, he'd ignore them.

Three more stops and George would be home. He closed his eyes and sighed contentedly. He would be safe then. He didn't want any more frogs falling in public. Not while he was around.

Something soft but firm pressed his lap, and George opened his eyes. He yowled. He couldn't help it. It was only a little yowl, but several people looked at him. And then they began to yowl, especially one buxom middle-aged lady. "It's indecent," she cried. "Utterly, thoroughly and obnoxiously indecent. Somebody call a policeman at the next corner."

The driver looked in the mirror, astonished, and nodded. George blinked his eyes, but when he opened them she was still there. She sat in his lap and she was very beautiful. She didn't have a stitch of clothing on.

"Please," George pleaded. "Go away! Please go away. Go away and put some clothing on and then come back if you want, but not like this!"

"You sent for me. You were in such a hurry you didn't even give me a chance to dress. Now you want to send me back. What's the matter, don't you like me?"

George felt the flush spread over his face. "Please," he said again. "Go away. Everyone's staring at us."

"Okay," she pouted. "Okay. I'll go away. Just put that call out again and I'll be able to do it." Her hair was long and billowing, the color of copper, and it tickled George's face. "But I'll be back. Don't you worry. I'll be back. And—if you see Arl—tell him I'm looking for him. Just wait till I get my hands on him. You just wait—"

George blinked. The lovely creature was gone.

He had not been aware of the fact that the trolley had stopped. Now a policeman stood in the aisle next to him.

"How'd you do it, pal? Come on, how'd you do it? I saw the girl and she was naked as Lady Godiva. Just try to explain your way out of this one..."

"It was utterly indecent," the buxom woman said. "I was going to visit my little grandchildren, but how can I after that? How can I?"

"That," George told her acidly, "is your problem."

"A wise guy, too, eh?" The officer was belligerent.

"It's not too difficult to explain, officer. Something like hypnotism. Something very much like it. It's called psychokinesis, I think."

"Psychokinesis, psychoshminesis. You just come on down with me and explain it to the sergeant."

George went with him and he explained it to the sergeant, but it did no good. The sergeant listened and then his face got very red. He had a thick neck and his uniform collar was too tight for it, and his neck got all red, too. He told George he could cool off his mental powers in jail overnight and pay a twenty-five dollar fine.

...They gave George breakfast early in the morning. It wasn't very good, but he was hungry and he ate all of it. Then he hurried out of his cell and left the stationhouse. The whole cell was filled with little red frogs, and he could hear the patrolmen bellowing as he left, but he hurried down the stairs and flagged a taxi.

HE tried to relax in the apartment, but it was no good. He thought of the girl who had materialized in his lap, and he knew she was Narka. He wished she would come back because he wanted to see what would happen when she met Arl. And there were other reasons, too. He wondered if she would be wearing clothing. And the next thought, of course, was a logical one: what kind of clothing would a fourth dimensional queen wear?

At ten the doorbell rang.

He opened the door, and Myra came in. Behind her was Arl, and George had never seen anyone so frightened as Arl looked.

"What the hell is wrong with you?" George demanded.

"Nothing—yet. I just read in the newspaper about you and the naked girl in your lap—mass hypnotism, the report said. But we both know it wasn't. It was Narka. Where is she?"

George said not to worry because she had gone back to the world of the red frogs; and then Myra grabbed his shoulder and spun him around sharply. She often did that when she was angry and wanted his attention, and George had never done anything about it. He didn't do anything this time, either. He just looked at her, and she removed her hand from his shoulder. Her face was very white when she spoke.

"What was she doing in your lap, George?"

"What do you think she was doing?"

"That's what I'm asking you. Please, George. I'm sorry about yesterday. I don't know what got into me. I never should have tried to hit you. A wife has no business trying to hit her husband."

"Nuts," George said. "You just thought you could get away with it, that's all. Now that you know you can't, you're trying to say you're sorry. Nuts."

Then he looked at Arl fondly. Arl was to thank for all this. If it hadn't been for Arl, he would still be henpecked. Myra didn't look like the type that would henpeck her husband, but George smiled ruefully at this thought. She was the type, and she did it every chance she got. Only she wouldn't do it anymore. Arl had been *that* catalyst. "Arl," George said, "I could love you like a brother."

"What about my wife?" Arl still wanted to know. "Where's my wife?"

"I told you, she went back. For some clothing, I think."

"Then she was sitting in your lap with no clothing on!" Myra said indignantly.

"Yes, she was."

"What was she doing in your lap with no clothing on?"

"You asked me that once."

"Please, George. What!"

"She was sitting," George said. He winked at Arl, but Arl only shuddered. Now *there* is one henpecked king, George thought.

Then he stood up expectantly. A frog had plunked down on his head.

THE look of expectancy on George's face faded. He waited, but there was nothing of Narka. No more frogs fell.

"That was tentative," Arl said.

"What do you mean, tentative?"

"I mean a tentative breakthrough into this dimension. Someone changed his mind. But I shouldn't say someone and I shouldn't say his. It was Narka." He was trembling.

"Get a hold on yourself, Arl. This is not the end of the world."

"You don't know Narka."

"You've just got to know how to handle women, that's all. Let them think they have the upper hand, and you're through. Just show them who's boos, that's all."

Myra seemed on the verge of snorting. But instead she smiled brightly at Arl. "George is certainly right."

"Of course I'm right. Buck up, Arl."

"Well, it's easy to say. But I can't."

George snorted himself and went for the bourbon bottle. He had never taken a drink before midafternoon in his life, but now he figured a lot of changes had to be made. Necessary changes.

"I have a terrific idea," Arl said.

George didn't think it would be terrific, but he said: "What's that?"

"Well, you have to put the call through, you know. So, why don't you just—don't?"

"Eh? Say that again."

"Don't put the call through. Don't put it through and Narka won't be able to come."

Myra nodded her head vigorously. "That sounds like a fine idea," she said.

George said, "It stinks. It so happens I want to see Narka again."

"After you see her, you'll be sorry. I'm not saying you can't handle women, George. Don't misunderstand me. Myra is a spitfire a lot like the Queen, but you certainly can handle Myra. I don't mean that."

George was pleased. "Of course. What do you mean?"

"Well, Narka is—"

HE stopped talking. Something fell to the floor at George's feet, and he stopped to pick it up. He held it in his palm—a necklace of flawless pearls, worth a small fortune. He held it in his hand, not knowing what to do with it.

"That's what I mean," Arl said.

"Oh, it's beautiful," Myra cooed. "Is it for me, George? Where did you get it?" Then she pouted. "It's not for—that Narka, is it? It's for me, isn't it, George?"

"That's what I mean," Arl said again. "Narka cannot resist the impulse to steal everything she likes in this dimension. She simply takes what she likes, and I know several cases in which one of your three dimensional men went to jail for a series of robberies committed by the Queen."

"That's ridiculous," George said. "How can she steal so many things?"

Arl shook his head. "You're forgetting the relationship between the three and four dimensional worlds again. Remember, it's like you and that square on the table. How would you get a necklace out of that square without crossing any of its lines?"

"Why—why, I'd simply lift the necklace up and then put it down on the other side of one of the lines."

"Exactly. That's what Narka's doing. She sees what she likes, lifts it up out of your three dimensional existence; momentarily carries it through the fourth dimension, and puts it down here. When she has all she wants, she'll come for her booty, then I'm afraid she'll take me home with her. Only she'll be very mad. She won't speak to me for a week— she'll do other things, bad things. I wish you had never called me, George."

Something went *plop*, and George saw a small velvet cushion on the floor. Like a pin cushion. And pinned to it were a number of jeweled brooches. George did not know too much about jewelry, but he didn't have to be an expert to know that these were valuable pieces. Even if he didn't know it himself, he could tell by the way Myra sighed. Myra would not sigh at imitations.

GEORGE laughed. "Now I know how Ali Baba must have felt after he said 'Open, Sesamee.'"

Myra nodded, but she hardly heard him. She walked from one treasure to the next, as each new one plunked down on the floor or the chairs or the tables. She was running, soon, with excited little gasps, feeling the jewels with her hands, caressing them, holding them to her throat and letting them caress her, raising them to the window so she could see the sun shine on them.

Arl said wearily, "I have seen this many times before. It's always the same the first time. Narka collects the treasure and someone here in this three dimensional world sees the treasure come in. The result is always the same. It's quite a sight the first time. Narka has sufficient jewelry here to buy this city."

179

"Well, it doesn't affect me that way," said George. But he only said it—he didn't feel it at all. This inter-dimensional travel was the answer to all his dreams. You saw something you wanted, you lifted it out into the fourth dimension. You came back with it to the world of three dimensions—and that's all there was to it.

"Don't tell me you're not thinking the same thing they all have thought in the past," Arl said. "I know you are. Everyone does. But I warn you, George: that way lies madness."

He could be a king, George thought. Not a titular king like Arl, but the real thing—a king in the true sense of the word, the old sense of the word. He'd want something—anything—and it would be his. Just like that.

"No more treasure," Myra said. "It isn't raining anymore."

George looked. The room was abrim with precious stones, and apparently Narka had enough for this trip. She had stolen a king's ransom—more than that. And there was that word again: with this power, George could be a king.

"No," he said.

"What's that?"

"Um, nothing, Arl. Nothing. Just thinking out loud." He did not want to be a king, not that way. Human values were too high, and he had moved on the straight and narrow path too long. Not that there was anything wrong with the straight and narrow path. Suddenly he liked it—it was very important to him, and although he remembered Narka as he had seen her, naked and beautiful, he thought of her now only as a cheap thief. The wild urge had gone—this was not the way to kinghood.

ABRUPTLY, Narka was there. One moment there were only the three of them and the treasure. The next, she stood next to George, and when she materialized, she was leaning on George's arm.

"I'm back," she said.

She wore a tunic, only it was more translucent than a tunic had a right to be. But George didn't mind. He didn't mind in the least. It was unfortunate, though, that he was so interested in the effects Narka's arrival would have on Arl. He looked at the woman only for a moment, and then he turned his eyes to her husband.

Arl was trembling. He looked ordinary compared with Narka. He wore what could have passed for a white linen suit, and it fit well. With that enigmatic smile, he could have been a good looking man, but right now he was trembling, and his mouth hung open.

"Narka—" he said.

"Don't you 'Narka' me. You know I didn't want you to come, but you came anyway. Just wait till I can get you home alone. Wait til I get you—"

"Wait is right," said Georg. He gestured to the jewelry about the room. "Right now there's another matter, a more important matter. What about your, ah, trophies?"

"What about them?" She gave George's arm a little squeeze, and George liked the feeling. But he saw Myra wince. "What about them? Why, nothing, I'll just take them home with me, that's all. I have a whole section of the palace filled with them."

"No you won't," George said.

"Don't be silly. Who's going to stop me?"

"I am."

She leaned more heavily on George's arm, and she looked up at him with her big round eyes. "No you're not."

"No? How are you going to get back unless I help you?"

"You'll help me. I'll leave some of these jewels here with you. Name any three items and they're yours."

Myra suggested, "That brooch, and that—"

"Shut up," said George.

Narka frowned. "Are you going to let him talk to you like that?"

Myra looked at George. "Y-yes," she said. "But please stop holding on to his arm like that. If George says you take all those things back where they belong, then you'd better do it. I—I think George knows best."

"He does," Arl assured his wife.

"You shut up, Arl. I'll attend to you later." Narka made no move to release George's arm. She leaned closer to him and stood on her tiptoes. Then she kissed him. George liked it—he liked it a lot. This Narka was quite a girl, even if she was a crook.

"Now, George," she said, "send us back."

"No." George pulled his arm away and Narka was leaning over so far that she almost fell.

"Hah," Myra said.

Narka smiled. "Arl," she said, "pick up the jewelry, and we'll get started."

"How can we get started if George won't send us back?"

"Just be quiet and pick up the jewelry."

OBEDIENTLY, Arl went about the room, gathering the treasures in his arms. It took a few minutes, and George stood by patiently, smiling. Finally, arms full, Arl nodded to his wife. "That's all, dear."

Narka looked at George. "Now, send us back."

George shrugged. "I said no, and I wasn't kidding. You take all that jewelry back where it belongs, and I'll send you back. Not before."

For a long moment, Narka looked at him. "You know," she said, "I think I will get you in trouble. Yes, I think I will. You definitely deserve it."

The apartment was on the fourth floor, near the corner. Narka strode to the window and opened it. Behind her, George looked out. Down on the corner directing traffic was a cop.

"He's a law officer, isn't he?" Narka demanded.

George nodded, and before he could stop her, Narka took two brooches and a necklace from the pile in Arl's arms, called to the policeman, and, when she had caught his attention, threw the jewelry down to him.

"Oh, no…" Myra moaned. George shut the window. I n a few minutes the policeman would be in the room. He'd see a room full of jewelry, and he'd receive reports of all the thefts in the past few minutes, the incredible number of thefts in so short a space of time, and though he would not know how it was done, he would blame George. He would definitely blame George.

A few minutes…

"You shouldn't have done that," George said.

Narka stuck her tongue out at him. It was very unladylike, even less queen-like. "No?"

"No." George reached out and pulled Narka to him. He saw the look of triumph on her face.

"George," she said coyly.

Holding her arm and retreating to a big chair, George sat down. Because he was still holding her, Narka sat on his lap, and from there it wasn't hard for him to turn her over. He did and then she got the idea, but it was too late. She struggled and she writhed but she couldn't do a thing about it.

"What you need," George told her, "is a good three-dimensional man to take care of you."

"Let me up or I'll—I'll beat you."

"You'll *what?*"

"I'll beat you. Ask Arl, he's a man, but I beat him. When I get him home, I will beat him."

GEORGE lifted his hand, but Arl caught it in mid-air. "Wait, George. I think I am learning." Arl was still trembling, but he attempted a smile. "I think I am learning."

George smiled and got up. Arl sat on the chair next to his wife. Men could be henpecked just so long, George thought—even in the fourth dimension, it couldn't go on forever.

But Arl's smile was uncertain, he was trying to bolster his courage with it, and Narka stared grimly, certainly. Suddenly, she and Arl were locked together, struggling. George breathed hard. The cop would be here in another minute or two, but he had to let Arl fight his own battle. A king could not be a king in name only, and he had tried to show Arl the way.

Narka wrestled Arl to the floor and held him there, next to the remainder of the jewelry. Arl began to moan, and then Narka laughed triumphantly up at George. "There's one thing you didn't know, third dimensional man. One thing you couldn't know. In the fourth dimension, the female is superior physically."

Arl moaned.

George didn't know a thing about fourth dimensional culture. He had never thought of this possibility, but now Narka held her husband firmly, and she began to do something to his arm.

"Give up?" she said.

Arl looked up at George. "I tried."

"Nuts," said George. "You may think the female is stronger in the fourth dimension, but you're in the third dimension now. If Arl—"

Arl needed that encouragement. He smiled now, and this time his smile was the grim certain one. "Why not?" he said. "Something there—different dimension, different laws apply, and if I can do it once, do it now—"

He writhed fiercely in Narka's grip, and George watched. Someone was knocking at the door. "Open up. Hey, open up in there! I saw you at the window, so I know you're there. What the hell did you throw them pins out for? Open up!"

The knocking became more urgent.

It was important, it was vital. But George hardly heard it. Here at his feet he saw a culture changing. Arl forced his wife slowly up and back, and then Arl was in control. He sat on the floor and Narka was draped across his lap and he was spanking her.

"Remarkable," Myra said.

Narka began to cry. With each downward stroke of Arl's hand, she cried. And by the look on the king's face, George could tell that Arl was having the time of his life.

He didn't want to stop. He was enjoying himself too much, after all these years, and he was in no mood to stop. But George pulled him away. "She's had enough."

Arl was cocky. "Will you be a good girl now, Narka?"

The queen sighed and nodded. She had a look of disbelief on her face, but she walked off into the corner of the room. She looked as if she wanted to sit down, but then she thought better of it, and she stood there, sulking.

"Quick," George said. He helped Arl gather up the jewels, and even Myra helped, and then Narka was telling Arl, listlessly, where she had gotten them. Arl winked at George, his arms loaded with the treasures, and then he disappeared.

GEORGE opened the door. The cop stalked in, belligerently. "Now, what's going on? What's going on in here, that's what I wanna know!"

George frowned. "What do you mean, officer?"

"I mean, these jewels." He held out his hand, showing the three expensive items he had caught. "Better explain this good, bud."

There was only one thing to do, George thought. "Explain it? Explain what? What jewels are you talking about, officer?"

"These damn jewels in my hand, that's what!" The cop held his hand out, showing the two brooches and the necklace.

"I don't see any jewels," said George. "Myra, do you see any jewels?"

"Huh? Why, of course not, I don't see anything."

"Narka?"

The queen looked sullen, but she shook her head. "No."

George looked at the policeman. "Tch, tch," he said, shaking his head.

"What do you mean, no jewels? You hinting I'm nuts?"

"Maybe just a few drinks too many," George suggested, looking at the jewelry.

"Why, listen—" But the policeman scratched his head.

He didn't see Arl come up behind him. Arl reached out and grabbed the two brooches, the necklace—and then disappeared.

The policeman looked at his hand. For a long time he stared at it. His jaw went slack.

"Jeez—" he said.

"We'll forget it," George told him. "We'll forget all about it. Now just go home and behave yourself—and no drinking on duty, eh officer?"

"Yeah. Yeah, sure." The cop went out the door, still staring at his hand.

In a moment, Arl was back. Narka looked at him, and George had seen that look in Myra's eyes yesterday at their

186

bungalow. Arl took his wife's arm in a firm grip. "We're going home," he said.

She looked dubious, but then she rubbed her posterior, and she smiled ruefully. "Yes, m'lord." Arl shook hands with George, waved to Myra—and then they disappeared.

George smiled. "Let that be a lesson to you, dear."

Myra kissed him, shyly. They had been married for six years, but it was a shy kiss.

"I don't need any lesson, George."

"No more Fort? No more psychokinesis?"

"No more, if you say so, George."

"I say so."

"Yes, sir," said Myra. "Yes, sir."

Anything Your Heart Desires

They wished for wealth, power, love. And their desires were granted.
But then they wanted more—and the Martian god laughed.

MURCHISON blinked hard to clear the burning, stinging sweat from his eyes. "Stop shooting your mouth off and let me think," he said. "I can't help it if we're lost."

Kincaid grimaced, fingering the stock of his blasting rifle. "Don't give me any excuses," he told the guide. "We didn't pay you to get us lost in this stinking red desert. "We paid you to find a herd of guru beasts so we could do some hunting."

"I don't think you understand. We're lost. L-o-s-t. All I want to do is find our way back to Canal City. The hell with your guru beasts."

"They said you were the best damned guide in the Syrtis Major."

"I get by. But Mars ain't anybody's backyard. Not yet. There's a mess of wilderness out here north of Canal City, and if you're lost you forget all about hunting. You concentrate on just trying to live, and sometimes it ain't easy."

"Christ! We should have hired a native Martian. He'd have known his way around."

"Sure," Murchison smiled. "He'd probably have slit your throat and taken your money. I've seen it happen. Martians don't like Earthmen."

"And what the hell do you think you are?"

"That's different. I'm just trying to make a living, and they don't mind me. But you guys who come poking your noses' around their sacred ruins and call them animated walking sticks to their faces, they don't like you."

"Forget it," Elena Kincaid pleaded, joining them. "If Mr. Murchison says we're lost, we're lost. Can you get us out, Mr. Murchison?"

Murchison shrugged his shoulders, but the woman's husband said: "Oh Lord, not you too!"

"I'm just trying to be sensible."

"Sensible? You've been making eyes at Murchison ever since we left Canal City."

"Please, Alan. You're acting mean because we're lost."

He ignored her. "Go ahead, Murchison, deny it. Hasn't she been making eyes at you?"

"No," said Murchison. He turned his back and stalked away, crouching over their pile of gear and sorting it into two heaps. One heap was much larger than the other, and it contained the expensive cameras, hunting clothing, fancy hand weapons, all the excess baggage.

"What do you think you're doing?" Kincaid demanded.

"We can't take all this junk with us. I'm sorting out what's necessary."

"That stuff costs money."

"From what I heard," Murchison told him blandly, "you're swimming in money."

"Don't get insolent, Murchison." Kincaid placed a soft hand on the guide's shoulder, but there was surprising strength behind it. "Put that gear back together again."

MURCHISON sat down in the ochre sand, lacing his long fingers behind his head. "Okay. You find the way out of here."

"What do you mean by that?"

"Just this. I give orders, all the orders. My neck's in this with yours, Kincaid. I'd like to get it out. Is that clear?"

"No!"Kincaid roared. "You're an inept, snotty—"

Murchison's lanky frame sprang up from the sand like an oversized dart. He grasped the collar of Kincaid's shirt with both his hands, shaking the man until his teeth rattled. "Is this clear?"

Kincaid swung his right fist up, but Murchison caught it and twisted until his employer bellowed.

Softly, Elena Kincaid was laughing. "You know, he's done that to me more than once, Mr. Murchison. Just what you're doing now. But that's enough. You'll give the orders, and I'll triple your pay if you pull us out of this."

"You'll triple it?" her husband snorted.

"That's what I said, Alan. It's my money, not yours. Now, shut up. Mr. Murchison, do you think I'm pretty?"

God, Murchison thought. *What a pair to be stuck out here with. No, you scrawny, flat-chested, washed-out checkbook of a dame, you're not pretty. Your husband married you for your money, he got hitched to you because he recognized a meal-ticket he saw one. Sure, I lied before. You've been making eyes at me. You'd make eyes at the two Martian moons if you thought they'd tell you you had looks to go with your money. As for you, Mr. Kincaid, you'll listen now, because your wife will start dangling that pocketbook just out of reach if you don't. God, what a mess.*

They left the discarded equipment behind, a shining mound in the sunlight. They staggered ahead through the shifting, wind-blown sands, the heat beating down like an oppressive blanket. Murchison smiled in spite of himself. Before man came to Mars, he pictured a frozen world where the cold would probe its icy fingers through half a dozen layers of the best insulation. Oh, that happened at night, all right, but during the long equatorial day the sun burned down through an atmosphere too thin to offer much protection, and the Gobi Desert was an oasis by comparison.

AN HOUR before sunset, they sighted the ruins over the low sweeping dunes which faded away to the horizon in all directions. Gaunt and ruby red in the fading sunlight, the long-dead city beckoned them.

"We're lucky," Murchison grunted. "Generally, those cities extend underground, so we'll be warm. I'd hate to think what it'd have been like out on the sands tonight."

"Well," said Kincaid, "no one asked you to leave our aircar behind."

Murchison ignored the remark, but Kincaid's wife said: "Don't be ridiculous. The aircar broke down. Sure, we could've had warmth there, but we'd also have starved to death. Mr. Murchison, will we find life in the city?"

"No," he assured her. "Maybe the Marties come here on religious pilgrimages once a year, maybe they don't. But the city's dead. Probably it's been that way since before your ancestors came down from their trees."

As it turned out, Murchison was right. They entered the city through a chink in its ancient stone walls, the twilight desert winds knifing in behind them. For a time they explored around among the ruins of a civilization which died before it reached the stars, leaving the uncultured Marties as its heirs.

Soon Murchison flicked on their band torch, and it cut a pale swath through the night. Mars' thin atmosphere lost its daylight fast, once the sun set, and the icy night winds knifed in through the city's broken walls. "We'd better find our way underground," Murchison said.

He didn't wait for an answer, stalking ahead of the Kincaids through an ancient archway, probing around with the beam of his torch. The archway opened on what had been a great courtyard, and all around them the gaunt shadows of Martian buildings which might be as old as the desert itself loomed mysteriously.

Murchison found what he sought, calling the Kincaids to follow him as he ducked down into a pit at the center of the courtyard. They went down a twisting staircase hewn out of the living rock, and it was a long time before they reached bottom.

Elena Kincaid gasped. "Why, it's—it's light down here!"

"Of course," her husband said, crossing to the far wall and running his hands over it. "Look at the wall—it glows."

MURCHISON NODDED. "Radioactive," he told them, then laughed when Kincaid withdrew his bands as from fire. "Don't worry," the guide explained. "The old Martians couldn't stand radioactivity any more than we could. There's just enough in the walls to give light and a little heat. But you could spend your whole life down here and you wouldn't get a dangerous dose."

Kincaid shook his head. "Well, I wish we had a Geiger counter."

"I said you don't need it."

"You said. You said! Listen Murchison, you got us into this, and—"

Here we go again, Murchison thought grimly, and he hardly listened when Kincaid went into his tirade. Instead, he studied the chamber in which they found themselves. The staircase came in through a hole in one of the three walls, and there seemed no other means of egress. Three walls. The room was a huge triangular vault, and Murchison eyed the walls keenly. Equilateral, he figured. Each wall the same length, perhaps fifty feet. Each of its three corners—the angles of the triangle—sixty degrees.

Murchison licked his dry lips. He'd heard stories about the ancient Martian cults, about a lost science, which died when the red planet took on the color which gave it its name, an age ago. And in every story the triangular vault took on special significance, coupled with a two-line fragment from an ancient chant. What was it? Murchison tried to remember, mumbled to himself. "Anything your heart desires, food or drink or gem of fires—"

"What say?" Elena Kincaid demanded.

Murchison grunted something noncommittal, went on with his thinking. No one had ever found one of the triangular vaults, not even the degenerate Marties. But the Marties stumbled through the shifting red sands of the desert, looking for them, saying that their civilization would be born anew when one of the vaults turned up...

Murchison shrugged. Hell, probably just a fancy myth with no more meaning that any one of dozens of similar myths on Earth. Even the three angles of the triangle might be explained by the Freudian school of psychology. The mystical number three...

THE VOICE changed his mind. Grating, metallic, it seemed to emerge from one of the walls. It carried somehow a feeling of hoary age. "Welcome to the vault of the three-sided abstraction, the deity Kron!"

"Hey!" Kincaid barked. "Did you hear that?"

Murchison nodded, and the woman said: "It spoke in English. In English! How can that be, Murchison?"

"Don't ask me. On Venus there are talking trees which speak more in the mind than any place else, using the language of the listener. Sort of like telepathy." Murchison tried to brush it off that way, but he felt oddly frightened. Voices just don't talk to you, not in million-year-old Martian cities, not in your own language.

The voice droned on, "Fair Mars is dying, and the three-sided abstraction which is a deity only for the superstitious will provide for its children. You have only to wish—wish for anything your heart desires here in the vault of the three angles. You will notice that one angle is red, one is blue, one is yellow."

Murchison stared, saw it was true. Each of the room's three corners had a different color—bright red, somber blue, pale yellow.

The voice had not yet finished. "The blue angle is for dreaming. Wish an abstraction there, and you will dream it. The red is for reality. Demand a particular there, and you will receive it. Dream wisely, demand sagely, for Mars is dying…"

The voice faded. A lot of hogwash, naturally. An old fanatic cult which couldn't reconcile itself to the death of a planet. But why hadn't the voice mentioned the yellow corner?

"…ridiculous," Kincaid was saying. "What I want to know is this: How the devil are we going to get out of here?"

"We'll wait until dawn," Murchison told him. "Then we'll burn this whole darned city, if necessary, to make a signal. Don't worry, they'll find us."

"Okay. Okay, it sounds good. Meanwhile, I'm thirsty, and hungry." Elena Kincaid had skipped jauntily into the red corner, her plain features looking almost ugly in the harsh light. "Well, what was it the voice said? Red for reality. I demand food—and drink."

Silence. Then, from somewhere far away, a rustling sound. Softly at first, then louder. Murchison felt his jaw grow slack. Elena Kincaid crouched in her corner, terrified, surrounded on all sides by savory dishes, by flagons of wine and water!

Murchison felt his salivary glands working overtime; he hadn't realized how hungry he was. And you don't go around rejecting an obvious impossibility, not when it offers you food and drink!

THEY SQUATTED in silence, the three of them, eating. Murchison dug in with gusto, only half aware that the roast meat did not quite taste like beef, that the vegetables and fruits had a strange but delicious tang to them, that the wine's color was a deep purple. Synthetics, obviously. Stuff like this didn't exist on Mars, not now. Perhaps long and long ago, in the dead past of the planet. Perhaps then, but not now. And only one conclusion could be drawn: synthetics, yes—but based upon the flora and fauna of the old Mars which had been dust a million years…

When they finished, Kincaid didn't have a word of complaint. A handsome man who had attracted the plain but wealthy Elena, only his petulant mouth and too-bright eyes showed weakness. But the lips trembled now, and the eyes stared fixedly, as if trying to penetrate the secret of the vault. "Imagine," he mused. "That voice wasn't fooling! Anything we want—anything—right here for the taking. Like a Djinn of Earth fairy tale, only this is based on science!" He stood up, bathed himself in the scarlet glow of the red corner. "I want jewels," he said. "Jewels, jewels, jewels—"

The stirring again, the rustling.

Kincaid let the rubies run through his fingers, tossed the handfuls of diamonds into the air, caught them, fondled the emeralds and sapphires.

"See?" he babbled. "See, see?"

Murchison saw. A fortune in uncut gems, fresh from their matrix. Kincaid didn't waste any time. He gazed scornfully at the plain features of his wife, this woman upon whom he'd depended for his wealth. He said, "Naturally, I'll want a divorce when we get back." Just like that.

"You'll what?" Elena Kincaid demanded.

"I'll want a divorce, of course. What do I need you for? What do I need anything for? I have this, don't I?"

The woman sobbed softly, but then she looked up, and she was smiling. "Not you alone," she said. "You're not the only one who has it." She went herself in to the red corner, said: "I want beauty. I want to be more beautiful than any woman in the solar system."

Somehow, he did not know why, Murchison had no desire to join them. Kincaid always had coveted wealth and power—he'd have these now. And Elena—she carried her plainness around like a wound which would not heal, and so first she asked for beauty. Now Murchison sat in the middle of the room, watching them, playing the role of an impersonal observer. He wondered how long he could maintain it.

Elena...changed. Murchison didn't see the change. The rustling came, and with it a cone of brilliant amber radiance, which cloaked the woman from head to foot. Other colors flashed through the cone, caressing the dim shadow which was Elena. Murchison thought he heard the woman scream, but the cone maintained a shrieking clamor of its own, and he couldn't be sure.

The cone faded.

MOUSEY HAIR swept back into a bun, sallow, pinched-out features, flat, uninspiring figure, thin legs—all were gone. Elena stood there, head tilted back, the glorious cascade of golden hair billowing halfway down her back, full red lips parted invitingly, breasts arched proudly, haughtily, long bronzed legs flashing as she pirouetted around the room after she stood for one moment and let their eyes take her in. This was the new Elena, fashioned not by a deity, Murchison knew now, but by a long-perished science.

Kincaid ran to her, reached out with his hands, but she eluded him. "Keep away!" she cried.

"Keep away? But you're my wife!"

She laughed, a musical sound. "You didn't want me, remember? You wanted a divorce. Very well, I'll grant it. Meanwhile, keep away."

"Elena—"

Still laughing, she skipped across the room to Murchison. "Do you like me?"

The guide's pulses were hammering furiously. Like her? The way she looked now, she'd make an octogenarian chase her around the solar system in a life-jet. "I—I think you are very beautiful."

"You may kiss me, Murchison." Red lips parting, waiting—sure, she'd had a crush on him from the very first, Murchison knew that. And now it could be a two-way proposition, despite the fact that Kincaid bellowed his rage. Hell, he could take care of Kincaid, soft, dissipated Kincaid. And this woman, this new Elena… Still, did he hear laughter, far away, through the walls of the room—an ancient voice mocking him? Did he?

He stepped away from the woman, feeling like all the varieties of a damned fool wrapped into one.

She did not pout. Instead, she laughed. "What's the difference? There'll be hundreds, thousands; I'll have the men of the solar system at my feet. No, Alan. Keep away. Away!"

She spoke like you might talk to a pet which refused to obey, and then struck out at her husband, slapping his face once with her left hand and once with her right. When he snarled and balled his fist, Murchison got between them. "That's enough," he said. "We still have to get out of here."

Kincaid relaxed visibly. "What's your hurry?" he said. "I don't feel like leaving this place. You can go when morning comes, if you want, but I'm stay right here. Oh, I'll leave eventually, but first—ah, what did the voice say? You can dream in the blue corner? Well, I will dream for a time."

He walked stiffly into the area of blue light, stood still for a moment, then said: "I want a dream of power. Any kind of power…"

He slumped to the floor.

Elena smiled demurely at Murchison.

LATER, KINCAID awoke. "Lord, what a dream."

"Very well, tell us about it." Elena yawned indifferently.

"Well, I was— I wasn't me! I was some kind of contraption, a robot, I guess, sliding on runners atop a big tank-like machine. Another robot faced me, like a dragon made out of metal. We fought. Voices shouted in my head, told me this dragon thing was the strongest creature in—what was the word?—in the galaxy. We fought, and I won. I can't describe the feeling, but I was like a god after the fight. I pounded my metal chest and the sound it made roared out all over the world. And people bowed and scraped their noses in the dirt before me. I let them kiss my metal arms…"

He chuckled. "Hell, while we're here I might as well enjoy myself with dreams like that. But I'll take more than enough out of this place to have the real thing. Power! What's power but a lot of wealth, used properly? I'll have everything. And you, Elena, you'll come crawling to me like all the others. You'll see—"

"My, how you've changed," Elena scoffed. "You used to say you loved me. Murchison, would you believe that he said it every night for a year until even I began to tire of it? Lies, all lies—and now, well, I'll have a hundred men to tell me that. But," she smiled, almost sadly, "none of them will mean it. Alan wanted my money. All the others will want my beauty. Even you, Murchison—no, don't deny it. If only I could have one man, one man as handsome as I am beautiful, who will love me always, deeply, sincerely…"

"I love you!" Kincaid said.

The woman ignored him, crossed to the red corner. "I want a human being, a glorious hunk of man, an Adonis in the flesh. And he must love me to the exclusion of all other emotions. Give him to me!"

"She's crazy," Kincaid muttered, playing with his jewels.

MURCHISON watched the amber cone return, hovering over emptiness. When it faded, a man stood there, a personification of the old tall-dark-and-handsome cliché. "Which one of you is Elena?" he demanded in a mellow baritone,

Elena smiled. "Suppose you figure that out for yourself."

"You are. Yes..." He swept her up in his arms.

"Oh, Lord!" Kincaid groaned. Jealousy flashed briefly in his eyes, and he forgot his jewels. He spun the handsome man around, but his fingers caught in the lapel of the man's trim white suit, and Murchison heard the cloth rip.

The man shook his head. "You shouldn't have done that. I must look my best for the woman I love—"

"Oh, shut up!" Kincaid cried, still holding the torn lapel. "You're not even real. They took a lot of chemicals and made you, that's all. Now, stop pawing my wife."

"Please," the man said.

"I told you to stop pawing her."

"Please."

"Nuts!" Kincaid let go of the lapel and swung clumsily with his right fist. The man caught the blow on his open palm, shoving Kincaid back. He tripped and fell, and when he got up he was bellowing again.

"Really," the artificial man told him, "this is regrettable. You're keeping me from my work." He shoved once more, this time harder, and Kincaid crashed into the wall. He got up slowly, and Murchison tried to hold him back.

"Stop it, Kincaid. Use your head. That thing was created to love your wife, and it won't let anything interfere."

"Yeah? Well, no bunch of chemicals is going to love my wife. Hey, you, get away!"

Shaking his head sadly, the artificial man hit Kincaid, a hard blow which caught the point of his jaw and lifted him half off the floor. He sat down hard, and for a few moments he did not try to get up. When he did, he took out a handkerchief and patted his bleeding lips, then lurched across the room to the red corner.

"Give me a blasting pistol!" he pleaded. Murchison had left the hunting rifle behind on the desert.

Out of his corner wheeled Kincaid, the pistol clutched in his fist. "Okay, you, get away from her!"

The artificial man turned to face him, blanched when he saw the weapon. "Please, no violence. I want to love—"

Kincaid shot him through the chest.

HE STAGGERED, and now Elena was screaming, because although he should have been a corpse, the artificial man staggered around the room after her, his arms outstretched.

Kincaid shot again, and the thing stumbled to its knees. "Please, I want to love—"

Again, and the artificial man shuddered, lay on the floor trembling. "Don't you understand? I can't die. I can only love. Love Elena..."

Murchison wrenched the pistol from Kincaid's nerveless fingers. "Let's get the hell out of here!" he roared. He looked at the thing on the floor, broken and twisted but not dead, and he felt sick.

"You killed him!" Elena wailed, striking at Kincaid's chest with her fist. He brushed her away, ran to the red corner. "Make that thing disappear!"

It disappeared.

"See?" Kincaid said, trembling. "N-nothing to worry about."

Elena stood in the red glow, pointing to her husband. "Kill him! Destroy him!"

Murchison knew it was a mistake. The science of the vault could do anything you demanded, but it didn't concern itself with the method. Kincaid's dream of power might have been one an old Martian could understand. Kincaid certainly had not understood it, and he'd tired of it soon enough.

Now the vault had been given an order: destroy Kincaid. It could do that, but no one had bothered to stipulate how. So the room would decide for itself...

Murchison heard a rumbling, looked up and saw rock dust sifting down from the ceiling. A crack appeared, spreading ominously. The rock grumbled.

A half-ton chunk detached itself and fell.

Kincaid screamed once, horribly, shielded himself futilely with his hands. Then the rock hit the floor with a booming crash, and Kincaid was under it.

Smaller stones fell. More cracks opened in the ceiling. The dust made it hard for Murchison to breathe.

He took Elena by her arm, cried: "This whole place will cave in! We'll have to make a run for those stairs!"

She pulled herself away from him. "Don't be foolish. All I have to do is stand again in the red corner, and tell them to stop. See—"

She skirted the slab of rock which was her husband's tombstone. Dimly through the clatter of rocks Murchison was aware of her sobbing. Perhaps at the very end, she realized what she had done. Perhaps...

He hardly had time to think. The first rock had started a fault in the ceiling, and once the thing was set in motion it wouldn't stop until the entire vault was buried. Something slammed against Murchison's shoulder, staggering him. He fell, picked himself up, saw that Elena had reached the red corner. A crack slit the ceiling over her head, and Murchison tried to shout a warning, tried to run at her across the rock strewn floor.

He didn't make it.

A score of boulders thundered down, forming a cairn for Elena.

MURCHISON plunged toward the stairs, tripped and fell. When he got up a fresh fall of rock had sealed his path to the exit. He flung himself about the room wildly.

The red corner—gone, buried under a dozen tons of rock. The same for the blue. Murchison backed away as the rocks pelted down.

He crouched in the yellow corner, and the metallic voice came back, sadly this time.

"It never works, does it? I'm only a robot here in these walls. And I—I can die. I will die when the rocks finish their bombing. Ten vaults—ten of these vaults all over Mars, built a million years ago to give the people what nature had taken from them.

"The people did not know how to use their gift. Greed, avarice, trickery—each had his own idea how to use the power. Nine vaults are gone. This is the tenth, and I am dying…"

Murchison hardly heard over the clatter of stones.

"You who have watched this night. You were not responsible. You merely watched, while others acted foolishly. For you, one more wish. Anything you want. But just one. I am weak, weak…"

Thoughts flashed through Murchison's delirium. Riches? Power? A final dream to combine all the raptures obtainable through an unknown science. He laughed insanely when he remembered the old legends of Earth. Three wishes, or four, or whatever number. But in the end you had to be content with something simple, and it was exactly as if the wishes had never existed...

The Martians had not known how to use their power any more than the men of Earth.

"Better get me out of here," Murchison said wearily. "Put me in Canal City. That's about all..."

HE STOOD on the quay near the old canal, radiant heat from the artificial sidewalks pushing back the cold of night. People moved about on all sides of him, gay, carefree people, enjoying nightlife in Canal City...

His memories were hazy. He'd been on the desert with the Kincaids. Now he was back. The Kincaids—dead. He knew that, without knowing how. He'd have some explaining to do to the authorities, but it would turn out all right. He knew it would. And meanwhile he'd better stop into Kelly's Marsport Bar and have a few stiff shots. Something told him his memories might return, and then he'd need those drinks.

Black Eyes and the Daily Grind

The little house pet from Venus didn't like New York, so New York had to change.

HE LIKED the flat cracking sound of the gun. He liked the way it slapped back against his shoulder when he fired. Somehow it did not seem a part of the dank, steaming Venusian jungle. Probably, he realized with a smile, it was the only old-fashioned recoil rifle on the entire planet. As if anyone else would want to use one of those old bone-cracking relics today! But they all failed to realize it made sport much more interesting.

"I haven't seen anything for a while," his wife said. She had a young, pretty face and a strong young body. If you have money these days, you could really keep a thirty-five year old woman looking trim.

Not on Venus, of course. Venus was an outpost, a frontier, a hot, wet, evil-smelling place that beckoned only the big-game hunter. He said, "That's true. Yesterday we could bag them one after the other, as fast as I could fire this contraption. Today, if there's anything bigger than a mouse, it's hiding in a hole somewhere. You know what I think, Lindy?"

"What?"

"I think there's a reason for it. A lot of the early Venusian hunters said there were days like this. An area filled with big lizards, and cats and everything else the day before suddenly seems to clear out, for no reason. It doesn't make sense."

"Why not? Why couldn't they all just decide to make tracks for someplace else on the same day?"

He slapped at an insect that was buzzing around his right ear, then mopped his sweating brow with a handkerchief. His name was Judd Whitney, and people said he had a lot of money. Now he laughed, patting his wife's trim shoulder under the white tunic. "No, Lindy. It just doesn't work that way. Not on Earth and not on Venus, either. You think there's a pied-piper or something which calls all the animals away?"

"Maybe. I don't know much about those things."

"No. I don't think they went anyplace. They're just quiet. They didn't come out of their holes or hovels or down from the trees. But why?"

"Well, let's forget it. Let's go back to camp. We can try again tomor—look! Look, there's something!"

Judd followed her pointing finger with his eyes. Half-hidden by the creepers and vines clinging to an old tree-stump, something was watching them. It wasn't very big and it seemed in no hurry to get away.

"What is it?" Lindy wanted to know.

"Don't know. Never saw anything like it before. Venus is still an unknown frontier; the books only name a couple dozen of the biggest animals. But hell, Lindy, that's not game. I don't think it weighs five pounds."

"It's cute, and it has a lovely skin."

Judd couldn't argue with that. Squatting on its haunches, the creature was about twenty inches tall. It had a pointed snout and two thin, long ears. Its eyes were very big and very round and quite black. They looked something like the eyes of an Earthian tarsier, but the tarsier were bloody little beasts. The skin was short and stiff and was a kind of silvery white. Under the sheen, however, it seemed to glow. A diamond is colorless, Judd thought, but when you see it under light a whole rainbow of colors sparkle deep within it. This creature's skin was like that, Judd decided.

"If we could get enough of them," Lindy was saying, "I'd have the most unusual coat! Do you think we could find enough, Judd?"

"I doubt it. Never saw anything like it before, never heard of anything like it. You'd need fifty of 'em, anyway. Let's forget about it—too small to shoot, anyway."

"No, Judd. I want it."

"Well, I'm not going to stalk a five-pound—hey, wait a minute! I taught you how to use this rifle, so why don't you bag it?"

Lindy grinned. "That's a fine idea. I was a little scared of some of those big lizards and cats and everything, but now I'm going to take you up on it. Here, give me your gun."

Judd removed the leather thong from his shoulder and handed the weapon to her. She looked at it a little uncertainly, then took the clip of shells that Judd offered and slammed it into the chamber. The little creature sat unmoving.

"Isn't it peculiar that it doesn't run away, Judd?"

"Sure is. Nothing formidable about that animal so unless it has a hidden poison somewhere, just about anything in this swamp could do it in. To survive it would have to be fast as hell and it would have to keep running all the time. Beats me, Lindy."

"Well, I'm going to get myself one pelt toward that coat, anyway. Watch, Judd: is this the way?" She lifted the rifle to her shoulder and squinted down the sights toward the shining creature.

"Yeah, that's the way. Only relax. Relax. Shoulder's so tense you're liable to dislocate it with the kick. There—that's better.

Now Lindy's finger was wrapped around the trigger and she remembered Judd had told her to squeeze it, not to pull it. If you pulled the trigger you jerked the rifle and spoiled your aim. You had to squeeze it slowly...

The animal seemed politely interested.

Suddenly, a delicious languor stole over Lindy. It possessed her all at once and she had no idea where it came from. Her legs had been stiff and tired from the all-morning trek through the swamp, but now they felt fine. Her whole body was suffused in a warm, satisfied glow of well being. And laziness. It was an utterly new sensation and she could even feel it tingling even at the roots of her hair. She sighed and lowered the rifle.

"I don't want to shoot it," she said.

"You just told me you did."

"I know, but I changed my mind. What's the matter, can't I change my mind?"

"Of course you can change your mind. But I thought you wanted a coat of those things."

"Yes, I suppose I do. But I don't want to shoot it, that's all."

Judd snorted. "I think you have a streak of softness someplace in that pretty head of yours!"

"Maybe. I don't know. But I'd still like the pelt. Funny, isn't it?"

"Okay, okay! But don't ask to use the gun again." Judd snatched it from her hands. "If you don't want to shoot it, then I will. Maybe we can make you a pair of gloves or something from the pelt."

And Judd pointed his ancient rifle at the little animal preparing to snap off a quick shot. It would be a cinch at this distance. Even Lindy wouldn't have missed, if she hadn't changed her mind.

Judd yawned. He'd failed to realize he was so tired. Not an aching kind of tiredness, but the kind that makes you feel good all over. He yawned again and lowered the rifle. "Changed my mind," he said. "I don't want to shoot it, either. What say we head back for camp?"

Lindy gripped his hand impulsively. "All right, Judd—but

I had a brainstorm! I want it for a pet!"

"A pet?"

"Yes. I think it would be the cutest thing. Everyone would look and wonder and I'll adore it!"

"We don't know anything about it. Maybe Earth would be too cold, or too dry, or maybe we don't have anything it can eat. There are liable to be a hundred different strains of bacteria that can kill it."

"I said I want it for a pet. See? Look at it! We can call it Black Eyes."

"Black Eyes—" Judd groaned.

"Yes, Black Eyes. If you don't do this one thing for me, Judd—"

"Okay—okay. But I'm not going to do anything. You want it, you take it."

Lindy frowned, looked at him crossly, then sloshed across the swamp toward Black Eyes. The creature waited on its stump until she came quite close, and then, with a playful little bound, it hopped onto her shoulder, still squatting on its haunches. Lindy squealed excitedly and began to stroke its silvery fur.

A MONTH LATER, they returned to Earth. Judd and Lindy and Black Eyes. The hunting trip had been a success—Judd' s trophies were on their way home on a slow freighter, and he'd have some fine heads and skins for his study-room. Even Black Eyes had been no trouble at all. It ate scraps from their table, forever sitting on its haunches and staring at them with its big black eyes. Judd thought it would make one helluva lousy pet, but he didn't tell Lindy. Trouble was, it never did anything. It merely sat still, or occasionally it would bounce down to the floor and mince along on its hind-legs for a scrap of food. It never uttered a sound. It did not frolic and it did not gambol. Most of the time it could have been carved from stone. But Lindy was happy and Judd said nothing.

They had a little trouble with the customs officials. This because nothing unknown could be brought to Earth without a thorough examination.

At the customs office, a bespectacled official stared at Black Eyes, scratching his head. "Never seen one like that before."

"Neither have I," Judd admitted.

"Well, I'll look in the book." The man did, but there are no thorough tomes on Venusian fauna. "Not here."

"I could have told you."

"Well, we'll have to quarantine it and study it. That means you and your wife go into quarantine, too. It could have something that's catching."

"Absurd!" Lindy cried.

"Sorry, lady. I only work here."

"You and your bright ideas," Judd told his wife acidly. "We may be quarantined a month until they satisfy themselves about Black Eyes."

The customs official shrugged his bony shoulders, and Judd removed a twenty credit note from his pocket and handed it to the man. "Will this change your mind?"

"I should say not! You can't bribe me, Mr. Whitney! You can't—" The man yawned, stretched languidly, smiled. "No sir, you can keep your money, Mr. Whitney. Guess we don't have to examine your pet after all. Mighty cute little feller. Well, have fun with it. Come on, move along now." And, as they were departing with Black Eyes, still not believing their ears: "Darn this weather! Makes a man so lazy..."

It was after the affair at the customs office, that Black Eyes uttered its first sound. City life hasn't changed much in the last fifty years. Jet-cars still streak around the circumferential highways, their whistles blaring. Factories still belch smoke and steam, although the new atomic power plants have lessened that to a certain extent. Crowds still throng the streets, noisy, hurrying, ill-mannered. It's one of those things that can't be helped. A city has to live, and it has to make noise.

But it seemed to frighten Lindy's new pet. It stared through the jet-car window on the way from the spaceport to the Whitney's suburban home, its black eyes welling with tears.

"Look!" Judd exclaimed. "Black Eyes can cry!"

"A crying pet, Judd. I knew there would be something unusual about Black Eyes. I just knew it!"

The tears in the big black eyes overflowed and tumbled out, rolling down Black Eyes' silvery cheeks. And then Black Eyes whimpered. It was only a brief whimper, but both Judd and Lindy heard it, and even the driver turned around for a moment and stared at the animal.

The driver stopped the jet. He yawned and rested his head comfortably on the cushioned seat. He went quietly to sleep.

A MAN NAMED Merrywinkle owned the Merrywinkle Shipping Service. That, in itself, was not unusual. But at precisely the moment that Black Eyes unleashed its mild whimper, Mr. Merrywinkle—uptown and five miles away—called an emergency conference of the board of directors and declared:

"Gentlemen, we have all been working too hard, and I, for one, am going to take a vacation. I don't know when I'll be back, but it won't be before six months."

"But C.M.," someone protested, "there's the Parker deal and the Gilette contract and a dozen other things. You're needed!"

Mr. Merrywinkle shook his baldhead. "What's more,

you're all taking vacations, with pay. Six months, each of you. We're closing down Merrywinkle Shipping for half a year. Give the competition a break, eh?"

"But C.M.! We're about ready to squeeze out Chambers Parcel Co.! They'll get back on their feet in six months."

"Never mind. Notify all departments of the shutdown, effective immediately. Vacations for all."

WHO SHUT off the assembly belt?" the foreman asked mildly. He was not a mild man and he usually stormed and ranted at the slightest provocation. This was at Clewson Jetcraft, and you couldn't produce a single jet-plane without the assembly belt, naturally.

A plump little man said, "I did."

"But why?" the foreman asked him, smiling blandly.

"I don't know. I just did."

The foreman was still smiling. "I don't blame you."

Two days later, Clewson Jetcraft had to layoff all its help. They put ads in all the papers seeking new personnel but no one showed up. Clewson was forced to shut down.

THE CRACK Boston to New York pneumo-tube commuter's special pulled to a bone jarring stop immediately outside the New York station. Some angry commuters pried open the conductor's cab, and found the man snoozing quite contentedly. They awakened him, but he refused to drive the train any further. All the commuters had to leave the pneumo-train and edge their way along three miles of catwalk to the station. No one was very happy about it, but the feeling of well-being which came over them all nipped any possible protest in the bud.

BLACK EYES whimpered again when Judd and Lindy reached home but after that it was quiet. It just sat on its haunches near the window and stared out at the city.

The quiet city.

Nothing moved in the streets. Nothing stirred. People remained at home watching local video or the new space-video from Mars. At first it was a good joke, and the newspapers could have had a field day with it, had the newspapers remained in circulation. After four days, however, they suspended publication. On the fifth day, there was a shortage of food in the city, great stores of it spoiling in the warehouses. Heat and light failed after a week, and the fire department ignored all alarms a day later.

But everything did not stop. School teachers still taught their classes; clerks still sold whatever goods were left on local shelves. Librarians were still at their desks.

Conservatives said it was a liberal plot to undermine capital and demand higher wages; liberals said big business could afford the temporary layoff and wanted to squeeze out the small businessman and labor unions.

Scientists pondered and city officials made speeches over video.

"Something," one of them observed, "has hit our city. Work that requires anything above a modicum of sound has become impossible; in regards to such work people have become lazy. No one can offer any valid suggestions concerning the malady. It merely exists. However, if a stop is not put to it—and soon—our fair city will disintegrate. Something is making us lazy, and that laziness can spell doom, being a compulsive lack of desire to create any noise or disturbance. If anyone believes he has the solution, he should contact the Department of Science at once. If you can't use the video-phone, come in person. But come! Every hour which passes adds to the city's woes."

Nothing but scatter-brained ideas for a week, none of them worth consideration. Then the bespectacled custom's official who had bypassed quarantine for Black Eyes, got in touch with the authorities. He had always been a conscientious man—except for that one lapse. Maybe the queer little beast had nothing to do with this crisis. But then again, the custom's official had never before—or since—had that strange feeling of lassitude. Could there be some connection?

A staff of experts on extra-terrestrial fauna was dispatched to the Whitney residence, although, indeed, the chairman of the Department of Science secretly considered the whole idea ridiculous.

The staff of experts introduced themselves. Then, ignoring the protests of Lindy, went to work on Black Eyes. At first Judd thought the animal would object, but apparently it did not. While conditions all about them in the city worsened, the experts spent three days studying Black Eyes.

They found nothing out of the ordinary.

Black Eyes merely stared back at them, and but for an accident, they would have departed without a lead. On the third day, a huge mongrel dog, which belonged to the Whitney's next-door neighbors somehow, slipped its leash. It was a fierce and ugly animal, and it was known to attack anything smaller than itself. It jumped the fence and landed in Judd Whitney's yard. A few loping bounds took it through an open window, ground level. Inside, it spied Black Eyes and made for the creature at once, howling furiously.

Black Eyes didn't budge.

And the mongrel changed its mind! The slavering tongue withdrew inside the chops, the howling stopped. The mongrel lay down on the floor and whined. Presently it lost all interest, got to its feet, and left as it had come.

Other animals were brought to the Whitney home. Cats. Dogs. A lion from the city zoo, starved for two days and brought in a special mobile cage by its keeper. Black Eyes was thrust into the cage and the lion gave forth with a hideous yowling. Soon it stopped, rolled over, and slept.

THE SCIENTISTS correlated their reports, returned with them to the Whitney house. The leader, whose name was Jamison, said: "As closely as we can tell, Black Eyes is the culprit."

"What?" Lindy demanded.

"Yes, Mrs. Whitney. Your pet, Black Eyes."

"Oh, I don't believe it!"

But Judd said, "Go ahead, Dr. Jamison. I'm listening."

"Well, how does an animal—any animal—protect itself?"

"Why, in any number of ways. If it has claws or a strong jaw and long teeth, it can fight. If it is fleet of foot, it can run. If it is big and has a tough hide, most other animals can't hurt it anyway. Umm, doesn't that about cover it?"

"You left out protective coloration, defensive odors, and things like that. Actually, those are most important from our point of view, for Black Eyes' ability is a further ramification of that sort of thing. Your pet is not fast. It isn't strong. It can't change color and it has no offensive odor to chase off predatory enemies. It has no armor. In short, can you think of a more helpless creature to put down in those Venusian swamps?"

After Judd had shaken his head, Dr. Jamison continued: "Very well. Black Eyes should not be able to survive on Venus—and yet, obviously the creature did. We can assume there are more of the breed, too. Anyway, Black Eyes survives. And I'll tell you why.

"Black Eyes has a very uncommon ability to sense danger when it approaches. And sensing danger, Black Eyes can thwart it. Your creature sends out certain emanations—I won't pretend to know what they are—which stamp aggression out of any predatory creatures. Neither of you could fire upon it—right?"

"Umm, that's true," Judd said.

Lindy nodded.

"Well, that's one half of it. There's so much about life we don't understand. Black Eyes uses energy of an unknown intensity, and the result maintains Black Eyes' life. Now, although that is the case, your animal did not live a comfortable life in the Venusian swamp. Because no animal would attack it, it could not be harmed. Still, from what you tell me about that swamp..."

"Anyhow, Black Eyes was glad to come away with you, and everything went well until you landed in New York. The noises, the clattering, the continual bustle of a great city—all this frightened the creature. It was being attacked—or, at least that's what it must have figured. Result: it struck back the only way it knew how. Have you ever heard about subsonic soundwaves, Mr. Whitney, waves of sound so low that our ears cannot pick them up—waves of sound, which can nevertheless stir our emotions? Such things exist, and, as a working hypothesis, I would say Black Eyes' strange powers rest along those lines. The whole city is idle because Black Eyes is afraid!"

In his exploration of Mars, of Venus, of the Jovian Moons—Judd Whitney had seen enough of extraterrestrial life to know that virtually anything was possible, and Black Eyes would be no exception to that rule.

"What do you propose to do?" Judd demanded.

"Do? Why, we'll have to kill your creature, naturally. You can set a value on it and we will meet it, but Black Eyes must die."

"No!" Lindy cried. "You can't be sure, you're only guessing, and it isn't fair!"

"My dear woman, don't you realize this is a serious situation? The city's people will starve in time. No one can even bring food in because the trucks make too much noise! As an alternative, we could evacuate, but is your pet more valuable than the life of a great city?"

"N-no…"

"Then, please! Listen to reason!"

"Kill it," Judd said. "Go ahead."

Dr. Jamison withdrew from his pocket a small blasting pistol used by the Department of Domestic Animals for elimination of injured creatures. He advanced on Black Eyes, who sat on its haunches in the center of the room, surveying the scientist.

Dr. Jamison put his blaster away. "I can't," he said. "I don't want to."

Judd smiled. "I know it. No one—no thing—can kill Black Eyes. You said so yourself. It was a waste of time to try it. In that case—"

"In that case," Dr. Jamison finished for him, "we're helpless. There isn't a man—or an animal—on Earth that will destroy this thing. Wait a minute—does it sleep, Mr. Whitney?"

"I don't think so. At least, I never saw it sleep. And your team of scientists, did they report anything?"

"No. As far as they could see, the creature never slept. We can't catch it unawares."

"Could you anesthetize it?"

"How? It can sense danger, and long before you could do that, it would stop you. It's only made one mistake, Mr. Whitney: it believes the noises of the city represent a danger. And that's only a negative mistake. Noise won't hurt Black Eyes, of course. It simply makes the animal unnecessarily cautious. But we cannot anesthetize it any more than we can kill it."

"I could take it back to Venus."

"Could you? Could you? I hadn't thought of that."

Judd shook his head. "I can't."

"What do you mean you can't?"

"It won't let me. Somehow it can sense our thoughts when we think something it doesn't want. I can't take it to Venus! No man could, because it doesn't want to go."

"My dear Mr. Whitney—do you mean to say you believe it can think?"

"Uh-uh. Didn't say that. It can sense our thoughts, and that's something else again."

Dr. Jamison threw his hands up over his head in a dramatic gesture. "It's hopeless," he said.

THINGS GREW worse. New York crawled along to a standstill. People began to move from the city. In trickles, at first, but the trickles became torrents, as New York's ten million people began to depart for saner places. It might take months—it might even take years, but the exodus had begun. Nothing could stop it. Because of a harmless little beast with the eyes of a tarsier, the life of a great city was coming to an end.

Word spread. Scientists all over the world studied reports on Black Eyes. No one had any ideas. Everyone was stumped. Black Eyes had no particular desire to go outside. Black Eyes merely remained in the Whitney house, contemplating nothing in particular, and stopping everything.

Dr. Jamison, however, was a persistent man. Judd got a letter from him one day, and the following afternoon he kept his appointment with the scientist.

"It's good to get out," Judd said, after a three hour walk to the Department of Science Building. "I can go crazy just staring at that thing."

"I have it, Whitney."

"You have what? Not the way to destroy Black Eyes? I don't believe it!"

"It's true. Consider. Everyone in the world does not yet know of your pet, correct?"

"I suppose there are a few people who don't—"

"There are many. Among them are the crew of a jet-bomber which has been on maneuvers in Egypt. We have arranged everything."

"Yes? How?"

"At noon tomorrow, the bomber will appear over your home with one of the ancient, high-explosive missiles. Your neighbors will be removed from the vicinity, and, precisely at twelve-o-three in the afternoon, the bomb will be dropped. Your home will be destroyed. Black Eyes will be destroyed with it."

Judd looked uncomfortable. "I dunno," he said. "Sounds too easy."

"Too easy? I doubt if the animal will ever sense what is going on—not when the crew of the bomber doesn't know, either. They'll consider it a mighty peculiar order, to destroy one harmless, rather large and rather elaborate suburban home. But they'll do it. See you tomorrow, Whitney, after this mess is behind us."

"Yeah," Judd said. "Yeah." But somehow, the scientist had failed to instill any of his confidence in Judd.

WITH LINDY, he left home at eleven the following morning, after making a thorough list of all their properties, which the City had promised to duplicate. Judd did not look at Black Eyes as he left, and the animal remained where it was, seated on its haunches under the dining room table, nibbling crumbs. Judd could almost feel the big round eyes boring a pair of twin holes in his back, and he dared not turn around to face them...

They were a mile away at eleven forty-five, making their way through the nearly deserted streets. Judd stopped walking. He looked at Lindy. Lindy looked at him.

"They're going to destroy it," he said.

"I know."

"Do you want them to?"

"I—I—"

Judd knew that something had to be done with Black Eyes. He didn't like the little beast, and anyway, that had nothing to do with it. Black Eyes was a menace. And yet, something whispered in Judd's ear, *Don't let them, don't let them...* It wasn't Judd and it wasn't Judd's subconscious. It was Black Eyes, and he knew it. But he couldn't do a thing about it—

"I'm going to stay right here and let them bomb the place," he said aloud. But as he spoke, he was running back the way he had come.

Fifteen minutes.

He sprinted part of the time, then rested, then sprinted again. He was somewhat on the beefy side and he could not run fast, but he made it. Just.

He heard the jet streaking through the sky overhead, looked up once and saw it circling. Two blocks from his house he was met by a policeman. The entire area had been roped off, and the officer shook his head when Judd tried to get through.

"But I live there!"

"Can't help it, Mister. Orders is orders."

Judd hit him. Judd didn't want to, but nevertheless, he grunted with satisfaction when he felt the blow to be a good one, catching the stocky officer on the point of his chin and tumbling him over backwards. Then Judd was ducking under the rope and running.

He reached his house, plummeted in through the front door. He found Black Eyes under the kitchen table, squatting on its haunches. He scooped the animal up, ran outside.

Then he was running again, and before he reached the barrier, something rocked him. A loud series of explosions ripped through his brain, and instinctively—Black Eyes' instincts, not his—he folded his arms over the animal, protecting it. Something shuddered, and began to fall behind him, and debris scattered in all directions. Something struck Judd's head and he felt the ground slapping up crazily at his face—

He was as good as new a few days later.

And so was Black Eyes.

"I have it," Judd said to his nurse.

"You have what, sir?"

"It's, so simple, so ridiculously simple, maybe that's why no one ever thought of it. Get me Dr. Jamison!"

Jamison came a few moments later, breathless. "Well?"

"I have the solution."

"You…do?" Not much hope in the answer. Dr. Jamison was a tired, defeated man.

"Sure. Black Eyes doesn't like the city. Fine. Take him out. I can't take him to Venus. He doesn't like Venus and he won't go. No one can take him anyplace he doesn't want to go, just as no one can hurt him in any way. But he doesn't like the city. It's too noisy. All right: have someone take him far from the city, far far away—where there's no noise at all. Someplace out in the sticks where it won't matter much if Black Eyes puts a stop to any disturbing noises."

"Who will take him? You, Mr. Whitney?"

Judd shook his head. "That's your job, not mine. I've given you the answer. Now use it."

Lindy had arrived, and Lindy said: "Judd, you're right. That *is* the answer. And you're wonderful—"

No one volunteered to spend his life in exile with Black Eyes, but then Dr. Jamison pointed out that while no one knew the creature's life span, it certainly couldn't be expected to match man's. Just a few years and the beast would die, and...Dr. Jamison's arguments were so logical that he convinced himself. He took Black Eyes with him into the Canadian Northwoods, and there they live.

JUDD was right—almost. This was the obvious answer, which escaped everyone.

But scientists continued their examinations of Black Eyes, and they discovered something. Black Eyes fears had not been for herself alone. She is going to have babies. The estimate is for thirty-five little tarsier-eyed creatures. No doctor in the world will be able to do anything but deliver the litter.

The Impossible Weapon

Stan knew that Venus's secret weapon couldn't possibly work. Yet Earthmen continued to die the thousands...

STANLEY STOKES stood on the balcony and looked up at the sky. He couldn't actually see the sky, since the tiny glowing pinpoints of light that made up the force field hid it quite effectively. He wondered idly how lovers fared without moon glow and starlight to give their passions impetus, but then he thought, to hell with lovers, I've got my own problems.

He turned and finished his fourth drink—or was it his fifth? Sixth? He said belligerently, "I hate bureaucracy. I particularly hate the Assistant Secretary of Defensive Weapons, Spatial Division."

Lila took his hand and led him back inside, plunking him down on a big overstuffed chair. "You're high," she told him severely. "And the A.S.D.W.S.D. happens to be my father."

"That makes it even worse," Stanley proclaimed. "The man who sired my girlfriend is a complete and utter nincompoop."

"Father is not a nincompoop!"

"Nor am I a hero, but I happen to be in a position to save the Earth. I can do it, despite the fact that I'm not a hero. So your father should listen, despite the fact that he is a nincompoop."

"He did listen."

"He did not listen. He merely sat there while I talked, and when I finished he smiled politely. I think he even winked at one of his aides. It took two months before I could get close enough to see him wink, and then, after ten minutes, he said no."

"The United Nations pays him for his work," Lila said acidly. "They believe he knows his business."

"Is that so? We're losing the war, aren't we?"

"Yes," Lila admitted, "but we weren't, not until last April. What could father do if the Venus-Mars-Ganymede League developed a new weapon? The way you talk, you'd think he was working for the League or something."

"I didn't say that, but...umm-mm. You have a point there."

"Stanley Stokes, you're terrible!"

"That's what your father said, only he used the word *crazy*."

"If you weren't high, I think I'd say goodbye. Permanently."

Stanley rocked back and forth gently, stood up and twirled around slowly until his eyes came to focus on Lila. "I am not high. But it looks like I'm having in-law troubles before we're married, because your father is a nincompoop."

"Stanley, I'm warning you—"

"Remember, I'm not high. Don't let that sway your decision. It's either...me or that nincom—"

"Here!" Lila removed the modest engagement ring from her finger, steadied Stanley's hand long enough to place the ring in his palm. "Goodbye."

There were tears in her eyes, but Stanley failed to see them, for his vision had become clouded on its own accord. Gulping audibly, he pocketed the ring, turned on his heel and stalked from the apartment. He tried to stalk in a straight line, his thin shoulders squared, as he had seen Clarke Townsend do so effectively on a score of video shows. But Stanley stalked in a weaving fashion.

Outside, he found an empty jet-cab near the curb. He punched his identification number on the record-box, took the cab up half a thousand feet to the local lane. He idled around purposely for a time, then set the controls in a northerly direction and leaned back. There was a time when he had liked night flying, watching the dark shadows of clouds scudding across the face of the moon, or on moonless nights watching the star-studded sweep of the Milky Way. But now all he saw was the glowing force field, and after a while he clamped his eyes tightly shut, surrendering the cab to robot control.

Ten minutes later he brought it down on the roof of the Queens County Spaceman's Bar.

STANLEY entered the place in time to see the tail-end of a brawl. It must have been a good one, although the cops had not been summoned. Three flunkies carted a mess of broken table and chairs to the waiting maw of a disposal unit; three others helped two battered spacemen to their feet and thence to the street-level door.

But a third spaceman needed no help whatever. His face was a near catastrophe. Not from this fight alone, but from a score of others. His crooked nose defied one further fracture; his huge jutting jaw would break knuckles, and not the other way around; his shining dome of a head—Stanley guessed a slight dose of radiation could account for that—was the canvas for lurid tattoos which bordered on the pornographic. But he was smiling, the over-large teeth giving Stanley the strong impression of a horse.

"A couple of puppies!" the ugly spaceman snorted, pounding his two huge hands on the surface of the bar. A frightened barman clambered across a heap of broken crockery and grinned shyly.

"Yes, sir! Oh, yes—a couple of puppies."

"No one asked you! I'll have Venusian brandy."

The barman gulped. "I'm sorry, sir. We haven't been able to get Venusian brandy since—"

"I know, dammit! Since they came up with that new weapon and chased our fleet out of space, its tail between its legs. Okay, give me cognac, a triple."

STANLEY gazed upon the proceedings with evident satisfaction. Here was a man after his own heart, even if it was a man endowed with about twice as much brawn. Hardly realizing it at first, Stanley found himself walking across the floor and joining the hulking figure at the bar.

"Name's Stokes," Stanley said in his best basso. "I agree with you. A shame that we have to run away with our tail between our legs just because they develop a new weapon."

"You think so, huh?" The huge spaceman seemed much larger from an eye-level proximity with his shoulder, and his booming voice lacked the faintest suggestion of anything but hostility. "I don't. Hell, it makes me sick, Stokes—but what can you do about it? You can't expect the boys to commit suicide by throwing themselves against a weapon they can't fight. Say, are you one of them damn pacifists who says we ought to surrender?"

"No," Stanley said at once, trying hard not to blanch when the spaceman looked down at him out of fuming eyes. "Quite the contrary. I believe I have the solution Earth has been looking for."

"You believe what? Just who the hell are you?"

"Technician second-class Stanley Stokes, Quantum Division. If you—"

"A quanto-tech!" The spaceman snorted. "What the devil can you do?"

"Let me finish and I'll try to tell you. All my plan needs is a spaceman and a ship, and then I think we can show the League a thing or two. Yes, bartender, I'll have cognac too. All right, a—a triple. Now—"

But Stanley didn't have a chance to finish.

Someone cried: "Holy Rockets, the cops!"

And someone else: "Let's get out of here! If O'Hanrohan decides to fight—"

O'Hanrohan was the hulking spaceman with the booming voice, and it looked like O'Hanrohan would decide to fight. He stood with his back to the bar, his feet planted wide apart. He picked up the bottle of cognac by its graceful neck, smashing it down against the mahogany with savage force. A lot of cognac and a lot of glass sprayed all around the immediate vicinity, but O'Hanrohan came up holding a shattered half-bottle, its jagged edges gleaming under the fluorescent lights.

With his free hand he grabbed Stanley around the neck and held him that way. "We're getting out of here!" he shouted. "Try to stop me and you'd be making a mistake." Then he hissed in Stanley's ear: "Did you leave a cab up on the roof?"

And when Stanley nodded weakly, his chin scraping against the hairy forearm: "Good. We'll take it and scram."

THE HALF dozen cops had an assorted arsenal of blasters, needle guns and heat-beams, but they couldn't use it, not with Stanley effectively shielding O'Hanrohan from their fire. O'Hanrohan backed slowly toward the roof exit, pulling Stanley with him. He didn't release his grip until they stood on the other side of the door. Then he kicked the door shut, bolted it and turned toward the waiting cab. Almost immediately, fists were pounding on the door. A moment later, its surface began to glow a dull cherry-red.

"They're using heat-beams," said O'Hanrohan. "That doesn't give us much time. Are you coming with me?"

"With an escaped criminal? A fugitive? Do you think I'm crazy?"

"I'm a fugitive, but not a criminal. One of those men I hit was an officer, but he had it coming. A lousy pacifist, he wants us to give up! You coming? Don't forget, sonny: I'm your spaceman, and I can get a ship."

Stanley looked at the door, glowing more brightly now. He watched the drops of molten metal dripping off sluggishly to the pavement below. If this wild giant of a spaceman wanted to help him...

"I'll go with you," he said, and together they ran for the cab. Behind them, the door dissolved into a bubbling pool and the first policemen stepped over it gingerly. A blaster seared air just below the cab as it flashed off the roof.

Stanley's thoughts were whirling. First Lila and his engagement ring—now this. Of his own free will, he had fled with a fugitive from justice, had helped him, in fact. Well, hardly that, but the police might think so. At least now he could lean back and think it all over. He thought he had the answer to the enemy's new weapon, but he could be wrong. And if he were, he'd gambled everything on a cockeyed theory—

Something made their cab bounce.

Something else made it spin and twist and turn upside down, bouncing Stanley's head momentarily off the ceiling.

"Strap your safety belt!" O'Hanrohan roared.

"What—what's the matter?"

"The cops followed us in their ship. They're firing."

"Even when you have a hostage on board?"

"Yeah. No! They must've heard us talking on the roof. I guess you're in trouble, sonny. Want to shake?"

They did, or they started to, but their cab bounced again, then shot skyward on a tangent. "I've never been shot at before," Stanley said.

O'Hanrohan grunted. "I don't believe you ever rode one of these cabs at three G's, either, but if we want to get away, you'll start doing it right now!" With a grin creasing his battered face, he pulled the jet-stick all the way back.

Something grabbed hold of Stanley's stomach and twisted, jamming him back against his chair at the same time, holding him there, squeezing all the air from his lungs. Spacemen encountered this sort of thing all the time, he knew, out in the bleak cold vault beyond Earth's atmosphere. But he was no spaceman, and a Sunday game of tennis was enough to give him a worn-out feeling.

O'Hanrohan laughed. "Look at that! Only three G's and they can't match it."

Stanley wanted t. shout encouragement, but he found that his voice couldn't leave the neighborhood of his throat.

"See?" O'Hanrohan continued. "We've left the local level. We're going up in a tight loop. By the time the cops reach express upstairs; we'll be on our way down again. They'll come down, only we'll be on our way up again. When they figure that one out, we'll be halfway to White Sands."

"White Sands?" Stanley managed.

"Yeah, White Sands, New Mexico. If you know what you're talking about, I think I can get us a spaceship there. Well, hold your ribs, sonny—we're going up again!"

Stanley started to hold his ribs, then blacked out. O'Hanrohan's wild laughter ringing in his ears.

"HOW DOES she look?" O'Hanrohan wanted to know. He stood with hands on hips, surveying the space cruiser.

"Isn't it a little small?" Stanley asked.

"Small? Of course it's small. Just a one-man cruiser. Did you think I could borrow a battleship or something? No, there's enough room for me to get inside, and if I can make sense out of your plan, I'll take her up."

"How did you get that ship?"

They had arrived in White Sands not more than six hours ago, Stanley realized. He had arrived with a mean headache, either from his drinking or the excitement, or perhaps a combination of both. O'Hanrohan had left him in a deserted little cabin out on the desert, and Stanley had been asleep almost at once. Now—when he awoke—O'Hanrohan stood outside, admiring his spaceship.

"Well," O'Hanrohan parried, "do I have to answer it?"

"We're going to work together as a team. I suggest that you do."

"Sure. Only—well okay! I know a gal who knows a man who guards a gate. The same old story, Stanley. She paid this man a visit, he got kind of busy. I went in and lifted the ship..."

"You stole it!"

"Hell, did you think the government would give it to me?"

"I thought you knew someone who would."

"I was thinking of this gal all the time. Anyway, important thing is I got us a ship. Now what?"

"I hardly know where to begin," Stanley admitted. "Also, I might as well tell you I'm afraid. Maybe my idea won't work after all."

O'Hanrohan said nothing, but the look he gave Stanley indicated plainly enough that his idea had better work.

"Let's take a look at the war," Stanley said. "At the beginning we almost lost, because the League started everything with a sneak attack. H-bombs and A-bombs—knocking out half our cities. That was five years ago. We countered, made a mess out of their military establishments. Then what happened?"

"Hell, everybody knows that. Roger Marshall invented his force field."

"Yes, the force field. And do you know precisely what a force field is, Mr., O'Hanrohan?"

"Call me Charlie. Yeah, I know. It's something damn strong, and nothing can get through it."

"Nothing?"

"Well, nothing except this here new weapon the League came up with. What are you driving at, Stanley?"

"THE LEAGUE has a new weapon which the force field can't stop. So far, they've only used it on our ships, and the ship force fields have been like so much paper. They haven't used it on Earth yet, because they realize Earth is a ripe plum and they'd like to get this planet untouched—after we're forced to surrender.

"All right so far? Good—now let's get back to the force field. Take atoms, any atoms, and strip away the electrons and protons, the neutrons—strip away all the subatomic particles. What do you have left?"

"Why...nothing!" O'Hanrohan scratched the tattoos atop his shining dome.

"You're wrong. What's left are the interatomic forces, the forces which bind subatomic particles together. Only they don't have to do that job anymore; there are no subatomic particles. Those interatomic forces become a force field! It can withstand anything, even direct H-bomb explosions. Anything, that is, except for the new League weapon. Our scientists call it an impossible weapon, for it behaves the way no weapon should. It goes right through a force field the way a knife goes through melting butter."

O'Hanrohan shook his head. "I know all that. Every time we send a ship into space, they knock it right out, and all the force fields in the universe don't matter. So we're helpless. What I want to know is this: what the hell can you do?"

Stanley smiled. "I think I know what that weapon is. And, if I'm right, I know what can nullify it, only the government won't listen."

"They're a little slow on the uptake, eh?"

"Uh...yes, a little slow on the uptake. I'm a quantum technician, as I told you. I work with light. Do you know what light is, Charlie?"

"Of course I know! Why, light is...umm-mm, light!"

"No one knows for sure. It reveals things to our physical senses, it travels at a speed of 186,000 miles per second in vacuum, somewhat slower in air or water, but not much. That's light, and that's all we know. We're not even sure whether it consists of waves, or particles, or a combination of both. I was fooling around with light, Charlie. That's my job, finding new and better ways to keep the lamps of Earth burning.

"Puttering around, I discovered a method to slow light. To slow it tremendously—all the way down to 10,000 miles per second. It still looks like light, I found—but it doesn't act like light at all. It acts more like a disintegrator. It destroys things, and a force field doesn't stop it! That's the League's new weapon, Charlie—slow light!"

O'Hanrohan looked amazed. "Yeah! Yeah! That's what everyone says. It looks just like a beam of light. So what will you do, speed it up again?"

"Don't know how. Instead, I'll simply use one of light's well-known properties. Come on, we're wasting time. We have to do a lot to this ship of ours."

NOT ONLY was O'Hanrohan a good spaceman, he also was a good mechanic—and something of a shoplifter. He got the supplies Stanley needed, and Stanley no longer bothered to ask him how. And then he set them up following Stanley's instructions. For his own part, Stanley found a book on astrogation and proceeded to study it. He found the subject intensely interesting, and he had time to kill while O'Hanrohan remodeled the ship under his tutelage.

A day came when Stanley felt sure that, if ever the occasion demanded it, he could pilot a spaceship adequately. But then he snorted at his fanciful thoughts. As if such a day would ever come!

He felt restless, nervous—and at first he thought the necessary delay for converting the ship could be blamed. But, as the final hours came, he still felt that way. He got increasingly morose.

Wandering about their little cabin, he found a bottle of O'Hanrohan's cognac, and he proceeded to drink it in a way which would have done the big spaceman proud. On his third drink, he began to think of Lila. On his fourth, he realized he still loved her. He determined to do something about it.

O'Hanrohan was out getting the final material, and Stanley entered the spaceship, sat down at its radio, and twiddled the dials idly. He'd acted like an idiot. Why hold Lila responsible for her father's behavior? Too many friendships had been ruined that way, let alone romances…

When the bottle was empty, he called Lila's home in New York. He got a lot of static at first, but presently Lila's voice followed it into his ears.

"Hello?" Faintly, listlessly.

"Hello. This is Stanley."

"Stanley?"

"Stanley."

"Stanley! Where are you? Where have you been? They gave a description of a man who helped a berserk spaceman escape New York, and—"

"He wasn't berserk."

"He was, according to the reports. Where are you?"

"Lila, I—I was wrong. I shouldn't have argued like that. I still—love—you—"

"Stanley! I love you too. Let's just forget it and start all over. Stanley?"

"What?"

"You don't sound so good, Stanley. Are you ill?"

"No, I've been drinking."

"Don't argue with me, you sound ill. Poor Stanley. Is there anything I can do to help?"

"No. But I'm all ready to try my plan, and I can give you back your ring—after I return, a hero."

"You are ill! Father told me all about this crazy plan of yours. I want to help you, Stanley, don't you see? I know, I can have Father trace this call, and we can come for you—"

"Don't!"

"Father! Father!" He heard her voice calling, muted, as though she had turned away from the radio. The call had been a mistake. He broke the connection, turned away from the radio. O'Hanrohan stood there, regarding him severely.

"I heard that, Stanley. She's going to trace the call. We'll be found before we can try your plan. Of all the dumb—"

Stanley stood up very straight. "No, I admit it, it was a mistake. But it merely means we'll have to work faster. You'll be taking the ship up in a few hours, Charlie, before they can get here."

O'Hanrohan swore under his breath, and they set to work with the final material.

FIRST, HOWEVER, Stanley brewed a pot of strong coffee. He drank it black and scalding and it made him feel better. Hours later, O'Hanrohan stepped back away from the ship. "It looks nuts." He scratched his bald head. "But I guess it's finished."

"Not quite," Stanley told him. "We still have to take out the force field."

"What? I can't go up there without a field. It'd be slaughter."

Stanley removed the tiny power plant, dismantling it carefully and storing the parts in their cabin. "The force field won't do any good against the League's new weapon, anyway. And they'll never get a chance to shoot at you with their more conventional weapons. You'll merely steer the ship into their beam, then desert it in a spacesuit. "

O'Hanrohan cursed softly, "It not only looks nuts, it sounds nuts! Stanley, I don't know why—hey!"

Stanley heard it too. High overhead, a droning. Coming closer every moment. They ran outside the cabin together and looked up into the twilight sky. Two dots.

"Maybe they're going away," Stanley suggested hopefully.

"Don't bet on it, sonny. See, they're circling. And coming down!"

They were, slowly at first—then faster. Soon Stanley could see them quite clearly against the darkening sky, two police fliers.

"They won't fire," O'Hanrohan guessed. "They'll want to get this ship back in one piece. But after they come down they'll use hand guns. If we're not public enemies number one and two, we're damned close, Stanley. You never should've made that radio call!"

"I know it, but that won't help now."

"Listen. I'm going to take that ship up. Five minutes is all I'll need to get her warmed, and you'll have to hold them off till then."

"How?"

"Here, with my blaster."

"I—I can't fire one of those things. I might kill someone!"

"More likely, you might miss. If you could return their fire and pin them down without hitting anyone…"

The planes came closer, their jets quiet as they prepared for landing. Stanley said, "Don't you see? I couldn't do that, but you could! You could pin them down, Charlie."

"Yeah? How would I take the ship up at the same time?"

"You wouldn't. I would."

"You! Very funny."

"I'm not kidding. It's the only way, because if they take us now, we'll never have another chance. I know how to pilot that ship. I think I know how. I read a book—"

"Oh no! Not a book. Tell me anything but that. You read a book!"

"I can do it," Stanley insisted. "We're wasting time. You hold them off till I get up—then surrender. Promise?"

"Yeah, sure. I don't want to kill no one. Hey, wait. Who said anything about letting you—"

BUT STANLEY didn't hear him.

Stanley was running toward the ship, darting and weaving clumsily, for already he imagined that blasters were searing the air behind him, crisping the ground under his flying feet.

Soon he heard a voice behind him, a very commanding voice which cried: "You! Stop—stop or we'll shoot!"

This time it wasn't his imagination. Blasters roared, little puffs of dirt kicked up at his feet. His breath came in sobs, his legs felt numb—and then, somehow, he was within the ship. He slammed the port shut, bolted it, looked for a moment through one of the view domes.

O'Hanrohan was down behind an outcropping of rock, old Wild West fashion, returning blast for blast, keeping the police busy. Good old O'Hanrohan!

Stanley kicked the eye-lever over, heard the atomic engine miss once and then catch on with a loud, steady droning. Dimly, he heard the blasters roaring outside, watched the needle climb slowly from warm to ready to—fire!

He thumbed down the rocket buttons, forgetting to strap himself in. The ship lurched crazily, then left the ground behind it, tugging Stanley's insides and making him scream. The ride in the jet-cab had been a three-G lark. Now he watched the dial climbing: four G's, four and a half, five. His vision blurred, his ears rang, his stomach was impossibly constricted.

Six G's...

Incredibly, it was over. The ship floated serenely in deep space, acceleration concluded. The fact that inertia carried it forward at fifty miles per second did not matter; Stanley felt nothing.

O'Hanrohan had done some checking. There should be a convoy of freighters out of Aukland base, heading for the asteroids. Fine. The League probably would be waiting for it. But, quite suddenly, Stanley felt afraid. He glanced at the planet meter, saw that he was seventy thousand miles up. Behind him in the rearview dome he could see Earth, a great gray-green globe, the pinpoint lights of the force field glowing like an infinity of fireflies. He was in space! In space. He had never been beyond man-made Satellite One before, a mere eight hundred miles up. But seventy thousand!

HE BUSIED himself with the radio-receiver, scrambling the dials the way O'Hanrohan had demonstrated, He listened: "*Silver Star* to *Ceres King*. To *Ceres King*, over."

"*Ceres King*," came another voice. "We haven't spotted anything yet, Mike. But Lord knows the Chief expects it. The League can pop us out of the sky like clay pigeons, any time it wants. I—Mike!"

The other voice again: "Yeah, I see it too. We ought to turn around and run, but we've got to get supplies through—"

Stanley picked up the little pips that were the convoy ships on his radar grid, followed them. He could see them through the fore-dome now, a score of freighters with a small military escort vessel flying each flank. And just ahead of them, not more than a thousand miles—a tiny mote of a League ship, and The Weapon...

It fanned out across the vault of space, probing. A wide beam of radiance, emanating from the League ship, spreading out across the heavens like a wide cone of light. Light—and yet not light. For at its speed of 186,000 miles per second, light seemed instantaneous. But Stanley could watch this beam groping, probing, leaping out across space. Light, slowed to a fraction of its ordinary speed, and behaving impossibly...

Stanley called into his radio: "Ships of the convoy! Convoy, do you hear me?"

A voice, perhaps one of the two he had heard before: "We hear you. What do you want?"

"Keep away from the beam! I think I can stop it."

"Who are you?"

"I—never mind. I can stop it, I said. Just give me five minutes."

He waited, heard nothing. Outside, the ships began to wheel around. But only some of them. Half a dozen either hadn't heard or refused to believe him. Six ships rocketed on toward the beam, trying to avoid it by speed.

The beam swung around, licked out—caught them! They flashed brilliantly for a brief instant, man-made novae. And then they were gone, completely disintegrated. The remaining ships broke their formation, hovered about in chaotic array. The beam swung toward them, knifed through, picked the ships out one by one and destroyed them.

STANLEY had never witnessed such carnage before. And now, with a first-hand view of the League's Weapon, he began to doubt his own theory. What if he were wrong? What if—

That was ridiculous! He'd staked everything on his theory. It had to work! If it didn't, the entire convoy would be destroyed. And Stanley, floating slowly in space in his spacesuit, could be picked off at leisure. Eventually, the entire Earth…

He set the robot controls carefully. His ship would hit the beam of radiance broadside, would plow directly into the brightest part. Stiffly, he rose from the pilot chair, climbed into the unfamiliar bulk of a spacesuit. Without realizing it, he'd swept dangerously close to the beam. He was vaguely aware of two more convoy ships puffing away into nothingness—and then the beam swung toward his own little craft!

He fastened the spacesuit on the run, got into the airlock, then activated his shoulder jets, spinning away from the ship, end over end, because he didn't know how to operate them.

After a time he righted himself, saw his ship a few miles off in space, entering the beam.

He waited breathlessly, hardly daring to blink his eyes for fear he might miss something. The ship disappeared within the beam, then swam into vision again, distorted, puffing—

It exploded!

Wildly, he looked again. He had failed—

No! Something flared brilliantly at the far end of the beam, and in an instant the radiance blinked out. Stanley sighed happily. This was the answer to the League, and it was so ridiculously simple. Sometimes you can nullify a super weapon with a good application of horse-sense…

O'HANROHAN grinned. "Sure, sonny. I held them off, but they were plenty sore afterwards. If the report hadn't come in on what you done—"

"The important thing is that it did come in, my boy." Lila's portly father beamed happily. And Lila squeezed Stanley's hand, flashing her reinstated engagement ring.

Her father said, "You'll have to make a full report to the United Nations, naturally. Want to give me some inside dope beforehand? Just how did that contraption work?"

"Well," Stanley said, "as I explained before, the League's new weapon was light. Just light. The force field couldn't hold it bac.,"

"But how can light destroy—"

"It can. When you slow light down to 10,000 miles per second, it isn't really light any more. It looks like light, but it seems to be concentrated at that slow speed, and it has a new property. It disintegrates."

"That much I know," Lila's father agreed. "But how did you stop it?"

"How would you stop any light? How would you turn light back to where it came from? Or, in this case, how would you make a dangerous weapon do an about-face and destroy the ship that produced it? Simple. O'Hanrohan and I coated the outside of my ship with silver paint, put a layer of plain, ordinary glass over that. See, the force field has no reflective qualities whatever: it absorbs light, as a matter of fact.

"O'Hanrohan and I fixed that up. When the light hit our ship it bounced back and knocked hell out of the ship that beamed it. You can take care of the League's super-weapon any time you want, now. It isn't much good as a weapon when all you need to stop it is a good-sized mirror!"

From Hidden Worlds

This silent watching was worse than open attack. In this war of nerves
who would win: mute aliens or imaginative Earthmen?

JEREMY sipped the drink mostly to taste what it was like,
Foamy McGann, the stewardess, now obliged him with her
company at his table.

But the routine of passenger life aboard the starcoach held
no further fascination for Jeremy. Everyone aboard had his
own particular reason for going to Sosiphon, everyone from
blustering Philip Ackeroyd who was to be the new governor
of Sosiphon Two, down to Jeremy himself, new professor of
extranthropology.

Now he nodded absently as the head waiter handed him a
note.

"A secret love tryst below decks, Professor Jenks?" Foamy
McGann said, smiling. "Honest, you surprise me."

Jeremy became mildly annoyed every time the stewardess
made fun of him. He said, very seriously, "Hardly. You're
the only woman aboard ship I call by her first name."

Foamy was still smiling. "My first name is Leatrice."

"Oh. By her nickname, then."

It turned out to be a note from Bart Dobson, the
astrogator. But Jeremy found none of Dobson's usual
wisecracks concerning Foamy, and he frowned. The note
sounded urgent.

Doc—Come forward. Hurry. Bart—

Jeremy got up. "Excuse me, Foamy. I've got to go
forward shall I order you another drink?"

Foamy stretched, stood up. "Don't bother, Jeremy.
Think I'll dance a round or two with Fred Parker over there."

She gestured to the blond haired young man sitting alone at a nearby table.

Jeremy winced. Why did that always bother him? He had to admit it was Foamy's job, among other things, to dance with the passengers. He also had to admit that Foamy and Fred Parker made a nice couple. Well, five months confined within a ship could do this to a man, and wait until he got his hands on some of those artifacts of the Sosiphonic subculture…

He shrugged, watched for a moment as Foamy reached the other table and sat down, then remembered Bart's note and hustled on forward.

He shrugged impatiently at the door, repeated his name three times before he got any response.

Then: "Oh, Doc." The voice sounded relieved. "Come on in."

Jeremy heard the buzzer which activated the lock, and in a moment he stood inside the control room.

Bart Dobson sat facing the controls, his back to Jeremy. Jack Cranshaw, the second astrogator, lay sprawled on a cot, a half-empty bottle of whiskey in his hand. "Have a snort," he suggested, rocking back and forth slightly.

"He shouldn't—" Jeremy began.

"Take it easy, Doc," Dobson said. "I've been tempted sure as hell myself, because then I could sit back in a fog and let whatever's going to happen, happen."

"What's that?"

"I dunno. I just know what's going to make things happen. Come here."

Jeremy started to advance and Cranshaw reached up from his cot clumsily. As Jeremy sidestepped, the bottle of whiskey fell, spilling all over the floor.

"Now look what you done, Doc," Cranshaw mumbled thickly. "You shoulda stuck to exnathro-up— Aw, g'way…"

"…over here, Doc," Dobson was saying. "The foreport."

Jeremy looked. "What am I supposed to see? We appear to be on course. We're skirting the Sagittarian cloud now, heading across the front of the dark Ophiuchus nebula, and then on to Sosiphos. Right?"

"Yeah," Dobson agreed. "But look a little closer at the Ophiuchus baby. Yeah, the middle. What do you see?"

"Hmm," Jeremy stared. "A tiny point of light. It looks like it might be a star."

"It's not," said Dobson. "There isn't any window in the Ophiuchus nebula, Doc. You know—just a dark mess of gas and cosmic dust, a door to the center of the Galaxy through which we ain't allowed to look."

THAT was true. Here at the fringes of the Sagittarian swarm and Ophiuchus lay Sosiphos, Earth's outpost on the frontier of the unknown. Beyond Sagittarius and Ophiuchus was the heart of the Galaxy, curtained by the swarm and by the nebula, unplumbed by man.

"All right," Jeremy nodded. "It's not a star. What is it?" Oddly—he did not know why—he was frightened. "'Sashipt'" Cranshaw cried. "'Saship, that's what it is!'"

"What did he say?" Jeremy demanded.

For answer, Dobson swung a scope over the foreport. "We first saw it six hours ago, and now it's coming closer. Take a look."

Jeremy peered within the scope, swung it across the great blackness of Ophiuchus.

"You see it, Doc? You see it?"

He did. It was not very big and it was round, utterly round, gleaming against the darkness. About its equator was a string of tiny circles, brighter than the rest, and even as he looked it grew appreciably in the scope.

"'Saship!'" Cranshaw cried, stupidly, and suddenly the thick strung-together words took on meaning for Jeremy.

"Yes," Dobson said, "it's a ship. Where no ship can be, Doc…" Dobson licked his dry lips. "Only it's round. No Earth ship is round, Doc. They're all built tapering, like this one. So—that thing out there isn't an Earth ship. It's from someplace else. It's not from this side of Sagittarius and Ophiuchus…"

He was trembling now as he continued: "I shut the radio both ways; we'll speak neither to Earth nor to Sosiphon, and we won't get anything in from them."

"Why did you do that?" Jeremy turned away from the scope.

Dobson sighed. "Take a look at this—the official history of space travel, Eddson's *An Account of Man's First Five Hundred Years in Space.* I know the book well, practically rave it memorized. The officials of Milky Way Starcoach see to that. We got no choice. We have to know this book backwards and forwards, especially the last chapter. Here—" Dobson reached into his breast pocket, dug out a much dog-eared, paperbound volume. "I've been reading it in my spare time, brushing up so I could pass the periodic written test when I get back to Earth. Only now it doesn't matter. I won't get back to Earth, won't even reach Sosiphon. Read the last part, Doc."

Jeremy read. By the fifth page he could imagine why Cranshaw was drunk, why Dobson brooded, by the tenth something was gnawing restlessly at his insides. He forgot all about Sosiphon Two and its University. By the end of the chapter he had even forgotten Dobson. He just sat there, staring straight ahead at the bright spot, which could not be in Ophiuchus and yet was, which now showed a tiny disc even without the scope.

"'Saship!'" said Cranshaw.

"FIRST," DOBSON told Jeremy, "we'll have to stop our flight, right now. Like this." He stood up and adjusted some dials on the wall. When he returned to his seat he was smiling grimly.

Jeremy said, "Why did we have to stop?"

"Use your head, Doc. We can't go on to Sosiphon. That alien ship might follow, might learn the location of Earth's colony. That might lead, ultimately, to the discovery of Earth's whole far-flung star-system. We can't high-tail it back to Earth for the same reason. Ditto, we can't change course and head for any of the other colonies."

"Umm, " Jeremy considered. "Yes. There are two hundred billion stars, more or less, in the Galaxy. Perhaps one out of three has planets. Of those, maybe one out of a hundred can support life. Not many, but it still leaves millions in the Galaxy."

Dobson nodded. "That's it exactly, Doc. If we don't head for any of the Earth planets, that alien culture might go another thousand years without finding them. It might go forever, which is what Earth Government wants. There's no telling if they'll be friendly or hostile. So—"

"Yes," Jeremy mused. "And what can an unarmed passenger ship like this one do?"

"We have one gun up front," Dobson told him. "Just a small job, but it's pretty deadly at close range."

Jeremy nodded, looked again through the foreport, saw the spherical ship hovering off in the void, the size of a kid's marble held at arm's length. "It looks like they had the same idea," he observed.

Dobson scratched his head. "What do you mean?"

"'They've stopped, too. They're waiting for us to make the first move."

"Nuts, Doc. I won't do anything until they—"

"Exactly. Nor will they. So we'll just sit back and relax, thanking our lucky stars this ship is a damned good balanced terrarium. Then we'll see."

"You hope," Dobson told him. "We might not get a chance to see anything. How do you know they ain't armed to the teeth?"

"I don't, but if they are, they've already had enough time to knock us out of space."

"Nope. Not necessarily so, Doc. Maybe they think we can lead them to the home planet, to Earth. Think of that. What the hell's one stinking ship when you come busting through a dark nebula to a new half of the Galaxy?"

JEREMY stood up and paced back and forth for a time. But the foreport drew his gaze like a magnet, and soon he stood in front of it, eyes riveted on the tiny mib of a spaceship hovering not too far off in the void. "All right, we have several alternatives," Jeremy said. "We can shoot right on to Sosiphon, we can return to Earth, or we can go on to one of the other colonies. But all three are out."

"Damn right. First place, there's an old law against it if we're found out, meant for the old military ships and punishable by death. I, guess that means we run away. We just keep on going until—"

Jeremy shook his head. "That's silly. This starcoach is no speed demon. They could run rings around us. But we could radio for help."

"Can't do that, Doc. It's against the old laws, too. They might be able to get a directional beam on our space radio. Then they'd know Sosiphon's location as sure as if we led them there. So—so maybe we oughta unload our pea-shooter and try to blast them. Maybe..."

Jeremy didn't even ponder over this one. He said, "One little gun? It would be pointless, because we'll have to assume they have more until we know better. We'll just have to stay put, right here, gawking out the port and watching them—God knows how long—until something happens."

"So what happens then, Doc? A day passes, a week, and they don't do anything. We can't just stay here."

Jeremy chuckled softly. "I wasn't thinking in terms of days or weeks at all."

"Oh, you mean just a couple of hours?"

"No. I was thinking in terms of months or years, all the rest of our lives, perhaps. I don't know that there's anything else we can do except stay right here. Maybe forever."

Jeremy felt strange saying it. That amounted to an exile in space, confined within the walls of the starcoach, cramped, unmoving, fed and given air by the hydroponic units arearships. It meant never setting foot on Earth again, not seeing the sun, not hearing the hundred little Earth sounds which you take so much for granted...

Dobson seemed a bit dazed. "I tell you what, Doc. Let me think. I can't answer that now. Just give me a chance to figure things out for a while. Meanwhile, we'll do as you say. We won't move, not an inch. We'll just sit on a bunch of nothing out here and watch that alien ship.

"But do me a favor? Don't tell anyone. I'll close the observation dome...for repairs...notify the passengers of a minor breakdown which'll delay us for a while. That's why we're not moving, see? But don't let the cat out of the bag, Doc."

Jeremy nodded, shook hands solemnly, got up and left the control room.

WHEN HE reached the dining room, he smiled. He'd better learn how to dance that Galaxy Special, he might spend all the rest of his life here on the starcoach. Foamy McGann, of course, could be a more than pleasant diversion, provided

Fred Parker didn't turn her head permanently in some other direction.

He found the two of them dancing, and suddenly he was doing something he had never done before in his life. He stepped up boldly behind Parker, tapped one of the broad shoulders. "I'd like to finish this dance with Miss McGann," he said.

"Miss—oh, Foamy! Sure, Prof, if it's okay with the lady, it's fine with me."

"Fine!" Foamy scolded him in mock severity. "I thought you said you liked dancing with me, Fred."

And then Jeremy took the girl in his arms and watched Parker drift away to one of the tables. They danced. Foamy's head nestling very close to his own. About the only thing Jeremy could find wrong with the dance was the fact that it did not last long enough. Suddenly, with no warning at all, the music stopped, and Jeremy found himself holding Foamy against his chest, not dancing.

She smiled, said, "Wake up, Jeremy. There's no more music, so won't you let me out of this bear-hug like a nice professor?"

Jeremy reddened and let her go. Then he was aware of a voice, metallic, coming from the loudspeaker. "This is Astrogator Dobson," the voice said. "We have stopped our flight three weeks out from the Sosiphon System. We are now drifting slightly, midway between the Swarm and the Ophiuchus Nebula."

Jeremy was aware of a rustling buzz of conversation all about him; it definitely was not ordinary for a starcoach to stop in mid-flight. Milky Way's ships were slow enough as it was, and this would only be an unnecessary delay.

Nearby, Jeremy heard Philip Ackeroyd, the new Earth governor for Sosiphon Two, talking to his wife. "Don't worry, my dear. It can be nothing serious. But still, they have a hell of a nerve stopping in mid-space like this. I'll be late for taking office..."

Dobson's metallic voice again: "Technical difficulties make it impossible for anyone to enter the observation dome until further notice. Radio communication to or from Earth, Sosiphon or any of the colonies is impossible. You will be notified further..."

Jeremy wondered if Bart Dobson had gone too far. The rustling buzz became an angry buzz, and he could hear Philip Ackeroyd's booming voice in particular. "...gal, that's what! I don't know what game this Dobson thinks he's playing, my dear, but I sure as hell intend to find out..."

Again, Dobson: "Passengers are to be confined to their staterooms, the library, the dining room and the recreation hall until further notice. That is all..."

"Confined, my foot!" Ackeroyd cried. "Confined to my quarters, to the library—"

Fred Parker grinned. "Whatsamatter, Governor? Don't you read?"

Ackeroyd ignored him. "My dear, if you will excuse me, I'm going forward right now."

HE GOT up and waddled toward the doorway, a little fat man with a booming voice. Foamy told Jeremy, "I don't know what this is all about, and I have a hunch you do, but never mind. Excuse me!"

In a moment she stood, arms akimbo, between Ackeroyd and the doorway which led forward. "It won't even take a minute, Mr. Ackeroyd," she said. "In fact, it will take no time at all, because you're not going. You've heard the orders, sir."

"Orders!" His face got very red. "Of course you're joking, Miss McGann. No one on this ship can order me around."

Foamy stood her ground, said nothing. The fat figure advanced until less than an arm's length separated them, and then Foamy spoke: "The only way you can get through that door, Mr. Ackeroyd, is if you hit a woman. Now, do you go back to your table while I lock this door, or...?"

Everyone was very quiet, and Jeremy knew that any authority that the ship's officers had would depend pretty much on what happened here. If Ackeroyd got his way, authority would be a hollow word with no meaning, and they couldn't afford anarchy now. The same would be true if anyone came to Foamy's aid; she must do this thing herself.

A chair scraped against the floor, and in the silence which followed, Ackeroyd's booming voice seemed to emerge from an amplifier.

"I've had enough, Miss McGann. Too much. Just get out of my way, young lady—or I'll push you right on ahead of me!"

Jeremy watched as Foamy leaned forward. She spoke earnestly, in a low voice, and only Ackeroyd could hear her. When she finished, the fat man stalked back to his table. Foamy turned, reached into a pocket of her blouse, came up with a key, swung the big door shut and locked it. She put the key back into her pocket and began to whistle. By the time she reached Jeremy's table, everyone was talking again, and there was enough laughter in the room to convince Jeremy that the first crisis had been met successfully.

FOAMY sat down. "Okay, Jeremy. Now, talk. What's going on?"

Jeremy shook his head. "Sorry, Foamy, I can't. Dobson may want to tell you, but that's up to him. I can't say a word. But you can tell me this; what made Philip Ackeroyd—"

"Ha—that was easy. This morning I met our governor friend in the corridor and he made a pass at me."

"He what?" Fred Parker demanded, sitting down.

"He made a pass at me. You know, got fresh. I slapped his face and he went away. It was the third time."

Parker chortled, and then he banged his hand down on the table. "That's rich, really rich. That little fat guy, and a governor no less. Tell me, Foamy, does Doc here make passes too?"

"Umm, no. Jeremy's a perfect gentleman. Really."

Jeremy frowned. He was definitely not happy because she considered him a perfect gentleman.

"Anyway," Foamy said, "I just told Mr. Ackeroyd this: He could walk right by me and I wouldn't try to stop him, not even slap him like I did when he made that third pass at me. I'd just go to Mrs. Ackeroyd and whisper something in her ear."

Parker slapped the girl's back, not ungently. "Well, I guess that settles his hash, all right. But now, how about Doc here? He knows something and he doesn't want to tell, and I think, even Mrs. Philip Ackeroyd, who isn't a genius, must know this breakdown of the ship is a bit on the phony side. Okay, Jeremy m'boy, spill it."

Jeremy shook his head again. "You're acting foolish, because if I won't tell Foamy, I won't tell you. Why don't you act like an ordinary passenger?" Jeremy winked at Foamy and found the startled look she gave him decidedly pleasing. "Well," said Jeremy, stretching, "it's been a long day. I think I'll turn in."

"Sure you wouldn't be going forward, Jeremy?" Parker wanted to know.

Jeremy gave him an acid look. "You figure it out. Only the door leading arearships is open. To go forward I'd either have to walk through metal or get the key by reaching into Foamy's blouse pocket and—"

Foamy's blouse swelled prettily with Foamy's firm, youthful flesh. "Good night, Jeremy," she said. "Definitely, good night."

Jeremy got up and started to leave, but he heard the sound of a key being inserted into a lock. Everyone in the room was suddenly very still, and he heard the tumblers fall. The door which Foamy had locked swung in.

JACK CRANSHAW entered the dining room, not as drunk as Jeremy had seen him before, but still drunk enough to cause trouble. "Hi, Foamy," he called out. "How's the girl?"

"I'm fine," Foamy told him. "Only I think it would be a lot better if the passengers didn't see you this way. Won't you get back inside like a nice guy?"

Poor Foamy, Jeremy thought. Lately, her job seemed to consist of keeping people in or out of the dining room.

"See that?" Philip Ackeroyd asked his wife. "We're in some kind of trouble. I was right. I demand to know what's going on, Mr. Cranshaw, if you can talk."

"Oh. Hi, Mr. Ackeroyd. No need to go off half-cocked, please sir. I ain't drunk. I woulda been, only some stinker spilled all my liquor... I just sat there with Bart, watching the thing. It drifted real close, real close. Now we're hanging two, three miles apart, and I can see all those little portholes in its belly, like a couple of dozen angry eyes. Nope. I don't want to go back and watch it."

"Shut up!" Foamy said, and she ran around behind the unsteady Cranshaw, circled his neck with one lithe movement of her arm, cupped her hand tightly over his mouth.

"No! " Ackeroyd blustered. "Let him talk! They say stay put and we stay put. Well, I'm the new governor of Sosiphon Two, and I want to know what's going on. I insist."

"He insists," Foamy said, letting go of Cranshaw and barring the door with her body. The action had gone to

Cranshaw's head now, and he fell down. He tried to get up, but he lay there, flopping about, mumbling under his breath.

"Yes. I insist," Ackeroyd repeated. "Now then, Miss McGann—will you make way for your governor?"

The stewardess stood her ground. "You don't govern this ship, Mr. Ackeroyd. I take my orders from Astrogator Dobson, and he said no one was to go forward. So, no one goes."

Someone said, "I think Governor Ackeroyd is right. They're keeping us in the dark about something, and if it's dangerous, we have a right to know. I'm with you, Governor!"

"You're damned right!" a man from across the room agreed. "This is the twenty-sixth century...we're all enlightened. Just who does this Astrogator Dobson think he is, anyway?"

Foamy seemed small standing there, just a pretty girl in trouble. People began to converge on the door, but Jeremy reached it first, and Parker was right behind him.

"I thought—" Foamy began.

"Baby," Parker smiled, "if there's any trouble, we're with you."

ACKEROYD turned his attention to Jeremy. "Out of my way, Professor Jenks. I mean it. There'll be trouble if you try to stop me."

The first sound to come from Jeremy's mouth was a dry clucking, and he could feel his heart, beating heavily against his ribs, but then he said: "Please keep back. I—I don't want to fight with you—"

After that, Jeremy didn't know quite how it started but Ackeroyd pushed him and he stumbled half way through the open door. He pushed back and Ackeroyd hit him. It wasn't a hard blow, but it caught him across the bridge of his nose and brought tears to his eyes. He hit back, awkwardly, and he heard a lot of air *woosh* out of the fat man's stomach, and then Ackeroyd was clutching him in a two-hundred-pound bear hug.

Dimly, he was aware of the fighting all about him—Fred Parker striking out with iron fists in all directions, Foamy darting in and out, hitting with her fists and clawing with her nails, trying to divert some of the men from Parker.

Jeremy felt himself borne back by Ackeroyd's ponderous bulk, and soon he was grappling with the fat man in the corridor. He hit the floor with a jarring impact, Ackeroyd on top of him. He writhed, and they rolled over and over down the corridor. Overhead, he could see feet flashing by, heading foward, and one pair of feminine legs kicking furiously, borne aloft. Someone had lifted Foamy bodily and was carrying her toward the control room.

Her voice faded down the corridor. "Put me down, you oaf! Just put me down and I'll break your neck. I'll tear you apart, one little piece at a time, but me down! If I were a man... *Ohh!*"

Ackeroyd lay back, panting, and Jeremy stood up. "They're all...inside," he said. "I—think we ought—to—follow—damn you..." He couldn't quite catch his breath. His legs were trembling.

Nearby, Parker propped his head up on an elbow.

"There's a discoloration about your eye," Jeremy informed him, almost cheerfully. "You'll find it difficult to be romantic with Foamy."

Parker snorted. "You should see yourself. Both eyes, Doc. You'll never teach extranthropology this way, Jenks, the terror. Your students will, quake every time you come near. Hey! There goes Ackeroyd—"

Together, they got up and ran down the companionway, and when Jeremy entered the control room the twenty-sixth century took a quick nose-dive—and plummeted down the long channels of culture, plunking down soundly in some prehistoric age where men wore skins, scratched lice out of each other's hair, and wooed their females with gnarled clubs.

WITHIN the control room Jeremy stood and looked about him, and his mind right then could only function in one way—it was just like a showcase lecture in extranthropology. He could see exactly what the lecture notes would look like.

One. Jack Cranshaw was dead. The assistant astrogator had probably staggered back to the control room to help Dobson, and someone had bashed in the side of his head with a blunt instrument.

Two. Three or four men and two women—including Foamy—sat around the room, dazed, with blood on their faces.

Three. Off in the foreport, the alien ship seemed the size of the full moon, with an ominous string of portholes around its fat belly. Waiting. Maybe watching.

Four. Someone kneeled near Jack Cranshaw, muttering. The muttering turned to babbling, and then he began to cry. The someone was Bart Dobson.

Five. Philip Ackeroyd stood at the radio, barking into it: "…of course I'm not drunk. I'm the governor, man. Yes, Ackeroyd. Yes, a ship, not an Earth ship. There's a mess here. Trouble. I tried to stop them, but when they saw it they ran wild, killed one of the astrogators, name of Cranway or Cranshaw, I think. What shall we do?"

Jeremy heard the answering voice: "Nothing. Don't do a thing. We'll contact the nearest patrol ship, but it won't reach you inside of a month. Just stay put. Don't move. Don't get hostile with the foreign ship. Don't move until the patrol comes."

Ackeroyd spluttered, "That's ridiculous, man! Who am I talking with, anyway?"

"Captain Sprague, Earth Military on Sosiphon Two. And don't tell me it's ridiculous. I don't care if you're the president of the Galactic Federation. That's what you do, understand? You stay put."

"Young man, you won't be a captain when I finish with you. I say this ship heads for Sosiphon Two and lands there. We're not going to be sitting ducks for your aliens, you can bet your life on that…"

Jeremy watched Dobson take one more look at the dead second astrogator, then stand up, shaking, and walk to the radio.

"Astrogator Dobson speaking," he said.

"Hello," the radio snapped back. "This is Dutch Sprague. You remember me, back on Sirius five years ago? Lieutenant in the navy then."

"I…remember. They murdered him, Sprague—for no reason at all."

"Who murdered whom?"

"Passengers. Ackeroyd instigated—"

"That's a lie!" boomed Ackeroyd. "The dead man attacked us first."

"They murdered him," Dobson said. "Killed—him—in cold-blood."

"Dobson? You all right?" Sprague's voice was anxious.

"Yes…no-o." Jeremy saw Dobson clutch his side in pain, stagger away from the radio. He dragged himself forward, spoke again: "They gave me—a pretty thorough-going over, Sprague. Internal injuries—I think. Feel lousy, but—awaiting your—orders."

"I gave them to Ackeroyd, Dobson. Did you hear? Dobson? *Dobson!*"

DOBSON didn't hear a thing. He crumpled to the floor suddenly, like a sack filled at top and bottom, with nothing to support its middle.

Foamy ran to him and ripped open his shirt. Jeremy, still standing on the brink of the room, not knowing quite what to do, almost afraid to plunge in lest he somehow become part of the carnage, looked. Dobson's abdomen seemed bloated, distorted, blue. From this distance Jeremy could detect no heartbeat. But Dobson's lips were flecked with a deep red.

Foamy stood up, stiffly. "He's dead," she said. She put a hand on Philip Ackeroyd's shoulder, spun him about. "He's dead," she said again.

Her palm struck his face, hard. Then she pulled it back and struck again, with both hands, hard, stinging blows. Ackeroyd grabbed her wrists, held her.

"Little minx! I could—"

Jeremy ran into the room. He couldn't walk. If he walked he'd have time to see the people with their hurt, bleeding faces, to see Cranshaw, dead, his skull bashed in, to see the dead Bart Dobson with his bloated torso. He remembered something someone had told him once. The harder you ball your fist, the harder you can hit. And don't push. Snap your blow.

Splat! Jeremy felt his knuckles crunch against the weak chin, Ackeroyd sighed once, fell on his back, lay still. Jeremy turned to Foamy, but she was busy with the radio.

"...Leatrice McGann, stewardess aboard the starcoach. Yes, both astrogators are dead. When we reach Sosiphon, I'd like to have a civil court—"

"Certainly, Miss McGann," Sprague's voice answered her.

"For, now, can I lock them up? Just half a dozen, Ackeroyd and some of the passengers. I can see why this Ackeroyd is a politician. He had them half-crazy with a couple of words."

Silence. Then: "Umm, no. Afraid not. Not on my authority. I can give myself just so much rope, Miss McGann. How do I know what really happened until there's an investigation? No, you can't lock them up. Now, who's left on your crew?"

"Just two of us," said Foamy. "There's old Hank Cobb in the hydroponics room. Past eighty. And there's me. That's all. I suppose you'll want me to be in charge, Captain. Well, I suppose I can try. I suppose—"

"Please, Miss McGann. Stop supposing and let me talk." Captain Sprague's voice sounded very tired. "I don't know what's going on there. All I have is an unofficial report of two murders, an unofficial report of an alien ship. I'll radio the patrol. In a month—"

"A month! Captain Sprague, I've got a bunch of scared, angry people on my hands! These aliens could be deadly, and—"

"I can't help it, Miss McGann. The nearest patrol ship according to my charts is about a month away, further than Sosiphon itself. And you haven't got a bunch of any kind of people on your hands, Miss McGann. I'm sorry, but I can't authorize you to govern the ship. You figure it out—a twenty-one year old girl—you just wouldn't command respect.

"I've checked your passenger lists with Milky Way's office here on Sosiphon Two, and the only man on your ship qualified to take charge of things is Governor Ackeroyd. So Miss McGann, while I don't want to seem arbitrary, you are to take your orders from Ackeroyd. Finally, do not use your radio. Hostile aliens might be able to put a directional beam on it. Anyway, Ackeroyd will tell you what to do." After that, the radio was silent.

So was Foamy.

ACKEROYD stood up, rubbed his chin ruefully. "Captain Sprague says we stay right here. All right, we stay. But we have two things to do. First, there are the dead men. We'll jettison their bodies into space, and—"

"Nuts," said Foamy. "They might be picked up by the alien ship. That might help them find Earth or its colonies."

"How, Miss McGann?" Ackeroyd was contemptuous. "You're talking like a frightened little girl. You want me to keep them here instead?"

Jeremy strode forward. "I'd say Foamy's right. Only—"

"Only," Fred Parker finished for him, "friend Ackeroyd's running this show, eh Doc?"

Ackeroyd's voice mocked them: "Well, gentlemen, thank you for your faith in me. I say further that anyone who doesn't cooperate with the decisions we're about to reach should be forcibly detained. So, first we jettison the bodies. I won't have them here on the ship—"

"Naturally," Foamy told him. "They'll only remind you you're responsible."

He ignored her. "Second, any trouble starters must be confined. By force, if necessary. Tomkins, Wilson—you'll act as the military."

Foamy knew the passenger list by heart. "Those two?" she said. "A cheap gambler and a night club bouncer!"

"Your first job," Ackeroyd told the two grinning men, "is to see that Miss McGann is confined to her quarters, permanently. As of now."

Tomkins chortled. "A pleasure. Come on, Foamy—"

She backed away from him slowly. "Keep away. No one's going to be locked up. Stay back or—" Tomkins came forward.

"Ooh, how I wish I were a man! I'd ram that stupid smile right down your throat. I'd—"

NOW, JEREMY knew, was the time to take sides. But if he tried to help the girl he'd probably wind up being confined, too. Since that wouldn't do any good, he'd have to wait.

Fred Parker took his stand. He edged close to Foamy and said, "You'll have to take me, too, if you take her. I won't stand here and—"

Ackeroyd shrugged, "It's just as well, Mr. Parker, to know what side you're on, don't you think? Anyone else? How about you, Professor Jenks?"

Jeremy said, "Don't look at me. I've had enough fighting for one day, thanks."

"Sensible. Sensible. Then that's the way we line up," said the governor. "Everyone on one side—the side of the law. Miss McGann and Mr. Parker on the other. Take them, gentlemen."

Jeremy met Foamy's eyes for an instant, and he turned away. If ever he saw contempt, loathing...

The fight was brief. Wilson soon had Foamy draped across one shoulder, writhing and kicking furiously. Tompkins' right hand lashed out and chopped across Parker's jaw, and as the blond man stumbled he was spun around, his left arm grabbed and forced up and in toward his body. Parker gritted his teeth and relaxed, deciding wisely, Jeremy realized, against a broken arm.

Philip Ackeroyd beamed upon his two henchmen. "The library will be as good a place as any. Keep them together there, locked up." He groped about the instrument shelf, came up with what he wanted, threw a ring of keys to Tompkins.

The bouncer and the gambler walked their two prisoners out of the control room.

Often in the days that followed Jeremy watched the passengers gather in the observation dome to look at the alien craft. Before long it became a game: You wagered what you thought the aliens would look like, or you bet a considerable sum on whether the aliens would be seen or not, or you wagered you would reach Sosiphon Two in time to celebrate Christmas.

Two or three times Jeremy tried to learn about Foamy and Fred Parker, but he'd only get routine answers to his questions. Yes, they were still in the library, and yes, they were being fed twice daily, and yessiree, Doc, I wouldn't mind being in that Parker's place, locked up with a gorgeous dish like that…

Jeremy blushed furiously, felt frustrated, and stopped asking questions.

NIGHT IN Jeremy's cabin. Someone prodded his shoulder, said: "Professor Jenks! Professor, get up."

He sat up and rubbed sleep from his eyes. "What time is it? Why'd you get me up in the middle of the night?"

"Three ayem, Professor Jenks. Governor Ackeroyd's orders—he wants you in control immediately."

Jeremy was annoyed. "Can I at least get out of my pajamas?"

"Nope. Governor says to hurry. Just hop into a robe and let's go."

Their shadows lengthened, then disappeared, then shot out ahead of them again under the green night lights in the corridor. Half a dozen people stood in the control room, close to the inner airlock door. There was Philip Ackeroyd, his wife, the tall gambler Wilson, others.

Ackeroyd said, "It's about time. I thought it would take you all night."

Jeremy ignored the remark. "What's the matter?" he said. "Why'd you call me?"

"Come over here and take a look, Jenks. Bet you never saw anything like this before."

Jeremy looked. He hadn't. "Where—what—?"

"Hah! Thought that'd get a rise out of you. Know where they're from, Jenks?"

"Of course I know. From the other ship. What I want to know is this: How'd you get them?"

"What do you think? We didn't kidnap them across a couple of miles of space, that's for sure. They just came. Must have been shot out of the other ship's lock with considerable force, got past it's gravity, were attracted here. A few men went hullside in space-suits and got these...things."

Things was right. Jeremy guessed each one to be about eight or nine feet long from the pointy top of the cranium down to the incredibly tiny feet. He wondered if bilateral symmetry might be a clue to intelligence. Men with their two arms and two legs located at opposite sides of the body, with their two lungs and two sets of bones, one the mirror image of the other, were symmetrical bilaterally. And now these things followed the same pattern. They didn't llok like men, not really; they had one pair of forelimbs too many, and both the arms and legs had not one, but two working joints above the wrist. They had no fingers to speak of, merely a set of four opposed fleshy hooks lined up two and two.

STILL, THE pattern existed. The creatures could have been symmetrical radially, or they might not have been symmetrical at all. But men and the green things of the other ship could be cut expertly down the middle with a huge pair of shears, and each half would be a mirror image for the other.

Ackeroyd shook Jeremy from his reverie. "Snap out of it, man! I figured you knew about things like this so I wanted to see you, but I didn't expect you to go into a blue funk about it." He frowned. "What I want to know is this: What kind of weapons do you think they have?"

Jeremy stood up from the green things. "How should I know?"

"Well, I can make some guesses myself, Jenks, but I want to see what an authority has to say."

"Not a thing, but thanks for the compliment. I can only think in terms of the sub-cultures, and I know, for example, that a radially symmetrical creature might have some form of sling-shot, say, instead of a bow and arrow. Necessity's the mother of invention, you know. You couldn't imagine how a radial creature could manipulate a bow that requires two arms, which can oppose—"

"Yes, yes," Ackeroyd cut him short. "Very interesting. But I want to know about these green things."

"Well, I can't say much. They're extremely similar to man—"

"You're crazy, Jenks! Four arms, a couple of hooks on each one, ears like mushrooms. They look like us, you say?"

"Yes, in a very general way. I'd say that the physical pattern in each case is the same, also the mental and emotional development."

"How do you figure that?"

"Well, we each have interstellar travel—so that sets a cultural level below which the aliens couldn't fall. Emotional, well—we're lingering here, daring not to move, not knowing what to do. Aren't they doing the same thing? Aren't they afraid, too?" He paused, cleared his throat. "I'd say all this puts them on pretty much the same level as it puts us. So, if I can say anything at all about their weapons, it would be this: Probably they're like ours."

"Ridiculous!" Ackeroyd stormed. "Look at those things. One has its head stoved in, like with a blunt instrument; the other two obviously were stabbed. Here's the way I say it shapes up, Jenks. We threw two dead men out in space, remember? So, they found the bodies. Apparently they thought it was an overture of some sort, and they were afraid. They felt the safest thing to do would be to reciprocate—so they sent us three of their kind, not to be outdone. Of course, they killed them by the most readily available methods, proving how primitive their military power is.

"So—I think we can blast them out of space and get the hell away from here It'll be a cinch, too!"

JEREMY SMILED. "Go ahead and think so. I don't think I could talk you out of it even if I wanted to." He intended that statement to cut deep. He had to prove Ackeroyd wrong. If he didn't, the governor might well decide to blast away at the alien ship with their little pea-shooter. The results could be disastrous.

"Bah!" stormed the governor. "Stupid pedant! Let's see what the rest of them think, Ursula?"

The woman had a squeaky voice which reminded Jeremy oddly of chalk scraping on a blackboard. "If you say it's true, dear, then it must be."

"Wilson?" Ackeroyd demanded. "Tompkins?"

"I don't know," said the gambler, and the bouncer shook his head too.

"Dr. Henderson?"

The gray-haired man frowned. "You just asked me in here to see if these…creatures were dead. They're dead."

"Entwhistle?"

"A guess. It's a good guess. That's all I know."

Jeremy could tell that none of the answers pleased the governor of Sosiphon Two. Jeremy spread his hands out wide, "Now what?"

"Okay, wise guy. What's your theory?"

Jeremy spoke slowly. "I've tried to show how these green things seem to parallel man in development. Right? Now, let's go a step further. Let's assume that big globe out there is a passenger ship, just like this starcoach. Just like we didn't, they didn't know what to do either. It worried them as much as it did us, way out here, half way across the Galaxy, on the fringe of the unknown. We had a fight, a panic, a riot. Two men were killed—"

"Their own faults!"

"I'm not arguing that now. Point is, two men were killed. How were they killed?"

"Beaten, that's how."

"Right. Just fists and blunt instruments, not even a knife. If the aliens found our two men, and if they followed your way of thinking, they'd say we were so primitive we didn't even know how to use knives..."

"Okay. What are you driving at? Damned if I can see the connection."

"Wait, I do," Dr. Henderson said. "You're saying, Professor Jenks, that very much the same thing happened on their ship as happened on ours. Panic, riot, and three men— uh, *things*—got killed. Someone decided to jettison the bodies—we found them—"

Jeremy nodded, earnestly. "Right all the way, doctor. So we just don't have any indication of what weapons we might expect the green things to have. But everything points to a culture similar to ours."

Ackeroyd was grumbling now, unable to argue with the sound logic, but Dr. Henderson smiled. "Brilliant, professor. I see it now—brilliant logic. I'll have to agree with you. I can't recommend that we fire on that ship."

Ackeroyd said, "That's all well and good, gentlemen. A lot of pretty theories. But I'm damned if I want to stay out in space like this a month and wait for a patrol cruiser, which *may* get here. When morning comes I'm going to find a passenger who knows how to use that gun and then we blast your sphere full of green things to hell and back. Understand?"

THE LITTLE meeting in the control room broke up soon after the governor's decision, and Jeremy waited until everyone left. Then he padded silently down the corridor in his slippers. Past several colored doors his way led him, and soon he reached the dining room. Within, Tompkins and Wilson, the bouncer and the gambler, were busy with their belated nightcaps.

"Hi," Jeremy said. "Mind if I join you?"

They looked at him queerly, and Tompkins snorted, "Don't tell me you drink, Doc?"

"I—uh—imbibe."

"Ha-ha. You hear that, Wilson? He imbibes. Okay, Doc, come in and imbibe with us."

Jeremy reached into the pocket of his robe and withdrew a bar of vitamin B concentrate. Since the appearance of the round ship, he had always carried a quantity of these bars with him. He knew from past experience that he often forgot to eat in a tense situation, and the concentrate would guarantee him a good supply of energy. But now he smiled. He'd use his vitamin B for a different purpose entirely: It would prevent the alcohol's toxic effects. He felt almost chipper as he munched his bar.

The first three rounds were hundred-proof stuff, a synthesized copy of what the Fomalhaut sub-culture called *askara*. Jeremy didn't bat an eyelash as he drank.

"Can you beat that!" Tompkins roared. "Old Doc's all right. What'll it be next, Doc? You just name it."

"Well," Jeremy said, "I've always meant to try Capellan brandy. The natives call it *smurth*, I think."

Wilson frowned. "That stuff's strictly one to a customer." But he got down the bottle.

It was the color of blood and the first *smurth* hit Jeremy a lot like liquid fire, making him gag. Two *smurths* later, Jeremy began to feel dizzy, in spite of the B concentrate. The room began to whirl, slowly and pleasantly, then faster. *Wheeeee!*

TOMPKINS AND Wilson were singing a raucous ballad about a female mutant on Deneb Three who could do several things at once because of certain anatomical duplications.

"S' good!" Someone pounded Jeremy's back with a hand like a slab of undifferentiated syntheplasm. "'Spretty good, Doc. Maw!"

Maw must have meant more, and Jeremy obliged with the *smurth*. The room commenced to whirl more rapidly, and Jeremy walked to the wall. It must have taken him five minutes.

He returned presently with a lot of torn curtain. Tompkins and Wilson sprawled in their chairs, listlessly. Jeremy went to work with the curtains.

"Hey, Doc—wacha doing? Hey, cut it out—*sblurp!* You're tying me up. *Down—?*"

The job was done sloppily but effectively, and Tompkins and Wilson looked like parts of the interior decoration, all trussed up. Jeremy next rammed a thick gag into each flaccid mouth, then staggered back to survey his handiwork. With trembling hand he reached into the pocket of his robe, took out another bar of the concentrate. He munched.

In a moment he ran his hands clumsily through Tompkins' pockets. Soon he came up with a ring of keys, mumbled thank you, observed that both Tompkins and Wilson were snoring quite profoundly, staggered to the door, closed it, locked it, spit on his finger and held it up gingerly to ascertain which way the wind was blowing remembered shamefacedly that he was indoors, on a spaceship in deepest space in fact, squinted in the green light until he saw a sign which said "library" and which pointed unwaveringly arearships, followed the arrow, reached the door and felt panic for a moment when he searched through his robe for his missing library card, smiled when he realized it was after hours, tried several keys in the door and finally found the right one.

FRED PARKER stood up. "Jeremy! Jeremy Jenks! I will be damned. You look green. Oh, it's the lights... What the hell have you been drinking?"

"*Smurth,*" Jeremy grinned foolishly. "Where's Foamy?"

"Sleeping back of ancient history somewhere. *Smurth*— and you're still walking? Amazing."

They found Foamy back of ancient history, and Jeremy prodded her shoulder dramatically with a slippered foot. "Get up, Foamy. Get up, you are delivered..."

Foamy rubbed her eyes. "Hello, Jeremy. Don't tell me they threw you in here with us, too?" She looked a little angry, but then when Jeremy shook his head and tittered she said, "Umm, get that aroma. I'll be right back."

She disappeared through classics of the English language, came back from the washroom with a pot of water.

"Fred, get our coffee down, will you? I'd say Jeremy needs about a gallon."

Jeremy giggled, watched them boil the water over a can of stored heat. Then he was sitting on the floor and Foamy forced cup after cup of strong coffee into his mouth. It burned.

Later, he told them everything that had happened. "...so, in a couple of hours Ackeroyd plans to fire on that alien ship. It's a mistake—an awful mistake."

"You're' telling me!" Fred Parker said. "But what I want to know is this : what do we do about it? I mean, right now?"

"Can we count on any allies?" Jeremy wanted to know.

"Hank Cobb," Foamy told him. "If you think he'll do any good. You know, Jeremy, the little old guy in charge of hydroponics. He has a set of keys and he's been bringing us food in here. Says that he hated Ackeroyd ever since he saw the man's face."

Jeremy smiled. "Sounds perfect. Okay, here's what we do. You get this Cobb and come with him, on the double, to the control room. Fred and I will be there. The first and most important job is to keep everyone else out, including Governor Ackeroyd. Can you and Cobb be there inside of ten minutes?"

Foamy ran for the door. "Make it five, slow poke. See you two in control. "

"SO THESE are the green things," Parker mused.

Jeremy nodded. "Yes, and there's a much more crowded sector of the Galaxy, out there beyond the Ophiuchus nebula. It's not too far-fetched to assume that there are other cultures, just as advanced, perhaps more…"

"Yeah. You think we'll ever get out of here, Doc?"

Jeremy nodded. "I think we have a good chance, provided Ackeroyd doesn't cause trouble. We'll see."

A buzzer sounded, and Parker barked, "Who is it?"

"Me, Foamy. Open up."

Jeremy slid back the bolt and opened the door. The old man who followed Foamy into the room was small and bent, with an almost leathery skin and a merry twinkle in his eyes. "Howdy, folks!" he greeted. "Hank Cobb at your service. When do I get a crack at this Ackeroyd jackass?" He ran on nimble legs to the foreport. "By gosh, there's the ship. They told me about it, everyone did—but hearing about it and seeing it are two different things."

Jeremy looked over his shoulder. "That's it, all right." Just looking at the silent globe hanging off there in space he almost could feel the size of the Galaxy. Perhaps when man climbed down from his arboreal womb a million years ago these green things had a similar birth. Evolution must have followed a similar path all the way. Two worlds, about the same size, cooling together across fifty thousand light years of galactic space, with the amoebal slime given genesis along a stormy sea-shore on each planet at about the same time, with the slow rise of life from—

"Jeremy! Jeremy, snap out of it. Someone's at the door." It was Foamy talking, and Jeremy turned away from the port, shaking his head to clear it.

Now he heard the insistent clamor of the buzzer, the metallic voice over intercom: "Open up in there! This is Governor Ackeroyd. Open up."

"Go fly an asteroid derelict!" Hank Cobb cried, his voice just below a shriek.

"Come on now, open up. I know who you are. We found the library empty and we found Tompkins and Wilson in the dining room. Open up, Jenks, and we'll be easy with you."

"I DON'T hear any angry crowd threatening us with righteous indignation, Governor." said Jeremy.

"Crowd? Crowd! I don't need it! I have Mr. Entwhistle with me. You remember Mr. Entwhistle, Jenks. He knows how to use this ship's blaster. That's what I'm here for. We're coming in to blast that alien vessel out of space before it does the same thing to us."

"This door is locked from the inside," Jeremy replied. "There's not a weapon on the ship. You can't force us out, so why don't you—"

"I can't, can't I? Our mutual friend Tompkins is in the 'ponies room. Yes, he has a nasty hangover, but he's there.

We'll just feed the pipes backwards for the control room. You won't get a fresh supply of air, courtesy of all the nice growing green things back in 'ponies. Instead, we'll pipe you the carbon dioxide. That could be lethal, you know—in about half an hour it will take the place of all the air in there. So—come out or die, Jenks. Come out or die!"

"Pleasant guy," Parker said. "Say, Hank, can he really do that?"

"You bet he can, Mr. Parker. Be a cinch. Half an hour after the start, like he says."

Ackeroyd's voice: "So—what's your answer, Jenks?"

Jeremy tried to stall. "Why don't you let us think about it, Governor? Give us, say—"

"No. I can't wait all day. I'm going back to 'ponies now to help Tompkins get things started. You can think in the half hour left to you. Better start now…"

Jeremy heard the intercom pick up the click-clacking of footsteps fading down the corridor. He turned to his companions. "Well, that's it. Up to us now." Suddenly he smiled. "Listen! Hank and Foamy, you stay here. Don't let anyone in—"

"Where do you think you're going?" Foamy demanded.

"Well, we have just one chance. No one's outside the door now, so we can leave and—"

"Yeah!" Parker cried. "I see it, Doc. If we can get Ackeroyd in here, fast, he'll change his mind about the C02. And how he'd change it! Only how are we going to get him?"

Jeremy shrugged. "I don't know now. But maybe we'll know when we get outside. Maybe." He turned to Foamy. "Okay then—but promise me this: You two stay here and don't let anyone in. But when it starts getting hard to breathe, then you both get out. Promise?"

"Well…" Foamy hesitated.

"We won't go unless you promise. If you stay you'll only wind up killing yourselves, and that'll help no one."

"I—I promise, Jeremy."

"All right. And one more thing: I don't know what's going to happen out there. I—I hope it turns out the way we want. If not—Foamy—Foamy..."

She was in his arms, laughing and crying, so quickly that he didn't get a chance to be shy. He kissed her neck, her cheeks, her lips.

Parker was grinning. "I wondered how long it would take you to wake up, Doc? All she was talking about in the library was you. Jeremy this and Jeremy that—"

"*Shh*..." Hank Cobb raised a gnarled finger to his lips. "Shut up, Mr. Parker."

"Half an hour," Jeremy said, pulling away from the girl. "We'll be back. I love you, Foamy."

He stepped to the door, unbolted it, swung it open. Still grinning, Parker followed him down the corridor.

THEY MET gray-haired Dr. Henderson corning from the dining room. "I thought you two were locked up in control. Word got around—"

"We were," Parker told him.

"Well, it's none of my affair. I heard the argument last night. I'm not taking sides, but there's a lot to what you said, Professor Jenks. We all acted like a bunch of idiots, and I won't make the same mistake twice. I think you'll find most of us feel that way. And the murders—it makes me shudder. No one was responsible, really. Ackeroyd—"

Jeremy nodded curtly, and they were running down the companionway again. That speech, he knew, mirrored pretty accurately the feelings of most of the passengers.

They followed the bright green arrows which led toward the 'ponies room. Parker plucked a fire extinguisher off the wall along the way, hefted it experimentally. "This'll do, Jeremy," he said. "I wouldn't look at that Tompkins ape without an equalizer. "

A few moments later they burst into the 'ponies room. Jeremy was only half aware of the long rows of tanks, the dank odor of vegetation, the throbbing of the pumps, the wet slime on the outside of a score of pipes. Ahead he saw the three figures crouched over some machinery. "Hold it!" he called.

Ackeroyd whirled to face them. "You, Entwhistle," he said, smiling grimly, "keep feeding that carbon dioxide, there's a good fellow. Tompkins?"

"Yeah?"

"Can you handle them, fast?"

The big man rubbed his hands together. "You bet," he growled, lumbering forward.

Jeremy sidestepped his lunge nimbly and stuck out his slippered foot. The contact sent bursts of pain shooting up his leg, but Tompkins landed flat on his face. Parker lifted the extinguisher up high over his head just as the giant began to get up, then brought it down. Jeremy heard a crunching sound, saw Tompkins half sit up, stare stupidly for a moment, roll over on his back.

Jeremy ran for the row of valves. " All right, Entwhistle. You know how to put that thing into reverse and get some air into the control room?"

Ackeroyd made a run for it then, Jeremy took three steps in pursuit, left the ground. It was not a good tackle, because by all rules of the game he struck too high, near Ackeroyd's midsection. But the governor didn't know how to shake him off, and they fell in a heap.

For a moment Jeremy thought of their previous fight. It almost seemed ludicrous to him now. He struck out with both fists, and although Ackeroyd was striking back, he hardly felt the blows. Left and right, left and right—he drove his fists into the rat face until someone tugged at his weary arms.

"Get off him, Jeremy! Come on, Doc—he's unconscious."

Jeremy stood up. He watched Parker drag the fat figure to the door. He whirled, grabbed a fistful of Entwhistle's blouse.

"Reverse those valves!"

"You—you're hurting me. Yes, sir. I'll reverse them. But after that I'm getting out of here. I'm just an ordinary businessman. I sell vacuum cleaners. First he has me go out in a spacesuit and get those green things, then he wants me to fire a gun, then he has me monkey with these valves. I tell you now, I'm all through."

"Good," said Jeremy. He watched the man turn two sets of wheels, heard a hissing sound, then ran after Fred Parker to help him drag the governor through the corridor.

"IT WAS rough for a time," Foamy said. "But then the air began to clear suddenly."

Ackeroyd sat up, rubbing his chin. "Damn you, Jenks," he said. "When we reach Sosiphon Two—"

Parker snorted, "Public opinion on this ship has changed, governor."

"Yes," Foamy told him. "I think everything will be fine on Sosiphon Two. When what happened here comes out—"

Parker was smiling. "Just like a woman, Foamy. Doc, that gal friend of yours is forgetting one thing. Look—see through the foreport? There's the alien ship. Nothing of what we've done here has changed it one way or the other. It's still there. So—"

"Oh that," Jeremy grinned.

"Oh that, the man says," Foamy laughed. "There's the source of all our trouble, Jeremy—and you say oh that."

"Well, I've maintained that men and the green things have followed parallel paths of evolution. They're enough like us culturally to be our twin brothers."

"Those ghastly green things," said Foamy, looking at the trio, which still lay on the control room floor. "Our twins?"

"Yes. Bilateral symmetry, and anyway, they came through the Ophiuchus nebula and saw us just about the same time we saw them. Right?"

"Right," said Foamy.

"We stopped. They stopped. Everyone was scared. Everyone waited for the other guy to make the first move. We're still waiting. So are they. You see my point?"

"I suppose so," said Foamy doubtfully.

Ackeroyd got up off the floor and made a run for the door. This time Fred Parker came up with a first-rate imitation of Jeremy's tackle. He brought the fat man down and sat on his chest. "You were saying, Jeremy?"

"I was saying that if each ship could back out of this affair gracefully, everyone would be happy. Now, look at the nebula in Ophiuchus. It's the perfect curtain. If we back away from it and they ease into it, no one will see anything, and we can each go our separate way. We'll inform our government, they'll inform theirs—official ships loaded with politicians and scientists will return here. Anyway, that's not our problem.

"Point is, I think we can break up this stalemate. All we have to do is back up in little spurts and see if they follow suit, backing up until the nebula is between us. Then we can go our way. Foamy?"

"What, honey?"

"Start this ship moving backwards. Say, a little three-mile jump and wait, then see what they do. Then another three-mile jump."

"Me?"

"Of course you."

"But I can't pilot—"

"I thought because you were a stewardess you knew how—"

"No."

"Anyone else? Fred, you?"

"Nope, Doc. Don't look at me. I couldn't tell a firing stud from the stasis lever."

JEREMY sat back, dazed. That put a quick end to his plan. Probably no one aboard could pilot the starcoach. He had taken it for granted...

"You looking for a pilot, Mr. Jenks?" Hank Cobb demanded. "I been a 'ponies man for forty years, but I was a pilot, first class, before that."

"Bless you," said Foamy.

Jeremy told him what must be done, and old Cobb's grin split his face almost all the way across. "Should be fun," he said. "You want me to go back in little spurts, sorta like an upside-down frog."

"Sorta," Jeremy agreed.

They stood at the foreport eagerly, hardly hearing as Ackeroyd pounded from within the closet where Parker had locked him for safe keeping.

Old Hank Cobb played with the controls for a few moments, and then suddenly, soundlessly, the round ship in the port seemed to jump away from them. "Nearest I can figure it," said Cobb, "we've gone back three miles. Real fun. Now you want more?"

Jeremy told him not yet. They watched the port, grimly, silently. After that first jump there was nothing. Now a tiny mib against the Ophiuchus blackness, the alien ship stayed put.

"Jeremy," Foamy said, "maybe you were wrong…"

Then the ship jumped back! Perhaps four or five miles, on its own accord, the mib receded until it was a dot.

"Again," Jeremy told Hank Cobb.

"You mean now?"

"I mean now. Yes, now. Now!"

The alien ship was a tiny speck, a fourth magnitude star against the nebula. It faded.

It disappeared.

Only the nebula…

"A curtain," Jeremy said, "shielding us from each other for the time being, at least. We'll get to them, and they'll get to us, and I have a hunch the meeting will be a friendly one when it comes."

"Well," Parker said, "let's radio Sosiphon Two and tell them what's been happening. Then Hank can drive us in."

"You radio them," Jeremy said. "I want to study those green things more thoroughly."

Foamy grabbed his arm and spun him around. "No, you don't, Professor Jenks. You don't want to do that at all. You want to get to know the woman who's going to be your wife as soon as we land on Sosiphon Two, that's what you want to do."

He took her in his arms and hardly heard Fred Parker shouting into the radio.

Foamy purred. "Umm…Jeremy. Umm…see?"

Jeremy saw.

Pen Pal

All she wanted was a mate and she had the gumption to go out and hunt one down. But that meant poaching in a strictly forbidden territory!

THE best that could be said for Matilda Penshaws was that she was something of a paradox. She was thirty-three years old, certainly not aged when you consider the fact that the female life expectancy is now up in the sixties, but the lines were beginning to etch their permanent paths across her face and now she needed certain remedial undergarments at which she would have scoffed ten or even five years ago. Matilda was also looking for a husband.

This, in itself, was not unusual—but Matilda was so completely wrapped up in the romantic fallacy of her day that she sought a prince charming, a faithful Don Juan, a man who had been everywhere and tasted of every worldly pleasure and who now wanted to sit on a porch and talk about it all to Matilda.

The fact that in all probability such a man did not exist disturbed Matilda not in the least. She had been known to say that there are over a billion men in the world, a goodly percentage of whom are eligible bachelors, and that the right one would come along simply because she had been waiting for him.

Matilda, you see, had patience.

She also had a fetish. Matilda had received her A.B. from exclusive Ursula Johns College and Radcliff had yielded her Masters degree, yet Matilda was an avid follower of the pen pal columns. She would read them carefully and then read them again, looking for the masculine names which, through a system known only to Matilda, had an affinity to her own.

To the gentlemen upon whom these names were affixed, Matilda would write, and she often told her mother, the widow Penshaws, that it was in this way she would find her husband. The widow Penshaws impatiently told her to go out and get dates.

THAT particular night, Matilda pulled her battered old sedan into the garage and walked up the walk to the porch. The widow Penshaws was rocking on the glider and Matilda said hello.

The first thing the widow Penshaws did was to take Matilda's left hand in her own and examine the next-to-the-last finger.

"I thought so," she said. "I knew this was coming when I saw that look in your eye at dinner. Where is Herman's engagement ring?"

Matilda smiled. "It wouldn't have worked out, Ma. He was too darned stuffy. I gave him his ring and said thanks anyway and he smiled politely and said he wished I had told him sooner because his fifteenth college reunion was this weekend and he had already turned down the invitation."

The widow Penshaws nodded regretfully. "That was thoughtful of Herman to hide his feelings."

"Hogwash!" said her daughter. "He has no true feelings. He's sorry that he had to miss his college reunion. That's all he has to hide. A stuffy Victorian prude and even less of a man than the others."

"But, Matilda, that's your, fifth broken engagement in three years. It ain't that you ain't popular, but you just don't want to cooperate. You don't *fall* in love, Matilda—no one does. Love osmoses into you slowly, without you even knowing, and it keeps growing all the time."

Matilda admired her mother's use of the word osmosis, but she found nothing which was not objectionable about being unaware of the impact of love. She said goodnight and went upstairs, climbed out of her light summer dress and took a cold shower.

She began to hum to herself. She had not yet seen the pen pal section of the current *Literary Review*, and because the subject matter of that magazine was somewhat highbrow and cosmopolitan, she could expect a gratifying selection of pen pals.

She shut off the shower, brushed her teeth, gargled, patted herself dry with a towel and jumped into bed, careful to lock the door of her bedroom. She dared not let the widow Penshaws know that she slept in the nude; the widow Penshaws would object to a girl sleeping in the nude, even if the nearest neighbor was three hundred yards away.

Matilda switched her bed lamp on and dabbed some citronella on each earlobe and a little droplet on her chin (how she hated insects!). Then she propped up her pillows— two pillows partially stopped her post-nasal drip; and took the latest issue of the *Literary Review* off the night table.

She flipped through the pages and came to personals. Someone in Nebraska wanted to trade match books; someone in New York needed a midwestern pen pal, but it was a woman; an elderly man interested in ornithology wanted a young chick correspondent interested in the same subject; a young, personable man wanted an editorial position because he thought he had something to offer the editorial world; and—

MATILDA read the next one twice. Then she held it close to the light and read it again. The *Literary Review* was one of the few magazines which printed the name of the advertiser rather than a box number, and Matilda even liked the sound of the name. But mostly, she had to admit to herself, it was the flavor of the wording. This very well could be *it*. Or, that is, *him*.

Intelligent, somewhat egotistical male who's really been around, whose universal experience can make the average cosmopolite look like a provincial hick, is in need of several female correspondents: must be intelligent, have gumption, be capable of listening to male who has a lot to say and wants to say it. All others need not apply. Wonderful opportunity cultural experience...Haron Gorka, Cedar Falls, Ill.

The man was egotistical, all right. Matilda could see that. But she had never minded an egotistical man, at least not when he had something about which he had a genuine reason to be egotistical. The man sounded as though he would have reason indeed. He only wanted the best because he was the best. Like calls to like.

The name—Haron Gorka: its oddness was somehow beautiful to Matilda. Haron Gorka—the nationality could be anything. And that was it. He had no nationality for all intents and purposes; he was an international man, a figure among figures, a paragon...

Matilda sighed happily as she put out the light. The moon shone in through the window brightly, and at such times Matilda generally would get up, go to the cupboard, pull out a towel, take two hairpins from her powder drawer, pin the towel to the screen of her window, and hence keep the disturbing moonlight from her eyes. But this time it did not disturb her, and she would let it shine. Cedar Falls was a small town not fifty miles from her home, and she'd get there a hop, skip, and jump ahead of her competitors, simply by arriving in person instead of writing a letter.

Matilda was not yet that far gone in years or appearance. Dressed properly, she could hope to make a favorable impression in person, and she felt it was important to beat the influx of mail to Cedar Falls.

MATILDA got out of bed at seven, tiptoed into the bathroom, showered with a merest wary trickle of water, tiptoed back into her bedroom, dressed in her very best cotton over the finest of uplifting and figure-moulding underthings, made sure her stocking seams were perfectly straight, brushed her suede shoes, admired herself in the mirror, read the ad again, wished for a moment she were a bit younger, and tiptoed downstairs.

The widow Penshaws met her at the bottom of the stairwell.

"Mother," gasped Matilda. Matilda always gasped when she saw something unexpected. "What on earth are you doing up?"

The widow Penshaws smiled somewhat toothlessly, having neglected to put in both her uppers and lowers this early in the morning. "I'm fixing breakfast, of course..."

Then the widow Penshaws told Matilda that she could never hope to sneak about the house without her mother knowing about it, and that even if she were going out in response to one of those foolish ads in the magazines, she would still need a good breakfast to start with like only mother could cook. Matilda moodily thanked the widow Penshaws.

DRIVING the fifty miles to Cedar Falls in a little less than an hour, Matilda hummed Mendelssohn's Wedding March all the way. It was her favorite piece of music. Once, she told herself: Matilda Penshaws, you are being premature about the whole thing. But she laughed and thought that if she was, she was, and, meanwhile, she could only get to Cedar Falls and find out.

And so she got there.

The man in the wire cage at the Cedar Falls post office was a stereotype. Matilda always liked to think in terms of stereotypes. This man was small, roundish, florid of face, with a pair of eyeglasses which hung too far down on his nose. Matilda knew he would peer over his glasses and answer questions grudgingly.

"Hello," said Matilda.

The stereotype grunted and peered at her over his glasses. Matilda asked him where she could find Haron Gorka.

"What?"

"I said, where can I find Haron Gorka?"

"Is that in the United States?"

"It's not a that; it's a he. Where can I find him? Where does he live? What's the quickest way to get there?"

The stereotype pushed up his glasses and looked at her squarely. "Noq take it easy, ma'am. First place, I don't know any Haron Gorka—"

Matilda kept the alarm from creeping into her voice. She muttered an *oh* under her breath and took out the ad. This she showed to the stereotype, and he scratched his bald head. Then he told Matilda almost happily that he was sorry he couldn't help her. He grudgingly suggested that if it really were important, she might check with the police.

Matilda did, only they didn't know any Haron Gorka, either. It turned out that no one did: Matilda tried the general store, the fire department, the city hall, the high school, all three Cedar Falls gas stations, the livery stable, and half a dozen private dwellings at random. As far as the gentry of Cedar Falls was concerned, Haron Gorka did not exist.

Matilda felt bad, but she had no intention of returning home this early. If she could not find Haron Gorka, that was one thing; but she knew that she'd rather not return home and face the widow Penshaws, at least not for a while yet. The widow Penshaws meant well, but she liked to analyze other people's mistakes, especially Matilda's.

Accordingly, Matilda trudged wearily toward Cedar Falls' small and unimposing library. She could release some of her pent-up aggression by browsing through the dusty stacks.

This she did, but it was unrewarding. Cedar Falls had what might be called a microscopic library, and Matilda thought that if this small building were filled with microfilm rather than books, the library still would be lacking. Hence she retraced her steps and nodded to the old librarian as she passed.

THEN Matilda frowned. Twenty years from now, this could be Matilda Penshaws—complete with plain gray dress, rimless spectacles, gray hair, suspicious eyes, and a broomstick figure...

On the other hand-why not? Why couldn't the librarian help her? Why hadn't she thought of it before? Certainly a man as well educated as Haron Gorka would be an avid reader, and unless he had a permanent residence here in Cedar Falls, one couldn't expect that he'd have his own library with him. This being the case, a third-rate collection of books was far better than no collection at all, and perhaps the librarian would know Mr. Haron Gorka.

Matilda cleared her throat. "Pardon me," she began. "I'm looking for—"

"Haron Gorka." The librarian nodded.

"How on earth did you know?"

"That's easy. You're the sixth young woman who came here inquiring about that man today. Six of you—five others in the morning and now you in the afternoon. I never did trust this Mr. Gorka..."

Matilda jumped as if she had been struck strategically from the rear. "You know him? You know Haron Gorka?"

"Certainly. Of course I know him. He's our steadiest reader here at the library. Not a week goes by that he doesn't take out three, four books. Scholarly gentleman, but not without charm. If I were twenty years younger—"

Matilda thought a little flattery might be effective. "Only ten," she assured the librarian. "Ten years would be more than sufficient, I'm sure."

"Are you? Well. Well, well." The librarian did something with the back of her hair, but it looked the same as before. "Maybe you're right. Maybe you're right at that." Then she sighed. "But I guess a miss is as good as a mile."

"What do you mean?"

"I mean anyone would like to correspond with Haron Gorka. Or to know him well. To be considered his friend. Haron Gorka..."

The librarian seemed about to soar off into the air someplace, and if five women had been here first, Matilda was now definitely in a hurry.

"Um, where can I find Mr. Gorka?"

"I'm not supposed to do this, you know. We're not permitted to give the addresses of any of our people. Against regulations, my dear."

"What about the other five women?"

"They convinced me that I ought to give them his address."

Matilda reached into her pocketbook and withdrew a five dollar bill. "Was this the way?" she demanded. Matilda was not very good at this sort of thing.

The librarian shook her head.

Matilda nodded shrewdly and added a twin brother to the bill in her hand. "Then is this better?"

"That's worse. I wouldn't take your money—"

"Sorry. What then?"

"If I can't enjoy an association with Haron Gorka directly, I still could get the vicarious pleasure of your contact with him. Report to me faithfully and you'll get his address.

That's what the other five will do, and with half a dozen of you, I'll get an overall picture. Each one of you will tell me about Haron Gorka, sparing no details. You each have a distinct personality, of course, and it will color each picture considerably. But with six of you reporting, I should receive my share of vicarious enjoyment. Is it—ah—a deal?"

Matilda assured her that it was, and, breathlessly, she wrote down the address. She thanked the librarian and then she went out to her car, whistling to herself.

HARON GORKA lived in what could have been an agrarian estate, except that the land no longer was being tilled. The house itself had fallen to ruin. This surprised Matilda, but she did not let it keep her spirits in check. Haron Gorka, the man, was what counted, and the librarian's account of him certainly had been glowing enough. Perhaps he was too busy with his cultural pursuits to pay any real attention to his dwelling. That was it, of course: the conspicuous show of wealth or personal industry meant nothing at all to Haron Gorka. Matilda liked him all the more for it.

There were five cars parked in the long driveway, and now Matilda's made the sixth. In spite of herself, she smiled. She had not been the only one with the idea to visit Haron Gorka in person. With half a dozen of them there, the laggards who resorted to posting letters would be left far behind. Matilda congratulated herself for what she thought had been her ingenuity, and which now turned out to be something which she had in common with five other women. You live and learn, thought Matilda. And then, quite annoyedly, she berated herself for not having been the first. Perhaps the other five all were satisfactory; perhaps she wouldn't be needed; perhaps she was too late...

AS it turned out, she wasn't. Not only that, she was welcomed with open asrns. Not by Haron Gorka; that she really might have liked. Instead, someone she could only regard as a menial met her, and when he asked had she come in response to the advertisement, she nodded eagerly. He told her that was fine and he ushered her straight into a room, which evidently was to be her living quarters. It contained a small undersized bed, a table, and a chair, and, near a little slot in the wall, there was a button.

"You want any food or drink," the servant told her, "and you just press that button. The results will surprise you."

"What about Mr. Gorka?"

"When he wants you, he will send for you. Meanwhile, make yourself to home, lady, and I will tell him you are here."

A little doubtful now, Matilda thanked him and watched him leave. He closed the door softly behind his retreating feet, but Matilda's ears had not missed the ominous click. She ran to the door and tried to open it, but it would not budge. It was locked—from the outside.

It must be said to Matilda's favor that she sobbed only once. After that she realized that what is done is done and here, past thirty, she wasn't going to be girlishly timid about it. Besides, it was not her fault if, in his unconcern, Haron Gorka had unwittingly hired a neurotic servant.

For a time Matilda paced back and forth in her room, and of what was going on outside she could hear nothing. In that case, she would pretend that there was nothing outside the little room, and presently she lay down on the bed to take a nap. This didn't last long, however: she had a nightmare in which Haron Gorka appeared as a giant with two heads, but, upon awaking with a start, she immediately ascribed that to her overwrought nerves.

At that point she remembered what the servant had said about food and she thought at once of the supreme justice she could do to a juicy beefsteak. Well, maybe they didn't have a beefsteak. In that case, she would take what they had, and, accordingly, she walked to the little slot in the wall and pressed the button.

She heard the whir of machinery. A moment later there was a soft sliding sound. Through the slot first came a delicious aroma, followed almost instantly by a tray. On the tray were a bowl of turtle soup, mashed potatoes, green peas, bread, a strange cocktail, root-beer, a parfait—and a thick tenderloin sizzling in hot butter sauce.

Matilda gasped once and felt about to gasp again—but by then her salivary glands were working overtime, and she ate her meal. The fact that it was precisely what she would have wanted could, of course, be attributed to coincidence, and the further fact that everything was extremely palatable made her forget all about Haron Gorka's neurotic servant.

When she finished her meal a pleasant lethargy possessed her, and in a little while Matilda was asleep again. This time she did not dream at all. It was a deep sleep and a restful one, and when she awoke it was with the wonderful feeling that everything was all right.

THE feeling did not last long. Standing over her was Haron Gorka's servant, and he said, "Mr. Gorka will see you now."

"Now?"

"Now. That's what you're here for, isn't it?"

He had a point there, but Matilda hardly even had time to fix her hair. She told the servant so.

"Miss," he replied, "I assure you it will not matter in the least to Haron Gorka. You are here and he is ready to see you and that is all that matters."

"You sure?" Matilda wanted to take no chances.

"Yes. Come."

She followed him out of the little room and across what should have been a spacious dining area, except that everything seemed covered with dust. Of the other women Matilda could see nothing, and she suddenly realized that each of them probably had a cubicle of a room like her own, and that each in her turn had already had her first visit with Haron Gorka. Well, then, she must see to it that she impressed him better than did all the rest, and, later, when she returned to tell the old librarian of her adventures, she could perhaps draw her out and compare notes.

She would not admit even to herself that she was disappointed with Haron Gorka. It was not that he was homely and unimpressive; it was just that he was so *ordinary*-looking. She almost would have preferred the monster of her dreams.

HE wore a white linen suit and he had mousy hair, drab eyes, an almost-Roman nose, a petulant mouth with the slight arch of the egotist at each corner.

He said, "Greetings. You have come—"

"In response to your ad. How do you do, Mr. Gorka?"

She hoped she wasn't being too formal. But, then, there was no sense in assuming that he would like informality. She could only wait and see and adjust her own actions to suit him. Meanwhile, it would be best to keep on the middle of the road.

"I am fine. Are you ready?"

"Ready?"

"Certainly. You came in response to my ad. You want to hear me talk, do you not?"

"I—do." Matilda had had visions of her prince charming sitting back and relaxing with her, telling her of the many things he had done and seen. But first she certainly would have liked to get to *know* the man. Well, Haron Gorka obviously had more experience along these lines than she did. He waited, however, as if wondering what to say, and Matilda, accustomed to social chatter, gave him a gambit.

"I must admit I was surprised when I got exactly what I wanted for dinner," she told him brightly.

"Eh? What say? Oh, yes, naturally. A combination of telepathy and teleportation. The synthetic cookery is attuned to your mind when you press the buzzer, and the strength of your psychic impulses determines how closely the meal will adjust to your desires. The fact that the adjustment here was near perfect is commendable. It means either that you have a high psi-quotient, or that you were very hungry."

"Yes," said Matilda vaguely. Perhaps it might be better, after all, if Haron Gorka were to talk to her as he saw fit.

"Ready?"

"Uh—ready. "

"Well?"

"Well, what, Mr. Gorka?"

"What would you like me to talk about?"

"Oh, anything."

"Please. As the ad read, my universal experience—is universal. Literally. You'll have to be more specific."

"Well, why don't you tell me about some of your far travels? Unfortunately, while I've done a lot of reading, I haven't been to all the places I would have liked—"

"Good enough. You know, of course, how frigid Deneb VII is?"

Matilda said, "Beg pardon?"

"Well, there was the time our crew—before I had retired, of course—made a crash landing there. We could survive in the vac-suits, of course, but the *thlomots* were after us almost at once. They go mad over plastic. They will eat absolutely any sort of plastic. Our vac-suits—"

"—were made of plastic," Matilda suggested. She did not understand a thing he was talking about, but she felt she had better act bright.

"No, no. Must you interrupt? The air-hose and the water feed, these were plastic. Not the rest of the suit. The point is that half of us were destroyed before the rescue ship could come, and the remainder were near death. I owe my life to the mimicry of a *flaak* from Capella III. It assumed the properties of plastic and led the *thlomots* a merry chase across the frozen surface of D VII. You travel in the Deneb system now and Interstellar Ordinance makes it mandatory to carry *flaaks* with you. Excellent idea, really excellent."

ALMOST at once, Matilda's educational background should have told her that Haron Gorka was mouthing gibberish. But on the other hand she *wanted* to believe in him and the result was that it took until now for her to realize it.

"Stop making fun of me," she said.

"So, naturally, you'll see *flaaks* all over that system—"

"Stop!"

"What's that? Making fun of you?" Haron Gorka's voice had been so eager as he spoke, high-pitched, almost like a child's, and now he seemed disappointed. He smiled, but it was a sad smile, a smile of resignation, and he said, "Very well. I'm wrong again. You are the sixth, and you're no better than the other five. Perhaps you are even more outspoken. When you see my wife, tell her to come back. Again she is right and I am wrong..."

Haron Gorka turned his back. Matilda could do nothing but leave the room, walk back through the house, go outside and get into her car. She noticed not without surprise that the other five cars were now gone. She was the last of Haron Gorka's guests to depart.

As she shifted into reverse and pulled out of the driveway, she saw the servant leaving, too. Far down the road, he was walking slowly. Then Haron Gorka had severed that relationship, too, and now he was all alone.

As she drove back to town, the disappointment melted slowly away. There were, of course, two alternatives. Either Haron Gorka was an eccentric who enjoyed this sort of outlandish tomfoolery, or else he was plainly insane. She could still picture him ranting on aimlessly to no one in particular about places which had no existence outside of his mind, his voice high-pitched and eager.

IT WAS not until she had passed the small library building that she remembered what she had promised the librarian. In her own way, the aging woman would be as disappointed as Matilda, but a promise was a promise, and Matilda turned the car in a wide U-turn and parked it outside the library.

The woman sat at her desk as Matilda had remembered her, gray, broom-stick figure, rigid. But now when she saw Matilda she perked up visibly.

"Hello, my dear," she said.

"Hi."

"You're back a bit sooner than I expected. But, then, the other five have returned, too, and I imagine your story will be similar."

"I don't know what they told you," Matilda said. "But this is what happened to me."

She quickly then related everything which had happened, completely and in detail. She did this first because it was a promise, and second because she knew it would make her feel better.

"So," she finished, "Haron Gorka is either extremely eccentric or insane. I'm sorry."

"He's neither," the librarian contradicted. "Perhaps he is slightly eccentric by your standards, but really, my dear, he is neither."

"What do you mean?"

"Did he leave a message for his wife?"

"Why, yes. Yes, he did. But how did you know? Oh, I suppose, he told the five."

"No. He didn't. But you were the last and I thought he would give you a message for his wife—"

Matilda didn't understand. She didn't understand at all, but she told the little librarian what the message was. "He wanted her to return," she said.

The librarian nodded, a happy smile on her lips. "You wouldn't believe me if I told you something."

"What's that?"

"I am Mrs. Gorka."

The librarian stood up and came around the desk. She opened a drawer and took out her hat and perched it jauntily atop her gray hair. "You see, my dear, Haron expects too much. He expects entirely too much."

Matilda did not say a word. One madman a day would be quite enough for anybody, but here she found herself confronted with two.

"We've been tripping for centuries, visiting every habitable star system from our home near Canopus. But Haron is too demanding. He says I am a finicky traveler, that he could do much better alone, the accommodations have to be just right for me, and so forth. When he loses his temper, he tries to convince me that any number of females of the particular planet would be more than thrilled if they were given the opportunity just to listen to him.

"But he's wrong. It's a hard life for a woman. Someday—five thousand, ten thousand years from now—I will convince him. And then we will settle down on Canopus XIV and cultivate *torgas*. That would be so nice—"

"I'm sure."

"Well, if Haron wants me, back, then I have to go. Have a care, my dear. If you marry, choose a homebody. I've had the experience and you've seen my Haron for yourself."

And then the woman was gone. Numbly, Matilda walked to the doorway and watched her angular figure disappear down the road. Of all the crazy things…

Deneb and Capella and Canopus, these were stars. Add a number and you might have a planet revolving about each star. Of all the insane—

They were mad, all right, and now Matilda wondered if, actually, they were husband and wife. It could readily be; maybe the madness was catching. Maybe if you thought too much about such things, such travels, you could get that way. Of course, Herman represented the other extreme, and Herman was even worse in his own way—but hereafter Matilda would seek the happy medium.

And, above all else, she had had enough of her pen pal columns. They were, she realized, for kids.

SHE ate dinner in Cedar Falls and then she went out to her car again, preparing for the journey back home. The sun had set and it was a clear night, and overhead the great broad sweep of the Milky Way was a pale rainbow bridge in the sky.

Matilda paused. Off in the distance there was a glow on the horizon, and that was the direction of Haron Gorka's place.

The glow increased; soon it was a bright red pulse pounding on the horizon. It flickered. It flickered again, and finally it was gone.

The stars were white and brilliant in the clear country air. That was why Matilda liked the country better than the city, particularly on a clear summer night when you could see the span of the Milky Way.

But abruptly the stars and the Milky Way were paled by the brightest shooting star Matilda had ever seen. It flashed suddenly and it remained in view for a full second, searing a bright orange path across the night sky.

Matilda gasped and ran into her car. She started the gears and pressed the accelerator to the floor, keeping it there all the way home.

It was the first time she had ever seen a shooting star going *up*.

My Sweetheart's the Man in the Moon

Not everyone will think of the first moon-flight as the first glorious step on the road to space. There will always, for instance, be the fast-buck boys like Lubrano...

JEANNE turned off the radio and went downstairs slowly, watching how the gold-shot curtains on the landing window caught the sunlight in a multitude of brilliant flecks. She shuddered slightly. Up *there*, the sun would scorch and sear.

When she entered the living room, Aunt Anna looked up from her magazine, and Pop puffed on his calabash pipe, occasionally grunting with satisfaction. Mom looked at Jeanne hopefully, but soon turned away in confusion. She could not tell whether Jeanne wanted her to laugh or cry.

"Well," said Jeanne, instantly hating the flippant way she tried to speak, "he got there." She never quite knew why, but whenever emotions threatened to choke her up she would slip on the mask, the carefree attitude, the what-do-I-care voice she was using now.

"All the way—*there?*" Aunt Anna fluttered her eyebrows, allowing herself a rare display of emotion.

Mom smiled, laughed briefly and nervously. She touched Jeanne's cheek tentatively with a trembling hand, hugged her daughter quickly and drew back. "I didn't know," she said. "None of us knew. We were afraid to listen. I mean, it's so far."

"Knew he'd make it," said Pop, tamping his pipe full with another load of tobacco from the humidor. "Tom's got good stuff in him. Smokes a pipe, you know."

"Not up there," said Jeanne practically. "It would waste oxygen."

"It says here in this magazine the moon is 240,000 miles away," Aunt Anna told them.

"Did the announcer say how Tom felt?" Mom wanted to know.

"Just imagine how it will be," Aunt Anna said, "when we get Tom back here and he speaks to the Women's League. We'll have to make arrangements—"

"Can't," Pop reminded her. "Government hasn't said anything about when Tom's coming back. Liable to keep him there a long time. Do the boy good. See what he's really made of, I always say. Andrea, your roast is burning."

Mom scurried off toward the kitchen. A moment after she disappeared, the phone rang and Aunt Anna took the receiver off its cradle. "Hello? Yes, this is the Peterson home. Yes, she is. In a moment... Jeanne, it's for you."

"Hmm," Jeanne chortled. "Some fellow trying to make time because Tom's too far away to protest." She hated herself for saying it, and administered the mental kick in the pants, which never helped. She was missing Tom more acutely every minute. The distance was unthinkable, the moon almost too remote to consider, lost up there in infinite void, surrounded by parcels—parsecs?—of nothing.

Picking up the receiver, Jeanne turned her back to Aunt Anna, who appeared quite eager to listen to at least half of the conversation. "Hello? Yes, this is Jeanne Peterson. The *Times-Democrat?* I could see you today, I suppose. Why, here at home. I'm on vacation. But what—about Tom? Oh, I see. Oh, they told you down at White Sands. Well, all right. 'Bye."

"It was a man," said Aunt Anna.

"Who said my roast was burning?" Mom asked them all indignantly as she returned from the kitchen.

"Who was the young man, Jeanne?" Aunt Anna asked.

Jeanne grinned, brushed back a stray lock of her blonde hair. "Sorry to disappoint an old gossip like you, but—"

"Tom *is* a long way off!"

"That was just Mr. Lubrano, a reporter on the *Times-Democrat*. 'How does it feel to be the fiancée of the first man to reach the moon,' he said. Funny, I hadn't thought of it that way at all. How does it feel? Did he expect me to turn cartwheels? (*But, I am proud of Tom, so why don't I admit it?*) He'll be down to interview me this afternoon."

"After dinner, I hope," said Mom.

Awkwardly, Aunt Anna lit a cigarette—something she did only on rare, important occasions. "It never occurred to me," she said slowly, trying to remove tobacco grains from her tongue as delicately as possible with thumb and forefinger. "Not for a moment. But Jeanne, in her own right, is also a celebrity. The Women's League has watched her grow up, I know. But suddenly, all at once, Jeanne is different. Andrea, get May King on the phone!"

"May—the president?" Mom wanted to know, somewhat awed.

"Of course, Andrea. A little imagination, that's what you need."

Mom got up doubtfully, approached the telephone as if it might jump up and attack her.

"Forget it," Jeanne told them. *Use big words. Use words, which would have ridiculous double-entendres for them. Frighten them.* "I won't prostitute my emotional relationship with Tom for all the Women's Leagues in the county. Forget it."

"Jeanne!" said Aunt Anna.

"Jeanne," Mom echoed her, more than a little shocked. "What all this has to do with—Jeanne! Oh…"

But Jeanne was on her way upstairs to put on something gay and bright for the arrival of Mr. Lubrano. Now that she thought of it, she liked the almost electric crackle in the reporter's voice over the phone.

"GOOD AFTERNOON, Miss Peterson. Honest, I feel almost like a cub. In a few hours, you've become quite a figure." Mr. Lubrano was young, good-looking in a dark, dangerous, eager Latin way. He took Jeanne's proffered hand, held it and looked at her long enough to let her know he appreciated what he saw, briefly enough to indicate everything would be strictly business if she wanted it that way.

Jeanne had been firm with Aunt Anna and her folks. Their part in this was to be strictly a vicarious one. She would answer their questions later. As it turned out, Pop almost had to propel Aunt Anna from the room, and this only because Jeanne had insisted beforehand. Mom couldn't fathom the fuss or the secrecy, and contentedly did as she was told.

"You're younger than I expected, Miss Peterson."

"Come now. Tom's only twenty-five. You know that."

"Well, then, prettier."

"Then we're even. After a reporter friend Pop once had, you could be Tyrone Power."

"Lovely dress you're wearing." He fingered the taffeta at her shoulder, let his hand rest more heavily than necessary. When she pulled away and sat as primly as she could on a straight-backed chair he said the one word, "Business?" He made it a question.

"Business."

"Just how long have you known the Man in the Moon?"

"The Man—really!"

"Oh, that's him. That's your Thomas Bentley. He's the Man in the Moon now."

Jeanne suppressed an unfeminine snicker. "About nine years. High school together, dates, going steady, engaged. The usual middle-sized town sort of thing."

"Love him?"

"Of course. Really, Mr. Lubrano."

For the next thirty minutes, Dan Lubrano asked her the sort of questions that might make an adequate Sunday-supplement feature. Nothing startling, nothing very original—except for the fact that Jeanne, as the fiancée of the first man to rocket across interplanetary space and reach the moon, was an unusual subject. Did she plan on marrying Tom upon his return? Naturally, but only the highest echelon of government and military circles knew when that might be. Was she afraid the utter desolation of space would somehow—change him? Lubrano made the pause significant. Might make him more romantic if anything, although Tom never tended toward stodginess. Could she be quoted as saying she looked up at the moon every clear night and called softly, silently, secretly to Tom across the unthinkable distances? Yes, if it were absolutely necessary.

When they finished, Jeanne said: "Don't tell me that's all, Dan?"

"Officially, yes. Unofficially, I haven't started. Look, Miss Peterson—Jeanne—mind if I'm perfectly frank?"

Jeanne said she didn't mind at all.

Lubrano grinned, displaying his piano-key teeth. "Jeanne, all my life I've looked for something like you. Only it's something you almost never find. Either you're lucky or you're not. Me, I'm lucky. I've found the fiancée of the Man in the Moon. To make things even better, you've got your share of good looks—and you're not dumb, either."

"I don't understand."

"Jeanne, we can make a million bucks together. Quick, with hardly any work. Want to?"

"It sounds crazy, Dan. You're not making any sense."

"No? Then listen." He turned on the radio, waited for the tubes to warm up, dialed at random for a station. "...at this hour, we know only that the Man in the Moon has landed on Earth's far satellite, that he has signaled the success of his mission with a phosphorous flare, and that he has as yet established no radio contact, although that is expected momentarily. It is anticipated that the government will make an announcement shortly. This much is certain, however. In order to consolidate our position on the moon, we will have to send up another spaceman to join fearless Captain Bentley on our bleak satellite, eventually an entire crew of technicians—"

"Is that all?" Jeanne demanded. "Of course Tom is news. What's the connection?"

"News is right. The biggest since we exploded the A-bomb. Listen." Lubrano dialed for another station. "...dream of all centuries, all generations. A spaceship to the moon. The implications are so tremendous that man hasn't even considered all of them. American know-how, scientific ability and determination has once again brought a new era to mankind. Tonight before you retire, Mr. and Mrs. America, give a silent prayer of thanks to our Maker for giving us the Man in the Moon. This is—"

Lubrano flicked the dial again. "...presented by Crunchy Kernels, the cereal with the truly sprightly crackle. And here he is, ladies and gentlemen, in a direct interview from White Sands, New Mexico. Dr. Amos T. Kedder, assistant supervisor of electronics for the final stages of the spaceship's construction—"

"See what I mean?" Lubrano asked triumphantly, turning off the radio. "Assistant supervisor in charge of electronics. Well, a pat on the backside for him. Nobody yesterday, the feature attraction on the Crunchy Kernel Guest of Honor Show today. Startling, isn't it?"

"What's all this got to do with me?" Jeanne asked.

"Every place you turn," said Lubrano. "Can't avoid it. Honey, who wants to? Don't get me wrong. You won't just be my meal ticket. I'll have to do most of the work, but together, watch our smoke. A million bucks, honey! That's the goal. Want to get on the gravy train?"

"Maybe," said Jeanne. "But I still don't—"

"Look," Lubrano sneered. "I'm a newspaperman, struggling along at fifteen bucks a week over the Guild minimum. But I got ideas, honey. Public relations, that's the field. Public relations. There's millions in it.

"Get the right start and you got it made. We can't have Bentley here on Earth—tough. But we got his gal-friend. A red-hot item, if handled properly. Man! Commercial endorsements as a starter, then maybe a lecture tour, theater appearances, even cheesecake pictures for the magazines. Get it, honey?"

"Why, yes. I'm beginning to under—"

"Of course you get it! Jeanne Peterson reads *Cosmopolite* to while away her lonely hours. Jeanne smokes *Dromedaries*, relaxes in her bathtub with *Luroscent*, dreams of her lover on the moon on a *Softafoam* pillow, writes him letters and saves them for his return by using *Perma-blue* ink, wears a *Furform* coat to keep her warm while gazing at the crescent moon on chill autumn nights. Get it, honey? Get it?"

Jeanne laughed softly. "Talk about your prostitution," she said, half-aloud.

"Huh? What say?" Effusive with enthusiasm, Lubrano hardly heard her.

"Nothing. Nothing. It's been interesting, Dan." She stood up, led him to the door. "Let me think about it. I've got to think."

"Say, wait a minute." Almost, Lubrano seemed indignant. "You looked all hepped up about it, honey—why the quick freeze? If you think you can do this yourself without help from me, you've got another guess coming. I've got the contacts; you've got the name we want to sell. You can't do it alone. A fifty-fifty split, straight down the middle."

Mechanically, Jeanne's mind went to work. Also mechanically, she spoke. "Fifty-fifty baloney. You get twenty-five percent, Mr. Lubrano, and not another penny. You must take me for a yokel."

"Forty."

"I said twenty-five."

"All right. All right. There's still enough in it for me. Twenty-five percent. Meet me tomorrow morning at my—"

"That's *if* I decide the idea is worthwhile," Jeanne said, pushing him across the door-sill and watching him retreat reluctantly down the walk to the street.

WHEN Mom and the others asked Jeanne later, she was the picture of co-operation. She told them everything about Mr. Lubrano and his pleasant interview. She told them nothing about Dan and his not-so-fantastic plans.

Jeanne excused herself after dinner, her mind seething with proposal and counter-proposal, and went upstairs to her room, but found sleep impossible. Was it fair to Tom, capitalizing on whatever feelings they had for each other? Was it fair to herself? If Lubrano had his way, a glorified Hollywood love would result. Jeanne and Tom would be adopted by the nation as its favorite lovers. Their faces would grace pop-bottles, sipping cola together in an infinite regress of progressively smaller bottles. Their forms would loll on all the beach billboards, proclaiming in the latest, brightest colors that the Man in the Moon and his girlfriend insisted on *Sunburst* bathing suits. And Jeanne would be waiting with her *Chlorogate* toothpaste smile for her lover to return from the infinite distances.

When he returned, nothing would be left. Commercial love, exploited love, hounded love, a cheap, impossible, publicized and doomed-to-failure marriage, if Tom ever allowed it to go that far...

"Phooey on you, Jeanne Peterson!" Jeanne said aloud, and sat up in bed, surprised at the loudness of her own voice. She was imagining things. It wouldn't be as bad as all that. Exploitation for a few months—and a small fortune, if not the great wealth that Dan promised. And the physical comforts made possible by whatever she earned would, over a period of time, smother Tom's anger.

Still, the one honest emotional experience, which somehow had penetrated deeper than the veneer she exposed to the world, had been her relationship with Tom... But she could make money, make herself happy, make Tom happy— if not immediately on his return then eventually... But...

Soon after the milkman pulled his truck to the curb down on the corner, Jeanne fell asleep.

"HOLD IT! Hold it!" The agency director of photography, a small, round man with a thin voice, waved the photographer off his camera impatiently and scowled at Jeanne. "You're a nice girl, Miss Peterson. That's a nice nightgown, filmy, but not so filmy it won't get by the censors. You got a nice figure and the country will love you. So why don't you be a nice model too?

"That ain't just a mattress you're on, Miss Peterson. How many times I gotta tell you that's the mattress you're waiting for Tom on? 'I miss Tom so, I'd never sleep, thinking of him so helpless and far away, the first Man in the Moon. Except for my *Beautysleep* mattress which induces sleep with its special innerspring construction.' I ain't no copy-writer, Miss

Peterson, but it will be something like that. So, cuddle up on that mattress like it will have to do till Tom comes home from the moon. Cuddle nice, Miss Peterson, cuddle nice."

It took Jeanne exactly fifty-five minutes longer before she could cuddle nice. They then took the picture in a matter of seconds, and Jeanne was allowed to change into her street clothes. Hurrying, she was only fifteen minutes late for her luncheon engagement with Lubrano.

"Three months," Lubrano said, after they'd settled themselves over cocktails. "Not bad, honey. Know how much we grossed, including the *Beautysleep* account?"

"Yes," Jeanne told him. "Twenty-eight thousand, three hundred and four dollars."

"Not bad," said Lubrano. "It takes the right kind of press, naturally. That's me, honey, the right kind of press."

"Yes," said Jeanne. "We're a good combination, Dan. You're right, it can't miss."

"Funny, you never sound excited about it."

"Maybe that's the way I am. I don't excite easily. So what?"

"So nothing." Lubrano began cutting his pork tenderloin.

"What's next on the agenda?" Jeanne wanted to know. "Maybe I lasso the moon with smoke rings blown from *Buccaneer* cigarettes?"

"Maybe you do eventually. Not right now. Right now you have to hop a plane for New Mexico and have a chat with the boyfriend."

"What?" Jeanne felt something flip-flop madly in the pit of her stomach. "Dan! Oh, Dan!"

"That's right, honey. Through the courtesy of 'Hands Across the Ocean,' sponsored by Cleopatra Complexion Soap. A radio broadcast across a quarter of a million miles of space to reunite you and Tommy boy. At least, for three minutes."

"Oh, Dan, Dan—that's wonderful." Jeanne stood up, removed the napkin from her lap. "If I hurry home and pack I can make a night plane and be in New Mexico by—"

"Whoa. Relax, honey, there's no rush. The show is tomorrow night, 11 P.M. our time. I've booked your reservation for the morning."

"I'm too excited to eat, Dan. Really. But thanks for everything." Jeanne bent down as Lubrano prepared to attack his tenderloin again. She kissed his forehead playfully, turned to leave.

Someone snickered, "That's the moon girl, I think. I thought her boyfriend was way up there. Another cheap publicity stunt."

"Careful," Dan frowned. "So you're happy. Don't go around ruining everything,"

Still smiling, Jeanne left.

"SIT DOWN, Miss Peterson." The general waved Jeanne to a chair, half rose as she seated herself. "Frankly, these publicity things always make me nervous."

"*You're* nervous! Look who's talking!" Jeanne waited while the general lit a cigarette. "Only three minutes! I can hardly think what to say."

"Is that bothering you, Miss? Don't worry. They showed me a copy of the script."

"Script?"

"Script, yes. For tonight's program. Your part is all there, word for word."

"But I thought—"

"That it would be extemporaneous? I guess we're both new at this, Miss Peterson. I would have thought the same thing. But not with an audience of twenty million. That's what Mr. Pate said. Pate, he's the director of the show."

"But—but they can't do that. I want to talk to Tom. I want to tell him—things. I won't recite any prepared speech." How ridiculous could the whole situation become? Jeanne thought. She'd made a farce of their love these months. Now she wanted to forget that, make up for it at least in part by speaking to Tom, by pouring her heart out to him (as if she could even start to do that, in three minutes). If that fell through too...

"You'd better send for Mr. Pate."

"You don't understand. Mr. Pate's in charge, not me,"

"Then—then I won't speak at all. Let him tell their audience that."

"What? Why, Miss, you can't do that. They expect you on the show and—"

"Send for Mr. Pate." Suddenly, she was glad Lubrano hadn't come out here with her. He naturally would have agreed with Mr. Pate.

The general picked up a phone on his desk, dialed. "Afternoon, Captain. Have you seen Pate? What? Splendid. Of course I'll wait." He cupped a well-manicured hand over the receiver. "They're looking for him, Miss...Eh? Hello? Mr. Pate? I'm sorry to bother you, but—yes, important. I wish you could come to my office, whenever you... Splendid. Splendid." The general hung up. "Be right here."

TEN minutes later, Pate arrived. He was young, florid of face, and looked like he'd soon have a bad case of high blood pressure if he didn't already have it. He waved a hand carelessly at the general. Too carelessly. Like he was a recently discharged enlisted man who felt he didn't have to bow and scrape any more.

"You're Jeanne. Recognize you anywhere. Like to tell your Tom he has good taste."

"Fine," said Jeanne. "Tell him anything you want. I'm not speaking."

"Ha, ha. Good joke."

"It's no joke, Mr. Pate. I won't recite any prepared speech. I absolutely refuse."

"Say that again. No, don't bother." Pate's brick-red face assumed the color of good claret wine. "Not ordinary, this. You probably thought we wouldn't reimburse you. Five thousand dollars all right?"

"Please, Mr. Pate. I came here to talk with Tom. I want to talk, not recite. Tear up your speech and I'll do it for nothing."

"Can't."

"Don't, then. Goodbye."

"Wait! General, can't you do something?"

"She's not under my jurisdiction. I told her you know your business and she was being—shall we say—something less than sensible."

"General! You never said anything like that. Don't you think I have a right to speak to my fiancé?"

"There's something to what you both say." Now the general sounded like he was talking from a prepared speech. *If it's a matter of publicity, never hurt anyone's feelings. Straddle that fence. Walk that tight-rope.*

"Well, I'll be damned," said Pate. "Show's got to go on. Is that final, Miss Peterson?"

"You can bet your bottom dollar on it, as the expression goes." Jeanne almost felt like smiling, despite the situation.

"Don't say anything unprintable, then. Tear up your speech. We've got to. See you in two hours." Muttering a brief word or two, Pate left, not bothering to say goodbye to the general.

The general grinned professionally at Jeanne. "Any time I can be of further assistance..."

"Is THIS seat taken?"

Jeanne looked up from her third cup of coffee, which she'd been stirring nervously. She'd found a small restaurant outside the post's main gate.

"Why, no. Sit down, won't you?" Jeanne smiled at the girl who approached her.

"Th-thanks."

Kind of a plain type, Jeanne decided. Not pretty, though certainly not homely. Nice hair, if you liked it corn-silk color and long. Some men did, she supposed. "Cigarette?"

"I—I don't smoke, thank you. You—you're Jeanne Peterson. I recognized you. My name is Mary."

"Hello, Mary."

"Miss Peterson, I don't know how to begin. But I've got to talk to you. You're a stranger and—Miss Peterson, please. You've got to do something..."

"How can I help you if I don't know what you're talking about?" Jeanne almost felt like saying, *sister, I've got problems of my own.*

"It's Curt. Captain Curt Macomber. He's—maybe I shouldn't be telling you this. You won't say anything. I mean—"

"For gosh sakes, what *do* you mean?"

The girl sniffled.

"I'm sorry," said Jeanne. "Go ahead." Maybe she'd feel better herself if she heard someone else's problems.

"Curt is going—up there. To the—the moon. I still can hardly believe it. But they're sending him to join Captain Bentley. Tonight, at midnight."

"That's right, they did say something about sending a man to help Tom with whatever he's doing."

"Establishing a base, that's what. Curt told me. Curt said—he said he was going. He got two weeks of fast training and that's it. He told me the ship—the spaceship—

worked automatically, anyway. Captain Bentley will brief him when he reaches the moon. Your Captain, Miss Peterson. But—but I'm so ashamed."

"Ashamed?" The whole thing sounded more and more like a soap opera to Jeanne every minute.

"Curt—Curt and I, we got married. In secret. His folks didn't approve and—well, that's not important. But I'm— I'm—well, I haven't told Curt. I'm going to have a baby. I can't tell him now, not when he's about to go further away than anyone…Miss Peterson, please don't tell anyone." More sniffles. "Please."

"Forget about it. But I don't see where I can help you."

The girl spoke again, a quick rushing torrent of words. "You can speak to your captain and find out what it's like on the moon and discourage Curt, or maybe even tell Curt the truth that I'm going to have a baby and then he'll understand he can't go… He doesn't have to go, he's a volunteer. I mean, he can change his mind, if he wants to, if you can make him…" The girl's voice trailed off plaintively.

Aunt Anna would be all for doing it, and then telling her friends the full details for the next five years or so. Pop would smoke his pipe and grunt something about it doing the boy good. Mom would say, "Whatever makes you happy, dear," and retreat to her kitchen. You could never predict Dan Lubrano. He might tell her to don a pair of football shoulder pads, tackle Captain Macomber and sit on him until the automatic spaceship blasted off for the moon. (Weller's football equipment, of course. Nothing but the best, nothing but a cash-on-the-line endorsement.)

"I'll do what I can," Jeanne said finally. "After the show, kid. Meanwhile, all you can do is take it easy. But I don't promise anything. Your Captain Macomber is a big boy now and probably, he'll make his own decisions."

The thought of a naive, innocent girl like the one sitting beside her falling into the publicity mill of another Dan Lubrano was almost horrifying.

"YESSIR, ladies and gentlemen. Every week at this time we all get together and join hands across the ocean—in Cleopatra Facial Soap's famous human interest program, the show that tugs at your heart-strings as much as, Cleopatra Facial Soap tugs at the grit and oil, removing them from the pores of your skin—'Hands Across the Ocean.'

"Each week, Cleopatra Facial Soap extends a helping hand to men and women everywhere. Submit your story to us, and if it is judged a winner, you will speak with your loved one overseas—wherever he is, whatever he's doing—courtesy of Cleopatra...

Soon, across the distances that defied imagination, she would hear his voice—

"...Your master of ceremonies, Laird Larsen. Here he is, ladies and gentlemen, the man whose voice all lovers know— Laird Larsen!"

"Hello, everybody, hello! Here we go again, in another Cleopatra attempt to make young lovers happy." Larsen, an unprepossessing man who spoke like Clem McCarthy, smiled mechanically. "This time, though, 'Hands Across the Ocean' makes an unprecedented leap. The Pacific Ocean is a goldfish bowl compared to the empty space between us and the moon. But Cleopatra Soap, in conjunction with the Amalgamated Broadcasting Network and the United States Air Force, will attempt to reach the moon tonight—by radio. Here with us is the lovely Jeanne Peterson, who..."

On and on he rambled. *There was so much she wanted to tell Tom—*

"...and on the moon, on the unthinkably remote moon, Captain Tom Bentley, alone on a wild, utterly unexplored frontier. More alone than any man has ever been before him. Lonely, perhaps a little terrified, although we feel our Captain Tom is made of sterner stuff."

Our Captain Tom. All at once, it was sickening.

"Are you ready, Amalgamated? Very well."–appropriate tremble of the voice—"This is Cleopatra Soap, the planet Earth, calling Captain Tom Bentley on the moon. Cleopatra Soap and all its millions of listeners, calling the moon." Laird Larsen had picked up an unnecessarily complex microphone and was talking into it. "Earth and Cleopatra calling Moon. Do you hear me, Moon?"

But what could she tell him? "Just imagine what it will be like when Tom gets back here and speaks to the Women's League," said Aunt Anna. That? "They're liable to keep Tom on the moon a long time," said Pop. "Hmm," said Jeanne, "some guy trying to make time because Tom's too far away to protest." That? "I wouldn't prostitute my emotional relationship with Tom for all the Women's Leagues in the country," Jeanne said. Very funny. Tell him that? Tell him about Dan Lubrano?

"Cleopatra calling the Moon. Come in, Moon. Do you hear me?" Laird Larsen mopped his brow. "By now the radio waves have reached the moon and returned, ladies and gentlemen. But still, no contact with Captain Bentley."

Why hadn't she agreed to use the prepared speech? If she talked to Tom now, everything would be a lie. Nothing real. Nothing. And, she told herself, this would be one more step toward cheapening whatever they had. Twenty million people would gawk while they spoke. *Darling, I love you. I love you! Hooray!*

"Hello, Captain Bentley."

"This is Bentley." Tom's voice, faint, from far, far away— but unmistakably Tom's. It made Jeanne feel weak allover.

"Captain Bentley, I have a surprise for you. I have—"

Off in the wings, Mr. Pate stood, mopping his brow. The general was at his side, beaming.

"Jeanne? Did you say Jeanne?" Tom's voice, weak, so distant.

"Of course, Captain. Courtesy of Cleopatra Soap, the facial soap that…"

Jeanne wished he'd choke on all the bars of Cleopatra Soap that had ever been manufactured.

"And here she is, ladies and gentlemen. America's number one sweetheart, Jeanne Peterson, about to bridge the gap of interplanetary space to chat with her lover."

Jeanne looked at the microphone and cringed. She walked forward, then paused. She stared once at Mr. Pate, still mopping his brow in the wings. Then she turned and fled, oblivious to the rising tide of voices behind her.

ALMOST midnight. If Tom hadn't spoken so often of the White Sands Air Force base, she never would have come in here, never found the little-used gate behind the barracks, where Captain Macomber would enter to avoid publicity, never have mentioned the right few words to the master sergeant at the gatehouse. (*If ever you need anything, darling, see Sergeant Reed. We were in Korea together.*) Sergeant Reed had been reluctant at first, but then had understood…

She crouched behind the gatehouse in darkness now and listened.

"But I tell you I'm Macomber!" the captain cried. "You've got to let me through. The ship's blasting off on automatic in a few minutes."

"Just show me your identification," Sergeant Reed said.

"I already—"

"Show it to me in the light where I can see it, Captain."

Jeanne ran down the runway that led past the little cement mounds of the observation turrets toward the needle-like shape, which loomed up in the glare of a single floodlight. She had checked her wristwatch with Sergeant Reed's. Four minutes to midnight. Reed would delay Captain Macomber long enough. It was only a matter of minutes now. The sergeant would get a blistering chewing out, but could claim he'd only been doing what he thought was his duty...

He told me the spaceship worked automatically, the girl in the restaurant had said.

The spaceship's airlock was not secured. There was no reason to secure it. Jeanne found Macomber's pressure suit and with two handfuls of thumbs buckled it on herself. Footsteps pounded along the runway as she slammed the airlock door.

Seconds now. Less than seconds—

The last thing she told herself with a happy little smile, an instant before she blasted off in the second lunar ship, was that the Man in the Moon would get a real surprise in a little while.

THE END

If you've enjoyed this book, you will not want to miss these terrific titles…

ARMCHAIR SCI-FI, FANTASY, & HORROR DOUBLE NOVELS, $12.95 each

D-21 **EMPIRE OF EVIL** by Robert Arnette
THE SIGN OF THE TIGER by Alan E. Nourse & J. A. Meyer

D-22 **OPERATION SQUARE PEG** by Frank Belknap Long
ENCHANTRESS OF VENUS by Leigh Brackett

D-23 **THE LIFE WATCH** by Lester del Rey
CREATURES OF THE ABYSS by Murray Leinster

D-24 **LEGION OF LAZARUS** by Edmond Hamilton
STAR HUNTER by Andre Norton

D-25 **EMPIRE OF WOMEN** by John Fletcher
ONE OF OUR CITIES IS MISSING by Irving Cox

D-26 **THE WRONG SIDE OF PARADISE** by Raymond F. Jones
THE INVOLUNTARY IMMORTALS by Rog Phillips

D-27 **EARTH QUARTER** by Damon Knight
ENVOY TO NEW WORLDS by Keith Laumer

D-28 **SLAVES TO THE METAL HORDE** by Milton Lesser
HUNTERS OUT OF TIME by Joseph E. Kelleam

D-29 **RX JUPITER SAVE US** by Ward Moore
BEWARE THE USURPERS by Geoff St. Reynard

D-30 **SECRET OF THE SERPENT** by Don Wilcox
CRUSADE ACROSS THE VOID by Dwight V. Swain

ARMCHAIR SCIENCE FICTION CLASSICS, $12.95 each

C-7 **THE SHAVER MYSTERY, Book One**
by Richard S. Shaver

C-8 **THE SHAVER MYSTERY, Book Two**
by Richard S. Shaver

C-9 **MURDER IN SPACE**
by David V. Reed

ARMCHAIR MASTERS OF SCIENCE FICTION SERIES, $16.95 each

M-3 **MASTERS OF SCIENCE FICTION, Vol. Three**
Robert Sheckley, "The Perfect Woman" and other tales

M-4 **MASTERS OF SCIENCE FICTION, Vol. Four**
Mack Reynolds, Part One, "Stowaway" and other tales

If you've enjoyed this book, you will not want to miss these terrific titles…

ARMCHAIR SCI-FI & HORROR DOUBLE NOVELS, $12.95 each

D-31 **A HOAX IN TIME** by Keith Laumer
INSIDE EARTH by Poul Anderson

D-32 **TERROR STATION** by Dwight V. Swain
THE WEAPON FROM ETERNITY by Dwight V. Swain

D-33 **THE SHIP FROM INFINITY** by Edmond Hamilton
TAKEOFF by C. M. Kornbluth

D-34 **THE METAL DOOM** by David H. Keller
TWELVE TIMES ZERO by Howard Browne

D-35 **HUNTERS OUT OF SPACE** by Joseph Kelleam
INVASION FROM THE DEEP by Paul W. Fairman,

D-36 **THE BEES OF DEATH** by Robert Moore Williams
A PLAGUE OF PYTHONS by Frederick Pohl

D-37 **THE LORDS OF QUARMALL** by Fritz Leiber and Harry Fischer
BEACON TO ELSEWHERE by James H. Schmitz

D-38 **BEYOND PLUTO** by John S. Campbell
ARTERY OF FIRE by Thomas N. Scortia

D-39 **SPECIAL DELIVERY** by Kris Neville
NO TIME FOR TOFFEE by Charles F. Meyers

D-40 **JUNGLE IN THE SKY** by Milton Lesser
RECALLED TO LIFE by Robert Silverberg

ARMCHAIR SCIENCE FICTION CLASSICS, $12.95 each

C-10 **MARS IS MY DESTINATION**
by Frank Belknap Long

C-11 **SPACE PLAGUE**
by George O. Smith

C-12 **SO SHALL YE REAP**
by Rog Phillips

ARMCHAIR SCIENCE FICTION & HORROR GEMS SERIES, $12.95 each

G-3 **SCIENCE FICTION GEMS, Vol. Two**
James Blish and others

G-4 **HORROR GEMS, Vol. Two**
Joseph Payne Brennan and others

If you've enjoyed this book, you will not want to miss these terrific titles…

ARMCHAIR SCI-FI, FANTASY, & HORROR DOUBLE NOVELS, $12.95 each

D-41 **FULL CYCLE** by Clifford D. Simak
IT WAS THE DAY OF THE ROBOT by Frank Belknap Long

D-42 **THIS CROWDED EARTH** by Robert Bloch
REIGN OF THE TELEPUPPETS by Daniel Galouye

D-43 **THE CRISPIN AFFAIR** by Jack Sharkey
THE RED HELL OF JUPITER by Paul Ernst

D-44 **PLANET OF DREAD** by Dwight V. Swain
WE THE MACHINE by Gerald Vance

D-45 **THE STAR HUNTER** by Edmond Hamilton
THE ALIEN by Raymond F. Jones

D-46 **WORLD OF IF** by Rog Phillips
SLAVE RAIDERS FROM MERCURY by Don Wilcox

D-47 **THE ULTIMATE PERIL** by Robert Abernathy
PLANET OF SHAME by Bruce Elliot

D-48 **THE FLYING EYES** by J. Hunter Holly
SOME FABULOUS YONDER by Phillip Jose Farmer

D-49 **THE COSMIC BUNGLERS** by Geoff St. Reynard
THE BUTTONED SKY by Geoff St. Reynard

D-50 **TYRANTS OF TIME** by Milton Lesser
PARIAH PLANET by Murray Leinster

ARMCHAIR SCIENCE FICTION CLASSICS, $12.95 each

C-13 **SUNKEN WORLD**
by Stanton A. Coblentz

C-14 **THE LAST VIAL**
by Sam McClatchie, M. D.

C-15 **WE WHO SURVIVED (THE FIFTH ICE AGE)**
by Sterling Noel

ARMCHAIR MASTERS OF SCIENCE FICTION SERIES, $16.95 each

MS-5 **MASTERS OF SCIENCE FICTION, Vol. Five**
Winston K. Marks—Test Colony and other tales

MS-6 **MASTERS OF SCIENCE FICTION, Vol. Six**
Fritz Leiber—Deadly Moon and other tales

If you've enjoyed this book, you will not want to miss these terrific titles…

ARMCHAIR SCI-FI & HORROR DOUBLE NOVELS, $12.95 each

D-51   **A GOD NAMED SMITH** by Henry Slesar
WORLDS OF THE IMPERIUM by Keith Laumer

D-52   **CRAIG'S BOOK** by Don Wilcox
EDGE OF THE KNIFE by H. Beam Piper

D-53   **THE SHINING CITY** by Rena M. Vale
THE RED PLANET by Russ Winterbotham

D-54   **THE MAN WHO LIVED TWICE** by Rog Phillips
VALLEY OF THE CROEN by Lee Tarbell

D-55   **OPERATION DISASTER** by Milton Lesser
LAND OF THE DAMNED by Berkeley Livingston

D-56   **CAPTIVE OF THE CENTAURIANESS** by Poul Anderson
A PRINCESS OF MARS by Edgar Rice Burroughs

D-57   **THE NON-STATISTICAL MAN** by Raymond F. Jones
MISSION FROM MARS by Rick Conroy

D-58   **INTRUDERS FROM THE STARS** by Ross Rocklynne
FLIGHT OF THE STARLING by Chester S. Geier

D-59   **COSMIC SABOTEUR** by Frank M. Robinson
LOOK TO THE STARS by Willard Hawkins

D-60   **THE MOON IS HELL!** by John W. Campbell, Jr.
THE GREEN WORLD by Hal Clement

ARMCHAIR SCIENCE FICTION CLASSICS, $12.95 each

C-16   **THE SHAVER MYSTERY, Book Three**
by Richard S. Shaver

C-17   **THE PLANET STRAPPERS**
by Raymond Z. Gallun

C-18   **THE FOURTH "R"**
by George O. Smith

ARMCHAIR SCIENCE FICTION & HORROR GEMS SERIES, $12.95 each

G-5   **SCIENCE FICTION GEMS, Vol. Three**
C. M. Kornbluth and others

G-6   **HORROR GEMS, Vol. Three**
August Derleth and others

If you've enjoyed this book, you will not want to miss these terrific titles…

ARMCHAIR SCI-FI & HORROR DOUBLE NOVELS, $12.95 each

D-61 **THE MAN WHO STOPPED AT NOTHING** by Paul W. Fairman
TEN FROM INFINITY by Ivar Jorgensen

D-62 **WORLDS WITHIN** by Rog Phillips
THE SLAVE by C.M. Kornbluth

D-63 **SECRET OF THE BLACK PLANET** by Milton Lesser
THE OUTCASTS OF SOLAR III by Emmett McDowell

D-64 **WEB OF THE WORLDS** by Harry Harrison and Katherine MacLean
RULE GOLDEN by Damon Knight

D-65 **TEN TO THE STARS** by Raymond Z. Gallun
THE CONQUERORS by David H. Keller, M. D.

D-66 **THE HORDE FROM INFINITY** by Dwight V. Swain
THE DAY THE EARTH FROZE by Gerald Hatch

D-67 **THE WAR OF THE WORLDS** by H. G. Wells
THE TIME MACHINE by H. G. Wells

D-68 **STARCOMBERS** by Edmond Hamilton
THE YEAR WHEN STARDUST FELL by Raymond F. Jones

D-69 **HOCUS-POCUS UNIVERSE** by Jack Williamson
QUEEN OF THE PANTHER WORLD by Berkeley Livingston

D-70 **BATTERING RAMS OF SPACE** by Don Wilcox
DOOMSDAY WING by George H. Smith

ARMCHAIR SCIENCE FICTION & FANTASY CLASSICS, $12.95 each

C-19 **EMPIRE OF JEGGA**
by David V. Reed

C-20 **THE TOMORROW PEOPLE**
by Judith Merril

C-21 **THE MAN FROM YESTERDAY**
by Howard Browne as by Lee Francis

C-22 **THE TIME TRADERS**
by Andre Norton

C-23 **ISLANDS OF SPACE**
by John W. Campbell

C-24 **THE GALAXY PRIMES**
by E. E. "Doc" Smith

If you've enjoyed this book, you will not want to miss these terrific titles...

ARMCHAIR SCI-FI & HORROR DOUBLE NOVELS, $12.95 each

D-71   **THE DEEP END** by Gregory Luce
         TO WATCH BY NIGHT by Robert Moore Williams

D-72   **SWORDSMAN OF LOST TERRA** by Poul Anderson
         PLANET OF GHOSTS by David V. Reed

D-73   **MOON OF BATTLE** by J. J. Allerton
         THE MUTANT WEAPON by Murray Leinster

D-74   **OLD SPACEMEN NEVER DIE!** John Jakes
         RETURN TO EARTH by Bryan Berry

D-75   **THE THING FROM UNDERNEATH** by Milton Lesser
         OPERATION INTERSTELLAR by George O. Smith

D-76   **THE BURNING WORLD** by Algis Budrys
         FOREVER IS TOO LONG by Chester S. Geier

D-77   **THE COSMIC JUNKMAN** by Rog Phillips
         THE ULTIMATE WEAPON by John W. Campbell

D-78   **THE TIES OF EARTH** by James H. Schmitz
         CUE FOR QUIET by Thomas L. Sherred

D-79   **SECRET OF THE MARTIANS** by Paul W. Fairman
         THE VARIABLE MAN by Philip K. Dick

D-80   **THE GREEN GIRL** by Jack Williamson
         THE ROBOT PERIL by Don Wilcox

ARMCHAIR SCIENCE FICTION CLASSICS, $12.95 each

C-25   **THE STAR KINGS**
         by Edmond Hamilton

C-26   **NOT IN SOLITUDE**
         by Kenneth Gantz

C-32   **PROMETHEUS II**
         by S. J. Byrne

ARMCHAIR SCIENCE FICTION & HORROR GEMS SERIES, $12.95 each

G-7   **SCIENCE FICTION GEMS, Vol. Seven**
         Jack Sharkey and others

G-8   **HORROR GEMS, Vol. Eight**
         Seabury Quinn and others

If you've enjoyed this book, you will not want to miss these terrific titles…

ARMCHAIR SCI-FI, FANTASY, & HORROR DOUBLE NOVELS, $12.95 each

D-81 **THE LAST PLEA** by Robert Bloch
THE STATUS CIVILIZATION by Robert Sheckley

D-82 **WOMAN FROM ANOTHER PLANET** by Frank Belknap Long
HOMECALLING by Judith Merril

D-83 **WHEN TWO WORLDS MEET** by Robert Moore Williams
THE MAN WHO HAD NO BRAINS by Jeff Sutton

D-84 **THE SPECTRE OF SUICIDE SWAMP** by E. K. Jarvis
IT'S MAGIC, YOU DOPE! by Jack Sharkey

D-85 **THE STARSHIP FROM SIRIUS** by Rog Phillips
FINAL WEAPON by Everett Cole

D-86 **TREASURE ON THUNDER MOON** by Edmond Hamilton
TRAIL OF THE ASTROGAR by Henry Haase

D-87 **THE VENUS ENIGMA** by Joe Gibson
THE WOMAN IN SKIN 13 by Paul W. Fairman

D-88 **THE MAD ROBOT** by William P. McGivern
THE RUNNING MAN by J. Holly Hunter

D-89 **VENGEANCE OF KYVOR** by Randall Garrett
AT THE EARTH'S CORE by Edgar Rice Burroughs

D-90 **DWELLERS OF THE DEEP** by Don Wilcox
NIGHT OF THE LONG KNIVES by Fritz Leiber

ARMCHAIR SCIENCE FICTION CLASSICS, $12.95 each

C-28 **THE MAN FROM TOMORROW**
by Stanton A. Cobllentz

C-29 **THE GREEN MAN OF GRAYPEC**
by Festus Pragnell

C-30 **THE SHAVER MYSTERY, Book Four**
by Richard S. Shaver

ARMCHAIR MASTERS OF SCIENCE FICTION SERIES, $16.95 each

MS-7 **MASTERS OF SCIENCE FICTION AND FANTASY, Vol. Seven**
Lester del Rey, "The Band Played On" and other tales

MS-8 **MASTERS OF SCIENCE FICTION, Vol. Eight**
Milton Lesser, "'A' is for Android" and other tales

www.ingramcontent.com/pod-product-compliance
Lightning Source LLC
Chambersburg PA
CBHW050554260626
47157CB00002B/564